Praise fc

This brilliant novel introduces us to a dysfunctional man, Naughton, with a fountain of stories from his past, and tending to logorrhea, and Charlene, a woman who is tongue-tied in a close to catatonic state. The juxtaposition of these characters as they are trapped at either end of loquacity is an ingenious premise. Further, the novel is provocatively set in a world that seems to have taken Michel Foucault's insights in *Madness and Civilization* to heart. Here we experience how the telling of Naughton's stories gradually moves her out of her cocoon. But the real delight comes from the wit and economy of Garber's writing, as in all of his published prose. The high-level dialogs in the asylum of Maison Cristina bristle with quips, hidden agendas, and allusions. Read the book as an exploration of the power of stories to heal, or as an illustration of Foucault's relativistic view of mental illness, or just as a connoisseur of fiction writing at its best—you will be richly rewarded.

Joachim Frank, Author of *Aan Zee* and Nobel Laureate in Chemistry

Garber's *Maison Cristina* contains many elements of classic Gothic stories and novels written by Hawthorne, Irving, and Bradbury including an interesting anti-hero, a twisting, supernatural plot, and a dark setting. I would like to add that like his predecessors, Garber also possesses the genius of a great storyteller.

Francis X. Fitzgerald, *Heavy Feathers*

⊕

In previous novels by Garber, you enjoy at least one character who is a Paganini of language. In *Maison Cristina*, Peter Naughton, an octogenarian with a dark past, is our virtuoso. He sees horrific visions on the walls, for which he has been committed to Maison Cristina, a psychiatric institution run by nuns. Another patient, Charlene, a young woman unable to speak or to close her eyes, recalls a character in Garber's *The House of Nordquist*: Helene, the woman whose body and soul were to be transmuted into music. Both are emaciated, half dead, long suffering. In both novels, expression is expected to be salvific; music in *The House of Nordquist*, storytelling here. But there are remarkable differences. *Maison Cristina* has a unity of plot more organic than anything I remember having read by the master. Also, the nuns who run the psychiatric institution provide an aura of sacredness, especially Sister Claire, who, in her sessions with Naughton, offers pearls of thought-provoking spirituality like the following: "There's the silent waiting for the voice of God. And there's the silence of abnegation." Reading this book is a wonderful adventure of the spirit going back and forth among the living and the dead.

Ricardo Nirenberg, Author of *Wave Mechanics, a Love Story* and Editor of *OffCourse*

⊕

MAISON
CRISTINA

OTHER BOOKS BY EUGENE K. GARBER
Metaphysical Tales
The Historian
Beasts in Their Wisdom
Vienna ØØ
O Amazonas Escuro
The House of Nordquist

OTHER TRANSFORMATIONS PRESS BOOKS
The Art of Balance
Paths to Wholeness
52 Flower Mandalas
52 (more) Flower Mandalas

MAISON
CRISTINA

Eugene K. Garber

TRANSFORMATIONS PRESS

Cover design by Owen Gent

Published in Wenham, Massachusetts by Transformations Press.

Phone: 978-395-1292
Email: info@transformationspress.org
Website: transformationspress.org

ISBN: 978-0-9846994-8-3
Library of Congress Control Number: 2021907304
Printed in the United States of America.

The naked body lies some distance from the foot of the sheer cliff and just up from the water's edge. A male about forty years old. The flow of blood from the head and ribs has slowed now to a lazy rivulet. The pooling of the once copious stream has been dissipated by the gentle laving of wavelets at the bay's edge. Slack tide. The slowly fading bloom of encrimsoned water rises and falls not far from the glistening stones of the shoreline. Three small crabs are scavenging the broken flesh by the shattered ribs. They must hurry, clawing and nibbling. The gulls will be here soon and drive them away. The eyes are the prize, but they will be saved for the resident eagle. Out along the watery perimeter of blood an eel darts back and forth in search of the mother lode.

High up on a scarp of ragged rock a tall nude man stands with stern rigidity as if to distinguish himself sharply from the nearby wind-bent madrones that twist against the sky. Tubular white clouds, as though carefully racked, keep rank against the blue. The nude man is very tall. Germanic, sparse body hair of a light reddish hue, hair of head much the same, sharp features. He nods. "Just as I thought," he says in a tone that would be absolutely pitiless in its claim for prescience were it not for a slight involuntary hitch.

The eagle arrives, driving the gulls away, lighting on the body with an exultant cronk. His feast is selective, the eyes first, then a scrupulous extraction of glistening ropes of entrails, as if he were intent on unmooring the rejected remains so that the next tide can lift them off the rocks and commit them to lesser creatures unfamiliar with the higher precincts of the sky.

Now a scrim drops over the scene. The light changes. Across the face of the cliff hangs the tapestried image of a beautiful dark-haired woman, softly ruffled by the breeze so that, though silent, she seems intent on conveying her sentiments solely by means of facial expressions. Or maybe this subtle motility is a response to something being said or shown, invisible because behind the viewer.

The scrim disappears. The scene viewed anew is clearer. It's now obvious that the man on the rocks has hurled himself off the cliff, or he wouldn't be so far from the base of the precipice. It's an uncommon lot, not dust unto dust but flesh unto sea worms, crabs, eels, gulls, an eagle. Perhaps he meant to make a grand gesture, all the more grand because nobody was watching, unless it was the woman on the scrim. The Germanic man seems clearly to have arrived after the death.

"Shall we resume our talk, Mr. Naughton? We didn't get very far last time."

"I was detoxing. Yes, let's talk." Naughton, a man in his eighties, is sitting by a window in a neatly kept office. He's wearing a shirt printed with red and russet squares, the kind associated with lumbermen. He wears jeans, commodiously fitted. He's not a large man.

"We're sorry you didn't find Sister Kathleen a satisfactory companion."

"The chemistry was wrong. An Irish thing maybe. And so now you, Sister Claire. French extraction?"

2

"Yes, French. Maybe my French chemistry will be no more appealing than Sister Kathleen's Irish. But I'm afraid you're stuck. There're only two of us."

Naughton smiles. "Claire de lune. Light of lunatics."

"You're not a lunatic, Mr. Naughton."

"I offer a syllogism, Sister. Persons confined to Maison Cristina are lunatics. Peter Naughton is confined to Maison Cristina. Therefore, he's a victim of filial betrayal."

"Your son brought you here because he's concerned. Would you like to talk about him?"

"No. But I would like to know what he said or wrote when he had me brought here."

"He sent a very brief report. It said you were sitting alone in your house drinking whiskey and waiting for a drama to appear on a wall."

"That's accurate."

"What did you expect to appear?"

"I don't know. Shadowy figures were beginning to appear. They might've taken shape if I hadn't been taken away by Joshua's agents. I declined to accompany them, but they were armed with a court order. No doubt it specified Maison Cristina."

"Yes, we agreed to welcome you here as a guest." Sister Claire studies Naughton's face.

"You expected more discoloration, Sister?"

"I wasn't thinking of that, Mr. Naughton. I was thinking of something else that your son's report said, that you're essentially a man of words." Sister Claire smiles. "Many words."

Naughton returns the smile. "Yes, a good number, but it seems they've come to naught."

"Nothing comes to naught, Mr. Naughton. This isn't wordplay. It's a promise we have. All our deeds and thoughts are saved."

"Are you speaking of Judgement Day, Sister?"

"I wasn't thinking of judgement, Mr. Naughton. You're not under judgement here. But I do have a favor to ask of you."

"What is it, Sister?"

"I believe you may find a wall here suitable for your dramas. If that happens, will you share them with me?"

Naughton is openly surprised. He pauses. "Didn't Joshua say that my walls were the illusion of a mind fed on fumes of alcohol?"

"Yes, something like that. In any case, I take it you've been waiting a long time for something to appear."

"Yes."

"We don't wait for nothing, Mr. Naughton. Waiting is a great virtue and always rewarded, though often in unexpected ways."

Naughton looks fixedly at Sister Claire. "Maybe that's been the problem, Sister. I've been afraid of what's going to appear. So I veiled everything in whiskey."

"Quite possibly. But what's your answer, Mr. Naughton? When the wall comes alive, will you share it with me?"

"What if the thing that appears is hideously ugly?"

"I suspect it will be. Not because you're ugly of course."

"Then why will it be ugly? Is it because my mind is ugly, my memories are ugly?"

"Your mind isn't ugly, Mr. Naughton. No one's is. The mind is a stage where many dramas are played, some of them very strange and dark."

"Why are they dark, Sister?"

"Because we're fallen."

"Are the mind's dramas always battles between good and evil?"

"No. Visions are much more complicated. The only constant thing in them is the call of love."

Naughton nods meditatively. "All right, Sister, you may share my walls if they ever become animate. But I've given you warning."

"I'm warned. You say walls, plural."

"Yes. In the house, before Joshua had me taken away, I moved from room to room, wall to wall, waiting. They all seemed charged, but in the end nothing appeared."

"I believe there're walls here that will answer to you. I'll keep my eyes and ears open."

Naughton leans back in his chair and inspects the woman sitting patiently in front of him. She's dressed in a sky-blue outfit—long skirt and jacket, buttoned, lapels of modest width. Beneath is a crisp white blouse against which hangs a small plain Latin cross on a gold chain so thread-thin that the crucifix seems to hang in midair or to be pinned to her breast. White stockings, tan suede shoes. At last Naughton says, "They make you wear your hair like helmets." He smiles. "Sister Kathleen's rebellious red has had to be tamed by pomade, quite fragrant."

Sister Claire smiles. "The helmets, I'm afraid, are less protective than merely modest."

Naughton chuckles. "I'm familiar with the temptatious nature of women's hair. Pardon me if I seem to stare. It's not the helmet of hair but your hazel eyes that have arrested me. My daughter's eyes are hazel. The story is that she took the color from the irises of an Egyptian cat she named Man Two."

"Someday I'd like to hear that story, Mr. Naughton. Joshua said you are a master wordsmith."

"Well, my classmates at Jesuit High School called me Doc Logos. But I wish you would just call me Peter."

"I'd like to oblige you, but first names are discouraged."

"Of course. Professional protocol." Naughton smiles wryly. "Just as well. I'm not Peter the rock but Peter, Peter pumpkin eater, had a wife and couldn't keep her."

"Would you like to talk about your wife? Cam, right?"

"Right. Now, like hundreds of others, you're supposed to ask, Cam is short for, Camelia? Carmela?"

"And what do you say when they ask?"

5

"I say Camouflage. But I don't want to talk about her."
Naughton slips into a deep silence.

"What are you thinking, Mr. Naughton?"

"A strange thought."

"Tell me."

"I'm afraid you'll be offended."

"I doubt it. Please go on."

"I was thinking you can make a wall out of anything. A nun's white blouse for instance. Preferably with the decorative cross removed."

"It's not decorative. I could move it to the side. But it would make me feel very queer to have a scene on my blouse. However, if that's what you need, Mr. Naughton, it will be done."

After a pause Naughton says, "I'm not sure this is going to work, Sister."

"What?"

"You and me working together."

"Why?"

"Well, I'm not completely sane, obviously. And I'm not sure you're the right counterbalance."

"Why would that be?"

Naughton looks steadily at Sister Claire. "Frankly, you seem a bit too susceptible."

"Go on."

"All right. Here's another thought. I might make a wall out of one of your eyes, way down at the end of the optic nerve. I see there a sheet of weathered bronze, verdigris, dating back many centuries before your faith."

"My faith is from the beginning of time. So if one of your dramas plays out on the back of my eye, both the stage and the action will be relatively new. Quite new to me of course." Sister Claire smiles agreeably.

"Well, it's no doubt an absurd fancy. Joshua must've reported my predilection for the irrational."

"His report says you claim to be eidetic and telepathic."

"Yes, but I think I told him that just to hear him explain it away. His explanations can be hypnotic. They're like the black holes he studies. Anything that comes close gets swallowed up in irresistible logic."

"Really? He seemed quite sympathetic to your circumstances."

"Oh he knows there're things science hasn't explained. But he believes it will someday."

Sister Claire pauses. "In any case, I don't think our relationship will have much recourse to science."

Naughton nods, but absently. "I think what we're doing, Sister, is called the talking cure. It must be a trial for you. How many patients do you have?"

"At the moment just two."

"So you've got plenty of time to pray and meditate on the sacred wounds." Naughton breathes deeply. "Do you think the wounds I've inflicted are sacred, Sister?"

"All wounds are sacred, Mr. Naughton."

"And the one who inflicts the wounds? Is he sacred?"

"Such a one is dear to God, but he must make an act of contrition."

"How do I do that?"

"That's something we'll have to discover. Perhaps it'll begin on a wall. Walls are clearly essential to your person."

Naughton turns his head. "I'm looking out your window. Windows are the opposite of walls. Maybe better."

"No doubt in some cases. But for inward looking, Mr. Naughton, walls are better than windows."

Naughton is silent for some time. "I'm sure you're aware there's an autonomic blink that moistens the eye."

"Yes."

"That means your eye creates a scrim that hangs in front of the stage we call the world."

"Interesting, Mr. Naughton. What's the purpose of the scrim?"

"The viewer can adjust his eye so that the scrim either hides the stage or opens like a curtain." Naughton looks out over Sister Claire's head. "Walt Whitman wrote me a poem about scrim, 'Eidólons.' It went looping off like a lot of his work, but the idea is that we have to refocus our eyes to see the Oversoul that embraces everything. Not in your theology, I don't think."

"So you knew Walt Whitman?"

"Yes, intimately. But we parted. For the best."

Sister Claire nods. "I'll want to hear more about your friendship with Walt Whitman, but now I want to go back to the stage on the wall. Tell me if this seems right to you. What appears on the stage is memory."

"No doubt, but memory much altered by the needs of the one who remembers. Everything gets changed, images, sequence, even identities."

"Yes, all that and more no doubt. But we try not to think too much about sequence. It gets us into a trap of clocks and calendars."

"Instead of what?"

"Instead of a quilt. On a quilt everything's already there. It's the movement of the eyes across a pattern too large to take in at a glance that creates the illusion of time."

Naughton nods. "Walt would like that. But it's not only the eye roving through patterns, Sister, it's also language. Tenses, moods, inflections. You and I are talking, a great pleasure for me, but as long as we use language we're trapped in time."

Sister Claire smiles with amusement and pleasure. "Suppose we use only nouns?"

"Won't work. For instance, I say wall. Before you can respond, history crowds in on us—Jericho, the Great Wall of China, Trajan. We're trapped in time."

"What if we said nothing, but sat silently, looking at each other, waiting for the wall to reveal itself to us, not from the past, but just there where it always was."

Naughton hitches back in his chair. "You amaze me, Sister. It makes me think of something Josh told me, about retro-causality."

"What is it?"

"It's the idea that something in the present causes something in the past. This conversation you and I are having now could be what caused Nicodemus to wonder what being born again could mean."

"You may be surprised, Mr. Naughton, when I say my faith can handle retro-causality, but I'll have to think about it."

Naughton looks out the window for a while before returning his gaze to Sister Claire. "I assume your other patient is Charlene."

"Yes. You've spent a little time with Charlene, I believe."

Naughton nods. "Propped up in a wheelchair. I'm afraid she's lost in the pattern of your quilt. Hard to tell where the white robe ends and the flesh begins. A whisper of cold air would blow her off into a dark tale."

"What tale?"

"That was just a figure of speech. I didn't have one in mind."

"But now you do. I saw it cross your face like a shadow."

Naughton wags his head compliantly. "All right. A wicked witch has transformed a beautiful girl into scraps of birch bark and thrown them on a forest floor. A gummy granny gathers them up to make a fire under a pot of cabbage soup, which she eats with a crust of molded bread that gives her visions of a witch and a beautiful girl. So the ecclesiastical authorities have to burn her."

"A dark tale indeed. Fortunately, we don't burn witches anymore, Mr. Naughton."

Naughton looks at the wall behind Sister Claire's desk. A small wooden crucifix hangs there. "I look at Charlene's face. A memento mori with two giant black eyes. Inside, a dramatic scene in progress. It could be called the Dance of Death. You can hear the clatter of bones. Can you make these bones live? Nurse Vera tries to feed her soup. Charlene makes a thick bubble that hangs on her lips like a hangman's noose."

Sister Claire fixes Naughton with a penetrating gaze. "Maybe you could talk to her, Mr. Naughton. Make for her a wall with a blue sky and birds. Patients have been known to help each other when nobody else could." There's a silence. "What're you thinking, Mr. Naughton?"

"I'm thinking no wall of mine will have blue skies. And anyway, I won't share walls with Charlene. They're for the two of us."

"All right. But think what you might do. She's in great need."

"More than need, Sister. On the edge of a cliff. I don't know what I can do, but I'll think about it."

Sister Claire studies Naughton's face. She stands up. "I'm going to let you go now, Mr. Naughton. But I'll tell you what I worry about. Not ugly walls. I worry about waiting and silence."

"I thought waiting and silence were practices of your order."

Sister Claire goes to her desk and lays her hand on its smooth surface as if it has always been there as a surety of her office as mistress of Maison Cristina. "Mr. Naughton . . ." She stops as if she hadn't meant to begin with a name, then goes on. "There's the silent waiting for the voice of God. And there's the silence of abnegation."

A cloudy late morning. Naughton walks down the short narrow hall, three doors on each side, two for the nuns' quarters, one each for the four residents. From one a murmurous complaint, from another a clatter so muffled it may be a cracked human voice or the rattle of dishes and silver, though it's long after breakfast. He walks past them without turning. At the end of the hall is a large window that looks out on a small rough greensward rounded with a motley of untrimmed greenery—thistle, spiderwort, vetch, pokeweed with its cones of red-black berries, a rare but hearty patch of wild geraniums, its shy violet stars half hidden among the green, and the inevitable floating white of Queen Anne's lace. Behind them in soldierly rows is a deep stand of yellow birch extending left and right beyond the confines of the window frame. There's no sun, no shadow, only a dull pewter, the source of light off somewhere in the gray sky. Just to one side of the window is a wheelchair, in it Charlene. Naughton stops and stands before the window surveying the drab scene and then turns to Charlene. Her huge black eyes are wide open, but there's no evidence she's looking at him. He comes a step closer. "You know, Charlene, eyelids are common walls. But they're moveable. You can lower them, like the portcullises of old castles."

Nurse Vera appears in a blue uniform. She's large, face and hands bronze against the pale fabric of her uniform. Naughton says, "I think Charlene may need to shut her eyes, Vera."

"She does not shut her eyes, even when she sleeps." It's obvious that English isn't Vera's native language. She speaks with a practiced precision.

Charlene moves as if to retreat farther into the chair, but there's no space between its back and her spine.

"Was she born without eyelids?"

"No. She does not use them."

"And she never says anything?"

"One time she said no, we believe."

Naughton returns his attention to Charlene. "I'm the wall man, Charlene. Sister Claire said I could talk to you."

Vera looks pityingly at Charlene and steps away. "I must go to Mr. Gerrity."

Naughton puts his hands behind his back and speaks in a meditative tone. "It was just recently, Charlene, that I began to search for walls. I had the idea, and still have it now, that I could find on walls everything I'd lost."

Under her white robe Charlene tightens as if to shrink, but there's little of her to shrink.

Naughton nods. "I understand." After a pause he says, "Do you like visions? Here's one. You're up on the highest wall in the world, Charlene. Perched right on the edge. The sky is all around you. Not a blue dome, welkin, that kind of poetic stuff because it doesn't matter to you if it's glowing or weeping. You don't care what your talons are grasping at the moment, scrabble, saxifrage, a sapling in a crevice. You depend on no such frailties. The updraft is ruffling your feathers. You feel the power. You move your telescopic eyes over the world below. Lots of quarry down there you could easily seize. Wandering wobbly calves and kids, a neglected infant in a crib, fat pigeons, rabbits, downstream salmon washed up in the shallows, the whole world in your talons. But you don't want any of that easy prey. You're after something bigger."

A hint of movement crosses Charlene's face, but there's not enough flesh to tell exactly what it is—a twitching in the corners of her mouth, a flaring of her nostrils.

"What do you want to strike, Charlene? You launch and furl your wings. A hundred miles an hour, all the resistant air will allow. Who do you want to strike, Charlene? They'll never know what hit them."

Naughton abandons his meditative posture and tone. He paces like one in a state of urgency and anger. "Charlene. Listen. We're not going to let them take what's ours."

Now Charlene's eyes roll left and quickly back to their steady forward stare, at nothing.

Naughton bends down until his mouth is not far from Charlene's ear. "Charlene. They're gentle folks here. Lovely folks. Even smart, like Sister Claire, but they can't help you with this. Because we're talking about eating or being eaten. It's not in their theology. And those others are dining on us, Charlene, one morsel at a time, at their leisure. Sure, we could slip out death's back door. The good sisters have tried to lock it, God bless them, but they've got no head for numbers, Trinitarians. You and I could crack the combination in a minute. I learned how from my son Joshua. But we're not going down that dark hall, Charlene."

Naughton steps back, looks out the window for a long moment, nods as if to himself, then turns back to Charlene. "I'm your friend, Charlene. I'm the wall man. You're the eagle. We're in this together."

On Charlene's face a faint hint of rubescence.

Vera reappears, surveys the scene. "What have you been saying to her, Mr. Naughton?"

A mumbling of indecipherable sounds issues from Charlene's mouth.

Vera narrows her eyes.

"She says she wants something to eat."

"Vera says you talked to Charlene." Sister Claire, sitting behind her desk, looks at Naughton with keen interest.

"Yes. You wanted me to try to think of something."

"That's right. I'd like to know what you said."

Naughton smiles. "I told her I'm the wall man, she's the eagle. We're both up high, very high."

"Are you going to tell me what these symbolize?"

Naughton laughs. "I couldn't, Sister. Symbols unfold as they will, in the lower depths of the mind. If you want to rationalize them, we'll have to call on Josh, our man of logical connections and precise quantifications."

Sister Claire sits quietly for some moments. "I have an intuition that someday a wall will appear that will reveal what went wrong between you and your son. A wall of reconciliation."

"Walls, like symbols, Sister, you have to take as they come. Like the great murallas of Ávila when I went to see Santa Teresa."

"And Joshua was with you?"

"Yes, but he wasn't paying attention."

"What did you and Santa Teresa talk about?"

"How to put together a geographically disperse operation. I was thinking of going into retail. Wooden pillows, sack cloth, ashes, other mortification products. But the plan fell through. All my plans fell through." Naughton lifts his hands up apologetically and drops them. "I'm sorry, Sister. Sometimes I'm seized by an imp of perverse and say silly things."

"You said Joshua wasn't paying attention. What did you mean by that?"

"He was supposed to remember the way out. King Philip's men had closed all the gates but one."

"But you did finally get out."

"No. It's not the kind of place you get out of. You just have to go on living your life elsewhere."

Sister Claire nods. "You can be trying, Mr. Naughton."

"We lunatics are always trying, Sister. We're immured in our own minds and can't get out."

"You're not a lunatic, Mr. Naughton, but even if you were, there's always a way out. But let's go back to Charlene? What did she say to you?"

"Nothing. I tried telepathic powers. I figured if they don't exist it wouldn't do any harm."

"And?"

"Nothing but a buzz, a sort of carrier wave, no content."

"Use your extraordinary command of ordinary language, Mr. Naughton. That will carry the day."

"Is there any such thing as ordinary language? Doesn't every language shine with the moisture of the many tongues that have spoken it?"

"Of course. I'm corrected." Sister Claire presses on. "If you can break Charlene's silence you'll be blessed."

"Blessed. That would be wonderful." Naughton tilts his head. "You know that Charlene never shuts her eyes."

"Yes. It's hard to imagine."

"Someone probably told her the story of the Sandman. You know it?"

"No, I don't think so."

"Your mother never told you if you don't shut your eyes the Sandman will come and put sand in them?"

"No."

"The Sandman comes in the night and steals children's eyes as the story goes. So Charlene has to keep her eyes open all the time or the Sandman will pluck them out and eat them."

"Who's the Sandman in this version of the story?"

"When she knows, she'll get up and walk out of here." Naughton leans back and looks up. "My sister Stella slept with her eyes open. It was spooky. I saw it once and never went in her room again."

"Who was your sister's Sandman?"

"God, I think."

"Surely not."

Naughton looks abashed. "Sometimes I speak hastily. In this case maybe bitterly. I wanted Stella to stay in the house where I was. But she went in search of perfection."

"Did she find it?"

"I don't think so."

"That was a trick question, Mr. Naughton. Nobody finds perfection. That comes later."

Naughton nods. "That's something to pray for."

"I never pray for anything, Mr. Naughton. My prayers are solely a way for me to try to align my will with God's will."

Naughton takes a deep breath as of one coming at last to the end of something. "I don't think I was ever really aligned with anything, Sister. Once or twice I convinced myself I was. What you might call a human necessity."

"When did you think you were aligned?"

"When I talked to Walt, when I wooed Cam."

Sister Claire leans on her desk, hands carefully folded. "You'll align yourself here. You'll find your walls. We'll share them. Whiskey was a way of hiding them."

Naughton nods, but dubiously. "May we leave it at that for now, Sister?"

"Of course, Mr. Naughton. I never want to hold you here beyond what we both believe is useful."

A Kitchen in New Orleans

On the wall near the foot of his bed Naughton's mother and father are putting on one of their shows for him. A familiar scene with variations. The three of them are in the kitchen, which has the usual sink, appliances, cabinets, chairs, table, walls, linoleum floor, but is really just a broad slash of stained and chipped white. His mother and father are drinking bourbon and smoking cigarettes. The alternately glowing and ashy-white tubes are essentially extensions of their bodies, bobbing up and down as they speak, pointing fiercely toward addressees, supping the oxygen necessary for their perpetuation. In his father's case the mouthing of the cigarette is a circus trick because his father is an ape dressed up to resemble a man. Matted tufts of black hair escape from the portals of his tank top. His arms and hands are matted with wet black hair. His neck is encased in a black muff. Hair bristles along the porch of his nostrils and pours from his ears.

"Your father does not sweat," his mother has informed him. "What you see is actually an oil characteristic only of futuristic anthropoids. Breathe in its celestial fragrance, Peter, and thank the gods for such grace."

After further silent blooms of smoke his mother proposes a profound question. "In this latter age how many does it take to make a man? In the case of Peter Naughton on display here more than six, because six have failed to accomplish the feat. Let us catalog these ineffective persons. There is the child bearer of course and the inseminator, the child bearer's mother Helen, the child bearer's sister Marietta, the homunculus's sister Stella, and the inseminator's mother. This last we do not indict on grounds of dementia."

The inseminator makes a jolly grunt. "You've done what you could, Liz."

"No. And neither have you, Marty. We haven't been proper models. And it's unfair to lay any blame on his beloved sister Stella, now off to a nunnery, because it's impossible for a highly spiritualized ectoplasm to have a formative influence on anybody."

"What about your mother Helen?" Playing the straight man comes naturally to the inseminator. "She's an upright woman."

"A fading old gossip."

The ape clamps his cigarette firmly between incisors so he can reward his wife's cleverness with a chittering laugh.

"That," his mother says, "leaves us with only his aunt Marietta, Ettie, my beloved sister."

"Tough enough to raise a tiger." A soggy shred of tobacco appears, undetected by its host, on his upper left incisor.

"Yes, but she's out in San Francisco determined to bed the Ur-Marine. Peter would be further unmanned."

"She'd love to have him though."

"I didn't love to have him. I screamed the loudest on record at Hotel Dieu and expelled the greasy thing from my body with such projectile force that the nurse had to catch him in midair. And when they wouldn't let me have cigarettes, I pretended to smoke Q-tips and flick the ashes on the floor."

"I smuggled in some bourbon for you." The ape smiles and pushes his shoulders forward and together in a gesture belonging perhaps to a semantic shared only by husband and wife.

"They wanted a name. We hadn't thought about that. A sometimes Black nurse was around, nice, pretended not to smell the bourbon on my breath. Savarina or something like that. You name him, I told her. I was hoping for something exotic from the dark continent, like Atolasi or Satachi, something with a little snap to it. Peter she said."

The boy speaks for the first time. "What do you mean, sometimes Black?"

"I don't mean mixed, mulatto, quadroon, whatever. I mean it depended on the light and the angle. By the window she was Ethiopian with a sharp nose. Straight on, the face flattened out, Negroid. She was the only thing in the whole obstetrics wing of any interest. Certainly not the crying babies."

"Why didn't you just not pay attention to her and give me some high-powered southern name like Beauregard or Braxton or Ridgeway?"

"If it had been one of those, I would've chosen Bedford, but at the moment your father, Martin Naughton, was just outside the hospital window amusing me with an old trick of his. Show Peter how you can blow smoke rings."

The inseminator takes in a huge mouthful of smoke, purses his lips and taps his cheek with a perfect tattoo so that the rings of smoke come out in rapid succession, each passing through the widening diameter of the preceding one, sometimes as many as four or five in a row, until they begin to disperse chaotically. His mother claps. "Do the next part, Marty."

The ape blows a single large ring, does a summersault, hangs, or seems to hang, for several moments to the bottom of the loop until it gives way and he flips back down on his feet. His mother claps again.

19

"Is that why you married him?" That might seem a daring thing for a fourteen-year-old to say, but that's part of the game. He's allowed ironic interlocutions as long as they're kept within bounds. The game is to edge close to the precipice of the unseemly or the revelatory.

"Only one of his many charms, Peter. Did you notice the way the rings started to wobble suggestively and then veer off into chaos? Chaos and Eros, close cousins." His mother pops a ball of smoke from the left side of her mouth. "Are you paying attention to me, Peter? These things I'm telling you aren't airy nothings."

"I'm listening to every word."

"Airy nothings. It's from the Bible, isn't it?"

"'Tis, Liz." The ape often stumbles into rhymes and puns, which please him greatly.

"Marty, in all candor, you wouldn't know if it was from the Bible or not because you were brought up Catholic and not allowed to read the Bible. Peter, you knew your father was a Catholic before I converted him, didn't you?"

"Converted him to what?"

"To the religion of Eros and Chaos. See? I knew you weren't listening."

His father wags a finger at him and does a double lift of his eyebrows.

"I didn't know it was a religion."

"It is, but you'll never belong to it, Peter, because your brains will get in the way. Brainy people are always irreligious, and unhappy in other ways as well."

"You're a brainy person, Mama."

"Maybe I might've been, but Mama Helen kept talking at me all while I was growing up so I didn't have any time to think. Which brings us back to the Bible. Mama Helen's reading of the Bible was selective. A lot about Ham, which explained to her why Blacks are inferior. She wouldn't have noticed much difference between Blacks and whites if it hadn't been for the Civil War. Well. People swear on the Bible all the time without having any idea what's in it."

The supply of bourbon and lit cigarettes has been refreshed. His father has lit two cigarettes at once, one on either side of his mouth.

"Isn't he talented, Peter?"

"What would you do, Mama, if you were in court and had to swear on the Bible?"

"That's a very hypothetical question, Peter, because long before the case ever got to that point, a murder or whatever, the lawyers would've decided that I was an unreliable witness, wearing a short sassy orange dress with Eros and Chaos written all over it, and enough rouge and lipstick to light up the night. Ask a more interesting question."

"All right. What did Aunt Ettie think of your marriage?"

His mother laughs a hiccupy laugh that this time does require her to remove her cigarette. "She got somebody to write a poem for her. Rare it is for a damsel to desire to marry a man made of wire."

"Damsel!" His father rolls his cigarette around a whooshing laugh.

"Marty, I don't appreciate that."

"How did the rest of the poem go, Mama?"

"I don't remember. But whoever helped her was very learned. She attracted all kinds. It had Centaurs and Minotaurs and other highfalutin rimes in it. Now if I wrote a poem about my sister Marietta it would be an ode to her perpetual virginity."

Another whoosh of laughter from his father.

"Marty, as you well know, we aren't talking about carnality. You're confusing the condition of virginity with the god Hymen. Marietta, pleaser of many men, is impenetrable and will always be a virgin." His mother continues to address the ape. "There's another trick he can do, Peter, which is connected to what I'm telling you. If I threw a coin on the floor, your father could press his right big toe on it and tell you whose head is on it and the date, even if it's an Indian. But we've had enough tricks for tonight. Tomorrow maybe."

Now on her fifth drink, eyes unnaturally bright, opposite of the bleariness one might expect, his mother looks at him inquisitively. "Who are you, Peter? You're an enigma. I should've named you Mysterioso. You could've been an opera star."

"I'm going to be a rock star, Mama. Peter the Rocker. We'll call ourselves the Punk Papists and dress in gold lamé."

His father grunts. "I knew we never should've sent him to the Jesuits."

His mother flicks an ash off of her cigarette onto the linoleum. "Go to bed, Peter. And may the guardian angel of brains watch over you."

Today the birches are bathed in golden light. Along the edge of the greensward, neon-bright in the sun, the weedy wall sways unevenly in a capricious April breeze. Charlene's wheelchair is turned so she can look out the window, though it's still not known if she actually sees anything. Vera passes a hand between Charlene's black eyes and the world. Nothing is registered.

"Has she eaten?" asks Naughton.

"Some broth, but it does not sit easy on her stomach."

"Of course not. I served with a sailor who was adrift on a raft in the Pacific Ocean for twenty-nine days. He caught a fish or two and dried jellyfish in the sun. When they brought him aboard the USS *Preston* they had to feed him little bits at a time, or, they knew, he would vomit everything back up. He was infuriated and threatened to eat the commissary men. He had seen Jesus walking across the waves but couldn't attract his attention."

Vera's face is expressionless, as if she has entered a pact of unresponsiveness with Charlene. "Is that the end of the story, Mr. Naughton?"

"There aren't any ends of stories, Vera, that I know of. Anyway, when they'd weaned this sailor from starvation and he was in his right mind again, he could eat everything but butter, which made him nauseous."

"It should have been fish."

"Or Jesus."

"Blasphemy is forbidden here, Mr. Naughton."

"Understood. But I'll tell you something, Vera. You have to show that you believe my stories. For Charlene's sake. She needs to believe."

"There are other things for her to believe."

"It doesn't matter what she believes as long as she believes something. She can always trade later. For instance, suppose I told Charlene that I was in love with her."

"If you did, I would report it to Sister Claire."

"Why would you do that? The order believes in love above all else." Naughton steps around Vera and faces Charlene. "Charlene believes in love. Remember me, Charlene? I'm the wall man. You're the eagle. Here's what we know. When the eagle stoops, not just on some dead fish for her daily bread but on the thing that's been taking everything away, the wake of her plummeting can never be stitched back together. It stays there in space like a gash and any hapless bird that flies into that wound disappears forever."

"Mr. Naughton, if Sister Claire had not instructed me to let you talk to Charlene, I would send you away. Now I have other people to attend to." She wheels herself around emphatically and walks away.

Naughton pulls a chair up and looks alternately out the window and at Charlene. "The idea isn't so much to get your toes down in the grass, Charlene, or grasp a nettle. Not yet. That comes later if you like things botanical. The idea now is to make these everlasting green walls of Maison Cristina talk to you. True, you won't ever be able just to snap your fingers and start them up. I can't do that either. But I know they're out there, the actors waiting for their turn on the walls." Naughton nods. "I just thought of something. You and I would never say mirror, mirror on the wall, who's most loved of all. We'll say wall, wall, what do you mirror?"

Charlene makes a muffled sound suggesting a negative.

"You're right, Charlene. Mirror is wrong. We don't want to see ourselves as we are now. We want to see deeper, what's hiding there in the wall like some old crypt with an ossuary. Pick up any skull. It's easy to see from the cracks and dents how the person was done in. Or there might be a whole skeleton all broken up, fallen from a high place, as often in tragedies. However, suicides are not allowed to be buried in the consecrated grounds of this order."

"That's not so, Mr. Naughton." It's Sister Kathleen. Her graying red hair doesn't profit from the day's radiance, but her blue eyes shine brightly.

"Still, Sister, we surely don't want to encourage the taking of one's own life even if the taking goes on for years."

"Of course. It's the gravest of sins."

"I wouldn't have thought that graves cared a great deal about whom they housed."

"You're too clever by half, Mr. Naughton."

"I rescind my pun. It was odious. I was showing off for Charlene. But tell me, Sister, what may a person be buried with? Say a treasured ring or the remains of a beloved dog kept for some years in the rose garden. Or a significant other."

"I don't know about the law, Mr. Naughton, but our order doesn't allow that." Sister Kathleen departs.

Naughton says, "Sister Kathleen's gait is almost regal, don't you think, Charlene? She may be a descendant of Cuchulain. She could slay the ones that injured you, but she's chosen a different calling. So you're stuck with me." Naughton snaps his head back, startled. "I don't mean to discount Sister Claire, Charlene. She'll shower you with blessings and love, but she's not an eagle high in an aerie." Naughton turns and looks out the window. "All this golden light can be misleading. First, we have to start walking again, Charlene. And remember that walking is just falling and catching yourself. Over and over again. My son Joshua could explain this to you in scientific terms, something about the center of gravity falling outside the base. Not so for dogs. And eagles don't walk. Even to traverse short distances they unfurl their wings and glide. But you and I can't fly yet, much less dive. We're fledglings. We would batter ourselves against the rocks."

Naughton turns and leans toward Charlene. "I'll tell you a secret, Charlene. My father could defy gravity. You know how? He was an ape, and apes are born with buoyant brains." Naughton laughs. Charlene's eyes move a little, up and down. "He and my mother could've gone into show business, but they wasted their talents on each other and me. Think of it, Charlene. A gravity defier and a woman who could make smoke speak in tongues."

There follows a silence. "I'm going now, Charlene, back to my cell. Sister Claire will come and give you a blessing. Will you pass it on to me? You could touch my hand or just move your eyes. There could be a tear. Virgen Lachrymosa."

Just as Naughton arrives in his room, Sister Claire knocks.

"Come in, Sister." There's an awkward silence, broken at last by Naughton. "Take the chair by the window, please, Sister. I'll sit over here."

Backlighted, Sister Claire's spare helmet of hair appears decidedly metallic. And when she speaks, the sharpness of the light seems to invade her voice. "Your mother was right. There was nobody to serve you as a proper model."

"No, there wasn't."

"You hesitated."

"I had a model, a Jesuit scholastic, but he was far beyond me."

Sister Claire nods. "You were lost in a haze, not just of cigarette smoke, but also of moral confusion."

"I'm sorry you had to witness that travesty of parental guidance, Sister."

"Judge not, Mr. Naughton."

"I know what you mean, Sister, but some judgements have to be made. You have to judge whether I'm going to help Charlene back toward her true self or darken her way."

"Exactly. I and my superior, Mother Martha. Can you help us with that judgement?"

A movement of Naughton's hands suggests that he thinks of turning his palms up empty but decides not to. "Here's one way to think about it, Sister. A scrim has fallen between Charlene and her self."

"You talked about scrims before."

"Yes. Did I say that some scrims add dimensions. Others occlude. Like the smoke in the kitchen."

"Go on, Mr. Naughton."

Naughton presses his hands against his forehead and rotates his palms. "Actually, it's more complicated. In a theater the operator changes the lighting so that the eye's focus alternates among images that are on the scrim, or in front of it, or behind it."

"Can you apply this to the scrim you say hangs between Charlene and her self?"

"Only that the hiding or revealing in Charlene's case must surely have a lot to do with memories."

"As also in your case."

"Yes."

"Do think Charlene has evil memories?"

"I think they must be."

"What more do you know, Mr. Naughton?"

"I know that I'm afraid."

"Of what?"

"I told you, Charlene and I are up very high. One false step and we end up on the rocks below."

Sister Claire leans back in the chair.

"May I turn on the light, Sister? I can't see your face."

"Of course."

The dim yellowish light of the lamp gives Sister Claire's fair skin a jaundiced look. She says, "Whether you believe it or not, Mr. Naughton, you're in God's hands. So is Charlene."

Naughton nods. "I'd like to believe that, Sister. The fall of a sparrow, the hairs of my head numbered."

"They are. So, act with good will. Believe in providence."

"What's providence?"

"Providence is God's will, what must be, but we have to work it out. A paradox."

Naughton shakes his head. "I have a hard time believing there's a what must be, Sister. It's something Joshua used to lecture me about. Determinism, prediction, probability, indeterminacy, all that."

"Give me an example."

Naughton thinks. "Suppose you're telling your beads. Credo, Our Father, Hail Mary, Glory Be, all in proper sequence, all the thousands of times you've prayed them. Then one day a bead says libera me, Lord, from eternal death. You've suffered the first death without knowing it. What will the next bead say? Nobody knows." Naughton taps his forehead. "I told you, Sister, I'm given to flights."

"The idea of a talking bead is interesting. Such a thing might happen. But there's only one death and then resurrection. No bead would say otherwise." In Sister Claire's tone a hint of exasperation.

Naughton leans forward. His chair creaks. "I know you want me to try to describe Charlene's case rationally, but I can only speak metaphorically. Charlene has died many times and keeps on dying. Assailants keep coming out of the dark over

27

and over like a looping film caught on a ratchet." Naughton breathes. "You've heard of sleeping with one eye open. Charlene has to keep both eyes open all the time."

"Who're the assailants?"

"They're behind the scrim."

"Can you help her see through the scrim?"

"I'm not equipped, Sister. The seeing through will come as it wills."

"Isn't that just another form of the what must be that you and Joshua disapprove of?"

"You're sharp, Sister." Naughton turns his head away and then emphatically back again. "I could go over the edge. Not unlikely. Then you'd have to take my place with Charlene. The scrim lights up. Someone is speaking maybe in a language you don't understand. You tilt your head, shift your gaze, tune your ears, judge the trustworthiness of the rocks with your toes. Are you following me, Sister?"

"Go on."

"You're where there's no what must be, Sister. You have to act. Or do nothing. Either way the scrim may part, the wall of the cliff play its scene. Voices gabble. Images swirl. Charlene falls."

Sister Claire looks at Naughton intently for a long time. "You test me, Mr. Naughton."

"We'll experience the test, Sister, when we're clutching the edge of the cliff. Look at Charlene's fingers. Flesh scraped from the bone." Naughton shrugs. "OK, a self-damaged old man on borrowed time. But Charlene."

"Yes. Charlene is the issue here. I want you to talk to her." Sister Claire speaks sternly and knits her fingers tighter. "I'm opposed in this. Mother Martha listens to my reports. Yes, Mother, Mr. Naughton is definitely a risk. But Charlene has moved her eyes. Her voice has awakened, though it still sounds half throttled. She's swallowed some broth and eaten a few crackers."

"Doesn't she ask how you know what I'll say to Charlene?"

"Actually she's proposed the prior question. How do I know what Mr. Naughton is? I don't have an answer yet."

"You have Josh's report. I'm one who comes bearing a multitude of failures and a fiery event."

"That helps very little, Mr. Naughton."

"OK. But if I'm something of a mystery, Charlene is totally shrouded in darkness."

"Yes. Somebody has to shine a light. You seem to be able to."

Naughton shakes his head slowly, more in mystification than denial.

Sister Claire rises from her chair. "You want to be a light bearer, don't you, Mr. Naughton?"

"Light bearer. That's Lucifer, isn't it?"

"Don't play word games with me, Mr. Naughton."

Naughton replies with surprising assertiveness. "If I bring any light, it'll be in the form of words."

"Exactly. We know that. It's the gift God has given you. Put it to work."

A Rented Room in New Orleans

It's almost midnight. Peter sits at his desk turning the pages almost idly of *Leaves of Grass*. Looking up one way, he can see the single window, which is mostly black with only vague images of street and houses beyond. Another way he sees the blank wall adjacent to the doorway of his room, dimly lit by a glow from the hall light outside.

A mounting hullabaloo comes down the street outside the window. He gets up from his desk, pushes the scrim of ragged curtain back and looks out. Two dozen or so frat boys. The leader lifts high a flambeau that throws a lurid circle of red light over the throng, fading along the outer perimeter of shouting celebrants. The glow of an antique streetlamp creates a pale nimbus around the red ring. New Orleans. March, 1961. The day before Mardi Gras. The curtain lollops and wrinkles in a slight breeze, picking up the flare of the flambeau like a nexus of shifting lacerations. A brief quiet ensues while the leader issues instructions, waving the flambeau aloft so that it flares and whooshes. Presently a staggered addition of inebriate voices raises a song of sorts, but many do not know the words, others off timing, some just shouting for the joy of it. The song contains a chorus-like repetition of the words "Peelers defeat," but that is all that is distinguishable in the raucous gabble. Just before Peter turns away, a lone figure in white appears far behind the rabble. A girl. She walks with a soft stately gait that does not permit vagrant breezes to billow her gauzy dress. Peter watches her for some moments. The pale light of the streetlamp so blanches her blond hair that it resembles a wimple. He shuts the window, streaked and pocked by old rains falling on dust. The now distant red of the moving flambeau stipples the glass like fading stigmata.

Peter goes back to his desk, looks up. Vogt is standing in the doorway to the hall, leaning against the jamb. The creases of his stained polo shirt seem an extension of the flaking wood. "You called."

"I don't remember calling."

"You did. If you don't call I don't come. I stay in the Unterwelt."

"I don't believe in the Underworld."

"Well then, I'm an apparition."

"Apparitions don't stink."

"That's unkind, Peter. You should know it's hard to keep fragrant among the dead. O Mensch, gib acht. Was spricht die tiefe Mitternacht? Did you find out from your marching brothers what the midnight says?"

"They're not my brothers, and you're not Nietzsche."

"Right. I'm a sort of mirror, sometimes inverse."

"I'm not looking into it. What did I call you for?"

"The subject is rebirth."

"Big topic." Peter goes back to his book.

"You know, you shouldn't disdain the marchers. In their own benighted way they understand something."

"What?"

"That frenzy, however juvenile and vacuous, is still better than the lowing of the herd."

31

"They're nothing but a herd themselves. I was once one of them."

"The herd is everywhere, Peter. That's why you called me. You don't want to be a member of a herd. You've been moving from one herd to the next. Child of alcoholics, Jesuit boy, frat boy, naval officer, and most recently a member of the literary elite in the American academy. Right?" There's a silence. "You've got to pitch in here, Peter. Even emissaries from the Unterwelt need Gesprächspartners."

"I'll have something to say when the time comes. Proceed, mirror man."

"OK. Now, to your credit, you've decided to fail and sever yourself from the herd of the academy."

"I didn't decide to fail."

"Of course you did. You proposed an impossible dissertation. Peter, the stone, hurled himself futilely against the impenetrable outworks of the academic brother hoard and lies broken below the walls of ivy."

"OK. I'm unherded."

"So you have a chance to be reborn."

"That's what I was going to do through my dissertation, achieve rebirth."

"Right. Whitman. Tell us more about that."

"OK. The Ninth-month midnight. I was going to go out to Montauk and read the midnight poem to the wind and the birds. After that lilacs. I was going to follow the long train of grief and lay a blossom on the tomb in Illinois in the black murk of midnight. I was going to know what your deep midnight says. I was going to tell it all, just as it happened to me."

"And what made you think the academic herd would allow such subversions of scholarly standards?"

"I don't know. But I was obviously mistaken."

"You weren't mistaken. You knew the herd wouldn't allow it, so you chose to break yourself against the wall of the academy. You thought that would bring rebirth."

"I'm not broken."

"You've broken an old shell of yourself, but you haven't remade yourself." Vogt crosses his arms and looks up contemplatively. "You're about to join a new herd, called happy husbands. I've seen her."

Peter says nothing.

"She's very beautiful. Probably of noble birth."

"She was an orphan."

"Maybe a royal foundling."

"Hardly. Adopted and brought up by an Asian-American family."

Vogt pauses, as one weighing words. "This is not a good pairing, Peter. A beautiful thing in flight, a broken creature struggling to break out of an old shell."

Peter looks up angrily. "How do I end this call?"

"Just say the word, Peter. But know that I'm always at your service."

Naughton, on his way to see Charlene, meets Sister Claire. "Guten Morgen, Schwester."

"Good morning, Mr. Naughton. I assume this is a little test. Yes, I've met your friend."

"I would've spared you, but you wanted to share fully."

"Yes."

"Do you think he's a demon?"

"At this moment I would say no, but I expect to see him again."

"What do you think he is?"

"When I think I know, I'll tell you. As I said, I expect to see him again."

Naughton cocks his head. "Demons are very smart, as you know, Sister. The demons knew who Jesus was before the disciples did."

Sister Claire smiles.

Naughton slaps his forehead. "Oh my God. I didn't mean to compare . . ."

"I know that, Mr. Naughton. And Vogt seemed to have had a good idea of who you were at that time."

Naughton's eyes redden. "I can't make him go away."

"I guessed that."

"What if he's capable of making us fall?"

"We walk on with the faith that we won't."

"If we fall, will an angel snatch us out of midair?"

"No."

"What about that demon in the story in the desert. What if Jesus had flung himself off the precipice, would an angel have saved him?"

Sister Claire is silent for some moments. "For some stories, Mr. Naughton, there are no what ifs. You're a storyteller. You know that some eventualities don't fit."

Naughton nods. "What will you tell Mother Martha?"

"I've already told her. I believe that through the power of words you can help Charlene."

Naughton looks troubled. "You understand, Sister, my words to Charlene, these scenes come unbidden, uncensored."

"I understand that, Mr. Naughton." Sister Claire looks down at some papers in her hand. "Reports, Mr. Naughton. Words. Inescapable. We must do our duty."

A Lake Near New Orleans

Rest. Let go. Naughton lies in his bed drifting slowly back in time, which in this case is not filled with smoke and bourbon fumes but with the sound of water, the taste of salami and provolone pressed inside a sliced baguette. He looks down at the quilt spread out below him, alternate squares of fleurs-de-lis and circles divided into four parts by crosses with equal arms. The land of counterpane. An old poem.

A scene begins to assemble itself— a small lake defined by a band of trees not quite fully greened. May. The class picnic, end of Peter's sophomore year at Jesuit High School. Mr. Donnelly, teacher, scholastic, had helped his students arrange it. And now he is in the water, cassock off, white swimsuit, beset by a half dozen of the class's more forward boys.

Peter, for some months utterly entranced by *Hamlet*, delivers a soliloquy. Who are these that dare to lay their hands on the sacred body? If I had their names in my hands I would crush them like so many overripe grapes, obscene clusters of vowels—Tuminello, Sabathia, LaNasa, even the trick French names that end sounding like vowels, Favrot, Garsaud, Grenier and the one Jew, God knows why, DaSilva, and even the one German, Kunow, and of course the legion of Irish, Brady, Kavanagh, McCrae, Donohue. Curse the fate that I am powerless to set it straight.

But Peter had joined his voweled comrades in the great fun of the fourth book of the *Aeneid*, secretly drawing Dido spread-eagled on her bed of lust, female concupiscence to them a glorious revelation.

The lake comes into sharp focus. The sound comes up of the splashing and hollering of the attackers of Mr. Donnelly, who will not go down. The scholastic, though his bones are thin and almost fleshless, though the hounds of roaring vowels seize, push and pull, will not go down. He laughs and slips their grasp like a sly serpent, his face and reddish hair streaming the tepid water of the lake, the sun challenged to light faithfully the shine of his teeth, the freckled skin, the blue eyes.

Peter resumes his soliloquy. O ignorant and doomed comrades, so I must call you, you have not long to live. I speak not of the infinitesimal time of our common tenancy on earth. Know you not that Mr. Donnelly by his very name is a descendant of the fabled King Niall of the Nine Hostages and a representative of Jesus. You laugh and call me Doc Logos, the class super scholar. And yet you best me in memorization and in your clownish acting of scenes. You call me the great tongue-tied stone face. Peter the rocky scholar.

Now Mr. Donnelly, who some moments ago had freed himself and run along the shoreline, plunges into the water again, his face flushed, his eyes bright with the joy of pursuit and escape, utterly confident, his subtly articulated limbs easily slipping the awkward grappling of the vowels.

A change in the lighting illuminates the scrim that had until that moment been invisible. Four ancient decapitated pillars stand in the foreground. A dais, still firm and flat, anchors the pediments of the columns. There is no entablature or cornice, nor a single fallen stone to attest there ever was one. But the scrim, agitated by a sudden breeze, nevertheless flashes a fleeting image of a brace of steed with flaring nostrils pulling the chariot of an armed traveler. Off to the side of the dais a devotee of a later god has raised an altar embossed with an encircled cross. Behind is a wall of variegated stone, some of rude masonry, some carefully laid in lattice-like patterns. Within the wall is a shallow oval recess, probably not for a throne. Above the wall lies a steeply sloped field of broken stones and weeds. Along one side the green pinnacles of three stately poplars pierce the cloudless sky. Near the top of the scene rises the sheer face of a cliff gnawed by years of sharp-toothed winds that have found the weakest veins in the granite. Along the top of the scene a cloudless sky burns with a cruel light that ignites all below—ruins, gray rocks, green trees. Behind the viewer of the scene a voice cries out, "He has killed his father." So hollow and toneless is the voice that the speaker must be either stunned by horror or oblivious to it. Against the far cliff the words take the form of a man falling. The doomed man has pulled his knees up under his chin and wrapped his arms around his legs as if to imitate an equilibrist's controlled plunge, but there is no net below. "He has killed his father," the voice repeats monotonously.

Mr. Donnelly comes ashore triumphant, coated with a glistening sheath of lake water. The vowels come panting behind. All sit on towels in the sand. It's time to open the picnic box and the cooler with many soft drinks and one beer for each boy. "Doc Logos is dry," says LaNasa. It's not a taunt, just a statement of disinterested wonderment. There follows brief laughter aimed at Peter's strangeness, but food and drink are the priority. A great rattle of wrappers and fizzing from cans follows. "Shall we have a blessing, lads?" An instant quiet ensues. "Bless us, Oh Lord, and these thy gifts, which we are about to receive from thy bounty. Bless the treacherous waters through which we have passed as did Moses and the Israelites the Red Sea. Bless the healing powers of the ointments which we must apply to salve our overexposure to your potent servant that beams upon our sinful bodies." Subdued snickers. "All this we ask through Christ, Our Lord. Amen." Now great laughter, gnashing and guzzling.

The scrim, lit again, reveals a deserted beach under a blistering sun. So oppressively hot is the air that the sea reluctantly stirs itself to wash the shore with an indolent lapping. A pistol hangs in the air near the rocks that define the beach. It is not suspended by a wire. Surely a hand will appear to hold the pistol. It will be painfully hot, black metal in the sun. The scrim sways though there's little breeze. It appears that the pistol is moving slowly, searchingly along the rocks. After an extended transit it finds its mark, a large crablike creature cowering between two boulders. "Bang!" says the pistol. "Bang! Bang! Bang! Bang!" Its voice sounds like that of a player in a boyish game. The creature hiding between the boulders recoils from the noise. It's not apparent that it's been struck until it begins to wilt like a punctured balloon. At last it lies deflated on the rocks, little more than a thick shadow. The pistol disappears. All that remains of the murder are the reverberations of the shots, creeping stealthily among the rocks, seeking niches and crannies in which to die.

It's time now for the swimmers to gather up the remains of the hastily consumed repast. A bit of muttering about this or that picnicker who isn't doing his share, but soon the effort is organized and they're on the way back to the bus, where Phillipe, a swart man of indeterminate race, lies dozing in the grass on the shady side of the vehicle. The turn in the road that leads out of the sun and into the dark wood prompts Peter to show off as Doctor Logos. "In the middle of our lives we entered a forest savage and dark . . ." Boo. Hiss. "We should've thrown him in the lake," says Brady.

"Wouldn't do any good," says Favrot. "He can talk underwater."

It's raining. Vera stands at the side of Charlene's wheelchair and looks out stolidly. Peter comes up beside her. "The heavens are weeping."

"It is just nature, Mr. Naughton."

A gardener in a yellow slicker trundles a wheelbarrow of rubbish across the greensward and disappears to the right of the window. Vera says, "It is easier to weed when the ground is wet."

Charlene's eyes follow the shining yellow movement and return to their fixed blankness.

"What about the gardener, Vera? Is he nature?"

"Humans are not nature, Mr. Naughton. We are the keepers of nature, as God ordained in the garden."

"But something went wrong in the garden."

"That is right. Sin."

"Charlene knows what went wrong. Everybody is afraid of snakes. But I'm not."

"You are not?"

"That's right. A long time ago I belonged to a cult of snake handlers up on top of Sand Mountain near Birmingham, Alabama. We went up there to escape the Sodom and Gomorrah below. We kept vipers and asps in one big barrel and fed them rats and mice brought up from the city. They're beautiful in their coils, like one long looping creature. Stripes, rings, diamonds."

"You will not tell me that you put your hands in that barrel." Vera's voice brims with repulsion.

"A snake handler has to hold snakes in his hand if he's going to be saved from what is going on down below the mountain."

"The women did not do it."

"Everybody. And the only one that died of a bite was a man who dropped the snake out of fear and lack of faith. Oh ye of little faith."

"That is Jesus walking on water, Mr. Naughton, not snake handling."

"That's right, Vera. A man of faith can handle a snake, but if he tries to walk on water he'll fail every time."

"That is because we are not divine. But it does not matter because I do not believe that you handled snakes, Mr. Naughton."

"I told you, Vera, you've got to be a believer. I never claimed to walk on water, just handle snakes. Paul astounded the barbarians, who didn't believe he could survive the viper's bite."

"I know how to read the Bible, Mr. Naughton. But I worry about this child hearing these strange things you say."

"Is she eating?"

"She is drinking more broth now and eating whole crackers, but that has nothing to do with your tales, Mr. Naughton."

"It may. But I defer to Sister Claire."

"Sister Claire is my superior," saying which Vera makes her well-established sharp turn and walks away.

Naughton watches the rain for a while. "You know, Charlene, water is a miracle." He approaches the window and moves his head close to the glass. "With these drops you could say your beads. Some drops would fall down. New ones would settle against the window. Father, Jesus, Holy Spirit, Mary, Pontius Pilate, the hour of our death. I don't remember it all. You wouldn't hold the beads in your fingers but in your eyes, like little tears of faith and joy. Don't forget to say a bead for protection against the fiend. He's prowling around, maybe out there in the garden in the rain, maybe right here in these hallowed halls. No place is sacred to him." Naughton rubs his face with both hands, then turns and looks at Charlene. "When you say your beads, Charlene, tell one for old Mr. Naughton that he may be protected from the Devil of denial."

Charlene's eyes remain unmoving and blank, or so it seems, but their focus may be different. That would be hard to detect. The expressionless immobility of the face remains, but the hue might change subtly. Also difficult to detect.

"Vera's not a believer. But it's in the Bible that one who passes the test of snake handling can become a healer and lay on hands and speak in tongues." Naughton makes a hovering motion with his hand as if tranced, then returns to the wet scene out the window. Sister Claire comes up behind Charlene's wheelchair, approaching softly on her soft-soled shoes. She stands there quietly for some moments.

"Hello, Sister," says Naughton without turning.

"I thought you hadn't heard me."

"My hearing isn't good, Sister, but I saw you coming down the hall in a big drop of rain, plump as in a funhouse mirror. You were tinted gold from the trees and the gardener."

"How nice, Mr. Naughton. I've never been plump since I was an infant, when I was also a bit yellowish. Jaundiced at birth according to my mother."

Naughton nods but not with great interest. "I envy Charlene. All day she watches little worlds beading and belling on the window and rolling down to make room for others. A display of cosmic dynamism in miniature."

Sister Claire comes around the wheelchair and looks down at Charlene. "It would be a wonderful thing, Charlene, if you would tell us about one of those worlds. I think I see one in your eyes."

Charlene's eyes do not move.

"May I touch your hand, Charlene?"

Charlene does not shrink back.

Sister Claire turns her hand palm up and moves the back of it over Charlene's flesh-bare knuckles and spidery fingers. It's uncertain whether she actually touches Charlene's hand or only conveys a subtle warmth. Something, an autonomic reaction maybe, causes the hairs on Charlene's hand to rise up

41

to Sister Claire's proximate flesh. Sister Claire is fair and virtually hairless. But Charlene has hair on her forearm and on the back of her hand, as black as the hair on her head. Charlene quietly settles deeper into the cushion of the wheelchair. Presently Sister Claire motions Naughton to follow her.

In her office Sister Claire sits in a chair not far from Naughton, who sits in an identical chair.

"I won't ask if you actually handled snakes."

Naughton smiles. "Thanks. But I'd like to ask you a question. Did you sense what you French call *une chaleur* when you put your hand above Charlene's, a living warmth?"

"Yes, I felt it." Sister Claire pauses. "But Vera fears the dark things you say to Charlene."

"What do you say to her?"

"I tell her that her fears are understandable. I tell her that your dark tellings are awakening Charlene. That, I tell her, is what people nowadays call counterintuitive. She understands that. And yet I have fears."

"I have fears. Can it be a good thing, Sister, for two to be bonded by fear?"

"What do you think?"

Naughton smiles grimly. After a long pause he says, "There has come to my mind another of what I call flights."

"Share it."

"I'm in a London tube while the rockets rain down. We, the desperate, cling to each other. We foul ourselves and stink. Our breath is like swamp gas." Naughton abruptly stops speaking. "Did I say rain?" He shakes his head like one trying to clear away a cloud. "Josh told me that fewer than 3,000 were killed in London, but over 20,000 forced laborers died making the rockets. At the time we feared the rockets, Sister, but we didn't know to fear the deadly tunnels of Mittwerk." Naughton stops, presses on. "The time comes when there's not fear of some thing, but just fear like a dense fog and you're perched on the edge of a cliff with wet rubble under your feet. And you're not an eagle."

Sister Claire nods. "At seminary it's called existential fear, the fear that there's no God."

Naughton moves his head almost randomly, casting about. "Cam would've said the numbering of the dead is meaningless. I would look in her eyes to see what was meaningful. I knew some meaning was deep down in those eyes, but I never reached it." Again Naughton pauses, but this time more purposefully. "Have you looked into Charlene's eye? How long can you look into her eyes, Sister?"

"I've never tested myself."

"I've tested myself. It's not long. I turn away and talk. Words."

"Words are what you have to give. Someday we may be given to know where the darkness in them comes from."

Naughton nods, provisionally. "A friend or a demon once told me that life is an inverted pyramid, the pinnacle nose down deep in the sand. Everything we are comes from the stone buried in the sand." Naughton churns the air with his hands. "The hot desert winds blow day long, curling around St. Simeon on his pillar, around the pyramid. The pyramid stands unmoving, caring nothing for the rote of the trillions of honed grains of sand that dart against it." Naughton keeps his hands aloft. "If we're going to be born again, Sister, we have to topple the pyramid, strew its stones around the desert, all that hardness of identity. Charlene's stones are blackened by horrible memories, abuse, God knows what. They're still buried in the sand pit."

"This is a fine metaphor, Mr. Naughton. Go on."

Naughton suddenly laughs. His voice turns completely about, from the vatic to the ironic. "Tourists on rented horses, wearing flowing white like Lawrence of Arabia, construct philosophical statements about the grandeur of the past and the ravages of time. Sic transom glory mundo, the learnéd guide says. Now we must quick ride about or the Bedouins will come on swiff camels and tax us heavy, for Ra the sun god has given them this land."

Sister Claire smiles.

"I'm a foolish old man who can't keep to the subject."

"I'm graced by your foolishness, Mr. Naughton. I'll tell Mother Martha you have a comic side. She'll be reassured."

"Do you tell her everything?"

"Let's stipulate that I do? Your father hangs on a wraith by his toes. Your mother declines to name you. You disdain your schoolmates but love your teacher. You think maybe he's a hero of Irish myth or a water god."

"Is she appalled?"

"She says these are strange imaginings. I tell her Mr. Naughton's classmates named him Doctor Logos. Mockingly. It was probably their way of escaping the knot of his words. He tells about an eagle's flight slicing the air in half, about drifting on a raft for days at sea, about a figure walking on water, about handling snakes and receiving powers."

"What does she say?"

"Be careful. But it's hard to be careful with you, Mr. Naughton. You go flaring off in many directions. One has to run to catch up."

"The wind bloweth where it listeth, Sister."

A Hall in a Fraternity House

The residents of Maison Cristina are encouraged to get exercise. Small weights and thin rubber stretchers are provided. Naughton chooses to walk the hall from the securely locked front door to the large picture window outside Charlene's room. He may encounter Sister Claire or Sister Kathleen or Vera, in which case he will doff an imaginary hat and bid them good morning or good afternoon, sometimes deliberately mistaking the time of day in order to elicit a kind correction. The trip from one end to the other is about one hundred and twenty paces. The length of stride can be adjusted to achieve variety. The walls of the hall offer little to arrest the eye, a sprinkling of simple wooden crosses, an idealized portrait of the founder of the order in a modern wimple, spare, tight and white, something like a bandage for an extensive head wound. Naughton often pauses and fixes his gaze on the off-white paint. It's easy to see where the painter's hand has slipped and left an old coat showing, holidays they called them in the Navy. These miscues can from time to time afford escapements.

The second-floor hall of a fraternity house. The phone rings. Peter, a senior now, is in charge of answering. "Hello, Aunt Ettie."

"How did you know it was me?"

"Nobody else calls here at 3 am in the morning."

"Your frat brothers must be a bunch of deadheads."

"Yep. So what's the subject for this morning, the usual?"

"Don't get smart with me. The subject is that I have just gotten home from a date with another weenie, Sergeant Prescott, US Marines, decorated, but don't ask me what for."

"Maybe, Aunt Ettie, the chosen one you're looking for isn't a Marine after all."

"Who would it be then, Sonny, my horny boss Albert Riemensperger? Good morning, Mr. Riemensperger. Who did you dream last night?"

"I wish you wouldn't call me Sonny, Aunt Ettie. Twenty years old. Why don't I get to be called by my real name?"

"Two reasons. Peter's not your real name. Your mother, my beloved sister Lizzie, let a Black nurse name you. Second, none of you frat boys are grown-ups. Sonny, Bubba, Dicky-bird, and worse."

"Well, what is my real name if it's not Peter?"

"I told your mother Alexander or Marcus or some other noble name, but she forgot because your father was sneaking bourbon into the hospital in Coke bottles."

"Actually, Peter's OK with me."

"It's not OK. It sounds like a tsar or a rabbit. Why didn't you put in to become a fighter pilot instead of a supply officer, or switch over and become a Screaming Eagle? You could've gotten your name changed to Baron von something after you'd won a couple of dog fights in the sky."

"I don't think they have a lot of dog fights anymore. Anyway, my eyes are bad and my inner ear is defective. Up in the air I can't tell the earth from the sky and the clouds."

"That's because your mother whenever she got a break from barfing during morning sickness kept drinking and smoking and losing her balance. You're lucky you weren't born a fetal alcohol monster or whatever they call it."

"There was a Jewish philosopher who said it would've been better not to be born."

"Who knows what Jews might say? They've been in captivity forever. It screws up your head. Anyway, is that the kind of junk they're teaching you in college on a Navy scholarship?"

"Never mind the curriculum. I'm interested in your case, Aunt Ettie, and your never-ending search for a high performer. Did you ever consider a Centaur?"

"What is it, a club?"

"Sort of."

"If I get desperate, I'll get their number from you."

"You're already desperate."

"Listen, Peter. Millions of women in this town are desperate. You got any idea how many queers there are in San Francisco?"

"A million?"

"More. Every closet in the city."

"Better than letting them out on the streets. But you don't have to worry if you're dating Marines, right?"

"Are you kidding? Semper Fido. Locker room sodomates."

"Shocking. Why don't you come back down south?"

"You in New Orleans, queen city of queerdom, and you say that?"

"It wouldn't have to be New Orleans."

"Name one other interesting southern town." Aunt Ettie laughs a bitter laugh. "Maybe I'll try women. I got a catalog. The equipment looks interesting."

"Let me know how it works out."

"Or I'll try your centaurians. Roman, right?"

"Greeks."

"Greeks. Weren't all the big-shot Greeks queers? Like Sacrotus?"

"Not queers, pederasts."

"All right, pederasts. What's in a name?"

"Everything. You said it. I don't have the right name and it's messing me up. But let me know, Aunt Ettie, what you try next. I'll be waiting for your call."

"You're not hanging up. I'm not through talking to you. Listen. If any of those pervert profs make a move, which they will, because you're a pretty boy, put them in touch with me."

"OK. I will."

"But that's not what I want to talk about now."

"What do you want to talk about?"

"I want you to know that I loved your mother."

"I never doubted it. You couldn't have beat up on each other with such glee if you didn't love each other."

"That's right. And she always won."

"I wouldn't have said so."

"Sure she did. It was her vocabulary, which you have inherited. What's the average vocabulary of an American?"

"I don't know. Maybe ten thousand."

"Then she had a million. A word for every known thing and some she made up."

"Yes, but in your battles it wasn't the number of words, it was the amount of poison."

"No it wasn't. It was words wrapping around your neck like one of those boa constrictors Hollywood whores wear."

"Not all Hollywood actresses are whores."

"Name one."

"Irene Dunne. Member of the Knights of Malta. Practically a nun."

"Nuns. What do you think is under those black skirts, Sonny? Some kind of padlock? Your sister is the one who's a nun."

"Is that why you couldn't live with her?"

48

"No. I figured from the first she was either a saint or a lesbian. But that didn't bother me. She was welcome in my apartment. It was her that moved out."

"Maybe she was frightened of men, warriors in particular."

"Not one of them ever touched her. I would've killed them."

"I believe it."

"I don't even know where she is anymore."

"She's still right there in San Francisco, as far as I know."

"Don't you write or call?"

"I heard she invented some kind of sisterhood."

"It's because your mother never treated her right."

"What do you mean?"

"I mean she couldn't stand having a saint in the house playing the piano and floating around in white gauze. To tell the truth I didn't like it a lot either, but she was always welcome here. What about you? Did you like it?"

"She was gone when I started high school, but no, I didn't like it. I didn't understand it. But I liked the piano. I tried to learn."

"I know it. Your mother sent you off to a nun, but you didn't stick with it. I don't blame you. I visited once. That woman smelled to the high heavens. You can't go around in black in the South in the summer just touching water to your forehead."

"I never took piano lessons from a nun."

"Sure you did. You've just forgotten, or buried it. What do the psychology profs call that?"

"Suppression, sublimation, displacement."

"I don't think mine is sublimation because there's nothing sublime about any of the people I keep company with."

"I can believe that, Aunt Ettie. But anyway, I never had the talent to play the piano. I can, however, tell you who loved Stella."

"Who?"

"My father."

"Your father didn't love anything because whatever love is it was over his head. But it figures he'd be attached to Stella. The ape and the saint. They would've made a great movie team. Stella, Hollywood's only virgin, and Martin Numbskull in King Kong Meets Saint Mary."

"We're coming to the end of this conversation, Aunt Ettie. I've got to get up in the morning and go to class."

"One more thing. Peter. You can go to court and change it."

"And you could change Marietta."

"You can't change a nickname. Titta. How would you like to spend your early years being Titta because your sister, who started talking when she was forty-five minutes old, couldn't pronounce sister? Titta. All the cousins and neighbors thought it was the cutest thing. So I was never Marietta, which isn't a five star name either. Then you called me Ettie."

"What would you want to be named?"

"Something Irish, like Morna, with flowing red hair, instead of this black kinky stuff, probably from some Black way back. Everybody in the South has Black blood."

"So I've heard."

"Then there was the kitten we got, which your mother got to name when she was an hour and a half old. It was supposed to be Pretty Thing, which is already nauseating, but she couldn't pronounce that yet either, so it was Pity Sing. If she'd been oriental, like half of this town, it would've been Plitty Sin, which would've been more interesting."

"I think we're through for the night, Aunt Ettie."

"If you hang up I'll call you right back."

"I'm leaving the phone off the hook. Go look for your perfect man, but you won't find him in the bottom of a glass of bourbon."

"Sonny, you little prick."

"Like all your men. Goodnight, Aunt Ettie."

Naughton is sitting in one of two identical chairs in his room. It has a hard seat and back, no arms. The other chair, empty, is identical. The bed is an ordinary twin except that it has lifters under the legs at the head. It's made up meticulously—hospital corners, the top sheet and blanket folded down at a slant to create a right triangle. He's oriented toward the hall. Behind him and to the left the bathroom door is open. A toilet, seat closed, can be seen. The end of the roll of paper depending from a wall bracket has been folded to create a neat point like an unsealed envelope. Directly behind him is a window that looks out on a small area enclosed in a fence. A garden shed stands at the back. He's smiling, an inward smile at some thought or image.

Sister Kathleen pauses at the doorway. "Good morning, Mr. Naughton." Her tone is at once cheery and brittle.

Naughton tips an imaginary hat. "Top o' the morning to ye, Sister."

Sister Kathleen smiles. "Naughton has an Irish ring to it. County Clare maybe."

Naughton deepens his voice comically. "Send not to ask for whom the Nellies toll. They knell for thee."

Sister Kathleen laughs abruptly. "I'm afraid you've got it wrong, Mr. Naughton. The Nellies were the downstairs English girls. We were the Molly McGuires."

"In which case, Sister, I owe you, a double apology, national and personal."

"Personal?"

"Yes, because I was churlish when I first came and declined to be ministered to by you. However, I believe that in the end it was wise."

"Why is that, Mr. Naughton?"

"Well, I recall saying to myself something perspicacious, whereas most of what I say to myself is midnight palaver."

"What did you say to yourself?"

"I said, Peter, here stands before you, a true Gaelic with flaming red hair and sapphire eyes. Either she is one of the religiously ruthless kind or she is, beneath her prim garb, Irish wild. In either case we will make an unnatural couple."

"That may be, Mr. Naughton, but I would've been pleased with the assignment."

"Gracious of you, Sister. Especially spoken about a person here on grounds of insanity, perhaps homicidal or suicidal, depending on the account of my son Joshua, an account which apparently I'm never to see."

"The revealing or not is none of my doing, Mr. Naughton. But, turnabout, what do you suppose I said to myself looking upon yourself?"

"I would take a dander along the cliffs of Antrim to know it, Sister."

Sister Kathleen looks closely at Naughton. "Have you been to Ireland, then, Mr. Naughton?"

"I've been everywhere on the planet, Sister." Naughton taps his head. "I would've thought they told you. But you said you'd tell me what you said to yourself when you saw me."

"I did say so. Then, to follow your manner of speaking, I said, Kathleen, here stands before you a man who has wandered from his wits into a thicket of such confusion that he doesn't know what has actually happened. The case is interesting, but 'tis late in the day for me to become a detective. So, you see, Mr. Naughton, we caromed off of each other like billiard balls."

"Ah, there you have struck true, Sister. For nothing is so definitively imperial as the report of the collision of two billiard balls in the cavernous gaming parlor of the Vice-regal Lodge at Shimla. A ceiling fan of bamboo paddles whispered overhead. In a far corner an old gentleman turned with slow deliberation the limp pages of last week's *London Times*. Otherwise, the hush of the Indian summer lay upon us like a bolt of loosely woven silk. 1912, one of the hottest. It's likely that in some misfortunate precinct of Calcutta many succumbed to the heat. But that was of no consequence here. Meanwhile, it was of course necessary for an American visitor to mute his skills. In billiards the angle of incidence does not quite equal the angle of reflection. Slight imperfections of the ball, invisible wrinkles in the cushion, an eccentric strike of the cue causing spin, that sort of thing. One quickly learns, but it's better not to put such knowledge to use, especially among the British. I'm sure that in your life, Sister, you also have experienced the necessity of hiding a bit of your Irish brilliance under a bushel."

Sister Kathleen has been listening with amused admiration. "I've never thought I had any dangerous brilliance to hide, Mr. Naughton. The problem for us beyond the pale has always been the opposite, to dig out of the bogs for some glance of sun."

"Well spoken, Sister. You make me doubt my wisdom in declining your ministrations. But now I'm in the hands of Sister Claire, and the French are masters of reason and clarity."

Sister Kathleen's face, which up to this point has been handsomely suffused with amusement, darkens. "Sister Claire's a beacon, but it's we Irish that can't be thrown off balance by wild talk."

"I believe she will not be either."

Sister Kathleen takes a quarter turn. "I'm glad we had this talk, Mr. Naughton."

"Grace me from time to time, Sister, with your smile. It's different from all else here."

"I'll do that, Mr. Naughton." Sister Kathleen departs.

Naughton gets up from his chair, walks out into the hall and turns toward the window at the end. He stops to look into the room immediately adjacent to his. A woman of eighty years or nearly that sits in a chair with a table and tray before her. On the tray is an assortment of pebbles, beads, wads of rolled-up paper, a fragment of a gum eraser and a number of other objects. These she sorts into different piles, muddles them again, sorts them again with amazing rapidity and dexterity. The woman does not look up. She says, "Twenty-four. How many different fours?"

"You must ask my son Joshua, madam. I believe your problem involves a veritable thicket of factorials and sixes."

"Sixes!"

"Consider yourself blessed, madam. Six is the most beautiful of the digits, the only one with an angel's wing."

"How many different sixes?"

"I'll bet Sister Kathleen can help you make a proper sort. I myself am handicapped, a word man."

"I don't like Charlene." The woman lifts a hand from the board and points out into the hall.

"Nobody likes Charlene. She's not here yet."

"Ha. Ha. Shut the door as you go out."

Naughton obliges and moves on to the next door, which is only partially ajar. All that is visible of a human occupant is an acute hillock of feet beneath a blanket at the foot of a bed. The rest of the room is hidden. The sound of a broken stertor comes faintly to the doorway. Naughton says, "I think your feet need some air, sir."

A disapproving grunt is followed by coughing and wheezing.

"I'm sorry, sir. I intended just a little foray into the humorous."

At the end of the hall Charlene sits in her wheelchair untended. Naughton circles around her and looks out the window. "Every day has its weathers, Charlene. Today I've been exchanging some Irish palaver with Sister Kathleen, and have been unkind to two of our fellow inmates, thinking myself witty. One of our confreres, possibly older even than I am, is sorting objects into piles. The objects, of a remarkable variety, don't appear to be of any interest to her. It's the order of them that challenges her. The idea of order in an unraveled mind is moving. Another I passed had a snoring foot, his undetachable bedmate, but miles and miles from him down long white hills and dales where no horse knows the way."

Charlene's legs make a momentary odd motion, straight out and back, knees bent.

"I think you were dreaming of walking again, Charlene, climbing up above the seashore." Naughton pauses reflectively. "I asked, of course, what may I know of Charlene? Nothing they say. There is nothing to be known. You were delivered here on a litter by nervous bearers who immediately disappeared. This strains credence, Charlene. Lost heirs of vast fortunes, royal foundlings. That kind of fairy tale stuff. Still, I have to accept it. Both of us have to accept what's spooned into our mouths. When you wouldn't swallow, didn't Vera stroke your throat? You wanted to sing, not swallow."

Vera appears. She radiates always a combination of skepticism and vibrant stability. "Well, Mr. Naughton, what story have you got for us today?"

"I was telling Charlene about a time when as a boy I took a very long walk, out onto a spit to the very edge of the ocean and there I thought I spied a swallow, which, as you know, can fly straight up into the air. I was mistaken. It was a mockingbird, two of them in fact, transients like me. I had to hack my way through blackberry briers and wild winds rushing this way and that."

"What were you looking for, Mr. Naughton?"

"I didn't know, but I knew it was out there. What were you looking for when you found your calling?"

"I was not looking. God was looking for me."

"It was a demon brother that was looking for me."

Vera gives Naughton a sharp look. "Did he find you?"

"Yes, but then he left me with only a parting gift of words, which is all I have now to share with you and Charlene."

"What kind of words?"

"The words of the mockingbird. Didn't I say? The mockingbird can sing in four score tongues, Vera. But I only heard one."

Vera turns from Naughton to Charlene, who again makes with her legs a stunted walking motion.

Naughton nods. "You walk the halls and the rooms of us afflicted, Vera, dispensing the bronze heat of God's love. Charlene and I have to go a different way. But for now let us just sit together."

A whitecap rolls up outside the picture window. Nothing is more false than a whitecap in a painting. Try as the artist may to produce kinetic froth and spray, the whitecap stubbornly rears itself to the surface of the oil and stands there empty, unfinished.

A Rented Room in New Orleans

Peter sits at his desk. There's a clicking sound. It could be merely the eccentric vocables of old plumbing. Or the chittering of the window in its casing, for there's a stiff breeze in the street. But it turns out to be the onset of a familiar voice. Vogt stands in the doorway. "You called."

Peter remains at his desk. A squat glass half full of amber liquid sits on a writing pad once green, now faded and stained. His eyes are mildly bleared. He smiles at his visitor. "Vogt, you're my favorite caryatid. Most of your fellow capital bearers have busted arms and sooty skirts, but your polo shirt is intact, even if rotted and your limbs are intact even if pocked. I nosed you before you appeared."

The features of Vogt's face in the upward light of Peter's desk lamp are sharp. "And from the end of the hall I nosed fumes of booze intermingled with emissions from the corpse of your academic career floating over your quarters like swamp gas. Thus, Peter, we're always mirror images."

"In a carnival glass. Anyway, I've forgotten what I called you for."

"You called to talk about the body."

"We don't need to. You can go back down. We've just had a learned lecture by a Yale professor washed up on the shores of Connecticut in a bottle from France. It proves infallibly that the body is essentially a social construct enlisted primarily when necessary for control of the unruly or deviant."

"Another fad for the academics to low as they reorient the herd. Remember your Jesuit teachings. Corpus est radix omnium malorum. Which will it be then, Peter? The body as wraith or the body as the habitat of pre-mortuary worms?"

Peter sips delicately from his glass. "I'm consulting the spirits of corn."

"Ask the spirits of corn if they agree that your pursuit of an Asian beauty is tainted with a deadly sinful lust."

"A logical error, Vogt. The idea of lust as a deadly sin depends on the existence of God."

"No it doesn't. God is dead, an old metaphysical monster invented in primordial caves. Lust exists, an evolutionary hyperbole of the urge to perpetuate the species. Often mistaken for love, as in your case."

Peter sips. "What does the deep midnight have to say about this matter?"

"It says you're shattered and about to offer your shattered self to one too innocent to understand the perils." Vogt leans toward Peter. His thin neck, strung with taut tendons and veins of beating blood, penetrates the penumbra around the desk lamp, bearing at its extremity a heavy cranium and a tightly compressed shock of red hair. "You called for consideration of the body, Peter. Consider breaking off this disastrous relationship."

"OK. You've said your piece, Vogt."

"I'm dismissed. We'll meet again, Peter, more than once but I predict there'll come a time when you won't call me anymore."

"What will signal the coming of that happy day?"

"Call it the ascendency of imagination over flesh."

"Oh wondrous prophecy!"

"Ungrateful sarcasm." Vogt goes to the doorway, stays there for a moment and then slides slowly back into the hall.

Peter sits still and silent at his desk for some time. In his face, which is a little slack, and in his narrowed eyes there is evidence of an effort to recall something. After a while he takes a sheet of paper from a drawer and lays it carefully on the desk pad, smoothing it ceremonially under the palm of his hand. He unscrews the top from a fountain pen and writes at the top of the page, "The Bridge."

"For Cam."

He writes furiously as if recording the speech of a sovereign voice that proceeds at an inexorable pace.

Do not look down to the bottom of the ravine

Do not search for the silver sheen that once rose from the stream

Do not ask why the sun has stricken dry the skulls of rock

Or why the cliffs have sucked their gums back from their teeth

See the bowman has come through the forest on the other side

See he has a quiver of arrows sharp against the wind and deeply notched

See he has a spool of white line stronger than a thousand spider's threads

See he has around his neck serpentine coils of hemp no knife can cut

See the arrows hewn from ancient cedar are finely tapered to slip the wind

See the bow's layers of bamboo and maple are too fine for the eye to count

Watch now he ties the white line to the arrow's base and notches the arrow

Watch the glint of the feathers the fletcher has fashioned from hen and cock

Watch him draw back the bowstring that is woven of sinew and flax

Watch the bowstring quiver like the neck of a singer pitched to the top of desire

If the arc of the arrow's flight is too proud the arrow will fall short

If the tip strikes the face of the cliff it will fall into the dark ravine like a stricken bird

If the arc of the arrow's flight is too flat the arrow will fall short

If the tip lodges for a moment in a crevice it will fall broken like a fated knight's lance

Wait until you see the white line split the trackless air dividing forest and sky

Wait until you see the arrow come to your feet trailing the white line

Free the line from the arrow and wrap it thrice around the young beech tree

With spit and the oils of your body anoint the line and winch it to you

See now the brown hemp snakes his sinuous way toward you

Be not afraid for he is the messenger of the bowman

When you have the hemp in hand tie it to the trunk of the beech

Pull tight the clove hitch you have learned and tie off the bitter end

Suddenly Peter is stricken, as if a powerful force has staggered him and left him struggling for air. With a great effort he turns his chair around, gets to his feet and lurches to his bed, motionless the moment after he falls onto the blanket. Under the desk lamp the pen lies uncapped on the sheet of white paper, slowly drying, giving up its glister.

Naughton wanders the hall. At the door of the room of the counting woman he pauses to look in. Sister Kathleen sits in a chair looking at her patient across the surface of a small table. On the table lie the many diminutive objects. "Come in, Mr. Naughton," says Sister Kathleen.

Naughton walks in and stands by the table.

"Ms. Trask is working hard to sort her objects."

The quickness of the old woman's hands has not diminished since Naughton's last observation. He ruminates. "Trask," he says. "Are you of the famous railroad family, madam?"

"Nine hundred and ninety-seven cars."

"Ah. A prime number, Ms. Trask. Hard to apportion."

The old lady takes an interest in the visitor. "Are you a mathematician?"

"Not really, Ms. Trask. I was just guessing, but my son was at one time a Pythagorean."

"What is he now?" asks Sister Kathleen.

"Alas, a devotee of quantum indeterminacy. That's why I'm here, but the full explanation is abstruse and convoluted, as is everything to do with Joshua."

The old woman continues her rapid sorting. Sister Kathleen says, "Ms. Trask has many extraordinarily interesting objects, but I can't slow her down so that we can talk about them."

Naughton says, "One of them is an ossicle, worn by weather and sea. May I have a closer look?"

Ms. Trask shoves the little bone off to the side but taps it with her finger to indicate it may not be removed from the table. Naughton bends down over the small object and inspects it carefully. Now Ms. Trask's hands slow down, certain piles seem satisfactory and then at last all of them. Her hands grow still, she throws her head back and shrieks triumphantly, a sound so piercing that Sister Kathleen instinctively leans away from the old woman. When Ms. Trask has, red faced, at last finished hurling her flaming lance of defiance at the gods of combinations and permutations, Sister Kathleen says, "You've done it, Ms. Trask. I knew you would."

Ms. Trask leans back in her chair, eyes closed, mouth open as for an ecstatic inhalation.

"Bernini's Santa Teresa," says Naughton. "A little aged but just as surely pierced by the angel."

Sister Kathleen looks sharply at Naughton but says nothing.

"I wish I were a zoologist," says Naughton, still bent over the small bone. "I don't know what animal it came from. Under such circumstances I think we're free to speculate, don't you Sister?"

Ms. Trask continues her consummative inspiration of air.

"Go ahead and speculate, Mr. Naughton."

"Let's say, then, that it's a vertebra from a serpent. Once removed from the garden of Ms. Trask's objects, she easily completed her task. Of course, my son Joshua would offer an entirely rational and unsymbolic explanation, that the number of Ms. Trask's objects was prime and so she couldn't create even piles. Thus the removal of any object would have sufficed to compose Ms. Trask. That little golden medallion with the eagle and shield on it for instance."

Now Ms. Trask sits forward. Her eyes brighten. She looks with an expression of absolute disdain at the objects on the table, raises a hand and sweeps them all onto the floor, whereupon she redirects her gaze at Sister Kathleen. "Where did you get this pile of merde? And don't say I brought them with me. Where was I when you captured me?"

"You were living with your sister, Jeanette, Ms. Trask. We didn't capture you. A friend recommended you to us."

"Jeanette. That explains everything. She was a packrat. Her husband Lloyd called her anal. But it had nothing to do with their carnal congress."

"I'm glad to hear that, Ms. Trask."

"I'll be taking my leave soon, not that I have any great desire to return to Jeanette."

"I'm afraid Jeanette wouldn't be able to receive you, Ms. Trask. She died some months ago."

"Did the house burn down around her? She was a chain smoker. The fingers of her right hand were amber."

"No, she died in a hospital, well taken care of and without much suffering."

"Then I'll go back to the house. Lloyd left a long time ago. It will take me ages to clear the place out. It has to be done with care. One day I was flipping through an old copy of *Good Housekeeping* and a stock certificate fell into my lap. RCA."

"We'll have to see what we can arrange, Ms. Trask."

Ms. Trask leans back, tired it would seem. Sister Kathleen motions Naughton out of the room. He says, "I'm very sorry to . . ."

"Go."

Just outside the door of Ms. Trask's room Naughton encounters Sister Claire. "Am I summoned?" he asks.

"Not today. Just now I'm on my way to keep an appointment with our chaplain, Father Schneider. You'll have a chance to meet him someday."

"I caught a glimpse of him in the hall yesterday. Ichabod."

"You will come to respect him."

"No doubt."

"I'm eager to talk to you about Marines and dead gods."

"There are more congenial subjects."

Sister Claire waves her hand, departing hastily.

Naughton finds Charlene at the end of the hall. A gentle mist shrouds the greensward. Beyond the hedgerow the yellow birches stand like a loosely ordered soldiery in a faded photograph. He peers out the window as if expecting them to advance.

"Changa," says Charlene.

"Yes," says Naughton, showing no surprise at hearing Charlene make a word-like sound. "The weather here is indeed very changeable, but any element of variety is welcome as far as I'm concerned."

Charlene shakes her head angrily. "Cdannn!"

"Danger," says Naughton.

Charlene nods.

Naughton says, "I had a friend who fell off a cliff in exactly this kind of weather. It's a sad story but maybe you'd like to hear it since you've mentioned danger."

Charlene nods.

"He was an ace climber, repelling, pitons, all that kind of thing, a sworn enemy of gravity. A poor choice of enemies in my estimation. I see from your look you're interested in what my sworn enemy might be."

Charlene's eyes brighten and widen as with incipient mirth.

"You are very perceptive, Charlene, because you have guessed already that my chosen enemy will be comical, absurd even. I'll tell you what it is, but don't tell Sister Claire or Vera because they already think I'm a little off." Naughton lowers his voice. "It's games, any kind of game except word games. Take chess for instance, with its board of squares and prohibited moves, a veritable prison. But suppose the pieces were changed into metaphors, pawns as in dupes and shops, castles as in the sovereign domiciles of the bourgeoisie, the act of castling though I can't remember exactly what it is except that it has something to do with rookeries, reminding one of seals, reminding one of kings and royal decrees, or modern queens those poor creatures whose painted faces but not their illicit desires have faded, and knights oh well there you have armor and amour under the moon and so on. Now, you see, the movement of pieces is very flexible and often amusing."

"Schto," says Charlene.

"Story? Ah yes, I remember. The tragic story of the missed step in the mist, a story that might've turned out entirely differently by the introduction of a small fortuitous object, like say the bitter end of a misplaced or forgotten rope . . ."

"Mr. Naughton, you are rattling." Vera has come up quietly.

"True, Vera, but a day without rattling is a day lost, words asleep on the job."

"It could be, Mr. Naughton, that Charlene would enjoy some sensible talk. Anyway, Sister Claire would like for you and Charlene to rest for the rest of today."

Charlene makes a noise something like an harrumph.

"Patience, Charlene. Sister Claire's advice is always wise. I shall repair to my quarters, and you will lean back into the soft gray mist. But keep an eye on the garden and you may catch a glimpse of our ill-fated equilibrist treading ever so carefully the edge of the lawn."

The following afternoon Vera has words for Naughton. "You are not eating right, Mr. Naughton." The word eating is elongated, its initial phoneme powerfully accentuated.

Naughton and Vera look at each other across Charlene's wheelchair. So set is this flanking and repetition of exchanges that it has the feel of a ritual.

"Eating." Naughton repeats the word just as Vera has spoken it. She frowns. "I'm not mocking you, Vera, but you brought that word here from a distant land. It makes me think of green terraces, rain cascading from level to level with a precise plashing."

"I never lived where there are terraces, Mr. Naughton, but if you need terraces to eat, think of terraces and eat."

"I'll think of what grows on terraces in the month of May."

"Good." That clearly is Vera's final word on the subject. She turns and walks down the hall.

Naughton surveys the scene beyond the window. "The merry month of May, Charlene. Brings to mind a sunny play I attended in old London town. A poem. Lots of green, a queen, a nightingale, a lover's tale. A cuckoo and a kiss." Naughton smiles wistfully. "Can you believe, Charlene, I was once a would-be lover? Not a cuckoo, I thought. A much larger, handsomer bird, maybe a raptor, like your eagle. Alas, it was an illusion. I thought I'd caught my prey, a beautiful woman. She bore me two children and mothered them until they were old enough to fly from the nest and then she left. Nobody for me to talk to. I started looking for walls. I am the wall man. You are the eagle."

Naughton turns from the window and looks at Charlene. Her body is alive, not in motion or even with a visible throb, but subtly animated, tense, like a crouching runner at the block or a diver balanced at the end of a platform. Naughton says, "If I had permission, Charlene, I'd touch your hand. It's ruddier today and surely warm." He looks into her eyes. "I'd be frightened of that avidity, Charlene, if I thought that when the day comes for you to stoop you would stoop on me. But it's not me, is it?" Naughton walks back and forth in front of Charlene, his hands behind his back, then stops. "I'm not quite a powerless old man, Charlene. My walls have powers. My stories have powers." Naughton takes another turn. "The stories go their own way, Charlene. So do the walls. Staged of course and sometimes secretively masked. Once at a carnival ball on the Grand Canal I thought I would be impaled on the golden beak of one of the more vicious celebrants of license. I don't know what he wanted. My liver maybe. But there're no rocks in Venice to chain a Titan to. No rocks here in Maison Cristina either. We'll get out of here someday."

Ganglia, musculature, tendons, on signal from some autonomic reflex or from something more conscious, produce in Charlene's body a jerky motion verging on a seizure.

Naughton's eyes widen. "Someday soon, Charlene, you'll be able to speak that shudder. The dark thing clutching your spine and jamming your larynx will submit to your will."

Sister Kathleen has come from a patient's door and glances down the hall. Naughton calls out to her, "Come to the window, Sister. Lovely is the breeze from over the sea."

Sister Kathleen comes smiling. "Is it a poem, Mr. Naughton?"

"I think it must be. The world is strewn with poems. But like sprites and sylphs, poems are shy, offish. You have to be on the lookout and poke around a bit."

"I thought it was a poem because we aren't near the ocean. But then you've been a seafaring man, haven't you?"

"Yes. I'm even a shellback. Are you a shellback, Sister?"

"Not that I know of."

"Then you're a pollywog."

"I hope not."

Charlene's diaphragm contracts in what must surely be silent laughter.

Naughton says, "No offense, Sister, but this is one of those either or things. You have either crossed the line on a ship or not, the line in this case being the equator, not some margin of acceptable behavior."

Sister Kathleen chuckles. Her face reddens attractively. "I thought a pollywog was a tadpole."

"In general parlance it is that tiny bog creature, but to us old salts it's a person who hasn't crossed the line on a ship. On the other hand, the term shellback isn't in common parlance. This gives us shellbacks a unique identity you pollywogs can never quite have. The social consequences are negligible, but

the psychological benefits of being a shellback are considerable, though I'm not sure I can describe them."

"I would never ask you to, Mr. Naughton."

Naughton lowers his voice a little. "Finely tuned as my
instincts are to various currents, human and oceanic, I believe
I can say definitively that Charlene is a shellback."

Charlene's mouth twitches, but nothing comes from it. It's
dry, though only minutes ago Vera swabbed it with a pink gel.
Tiny lesions divide the lips, each into four parts.

"How is Ms. Trask doing?"

"Ms. Trask has recovered her little treasures and is now
writing down detailed notes about the history of each."

"A wonderful recovery. Ah. Another snippet of poetry just
came to me. History has many cunning passages, contrived
corridors and issues."

"It's not very poetic, is it?"

"No, I'm afraid not. It's an old man's poem."

"I worry sometimes about Ms. Trask, but what's the use of
it?"

"Well, she may find her way out, piece by piece. But I
suspect that's rare in your experience."

"Yes. But hope is a great virtue."

"Charlene will find her way out. She's already stirring."

Naughton and Sister Kathleen look at Charlene. There's
evidence of what Naughton has just said. The lines between
brain and limb, limb and limb, apparently long broken, seem
to be slowly reconnecting.

Sister Kathleen departs. Charlene is still. Naughton looks
at a leg that has slipped from sheet and gown. It's thin and
very white. Naughton muses. How should a leg look? There
should be at least a faint blush of blood or burnish of sun. It
might even have a porcelain glow hinting at depth. But
Charlene's leg, her gown, and the sheet have coalesced into an
expanse of unbroken white.

A Stone Wall on a Sunny Campus

Peter and Cam are sitting on a high wall on campus. The wall, made of large umber sandstone blocks, is knobby. Some of the stones are delaminated. Neither's legs are long enough to touch the scrubby grass below. Cam is bending over, looking at the stone. "If we know how, we can tell the age of stones." Something in the cadence of her voice, an unusual unmodulated evenness, suggests a foreign influence. Her legs, bare below the hem of her skirt, are lighter than the stone but belong to the same color family.

Peter's, lightly haired, are much paler. "I wouldn't be able to say anything but old. In a seminar we had to read some Tennyson, *In Memoriam* mostly, poems about a dead friend. Geology shook Tennyson up. It shook everybody up at that time."

"Why did it shake them up?"

"It proved that the earth is much older than we thought, and somehow that scared everybody. I don't know exactly why. I didn't get it quite straight. Tennyson is not my guy."

"Who is your guy?"

"Walt Whitman."

"Isn't he a lot about the body?"

Peter laughs. "Yes, but that's not what I was going to write about."

"What were you going to write about?"

"Awakening and sorrow."

"Those are beautiful, but now you are not going to do it?"

"No." Peter smiles. "You're a good inquisitor."

"I know what that is. Why are you not going to do it?"

"Because I couldn't do it my way, and any other way seemed false."

"What are you going to do?"

"What I'm doing now, trying to make you fall in love with me."

"There is no need to try because it just can happen or not."

"Men when they see what they want can't help trying to will it."

"They should help it."

Peter gazes at Cam. She is quite beautiful, Eurasian, eyes dark and wide set, nose narrow, the opening of the nostrils barely visible, ogival. The indentation under the nose, the philtrum, is distinct and evocative, leading down to lips shaped like an archer's bow. Her hair is black.

Cam sits back up. She reaches out and touches the back of Peter's hand with her index finger, as precisely as if she were a physician probing the exact locus of pain. "You don't know who you are now without your guy Whitman."

"I could be the guy who reads you his poems. You'd love them."

"No. I tried to read poems. I don't understand them. One poem I was taught I understand. It is very famous, by Li Po, 'Chuang Tzu and the Butterfly.' You know it?"

"No. What does it say?"

"It says that in a dream Chuang Tzu became a butterfly. Then the butterfly became Chuang Tzu. Who can tell which is which? The water of the sea comes back to become the stream.

70

The melon gardener was a prince. What is what? Why do we work and work?"

"Does the poem tell why we work and work?"

"I think it's because we forget that we are butterflies."

"I'm a butterfly. I've flown thousands of miles north to sip on flowers and make sure they blossom again next year. You're a flower."

"What kind of a flower?"

"Since I'm a monarch, king of butterflies, I sip only from brightly colored flowers."

"What happens to the flowers that are brown like me? Not like these." Cam moves her hand slowly across a broad arc. Within its compass are many women students. It's the season for pastel blouses and bare arms and shoes without socks.

"You're not brown. You're like the color of tea the first moment warm water touches the leaves. The colors of those you're pointing to are borrowed. The monarch knows true beauty when he sees it."

"The colors of all clothes are borrowed. What if we didn't have clothes on?"

"If I saw you naked I wouldn't be able to breathe."

Cam laughs. "Then I would be free of you flying around in my head."

"Am I in your head?"

"Yes. You won't go away. You won't take the hint."

"But if I flew away, wouldn't you be lonely?"

"Yes."

"They say great beauty is a curse. Helen of Troy, Cleopatra and many others."

"I don't know those persons."

"It doesn't matter. It was off the wall."

"No. We're sitting on the wall. You look scared, like you're afraid of falling off."

Peter laughs, a bit uneasily. "It's not very far down. What makes you scared?"

"If you don't know, I can't make you understand."

A scrim slides across the pleasant sun and shade of the campus, obscuring the couple on the wall. A crow flies across the scrim, croaking its dissident cry. A bodiless image of Vogt's face emerges, unframed this time by the familiar door with its peeling paint. Against the distant and hazy green of the campus the shock of reddish hair burns the air. The blue eyes shine defiantly against the azure blue above. The lips are thin and imperfectly shaped like a misplaced mensur scar. Now they move, suggesting the rictus of a sardonic grin. "I've been listening, Peter. A wordy void, an insect metaphor feeding on a vulnerable flower, itself caught between beauty and emptiness." The voice pauses. "Who in your rarified world of Logos would've guessed that an empty signifier had such a voracious appetite?"

A motion disturbs the scrim, a wrinkle of sound or time. "We talked about the body, Peter, and its potential for disasters. I tried to breach the walls of your verbal cleverness. Do you have any idea how obdurate they are? That you're immured in a dungeon of your own making?" Another pause, a strenuous inhalation of exasperation. But the voice keeps true to its ruthless insistence. "And this poor creature, alone and alienated, exotic even in this stew of whites, mulattos, Blacks, Creoles, descendants of murdered Choctaws. Her innocent beauty confounds the young gallants, Fornier and Velez and Honorato, who fearfully stay their distance. So she has only you, devious master of words, incarnation of mindless appetite."

Another pause. When the voice comes again it's diminished by distance. "You'll call me again, Peter, before the fatal bound of marriage and after. In the old story the Fathers taught you there are three denials. But you're a master denier, Peter, three times three. Still, the chances for repentance are endless. Let her go. Sooner or later someone, man or woman, will come up from the noisy herd and offer her something of value." The scrim fades out.

Peter is speaking. "Suppose I said that my loneliness may be as deep as yours."

"You don't know my loneliness."

"I only said may. And you don't know my loneliness any more than I know yours."

"I don't know your loneliness. It's hidden because you want me to fall in love with you."

"Yes, but just about everything in us is always hidden."

"But this time it matters."

Naughton is sick for a few days, just a cold, but Sister Claire orders him to bed. Vera brings him chicken soup and crackers. He asks for coffee with a little cream. "Milk is not good for your cold, Mr. Naughton. It makes the spit thick." She brings him warm salt water to gargle. "Then you can suck a menthol."

Naughton coughs wheezily.

"You are not going to die, Mr. Naughton."

Naughton winds up his coughing and takes a deep breath. "The cough, Vera, was just so you wouldn't feel that your ministrations are for naught." Naughton pauses for acknowledgement of his clever pun but gets none. "Anyway, thanks for the reassurance, Vera. It's the first time anybody has conferred immortality on me."

"Everybody is immortal, Mr. Naughton. There is nothing special about you."

"Still, I used to worry about death."

"Do not worry about it. Death is just when the body quits."

"Right. How is Charlene?"

"Charlene's eyes move now."

"And she's still taking broth and crackers?"

"Yes. But the crackers are a problem. She has not learned to swallow again, so I have to rub her throat, and still sometimes they come back up."

Naughton nods. "Four of us you have to take care of, Vera. Charlene, me, the irascible Ms. Trask and another man whose feet twitch and who hoots if he thinks you're looking in his door."

"That would be Mr. Gerrity."

"Is there another hall or wing with others?"

"No. The sisters just asked for four."

"Do you think we're some kind of experiment?"

"Experiment. You do not experiment with people, Mr. Naughton. Just rats and monkeys. I have to go now. You ring if you need something."

"Tell Charlene hello for me."

"I will. She misses you and your stories. She is just learning how to miss things."

"A necessity for survival."

"A necessity to be a child of God and know that we are incomplete." Vera leaves.

Naughton looks out the window. The undergrowth is closer here than at the end of the hall. It's a moodless day full of grayness and glare that comes dispersed from an invisible sun. He turns away and looks upward. "You're not a very interesting ceiling," he says after a while. "In the Navy we had ducts and electrical conduits and bolted plates on the overhead. The ducts cast shadows and were themselves sleeved with darkness. The kind of place Vogt likes to hide and come out from. But I'm not calling him now."

Naughton drifts into a suggestible drowse. There's a tap on the door. The figure of a priest appears in a black suit, white collar. He is composed entirely of angles and impossible facets like a Picasso. The black thing on his upper lip looks like a cross between a propeller and a mustache, in the latter case easily peeled off when another role is required. He moves methodically from the doorway to the foot of Naughton's bed, his many-jointed legs bending and straightening in a complex pattern as if the space between door and bed were a set of stairs with irregular treads and risers. "Herr Grossinquisitor," somebody says. Now the figure speaks, his jaws moving like one of those clever double-jointed nutcrackers in the shape of a squirrel's head with glistening incisors. "You claim to have powers eidetic and telepathic." As surprising as this allegation is, what is more interesting is the defective synchronization of speech and mouth movement as if the words have been dubbed. "This derives ives from the report of your son un." The echoes of certain of the figure's utterances bounce resoundingly off the walls of Naughton's room though this modest space has never before been resonant.

"Ah! You don't deny eye it. Good. Such powers ours are not by nature given to humans uns. Their source is demonic ick. Yet Sister Claire air persists in believing that you may have healing powers ours. Snake handling and the like ike. She raises the possibility that you may be assisting Charlene in a catharsis arsis. Aristotle, pagan." At this point the figure thrusts an arm out in a telescoping maneuver so that the limb extends two feet beyond the sleeve. The flesh of the arm is covered with wiry black hairs, crooked and variously oriented toward the parent body or off into space along many compass lines. At the end of the arm is a hand that hosts a long index finger aimed at Naughton's heart.

"It also appears that you are a practitioner of animism or totemism ism, forms of demonism ism. Charlene is an eagle. You are a vivified wall all where fantastical stories are performed ormed. Further, you have an attendant demon un though Sister Claire air does not regard the creature as such utch." The accusatory finger redirects itself to the side of Naughton's head and makes a delicate boring motion as one might imagine characterizes an earwig's entry. "Merely an alter ego or Doppelgänger anger. These are the modernistic explanations for the demonic. Ha! Vogt. Beelzebub bub. What's in a name?"

The face of the figure pulses red like a traffic signal. The finger goes up in the air and makes an imperfect circle, perhaps a noose. Then it makes another circle and slices it twice down the middle. "Ha! I see you take the meaning. You are lucky to live in this age, Naughton oughten, or you would be hanged, quartered and drawn, crisped in the purifying fire ire of stalks and stake ache."

The figure retracts the elongated arm back into its sleeve, the mechanism perhaps inaccurately set, as arm and hand disappear entirely within the black fabric. And now the other hand disappears into its sleeve. The figure stands straight and folds the flaps of empty sleeves across his chest. "You have sinned against filial fidelity, fraternal affection, marital love, and paternal obligation shun. You have deployed the demonic ick fires ires of hell against innocent fellow men. How do you plead?"

"Guilty."

"So be it. Amen." The figure turns about and activates its many linkages to recross the zigzag space between bed and door, where it turns about, revealing alternately three planes of its stern countenance. The mustache wobbles momentarily but rights itself. "Await judgement mint!"

After some time, indeterminate but short, Sister Claire comes to the door of Naughton's room. "Well, Mr. Naughton, you're an even more accomplished visionary than I've given you credit for. But Father Schneider was much maligned in your version, though I admit his thinness and sharpness are hard on the eyes."

"It was ill contrived, Sister. Cubist. Way out of date."

"Don't worry about that, Mr. Naughton. We make no pretense here of being au courant."

Naughton rolls up to a sitting position on the edge of his bed. "Where are my manners? Please sit down, Sister. I was in the arms of Morpheus, one of the few pagan gods still around."

Sister Claire seats herself, this time in the chair by the wall rather than in the one by the window. She smiles. "Would it be acceptable, Mr. Naughton, if we entered the territory of the actual at this point?"

Naughton returns the nun's smile. "I'll do my best."

"Then let me report that Father Schneider has asked if you've ever heard Charlene laugh."

"I've never heard her laugh, but I've seen her laugh. Contractions of the diaphragm. The laughter hasn't reached her mouth yet. Father Schneider's question is a good one, because she needs to laugh."

Sister Claire waits silently for Naughton to go on.

"You know the old saying, Sister. Laughter is the best medicine."

"For what in this case?"

"To heal the trauma." Naughton holds a hand up. "If Father Schneider wants to know what the trauma was, please tell him we have a long way to go, and we may never know."

"Some would say that the process of healing in a case inevitably involves recovery of memories."

"Yes, some would say that."

Sister Claire sighs. "Charlene underwent a thorough medical examination as soon as she came here. There was no evidence of physical abuse."

Naughton turns up empty hands. "I don't have anything worthwhile to say about that, Sister."

"Then let's go for your meeting with Charlene. I'm going to stay out of sight. I don't want my presence affecting the interaction."

"I understand, but at some point, Sister, I predict it will be useful for Charlene to know that you are with us."

"I'm always with you."

Vera is oiling the hub of a wheel on Charlene's chair when Naughton and Sister Claire arrive. "This is not making a pretty song."

Sister Claire, looking at Vera, holds a finger to her lips.

Vera says, "Mr. Naughton is here, Charlene. He has been loafing in bed pretending to have a cold."

Charlene's body makes a quaking motion.

Naughton comes around and faces her. "You look good, Charlene."

"She has been eating. I told her you could not tell stories to a starving person."

"That's right, Vera, especially the story I plan to tell her about when I was an old salt in the Navy."

Charlene wrenches her body into an unmistakable negative.

"Schto! High!" Spittle runs down Charlene's chin. Vera moves to wipe it off, but Charlene jerks her head away. Vera says, "She wants you to tell the story about the man lost in the mist. She has been watching out the window."

Naughton hesitates. "All right, Charlene, but there was no rope. I can't change that."

Charlene nods in her bobble-head way. Still, it's now easy to tell that this is a gesture of positive assent.

During the ensuing telling, neither Naughton nor Vera gives any sign of the presence of Sister Claire.

"The man in the mist is in search of a condor nest to steal an egg and bring it back to his master, a hard man. The servant knows what the nest looks like. It's under a ledge that has been columnated by the wind, a little cathedral that protects the mother and the egg from the sun and the driving wind. Once the chick is hatched, the mother will have to go in search of carrion. Something has happened to the father. Old age or disease because adult condors have no predators. The problem for the mother will be getting aloft again with enough carrion in her talons to feed her baby. The problem for the servant is that the mist is so thick he can't see his feet. He can stay close to the wall that fronts and defines the narrow walk along the edge of the cliff as long as he can feel it, but then comes a breach in the wall. What's within the breach he doesn't know. He shuffles carefully and pokes the rocky surface ahead with his wooden walking stick. The stick has a handle shaped by a natural bend in the wood. The rocks on the path become more numerous and bigger. He has to walk carefully around and between them. After a time of threading in this way he becomes disoriented and unsure of the course of the path though he thought he would remember the feel of it. He thinks he should sit down and wait until the mist clears, but that might take hours or even days, and his master is a hard impatient man."

Naughton paces in front of Charlene. Off to the side, on the windowpane, the dim reflections of the nun are stock still, her images hazed by distance and overborne by the green and yellow splashes of garden and birches without.

"The servant stops. He thinks if he makes a noise with his stick the echo from the wall of the cliff will tell him which way to turn. He knows not to call aloud for help from God because the sound of his plea would reverberate all around the canyon and tell him nothing. He strikes a rock with his stick. The echo tells him the wall is on the right. He starts to turn that way, but the sharp sound has split the rocky ledge beneath his feet. It falls apart. He goes down clutching for any scrap of outcropping, but there is none."

Charlene has tensed visibly in her wheelchair. Her body resembles that of a puppet when the puppeteer lifts both string boards at once.

Naughton sighs. "The fabric of the man's time is torn, but it takes a long time to fray while his feet scratch futilely on the side of the cliff's wall. He hits a ledge, but the momentum of his fall is too great for him to gain a purchase on the thin shelf,

79

and so he goes down swimming in the misted air having no idea where the bottom is or if there is a bottom. If he had been a condor he could easily have caught an updraft and mocked gravity, but he is only a man."

Naughton turns his back to Charlene and looks out the window. Charlene's body caves in on itself, a puppet again, this time all the strings slack. Vera takes a deep breath. "That is how we always knew it would end, Charlene."

Charlene also breathes deeply, her body beginning to expand a little.

The image of the nun remains unmoving against a gray wall of obscurity.

Naughton says, "That's not quite the end. The mountain patrol informs the master of his servant's death. Bring the body to me, he says. The captain says you wouldn't want to see it, sir. Some of it is unrecoverable. But the master insists. Under the eye of the captain, who must observe legal requirements, the master tapes the skull together, arranges the ribs in order of length, and places the limbs where they belong. Then he folds it all into a white cloth. Now you can take it to the coroner or whatever you're supposed to do, he says. The captain says he needs to take the man's papers with him. There never were any papers, says the master. He was a drifter. I took him in. What was he doing on the mountain trail in the mist, asks the captain. The master says, I don't know. He was an ignorant man. But he should be buried. I will pay for that. The captain says that the grave will be unmarked. So be it, says the master."

Now there is an absolute stillness. Naughton looks out the window. Sister Claire recedes. Vera stands still, her hand on the handle of the wheelchair as if it needed steadying. But in it Charlene lies safely curled as always, almost serene.

A Rented Room in New Orleans

The white expanse of sheet that covers Charlene's body follows Naughton back up the hall and into his room. He lies on his bed. Which bed?

Peter and Cam are lying naked in Peter's narrow bed in the dark, face up. Hardly an inch separates their hips. Cam says, "This is to test how you'll know when to touch me and where."

"How will I know how to pass the test?"

"At first I have to tell you. Then you'll learn for yourself."

"You know how much I would love to touch you."

"We're not going to talk about love."

"All right."

"I have to tell you I'm not a virgin."

"I don't care if you've had lovers before me."

"I haven't had lovers. I did it to myself." There is a silence. "You don't ask why? I'll tell you. I didn't want a man to do it."

Peter hesitates. When he speaks his voice is weak. "It's all right."

"Yes. It's all right. I didn't want to harm myself. But you don't understand, do you?"

"No."

"Because if another person does it to you, you can never be equal."

Peter raises himself up on his elbow and looks into Cam's face, his eyes accustomed to the dark now, only a faint light at the window. "We'll be equal but different."

"That's what I ask myself. How much difference before we're islands?"

There's a silence, but it's not absolute. Several blocks north the clang of the St. Charles Street streetcar makes a single attenuated stripe of sound in the dark room. That ushers through the open window the indistinct buzz of the city, like a mist of invisible insects. Peter says, "There's a famous story of a floating island where you can get a bag of winds and sail where you want to. I'll sail to you."

"What if I'm a floating island with my own bag of winds?"

"I can sail faster."

Cam is silent for a moment. "I think you miss your life at sea."

"Only a little."

"Tell me anyway."

"Well, there's a lot of poetry about the sea being our first mother, but to me from the deck of my ship it only seemed big and moody."

Cam laughs. It's an odd laugh as if her body has never quite organized itself fully for laughter, so instead of a gust it's a puff, something to be done quickly. "You can't tell me it was the sea that made you moody. What else about life at sea?"

"The ports made you feel strange, not the ones in the Mediterranean. That was only language and custom and skin tone."

Cam speaks again with a sharp playfulness. "When you were not in the Mediterranean did you find a woman with skin my color?"

"Yes. I kept an image of her skin with me all these years until I found you. All the rest of her I forgot."

"Then you can forget about me too."

"Not if we stay together."

"Tell me about the ports that were not Mediterranean."

"Once we were trapped south of the Suez and visited many ports. Bahrein, Aden, Abadan. And then around Africa. Mombasa, Cape Town, Sierra Leone. You couldn't think about women anymore."

"You thought about women, but not the ones you saw."

"Right. They were forbidden."

"Still, I wonder if you smelled one."

Peter makes a comic sniffing.

Cam says, "You're smelling me."

Peter says, "In Cape Town an older British couple invited several of us to dinner. It was very elegant, a lobster curry. I'll never forget it. The lady of the house wore a dress made of many layers of diaphanous organdy with pink flowers hiding inside. It rose in the air a little when she walked. She wore subtle perfume, maybe just rose water. But then a servant came into the room, a handsome Black woman. They'd made her powder herself, but the sheen of her skin came shining through and with it her natural odor. I thought it smelled like some kind of wood freshly sawn, but I didn't know what kind, and have never smelled it since."

"There're many Black women here."

"Yes, but that was different."

"The smell is what you are and what you eat. Tell me what I smell like, because I don't put any fragrance on."

Now it's Peter's turn to produce a puff of laughter, but his more resonant. "I'm not smelling you, but the air is swarming with your pheromones."

"I don't know what they are. What're they doing?"

"They're increasing my desire."

There is a silence. Cam says, "You can touch my breast now."

Peter leans forward and presses his lips gently over Cam's nipple, which is immediately erect. Her body arches gently. "That's not what I said, but it's all right. What did it taste like?"

"Like honey."

"I'm not a bee."

"No. A bee wouldn't tease his lover."

"Then you can touch my flower. It will be all nectar."

Peter proceeds gently. After stroking lightly, he opens Cam's thighs, lifts himself and enters. She has spoken accurately. Her hymen is broken. Her natural oils flow copiously.

The scrim falls slowly. Peter and Cam recede into the background, moving to the powerful swell of their sex. The face on the scrim is Vogt's, his expression neither disdainful nor sympathetic but fiercely attentive. It seems he will speak, and perhaps he does, but a different voice overrides his.

Sometimes with one I love,
I fill myself with rage,
for fear I effuse unreturn'd love
But now I think
there is no unreturn'd love—
the pay is certain, one way or another;
(I loved a certain person ardently,
my love was not return'd;
Yet out of that I have written these songs.)

On the bed, obscured by the scrim, Peter lifts his head for a moment from his labor of love. It may be that through the rush of passion he hears the song, or it may be that he lifts his head because in his climactic labors he requires a great inhalation of air. Cam clutches his buttocks fiercely. It seems that everything is exhausted at once, the passion of the lovers, the song, Vogt's fierce concentration. Everything fades.

Naughton has an appointment with Sister Claire, but he's early. He looks down the corridor. Charlene is not yet by the window in her wheelchair. He goes to the door of Mr. Gerrity's room. Under a light coverlet Mr. Gerrity's feet are dancing. Naughton cautiously looks in. Mr. Gerrity is making a barely audible hum. It has no emotional quality to it. It's like the subaqueous thrum of a ship's engine. From just inside the doorway Naughton says casually, "It looks like you're doing a foxtrot, Mr. Gerrity."

Mr. Gerrity makes a throaty sound.

"You remember it. Two steps slow, one step quick. There're lots of variations. Think of Fred and Ginger dancing 'Cheek to Cheek.' Very stylish in the twenties and thirties, and then it got zapped by the war like a lot of nice things."

Mr. Gerrity's eyes roll, perhaps down some dim lane of understanding or memory.

"Practice, Mr. Gerrity. With a gorgeous redhead like Sister Kathleen you could make a stunning couple at the Ritz. Just remember. Upper body still as statuary. Everything happens from the waist down. Smooth as silk."

Mr. Gerrity seems to direct his will toward his feet, but there is little difference in the jiggling beneath the coverlet.

A moment later Sister Kathleen appears.

Naughton says, "Mr. Gerrity and I were just discussing the art of the foxtrot."

Sister Kathleen smiles. "You were a dancer then, Mr. Naughton."

"I had to pretend. I was a fraternity boy. I was very bad at it. I can never forget that one of my partners, suffering the sweating grip of my desperate left hand, said, 'You're not driving a truck, you know.' I should've challenged her and asked her what she knew about truck drivers, but I wasn't quick enough on my feet." Naughton awards his joke a mild chuckle. Sister Kathleen smiles broadly.

"Maybe you were just afraid of losing control."

"No doubt. Which from time immemorial has been a fateful truism for my doleful gender."

Sister Kathleen steps to the head of Mr. Gerrity's bed and looks down into his rheumy eyes, which presently she touches at the corners and canthi with a soft tissue. "Give us a smile, Mr. Gerrity."

Mr. Gerrity screws his mouth around obligingly and farts.

"Vera will be by shortly and set you on your throne."

Mr. Gerrity seems unmoved by the prospect.

Naughton says, "Give him a scepter and I will recite for him one of the few passages I remember from my school days."

"Recite it for us now."

Naughton lifts his head as into an old sky of memory and begins somewhat haltingly,

"This royal throne, this scepter'd isle,
This majesty, this seat of Apollo,
This other Eden, demi-paradise,
This fortress built by Nature
Against infection and war,
This happy breed of men, this little world,
This precious stone set in the silver sea,
This blessed earth, this realm, this England."

Naughton shakes his head. "I didn't get it quite right. Some missing iambs."

"It was quite beautiful, Mr. Naughton, but as you know, my heritage is from a different island."

"God forgive England and all of her descendants for her savagery."

"Be assured, Mr. Naughton, God has, or we'd be smelling the smoke of the English rising from below. Aren't you of Irish descent yourself?"

"Possibly. In New Orleans the races were, you might say, miscible."

Sister Kathleen nods. "A new word from you every day, Mr. Naughton. Now, Mr. Gerrity, I'm going to stroke your feet. You like that, don't you?"

"Who wouldn't?" says Naughton.

Mr. Gerrity's hum, modulated if clumsily, surely signals assent.

"Let's give Mr. Naughton's foxtrot a try." Sister Kathleen rolls up the cover and exposes the twitching feet. "Have you ever seen more lovely feet, Mr. Naughton?"

"Never."

"Most feet have some toe that insists on its superior importance and thrusts itself forward. The sin of pride. But Mr. Gerrity's feet are a model."

"They might've been fashioned by Praxiteles himself for his Hermes, fleet of foot. In fact, I think I see the small clips in Mr. Gerrity's feet where the wings used to be that once winnowed the clouds above Mount Olympus. What message have you brought us mortals, Mr. Gerrity?"

Mr. Gerrity's hum assumes a deepening regularity then plunges down below the threshold of hearing though one can see his chest continue to vibrate. Sister Kathleen massages Mr. Gerrity's feet. The navicular bone above the left big toe is distended. Sister Kathleen works on it with her thumb as though she might persuade the protrusion to retract. She runs her thumbnail along the bottom of the foot, but the toes don't curl. "Someday, Mr. Gerrity, you're going to fool me and curl your toes."

"I wish I knew the Gaelic for kindness, Sister."

"So do I, Mr. Naughton, but the mother tongue was taken from us."

"Yes. Another travesty." Naughton shakes his head sadly. "I must go. I have an appointment with Sister Claire."

"Then go, Mr. Naughton."

"Good day to you, kind Sister, and to you, Mr. Gerrity, swift messenger of the gods."

Sister Claire sits at her desk writing when Naughton taps on the door. "Come in, Mr. Naughton." She comes around from her desk and sits in one of the simple chairs that are arranged to face each other. Naughton seats himself and waits for Sister Claire to speak.

"We haven't been talking enough about you, Mr. Naughton, because we've been so taken up with Charlene."

"The less talk about me the better, Sister."

"False modesty, Mr. Naughton. And in any case, you have graciously consented to share with me your dramas of trial, love and loss."

"I'm sorry to have inflicted them on you. They can be ugly."

Sister Claire tilts her head. "I've known such things before. Yours have the unmistakable quality of truth-seeking. If we're going to have truth, we'll have to endure some ugliness."

"And from your point of view surely sin."

"The deepest sins are sins of the heart, and I find none in you."

Naughton cocks his head but is silent.

"What're you thinking, Mr. Naughton?"

"I'm thinking about my son Joshua. I don't know why."

"Let me guess. Because he's your opposite."

"Perhaps. And yours too, Sister. Sin isn't a concept that would mean anything to him."

"I suspect he knows it by another name."

"Maybe. Anyway, I'm not asking you about his report."

"Good. Let's put that aside. Speak to me about your demon."

"Vogt? And sin? He would disdain the very idea if he entertained it at all."

Sister Claire resumes in an altered tone. "I find myself wondering about Alexandra."

"She's lost. I lost her, a worthless father. That's all there is to say about that."

"It's not all there is to say, Mr. Naughton, but I accept your reticence for now." Sister Claire pauses. "Speak to me about your wife Cam."

"All right, Cam. Let me ask you, Sister. Can you honor a person by not understanding her?"

"Did she want to be understood?"

"No."

"That's what I've gathered."

"But should one take in marriage someone who doesn't want to be understood? Shouldn't he decline the marriage for her sake and for his own?"

"Could he know that understanding would never come?"

"He had strong intimations."

"But also hope."

"I didn't try hard enough to understand. I gave up. Then some came who did understand and took her away. People I never would've guessed she could love."

"Go on."

Naughton twists in his chair. "Sometimes I think I should've stayed with Sister Kathleen. You're too empathetic. And I fear there's worse to come."

"I've already admitted you trouble me, Mr. Naughton. You're too much in my mind. But that's what I'm here for. So tell me, why did you give up trying to understand?"

Naughton dodges again. "I don't know."

"I suspect you know but don't know that you do."

"Right, Sister. I don't know what I know. I'm not sure I ever did. I hope Josh warned you in his report."

Sister Claire pauses to reflect. "Never mind the report. What I don't understand is your stories. Do you think Charlene understands them?"

"I don't think about that. I tell whatever story comes to me."

"Let's call it a long yeasting. The story was always in your mind, maybe for years, waiting for you to tell it to Charlene."

"A strange and wonderful notion, Sister. But more likely my stories are just scraps of association. Mist in the garden, man in mist."

"But there was also green in the garden and yellow birches behind. They're not in the story. And there're no cliffs in our windows here."

"Now you're grilling me, Sister. You think I'm hiding something?"

"Only what you've hidden from yourself."

"Do you have some idea of what it is?"

"Only a scrap. In reaching out so powerfully to Charlene, maybe you're compensating for not understanding your wife. What do you think?"

"I've never thought that. And I don't understand Charlene either."

"Really? Not even a little?"

"Question for question, Sister. Do you think Charlene wants to be understood?"

Sister Claire doesn't answer.

Naughton throws his hands up. "Does anybody really want to be fully understood by another, Sister?"

"It depends on who the other is. But we won't be fully understood until we stand naked before God."

"I thought that in your faith he already knows us. Minutely. Do you know how terrifying that is?"

"It would be, except that he lets us go on searching for ourselves."

Again Naughton is silent for a while, his face pained. "The search is like a walk along the edge of a cliff in a thick fog. Nothingness is below. And I don't have an angel to catch me."

"Fear of abandonment, nothingness. We all have it. It's the beginning of faith."

Naughton wanders. "Joshua assures me that in science there's no such thing as nothingness. Voids between things but not nothingness. Even zero is merely a mathematical convenience, not discovered until late in human history. But nothingness is very real to me, Sister."

"I know that. But you must not think of yourself and Charlene as nothing. That would be tragic."

Naughton looks dubious.

"The proof is in the persistence of a self, Mr. Naughton. Think of all your memories of your self. Peter the child, Peter the naval officer, Peter the student, Peter the lover, the husband, the father. They all have the same self, however imperfect."

Naughton cogitates. "You think Charlene is moving closer to a realization of self?"

"I have great hope. Because of you and your stories."

"If only I had your faith, Sister."

Sister Claire nods. "Or your sister Stella's. Are you in touch with her?"

"I suspect she's dead. She'd be in her eighties, with no interest in physical health." Naughton muses. "In the beginning she got her faith from a piano. I tried it, but it didn't work."

"What about your beloved Mr. Donnelly and his faith?"

"What I learned from him was not faith but the power of words, especially poetical words."

Sister Claire folds her hands. "Then this is where we are, Mr. Naughton, the three of us, you and Charlene and I. On a search. Your stories are our path." Sister Claire is silent. "What're you thinking, Mr. Naughton? I see something in your face."

Naughton hesitates. "A biblical passage."

"Let's hear it."

Naughton rubs his forehead, as one might shine an old lamp. "It's about God's power."

"Go on."

"He quickeneth the dead and calleth those things which be not as though they were."

Sister Claire is startled.

Naughton hastens to speak again. "No, Sister, don't think that for a moment I believe I have the creative powers of the divine."

Sister Claire waves away Naughton's disavowal, leans forward deeper into the darkness of the room. "It's not for us to say what powers may have been lent you, Mr. Naughton."

Naughton, silent, shakes his head, in denial or wonderment.

"May God be our guide," says Sister Claire.

Another day. Naughton walks past the doors of the rooms of his fellow inmates and straight down the hall. Charlene is in her wheelchair, positioned to look out the window. Intermittent puffs of mist pass across garden and trees like the broken breath of one in distress. Standing beside the wheelchair, looking out the window, Naughton says, "You have long acquaintance with the weather here, I believe, Vera. Will this murk last the day?"

"No, Mr. Naughton, it is just fog. The sun will drive it away."

"As a former seaman, Vera, I can tell you that fog is unwelcome."

"Shtor," says Charlene.

"Are you going to tell us a sea story, Mr. Naughton?"

"I'll try to think of one, but first I have to say that Charlene's hair shines brighter day by day. Raven tresses is the cliché."

"That is because in God's eye every hair of her head is numbered."

"Ah. Of course. But I have to say that in some circumstances numbers can be very troubling."

"Is that the beginning of a story?"

"Shtor." Charlene's imprecise verbalizations are now accompanied by a kind of communication of digits. Fingers tap against the arms of the wheelchair, not executing a code but rather performing an instructive dance—encouraging, demanding, anticipating delight.

"A story then. In your mind's eye call up the image of a US Navy destroyer escort, gray as granite, twice as long as the hall of Maison Cristina, sleek, single stack, armed with a five-incher, but mostly with depth charges and hedgehogs for use against wolfpacks of dread Nazi U-boats. That was a war I was lucky enough to miss. Too young. Hard to look at me now and believe I was ever too young for anything."

Charlene's fingers rap impatiently.

"Charlene and I are thinking of a gray ship, Mr. Naughton. That is all. Go on with the story."

"All right, aboard the ship was a young Paymaster. Think of a day when the ocean was angry. The ship rolled and pitched in heavy waves that broke over the main deck and sprayed sea even up to the conning tower. The Paymaster is in his office, charged with the safekeeping of a miniscule fraction of the US treasury. Tomorrow is payday. What'll the sailors do with their pay, Charlene, in the middle of the ocean?"

Charlene makes a wobbly shaking of her head, but a hint of a smile widens her mouth.

"You guessed it, Charlene. They'll shoot craps in their quarters below deck, where visits from officers are rare and unwelcome. What is the fascination of dicing?"

"Gambling is a venal sin," says Vera.

"Yes, well, maybe some sailors abstained for religious reasons. Older salts may have abstained from prudence." Naughton nods reflectively. "One thinks of the Roman soldiers dicing for Jesus' robe, swatches of which can be found in many churches."

"Do not speak sacrilege, Mr. Naughton. What is the story of the Paymaster?"

Charlene lifts a hand, points a wavering but insistent finger at Naughton.

"The task that confronts the Paymaster is calculating the pay due to each member of the crew. This would be easy in normal seas, but not in a north Atlantic storm. Why? Because the Paymaster has to use an old calculator that looks like a big typewriter. It's bolted to his desk, so he doesn't have to worry about it falling, but the carriage that aligns keys and tape for recording figures skips or hangs up when the ship rolls, shudders when the ship pitches, blackening the type or rendering it an unreadable gray. But he must complete his calculation, waiting for brief moments when the carriage of the calculator is level and still." Naughton uses his hands to show how the Paymaster must hover over the machine. At a precise moment Naughton strikes imaginary keys like a pianist playing fortissimo. Charlene's fingers lift and strike.

"Why does he not wait until the storm is over?"

Charlene shakes her head.

"Charlene understands. Why does Father Schneider not delay Mass when lightning and thunder besiege his chapel? Nothing is more sacred aboard ship than payday, the palpable transfer of value from higher powers into the hands of the crew, the holy coinage of service."

"Do not speak sacrilege, Mr. Naughton. We are waiting for the story of the Paymaster and the machine."

Exactly, says Charlene's pointing finger.

"Yes. We are coming to a crisis of calculation, but first there are flying fish."

"Flying fish? How far around do we have to go, Mr. Naughton, to get to the numbers?"

"Numbers relative to flying fish are important, Vera. While the Paymaster is trying to cajole sea and calculator to cooperate, the captain of the ship, once a daredevil flyer in Korea, is sending commissary men out on the sea-scoured deck at their peril to gather the flying fish that have brained themselves against the starboard forward bulkhead. His own salubrious experiences with near death lead him to wish to share the benefits with the gatherers of fish. Besides, he is an avid fish-eater, and in all candor a flying fish, self-tenderized, is truly a delicacy, especially straight from the salt, hustled into the wardroom galley, fried in butter and served with lemon wedges."

Vera emits a puff of exasperation.

"Ah. . . The numbers, Vera, of course. In towering seas the trajectory of a flying fish, launched from the crest of an epic wave, can reach a quarter of a nautical mile at speeds of forty knots. Meanwhile, in his office, desperate to charm sea and machine, the Paymaster has to listen to the constant tattoo of self-immolated fish against the bulkhead. 'Jesus!' he was heard to exclaim, perhaps inspired by the ancient Christian acronym formed from the Greek word for fish, ikhthýs."

"What is the meaning of that, Mr. Naughton?"

"Using the Greek letters as the first in several words, one can construct the phrase Jesus Christ, Son of God, savior of mankind. Thus did the early followers of The Way use the simple Greek word for fish as a secret code of recognition. In this story we have flying fish suffering death, eaten and so forth. I leave the rest to you."

"This is the third time you have spoken sacrilege, Mr. Naughton. Once more and I will call Sister Claire."

Charlene makes an angry hawking noise in her throat.

"They were not intended as sacrileges but as evidence of the way in which Christian symbolism has penetrated deep into our culture, even out on the open sea."

"Go on with the story, Mr. Naughton, if there is one. Leave Christianity to do its own work."

"Verily. The calculator has not been designed to perform in high seas. The Paymaster begins to enter a number of, say, three simple digits. The ship rolls to starboard. The carriage races forward. The digits skip, repeat, lunge into a different column. Three hundred becomes three thousand or thirty thousand. The ship rolls to port, the carriage with it. The three hundred becomes thirty or three or even a new mathematical function composed of superimposed threes and zeros, something maybe like a Mayan symbol for eternity. The Paymaster is terrified. The fundamentals of mathematics have been destroyed. Infinity haunts his machine."

"Infinity belongs only to God, Mr. Naughton."

"The Paymaster doesn't know that. He thinks that the huge fields of storm and oceanic gravity have destroyed the one thing that reason requires, numerical predictability. He cannot complete the payroll calculations. He imagines the horde of a hundred and fifty men hanging him from the mast. Better to join his winged brethren of the deep. He rushes out of his office to leap over the lifelines. But an adept fish gatherer wrestles him sobbing to the deck. In sickbay he's given large doses of laudanum and relieved of his duties. The laudanum produces exquisite visions. He is a flying fish cavorting in high seas. Rising to the crest of breaking waves he launches himself into the spumy air, no steel wall of warship to fear. Occasionally he glides down into a pocket of still water and feasts on plankton. Those in the shape of tiny angels are the most delicious. Below, tuna and swordfish rise futilely as he soars over their heads. But what of the terns and auks, Charlene, the eagles of the open sea? Will he escape those?"

Charlene wobbles her head imprecisely, but a definite negative.

"Is that the end of the Paymaster?"

"No. Some years later he will meet a woman who has abjured all numbers as not only meaningless but malevolent. With all his heart he would like to follow her into a universe of pure analogs shaped like the beautiful waves of the sea in its infinite variety. But the calculator haunts his dreams. Well, if he is doomed to inhabit numbers, maybe someday he will find the indivisible number, fountain of all numbers, and then he can rest in peace."

Charlene holds up a finger and then curls it down upon itself.

"Right, Charlene. It's not the number one." Naughton pauses. "Unless just possibly it's a one formed by the coalescence of two."

"Three," says Vera.

Naughton sits in the chair in his room casting his eyes about purposefully. Walls, ceiling, windowsills, molding. The carpenter, then the taper, then the painter. The taper's edges are harder to hide than the painter's brush marks. The carpenter's cuts on the miter saw are so precise that the corners of quarter round fit like lovers' lips.

A Rundown Living Room in New Orleans

The family has gathered. Stella sits at the piano in a white dress but turned away from the keyboard and looking out at those around her. A small tattered leather suitcase sits on the floor beside the bench. The light is dim, the drapes closed against the heat. It's a late Saturday afternoon, hot and still outside. Cigarette smoke hangs in the air, curling on itself. Much of it issues from a deformed cigarette captured now between the mother's index and ring fingers, which are ochre like the clay of Mississippi from which she sprang. The brown stuffed chair the mother sits in is stippled with small black holes, stigmata of wayward embers. On a small table next to the mother a large round bronze ashtray brims with old butts, and a bronze elephant stands in the middle.

Peter sits on the floor, lotus-like. "Did you know that elephants scatter the bones of their dead?"

The father sits in a deep depression in a sofa that lists to port, missing one of its legs.

"Much more sensible than walling people up in dank vaults for tourists to marvel at," the mother says. "Tell us,

Stella, on Judgement Day do the elephants get put back together like the rest of us?"

"Everything gets put to right, Mama." Stella's voice is bemused and musical.

"So, Stella, now that you have tried college and a regular nunnery, you're going to San Francisco, to find what?"

"The Paraclete."

"Who's that?"

"The one that's going to help me."

"You have a phone number or an address?"

Peter says, "He'll be waiting for her at the train station."

Stella smiles. The smile is not condescending. "Maybe not that quick."

The father says, "Stella's going to be all right, but don't get a job playing at a cocktail lounge, Honey, unless it's a high-class hotel bar."

"I won't, Daddy."

"Maybe you could play my favorite once more before we call the cab."

Stella turns and lifts her hands to play.

The father slugs down a quantity of bourbon. "I'll sing."

"It's not what they sing in high-class bars," says the mother laughing smoke out of her nose.

Peter laughs. Stella plays. The father sings:

"Alone from night to night you find me
Too weak to bust the chains that bind me
I don't need no dungeon to remind me
I'm just a prisoner of love."

The father rolls off the couch onto the rug, which releases a puff of dust. Peter gets out of the way. Stella keeps on playing.

"She's in my dreams awake or sleeping
On my knees to her I'm creeping
My whole life into her is seeping

I'm just a prisoner of love."

During this second stanza the father crawls toward the mother, his voice muffled. He moves forward on his elbows, keeping low like an infantryman in combat training. Stella continues to play very softly, chords lifted from the song, turned upside down, rearranged, all very melodic and sad. When the father reaches the mother he takes a foot and kisses the big toe succulently.

The mother says, "You understand that this creature is not your father. Stop it, Marty. You're tickling me."

The father crawls back to the couch and lifts himself up, half sitting, half supine. "Thank you, Honey."

The mother's cigarette has burned down to a stub, which she drops on the pile of butts in the elephant ashtray. The father does his trick of lighting two cigarettes at once and takes one to the mother. Now the pile of butts in the elephant ashtray begins to smolder and smoke. The mother says, "Peter, take that out to the kitchen."

Peter returns from his task quickly, having doused the offending butts and dumped them in the garbage. As he puts the ashtray back on the table beside his mother he says, "You can put the cigarette in the elephant's back, Mama, and not burn your fingers."

"Really?" The mother sees that the elephant has a slot in its back. She snugs her newly lit cigarette into the slot. "How cute. I never noticed." She looks at her daughter. "So, Stella, a little practical matter. Do you plan to stay with Titta until the Paraclete gets you a job? She'll have to kick her current man out for a while, which wouldn't likely be a big sacrifice as they tend to run out of gas rapidly."

"Yes, Mama. She has already invited me."

"Let her buy things. She has her war widow's pension and many gifts from admirers. And that pittance your daddy secretly gave you won't last long. Actually your daddy would've given his life for his country and left me a pension but he was burdened with two children, which made him old and sagging. And anyway, they couldn't figure out how to stuff all that hair into a uniform."

"I volunteered for the Seabees. Airstrips and docks."

The mother chuckles. "We probably would've won the war even if they'd taken you, Marty."

"Won it quicker." He turns to Stella. "You write us, Honey."

"I'll write," says Stella.

Peter says, "He means to us, not in your diary."

The mother dislodges her cigarette from the elephant's back, takes in a great gust of smoke, discovers a shred of tobacco on her tongue and stores it under a fingernail. "Keep writing in the diary, Stella. It's destined to be one of the great documents of spiritual growth in post-war America, where things spiritual are no longer in vogue due to victory hysteria. I'll bet at the nunnery they didn't teach you that victory is a major stumbling block to spirituality. They stuck to sex and worldly goods, right?"

Stella nods good-naturedly. "They taught that anything that separates one from God could be an impediment, even extreme devotion to one's family."

Peter's face registers pain.

The mother nods emphatically. "It's in the Bible. Jesus asks who is his mother and who is his brother, like he didn't know. Very callous. Not a short-term memory problem. So if your calling requires, you can write our names down in your diary and cross them out."

"Don't cross me out, Honey."

"Don't worry, Marty. She won't be able to cross you out because you're the missing link. And she doesn't need to cross me out because I went up in smoke a long time ago. And Peter is a floating brain that could disappear on the next wave. So, Stella, the only one you've got in indelible ink is the ape man."

Stella looks at her mother in a way that signifies these ugly exorbitances have long ago lost their edge. "I won't forget any of you, Mama."

The mother looks out from the smoke rising from her cigarette. "That might be true, Stella, selectively. I can forget my father any time he shows up in my mind for some unexplainable reason. He's transparent you could say. So all I have to do is focus on what's behind or in front. What would likely be there is Mama Helen, your deeply mourned grandmother. She and I would sit on her screen porch and smoke cigarettes and drink Cokes. It had to be the Coke that got her going because she never learned to inhale. Of course, I blew smoke her way so maybe she got some nicotine benefit." The mother twiddles the ash off of her cigarette. "Memories, Stella. But you're as strong-willed as they come. Do with your memories whatever you want. Now why don't you play us something nice and we'll call the cab."

Stella plays Chopin's Prelude in B minor. It's a perfect leave-taking piece, sad from the beginning, a little false lift of hope in the middle and then a dying away to silence. The father claps lightly. "That's my girl."

Tears come to Peter's eyes. He hides them by bowing his head and looking into the rug.

"I'll call the cab," the mother says.

The next day Peter sits at the piano playing the opening of the prelude, clumsily but recognizably. He gets about twenty seconds in, when the repetition of the opening passage changes too subtly for him to replicate. He tries several times to get past the wall created by the variation, then gives up, closing the lid over the keyboard. His father has come up behind unnoticed, even though the smell of the man precedes his voice. "That was good, Peter. We'll get you the sheet with the notes on it."

"No," says Peter, unmoving. The father goes away. From the kitchen comes the sound of a chair scraping the pitted linoleum, voices unaccustomedly flat. Peter goes to Stella's room and steps in cautiously. The room is barren, nothing on the walls or dresser top. The bed has been stripped of linen. One uncased pillow lies at the head, two or three shafts of feather protruding from the striped fabric. He goes to his room. An old armoire stands in the corner, no doors, only the fragment of a hasp torn halfway out of splintered wood. Inside hangs his uniform, a used Marine jacket and pants, given to the high school in exchange for a one-hour drill once a week on the school grounds conducted by a tough old vet. Beside it hangs his khaki shirt and tie. From the armoire comes a distinct odor, human, not acrid. Peter goes to his desk, a piece of thick plywood mounted on two sawhorses, varnished by his father. His schoolbooks are arrayed between two brass bookends that slide inward or outward on stout rails: Caesar, plain geometry, civics, Latin grammar, Shakespeare, an anthology of great Catholic writers, a theological primer with seven proofs of the existence of God—the Unmoved Mover, The Necessity of the One, the Ground of Universals, Essence vs. Existence, The Principle of Sufficient Reason, The Argument From Design, the Tautological Proof. Off to the side, separated from its companions, is a worn copy of *Leaves of Grass*.

Peter lays his head down on the desk, the wood uneven now, welted, the varnish mostly worn away.

Down from the top of the doorway of his room, like a slowly unfurling scroll, falls something like a cerecloth that has lost its stiffness. Once fully unrolled it displays weathered wooden crosses, one at each of the four corners. In the middle is an image of Stella in a diaphanous white dress without undergarments. She stands on a low circular pedestal that is divided into equal quadrants. The pedestal turns. The quadrants move randomly so that she performs a curious slow dance, legs splayed to the side or front and back, brought back together and separated again, all while the pedestal turns slowly, always clockwise, the turning subtly modulated, faster, slower. Somewhere someone is playing Chopin's Prelude in B minor. The striking of the piano keys is so delicate that it seems to come from a misted distance. The voice of a kindly teacher says, "Legato. If you're going to play Chopin, you must make the piano sing. Legato. Softly. Softly." A strong deeply lined hand holds his up so that his fingers barely touch the keys.

Naughton has developed the habit of making the rounds. At the door of Mr. Gerrity's room he announces himself. "Your daily visit from the Good Humor Man, Mr. Gerrity. Jack of All Trades. Raconteur, dancer, ventriloquist."

Naughton's words cause Mr. Gerrity's feet to wiggle against the fingers of Sister Kathleen's hands. She says, "Mr. Naughton wasn't speaking to your feet, Mr. Gerrity. He was speaking to your ears."

"Can you wiggle your ears, Mr. Gerrity? When I was a boy this ability was considered a mark of great versatility. All right then, I see you don't want to be a show-off. Let me recite some lines written by my friend Walt Whitman.

I do not doubt interiors have their interiors, and exteriors have their exteriors, and that the eyesight has another eyesight, and the hearing another hearing.

I share these lines with you by way of saying that you undoubtedly have thoughts within thoughts and inner ears within the ones you can't yet wiggle. In my humble opinion, Mr. Gerrity, you should make haste to share these hidden things with Sister Kathleen, upon whose loving care your very life depends."

Sister Kathleen releases Mr. Gerrity's feet, the navicular bones above his big toes bumping vigorously together. Naughton says, "Marvelous, Mr. Gerrity, but the ingeniously coded tattoo of your toes is beyond me. Even in my Navy days, I have to confess, I was not good at Morse code. It was in all the war movies, remember? The signaler with the blinking searchlight warning of the approach of a Nazi submarine. But maybe Sister Kathleen has decoded the message."

"I have. Mr. Gerrity is saying that he is a loving human being temporarily deprived of speech."

The big toes work upon each other as if attending to a pleasurable itch.

Naughton says, "Such gestures of intimacy make me blush, Mr. Gerrity, reserved as I am, though putatively Irish. To return to Walt's interesting observation that exteriors have their exteriors, let's put the question to Sister Kathleen. Have you detected an aura or any manifestation of a presence outside the mundane encasement of Mr. Gerrity's skin?"

"Most decidedly. What color of irises would you say is most beautiful, Mr. Naughton?"

"Mauve. Capable of tincturing a whole generation."

"That's the very color of Mr. Gerrity's spirit. Auras, however, Mr. Naughton, must be relegated to the realm of occult practices, which are not part of our ministry here. They're shifty. Here the Spirit is what's enduring."

"I'm properly instructed."

"Good. And now that you are, I must ask you to excuse yourself while I prepare Mr. Gerrity for Vera's visit and his bath."

"Blessed may those lavations be."

Naughton looks in on Ms. Trask. "Good morning, Ms. Trask."

Ms. Trask, having liberated her objects, now has at her small table pencil and paper. She's marking the paper diligently. She looks up but doesn't speak.

"Oh my prophetic soul. I sensed some time ago, Ms. Trask, that the spirit of an artist dwelled within."

"Art! Look at this if you have eyes to see." Ms. Trask holds up the sheet she's been working on and rattles it violently above the table.

"I do have eyes, Ms. Trask, but at this distance . . ." He approaches warily.

"Take a look, Mr. Nobody."

"Dear Ms. Trask, please don't use that appellation. If word gets out that I'm Nobody, I may be evicted. Not to be confused with the dread Nobodaddy, who is not evictable."

"Aww . . . Just look!"

Naughton bends close to the thin curling paper that trembles in Ms. Trask's hands. What he sees, as permitted by the unsteadiness of the maker's grasp, appears to be a domino-like set of rectangles with many randomly placed black dots. "I think you're very near the Ur-pattern, Ms. Trask."

Ms. Trask drops the paper back on her table. "What are you talking about, Mr. Nobody?"

"I refer, Ms. Trask, to the template that, placed over various particular realities, reveals the universal pattern."

"Pattern of what?"

"Ah, that would require a deep dive into discursive metaphysics. Your squares and points say what cannot be said in words, which are inadequate for the sublime enterprise you're engaged in."

Ms. Trask picks up the sheet of paper and launches it out into the room, where it slips and slides along currents from the floor register that circulates warm air. At last it lands at Naughton's feet.

"Don't touch it! Go!"

Just outside the door of Ms. Trask's room Naughton encounters Sister Claire and an older nun dressed in black. The nun suffers a cruel case of scoliosis that bends her to the left and forward so that she has to crane and roll her eyes up to meet his surprised gaze. "Good morning, Mr. Naughton. I'm Mother Martha."

"I'm pleased to meet you, Mother. Sister Claire has spoken warmly of you."

Sister Claire stands by, benign and composed.

Mother Martha says, "You're not to lay at Sister Claire's feet this unannounced encounter, Mr. Naughton."

"I can't imagine ever blaming Sister Claire for anything, Mother."

Sister Claire smiles. "Mr. Naughton is too polite, Mother, to ask what you thought you might surprise him doing."

Mother Martha nods affably. "I'll continue my round. I've already seen Mr. Gerrity, newly bathed by Vera and wrapped in a swaddling cloth like a newborn." She enters Ms. Trask's room. Naughton and Sister Claire come behind. "Good morning, Ms. Trask."

Ms. Trask, who has recovered her paper, looks up from her chair by the table. "What happened to you anyway? I'll tell you if you don't know. You've been collecting too many things. It happened to my sister Jeanette, a packrat. Until her husband Lloyd left her. And that black get-up won't do you any good if you think it's going to catch the heat and straighten you out. Jeanette tried it and got hives until it looked like she had tits all over her body, but Lloyd was gone by then." Ms. Trask hardly pauses for breath. "I had a lot of things myself, but Sister Kathleen and I threw them away. Good riddance."

"That was wise, Ms. Trask. Lay not up treasures, where moth and rust corrupt, and where thieves break in and steal."

Ms. Trask emits a sound just short of a screech. "Moths! We had rats, big Norway rats, the kind that eat babies. Fortunately Lloyd never favored Jeanette with a child. Thieves you say. No thief could've found anything worth stealing. And now that Jeanette's dead, who's going to throw it all away? I don't want to go back there and face it. Piles of rotten stuff. If I was a rat I wouldn't want to raise my pups in that place."

"You don't have to worry about going back right now, Ms. Trask. And when the time comes we'll see that you have plenty of help."

"Send them in with gas masks and six-shooters. That's what we did when the brakemen and firemen got uppity."

"We'll see that everybody is properly equipped. Sister Kathleen says you're working on a very interesting project."

"It's not ready."

"When it is, I'd be honored to see it."

"I'll show it to whoever I want to. Right now I've got to get back to work."

Outside the door of Ms. Trask's room Mother Martha pauses and studies Naughton for some moments. "In time, Mr. Naughton, I'd like to have a conversation with you about visions and demons, but now you have work to do, divinely appointed work, I believe. Time will tell."

Naughton nods, not so much in assent as in deference.

"Rely on Sister Claire."

"I will, in all things."

"Good. This afternoon I will accompany you and Sister Claire on a visit to Charlene. And we will hear a story."

Naughton puffs a little. "Stories are not easily summoned, Mother."

"I understand, but you have several hours to perfect the summoning."

Naughton goes to his room to rest. There he finds the door open. It has never been closed since his arrival. Odd. But then, what could be hidden? The very walls would speak the truth.

A Rented Room in New Orleans

What are the ratios? Air is to fire as water is to earth? Whatever they are, if violated, everything turns into a white cosmic dust that lies inert waiting for the Spirit to move over it. Peter is sitting at his desk. Near the back edge is the set of sliding brass bookends that he has carried with him from his parents' home to his room in the fraternity house to this room. While he was in the Navy he had hidden them and a few books behind the furnace at the fraternity house. There for three years they were attacked by molds that adapt expertly to seasonal changes. The pages display a slightly warbled deformity and a graininess to the touch that suggests antiquity. Miraculously they're still readable. Peter has taken one from the narrow rank and opened it on the desk, *Leaves of Grass*. Beside it is a sheet of paper:

Dear Cam,

I'm supposed to be a person good with words, but when I'm with you they fail me, or I fail them. How is it that your words never waste a breath and go straight to the heart? I don't know what to say. It's hard to write a love letter that talks about the candor and frankness of the loved one or about a pact of silence about families. I did definitely agree that we should not talk about our families. I'll never go back on that. They would be a burden.

How would I describe the sweetness of your presence or the sweetness of your body without becoming maudlin? And besides, if I try to say something to you that might be a little poetic, you have a wonderful way of bringing it back to the here and now, my words an arrow that aims at the sun and falls back to earth. But I don't think you're a daughter of gravity. Your gravity is inside yourself. And for me it has a huge field. I can feel it right now at my desk pulling me toward you.

So I give up. I'm going to borrow from Walt Whitman. You said I wouldn't know who I was after I gave him up. Maybe I'll go back to him and find myself in him, and speak through him to you instead of stumbling along like a blind man. This is what I've decided to copy because it has always moved me so much. Probably you will find it strange that I identify with a bird that has lost his mate. We could talk about that. Whatever you say will be right because it will go straight from your heart to mine, like an arrow.

Low hangs the moon, it rose late,
It is lagging—O I think it is heavy with love, with love.
O madly the sea pushes upon the land,
With love, with love.
O night! do I not see my love fluttering out among the breakers?
What is that little black thing I see there in the white?

With all my love,
Peter

The telephone rings, an old black piece, handset scarred, dial half obliterated. It sits on a table between the bed and the window. Peter does not get up. The telephone continues to ring. At last he gets up and answers it.

"Hello, Sonny. You didn't want to answer, did you? Then you thought about your Aunt Ettie alone out here in the wilds of San Francisco."

"Right, Aunt Ettie. All those tigers and crocodiles roaming the streets dressed like Marines."

"Don't get sarcastic with me, Sonny. The trouble with you gobs is that you were always jealous of Marines and afraid of them because they might throw you in the brig and feed you bread and water."

"That would've been against the Uniform Code of Military Justice."

"Would they care? But I didn't call to talk to you about Marines. I called to talk to you about your oriental girlfriend."

"I should've known."

"Is she a Jap?"

"No, the Marines killed all the Japs."

"Stop it. This is a serious phone call. I'm calling to tell you not to marry that oriental woman. An orphan, right?"

"She and I have agreed not to talk about family."

"In your case a good idea. An alky mother and an ape for a father. But in her case something worse."

"Like what?"

"A lot of guys knocked up orientals during the war and brought them back and dumped them."

"She's not an oriental. She's a Eurasian."

"You can skip the fancy talk. You know what I mean."

"No I don't."

"She's sweet and pretty in the pictures you sent, but you'll never know her."

"Is this the Mysterious Orient thing?"

"Partly. But also flying over an ocean when you're a motherless child jumbles your head, which was already different."

"What do you mean different?"

"The brains and eyes of orientals aren't totally connected. Go ahead. Look in her eyes and see how far you can see."

"I'll work on it."

"And the skin is pulled back. And the voice is wrong."

"What's wrong with the voice?"

"What's the matter with your ears, Sonny? Don't you hear that chingy thing no matter what language they're speaking? Like little bells and whispers mixed up. Which means it never says what it means. Take my word for it. San Francisco is crawling with orientals. I had a Filipino vet once, pretty as you. Nice hands, but I never knew who the hell he was."

"Maybe all this doesn't matter if you love somebody."

"You told me the two of you agreed not to talk about love."

"That's right, but you can still feel it. You loved Tom."

"We were right together. That's what love is. You're not right together with Cam. I told you. You're never going to know her."

"Maybe that's good, marrying a mystery woman, keep things interesting."

"That sounds like something your mother would've said on one of her worst poetry out of a bottle days. Men hate mystery women. It drives them crazy."

"Are you a mystery woman, Aunt Ettie?"

There's a silence. "I never thought about it that way, but maybe I am a mystery woman, a one-man woman and he's dead so all the rest just drift by and wonder why I bothered. There, Sonny, you taught me something. So learn something from me. Let Cam go and find the right one."

"My world would go dark if I lost her."

"Then take it from one who knows. They killed him at Tarawa and sent me a purple heart lined with gold and a gold George Washington in the middle, who didn't know anything about Tarawa. Do you? Over George Washington's head is a shield with red stars and stripes, which is OK for a military thing. But on the sides of the shield are two green stalks. What the hell is that? On the back is Tom's name and letters saying 'For Military Merit.' Doesn't mention he's dead."

"You had it tough, Aunt Ettie."

"I didn't have any choice. You say your world would go dark if you let Cam go. All right, you want a stiff shot of darkness you can get over now or you want to live in a gray fog for years?"

"I'll take the fog, but I'll turn it silver. I've got to go now. I'm writing a love poem."

"Tell it to the Marines. Remember that during the war? Tell them what? I don't know. Anyway, you were too young to tell them anything. But listen to what I'm telling you. Let her go. Write the love poem to that old queer you're hung up on."

The walk down the hall to the window where Charlene sits in her wheelchair is slow. Mother Martha sets the pace. Not arduous but deliberate and contemplative. Once in front of Charlene, Mother Martha gives her an inquiring but kind look. "How are you, child?"

"Nnnnn," says Charlene. It's now clear that she understands what's said to her.

Mother Martha smiles. "You may not want me to call you my child, Charlene, but you are. You are all my children." She reaches out and grasps Charlene's hand firmly. Charlene doesn't pull back. "I'll tell you something strange that I want to share with you. I didn't fully understand my motherhood until I read a book written by a holy woman a long time ago. She said that Jesus is our mother, who feeds us not with milk but with blood. So I thought if I'm in Christ and Christ is in me, as I've been taught, then I'm the mother of all." Mother Martha's tone is matter of fact, tinged only slightly with a sense of wonder. She nods, smiling. "Your friend Mr. Naughton has lifted his eyebrows. Do you think, Mr. Naughton, I'm speaking heresy?"

"I wouldn't know, Mother, but the heyday of heresies is long past."

Vera comes out of the door of Charlene's room where she's been cleaning.

Mother Martha says, "Sister Claire is laughing inside herself, Charlene. My naughty children. But they are also your mothers because Christ is in them and they are in Christ." She makes a gentle shaking motion with Charlene's hand. "And now, Charlene, you must bear a child." Now Charlene strains against Mother Martha's grip, but Mother Martha holds tight. "I know, Charlene. All childbearing is painful. So it was ordained when Adam and Eve ate the forbidden fruit. The child you shall bear is yourself. And that may be the most painful birthing of all. You've been for a long time in the womb of darkness. You haven't wanted to come out. None of us have ever wanted to come out. It's in our nature to want to stay where it's warm and safe. But come out we must. And you're coming out. Isn't she, Vera?"

"Yes, Mother. Charlene is coming out."

"So, Charlene, Vera has fed you the milk of kindness and Sister Claire has fed you the milk of wisdom, and Mr. Naughton has told you strange stories. He's going to tell us a story now."

Charlene is pleased, nodding, her eyes brightening.

Mother Martha says, "My intuition tells me it will be a story of fire. He's told you a story of falling through the air to earth and he's told you an ocean story. So I think this will be a story of fire."

"Fire." Charlene almost succeeds in repeating the word. The beginning is muffled, but the pronunciation is still more fire than ire.

Mother Martha releases Charlene's hand and turns to Naughton. "Will this be an old pagan story about the fire-bringer?"

It's difficult to tell what Naughton is thinking. He has seemed to be elsewhere, staring out toward the garden and woods. The images of the five of them in the window are faint, overborne by a granular veil as if carefully planned pricks of sand have pitted the glass with meticulous care.

At the Old
Pueblo Archaeology Center

Peter stands before a wall constructed of many uneven layers of characterless stone held together by a sporadic caulking of dun mortar. Either the stones were hewn or the mason got lucky and found pieces with smooth faces. The wall is obviously a restoration because there is little evidence of the rote of windblown sand. Some distance from the wall, out in the baked yard, a ritual fire has been started, three stakes enclosing a brittle mass of desert weed that has flared briefly against the sun. A mix of voices approximate an incantation, but there is little rhythm or intensity. A high nasal sound, almost equine, is the only thing that lends to the event a bit of authenticity. A dozen tourists stand quietly in a broken circle around the fire. When the fire has consumed the weed with a final crackling of flame, the tourists award the show a murmur of approval. Encouraged by the chanters to examine the three charred stakes, they approach respectfully. No doubt a deep symbolism is intended.

Peter's family is not near the fire ceremony. They have gone with a guide to the Enchanted Hills to view cactuses and to pretend they're archaeologists, digging tools provided. A few shards of pots have been buried in hummocks marked with chalky stripes of color, a rigged treasure hunt.

Peter continues to stare, but not at the wall. Rather he focuses on the space between the wall and himself. There, out of the swarming desert heat, rises an image, vague at first and then as clear as a perfectly focused photograph, black and white, taken with a high-end camera capable of capturing precise images on different focal planes. Peter finds himself in the hot interior of Penance Hall at Jesuit High School in New Orleans. Orr, the assistant to Father Finneran, Prefect of Discipline, is walking the aisles between desks carrying a stick like a riding crop with a spatulate end. Orr is a veteran, bald from exposure to the sun of the northern Sahara, having fought the Desert Fox from Tunisia to El Alamein, so the story goes. Orr's duty is to patrol the rows of desks occupied by the day's miscreants. If any penitent is caught laggard or dozing, the instrument of atonement comes down with a searing whack on the hand of the delinquent. The task for these sinners consigned to Father Finneran's purgatory is to copy nine, the mystic three times three, pages of the maintenance manual for the M1 rifle: nomenclature, assembly, mounting of scope, sight correction, cleaning, loading, unloading, servicing, firing pin check, spent cartridge ejector spring, safety. If one stays on task one can finish in about three hours. Peter is here because he and O'Shea traded shoves and cuffs in the mess hall, O'Shea a little red-headed demon adept at tricking others into infractions while himself adeptly posing as innocent. He is not here in Penance Hall. Actually, the mess hall monitor, Mr. Marelli, a portly scholastic, is onto O'Shea's trickery, but deems O'Shea a necessary agent of the Devil useful in testing the weakness of those who otherwise strive to remain lawful.

Across the grinder in another wing of the building the school band, a ragged bunch, neither athletes nor scholars, is practicing Lecuona's *Malagueña*. They're having a very hard time getting the accelerando of the base melody on cue, especially the brass. The bandmaster, Mr. Muñez, a scholastic from Cuba, can be heard shouting angrily at his inept performers.

Orr hollers in a raspy desiccated voice, "Get it right, you bone-head mouth breathers. This baby is accurate at one hundred yards." He aims down the length of his instrument of mortification. "Bang! One more dead Kraut for Balala." Balala? What is he trying to say? Valhalla? Peter goes on copying and gets out just before six o'clock.

Mr. Donnelly happens to be passing by as Peter emerges from Penance Hall. "Follow me, Naughton," he says. They go back to their home room. It is empty, the strains of the butchered *Malagueña* barely audible through the window. "Sit down, Naughton." Mr. Donnelly opens a book and writes on the blackboard: Ὡς οἱ μὲν μάρναντο δέμας πυρὸς. "Do you know what it means?"

"No sir, but I don't think it's from the *Odyssey*."

"Very good, Naughton. It's from the *Iliad*. It means they fought like fire. But you and O'Shea are hardly epic. I'm surprised at you. Everybody knows that O'Shea is a troublemaker. In Elizabethan drama he would be called the Vice, remember? If the Vice wins over the protagonist, as Iago wins over Othello, you have a tragedy. If he is apprehended and exposed, you have a comedy, as in *Much Ado About Nothing*. In the modern world O'Shea will not become a notable villain. He will be a petty larcenist or more likely a crooked small-time politician. Do you know why?"

"I think it's in his nature."

"Yes, but what exactly is in his nature?"

"Dishonesty?"

"No. O'Shea has been born and brought up to perceive that the world, which does not love him, is malleable and porous. He's driven to find its softness and its holes so he can lure the gullible into his trivial plots. In his own small way he's actually imaginative."

Peter nods. "It was stupid of me to fall for it."

"The O'Sheas of the world you will deal with easily. It's something else that threatens you. Do you know what it is?"

Peter's eyes narrow in thought. "Is it that I have a stone face when I recite?"

"That's related."

"What is it, sir?" Fear tinctures Peter's voice.

"Words." There's a silence. "Are you surprised?"

Peter's face is conflicted. "I don't know, sir."

"Words come to you easily, Naughton, too easily." Mr. Donnelly pauses. "You may be thinking of the Word that became flesh. That's not the Word we're talking about." Mr. Donnelly's mild grimace is so finely etched that it barely reveals the incisors that glisten within. He pauses in his speaking, but his prominent Adam's apple continues to move subtly above his stiff white collar as if it were just there, in his larynx, where flesh capitulates to words. "For all of you boys the war with the flesh will go on all your lives, and some will be defeated. But you won't be defeated by the flesh, Naughton. That doesn't mean it won't pierce you and torment you. Be on guard. But you won't be defeated by it."

Peter's stillness is as of one bound in chains. "What will defeat me?"

"What always defeats us. The Double that lurks in our strength."

"I don't know what strength I have."

Mr. Donnelly's blue eyes flare. "Let's always speak truth to each other, Naughton. You know what your strength is, your growing mastery of words. Behind all your writings and translations I see the thickets of diction and case and syntax— English, Greek, Latin—that every day ensnare your classmates. But they don't ensnare you. That's rare. I've never seen it before."

"So what is the Double that will defeat me?" Peter's voice quavers. The image of Mr. Donnelly in the slant sun of the afternoon has a numinous quality, the fiery hair, the deep liquidity of blue in the eyes, the half-hidden glister of teeth, the lean neck, the thin inviolable hands and wrists, all highlighted by the unbroken black of the cassock.

"I've never spoken like this to any other student about the danger of words. I'm unpracticed. So I'll ask you. What is the serpent under the beauty of words?"

Peter shakes his head apologetically. "I can only think of the words themselves. I can't see what's underneath."

"There. You've said it. One word leading to the next and to the next and to the next ad infinitum and never to the thing beneath. So there's nothing but words. They never come to rest on their objects. One lives in a world without objects."

"Couldn't that be a spiritual world?" Peter seems shocked by his own forwardness.

Mr. Donnelly leans back into the shadows, withdrawing everything—the fire of his hair, the crisped eyes brother to the fire, the lean neck and wrists. He looks inward, behind a veil of contemplation. At last he comes back and bends forward over his desk, looking intently at his student. "Imagine one who went into a darkness that was without words or objects, that was absolutely pure. And there he found God."

"Did he ever come back?"

"He came back and tried to tell of it, for our benefit, but all the while he knew the telling was a betrayal, wasn't it? Words."

It takes some moments for Peter to find his voice, and then what he says is surprisingly bold. "Is that how you found God?"

Mr. Donnelly looks up startled. "No."

"How did you find him?"

"I didn't. He found me." Mr. Donnelly smiles, but it's clear the smile isn't for Peter. It's a smile of remembrance. "I wanted to be an Irish hellion with such foulness in my mouth I would astound the world. Because I knew how we Irish are viewed. I was born in the Irish Channel flanked by Blacks and Italians, kept out of sight by the WASPs and French of the Garden District. I played in the shadow of St. Alphonsus, which I hated for its ugly mishmash of architectures, though I couldn't have known how to say that at the time. I hated the tasteless piety of the neighborhood, the blue-and-white Virgins in old upended bathtubs, Les Madonnas des Bains. The beads and bleeding hearts, all of it. I hated it. I was determined to make of myself its opposite."

"What happened?"

"What happened? Nothing happened. There was no event, no road to Damascus. Just bit by bit the ugliness of my bitterness began to rise up into my mouth and nostrils."

"How did you know it was ugly?"

"You're a good student, Naughton. What did you learn from our little exercise with Duns Scotus?"

"One can understand that some bit of goodness he knows must depend on a yet higher affirming goodness. And on up the ladder until we get to the ultimate goodness, which is God."

"Right. So a scrap of goodness came to me. It's called grace."

"What if no scrap of goodness had come to you there in the Irish Channel?"

"There's no place on earth so poisonous that there's no scrap of goodness. Such a place would have to be called Hell."

"Do you believe in Hell?"

Mr. Donnelly sits back and breathes deeply. "Probably not the way you're thinking about it. Dante." He pauses. "We've gone as far as we can go, Naughton. You'll have to work out your own salvation. We all will."

"Maybe I'll give up words. I'll take up art and paint, but not objects."

"I understand that in New York City there are some that do that."

"Then that's what I'll do."

Mr. Donnelly laughs a mirthless laugh. "No you won't Naughton. Your path lies through words. I'll pray for you."

Peter goes around to a side yard and finds some shade. He sits on the ground and leans against a pilaster that has at its base a span of smooth stucco. A few moments later a woman, fortyish, comes out into the side yard and sits down across the way on a pile of stones in the sun. She wears cowboy jeans and boots and a leather vest. On one of her arms is a tattoo, sun-bleared, indecipherable. She lights a cigarette and smokes with a curious insouciance as though the cigarette is among the least of things. She knocks off the accumulated ash expertly with her little finger. She looks at Peter, then changes the focus of her eyes as if sighting something beyond the pilaster. Suddenly she stands up and flicks the half-smoked cigarette across the yard, propelling it with surprising vehemence along a low trajectory that arcs several yards before the cigarette strikes the barren ground and rolls another few inches, giving up a dying puff of smoke. The woman walks away with a rolling but uneven gait. Metal studs define the back pockets of her jeans.

Peter walks back out to the baked yard with its charred sticks. The group from the Enchanted Hills is coming back, eight including Cam, Peter and Alexie. Peter is fourteen, Alexie ten. As they maneuver through the low brush and cactuses, they appear and disappear. Behind them rises a low ridge and behind that a higher mountain covered with low green-brown growth. At last they reach the gate in the mesh fence and come across the yard. Alexie is holding her cat, Man Two. The cat is a light-gray Siamese. It has blue eyes that are crossed.

"Well," says Peter, "what secret did you uncover?"

"They weren't any good at math," says Josh. "Nothing like the Mayans."

"How do you know?"

"Just a lot of pictographs on rocks, squiggly lines, some beads, all the same color."

"Well, I don't think counting would've saved them from the western movement."

Cam says, "Is that what they call it, the western movement, taking all the land?"

Alexie says, "That's why they have museums, to remember."

Cam says, "Remembering is not what you think it is."

"Right," says Josh. "Memory is subject to revision. They should bar it from courtroom trials."

"I remember," says Alexie, "what the lady said about Man Two."

"What did she say?" asks Peter.

"She said is it an Egyptian name? I told her it's spelled M-A-N-T-W-O, named after a cat my daddy's aunt had. She said it was descended from pharaohs' cats."

"There're about six hundred million cats in the world," says Josh, "and zero pharaohs."

"Does that count the cats and pharaohs in dreams?" asks Cam.

"No," says Josh. "It's just the numbers."

Cam nods. "Nothing that means anything has a number."

"There're about thirty thousand Pueblo people of various tribes living around the Southwest."

Cam says, "Do they keep the number in their head? Do they wonder if people like the six hundred million cats more than they like the thirty thousand Pueblo peoples?" There's no animus in Cam's voice. But the recitation of numbers falls on the air like the spikes of an engine of torture.

"I tell you what I think," says Peter. "I think the sun has overheated our heads and it's time to get something cold to drink and head for the motel. Tomorrow we have a lot of driving to do."

"Man Two doesn't care," says Alexie. "Sun or rain."

"Pagan fire-bringer," says Naughton, looking startled. "No, Mother, there's no Prometheus in this story."

"I don't dare to hope that it might be about the tongues of fire that sat on the apostles' heads at Pentecost."

"No, Mother. Actually it's based on something half remembered."

Sister Claire says, "Later, Mother, Mr. Naughton may tell the fully remembered version."

Mother Martha laughs. "I don't think so, Sister. I think it'll be just another variant. I don't believe there's a canonical bone in his body. What do you think, Charlene?"

Charlene makes a bubbly sound.

"What does she say, Vera?"

"I think she wants to believe it, Mother."

"Good, Charlene. We've all had to believe things in order to come into the world, though everything at first was very blurry. We touched and tasted. First the mother milk and then the whole world came flowing in. Never mind that it was a fallen world. It was still God's creation. A miracle. Now your fire, Mr. Naughton."

Sister Claire smiles. "I've warned you, Mother. Mr. Naughton's stories can be fierce."

Mother Martha says, "What do you say, Vera?"

"Sister Claire has spoken the truth, Mother. They are hard."

Mother Martha nods soberly. "If the fire comes my way, I'll try to seize it and wear it on my head. When I was a child my mother would use her thumb and finger to snatch the flame from a candle's wick. I asked her where she hid it. In her heart for me, she'd say."

"I'm afraid Mr. Naughton's fire won't be like that," says Sister Claire.

"I'm warned," says Mother Martha. "Tell your story, Mr. Naughton."

Naughton draws himself up and rocks a little from side to side as if the story has to be awakened from a deep sleep. "Imagine the driest desert on earth. So dry that one might believe it has been burned to igneous grit by suns older than ours. This was the nature of the sand on the island where we anchored, a US man-of-war, crew of two hundred men. From the deck we saw in the distance a low city and the Sheik's palace we'd been told about. Nothing shimmered. The heat had long ago disciplined the air to remain immobile. Out over the water stood a huge skyward shaft. Just barely we could distinguish out in the offing the serrated edge of the shaft gnawing the planar surfaces of blue sea and sky. At night the shaft netted the sky in sly corrugations so that the stars winked and faded inconstantly. We wouldn't have anchored off such a barren island if it hadn't been for an invasion of the Suez Canal to the north, a misadventure concocted by the British, French and Israelis.

"On our side of the island near the Sheik's palace was a huge Quonset building, an evening watering hole for the Gloucester Marines and the Kenyan police who were billeted on the island to assure the uninterrupted flow of oil to its imperial masters. Sprinkled among these, to complete the polyglot, were a few Dutch and French oil workers. The Gloucester Marines spoke their difficult version of English, the Kenyan police essentially East Anglia with a few African phonemes thrown in, the French French, the Dutch Dutch, and we Americans our American English, universally disdained wherever English had been learned from the British."

Charlene's eyes brighten. Mother Martha looks at her intently.

"The Gloucester chaps wanted to know if we Americans wur ainy gouda zingin. We proclaimed that we were all zingers until we understood that a song was what was needed.

Anchors aweigh, my boys, we sang, anchors away. The Gloucester reprise was a loud jolly lament about bereft fisherwomen. That's all we could get. The Kenyans didn't zing. The resplendent burnish of their skin was their song. We whites, in stained and stinking khaki, were a blemish on even the tainted air of the Quonset. The Kenyans shone like rare brown-ribbed obsidian polished by the green winds of the Indian Ocean, impervious to the rote of the island's eternally blowing pumice.

"As the evening wore thinner and the end of our liberty ashore loomed, the pitch of talk and sound bloomed inside the Quonset like an unearthly blossom. We who had heard the thunder of sixteen-inchers while standing by the USS *Missouri* off the Brittany coast had still not yet understood the fact that sound, when tightly woven, ceases to be waves. It solidifies, expands and foliates. I looked up toward the high ceiling of the Quonset, where the huge blossom unfolded and tilted down, magenta, vaginal, edges dentate. What if it came down upon us like a Venus flytrap and exacted the punishment our coarse references to women deserved? I couldn't see that any others were aware of our peril. A Gloucester Marine and a Dutchman were arguing about which was the greater nation in the Goolden Chine. They raised their dukes, shadowboxed for a moment and then threw themselves into each other's arms laughing drunkenly. The great flower remained aloft, aloof. We were merely unsavory worms below. Anyway, those were our nights in Bahrein until the riot and the fire."

Naughton abruptly stops speaking, swept away from the island and deposited in his chair. He's been looking at Charlene. Now he turns and looks at the two nuns. His expression is one of recognition and surprise, at persons known but unexpected here just now.

Mother Martha says, "You must leave Maison Cristina, Mr. Naughton, and return to the island and take us with you."

Naughton nods. "Sister Claire, or perhaps another mentor of mine, has taught me that air is the most treacherous for man because it can't hold up us fleshly beings. But what about fire? It will hold us up only as long as it produces great drafts of heat. The moment it's extinguished, we drop."

"That's true, Mr. Naughton. Nevertheless, you've promised Charlene a fire story, and fire we must have."

Sister Claire looks at Naughton with concern but doesn't speak.

Vera follows Sister Claire's gaze. "Mr. Naughton is not eating right."

Charlene sits forward in her chair with great animation and frustration. "Stowy," she says.

Naughton takes a deep breath. "All right, to the fire, swiftly. The young Arabs of the island were incensed by news of the invasion of the canal and by the Sheik's failure to express outrage. They knew that the island was a thrall to oil. Still, they cried out for revenge. The Kenyan police and the Gloucester Marines were capable of quashing with definitive swiftness the smallest seedling of a real insurrection, but in some office a Brigadier all in white with stripes of real gold on his epaulets decreed that the young Arabs must have a chance to vent. So, when the would-be insurgents marched toward the Sheik's palace and the Brigadier's quarters they were redirected by police and Marines toward the principal quay on the island. At the end of the quay was a warehouse, mostly unused, at that time a jumble of pallets, cartons, broken furniture and the like. Brandishing flambeaux and shouting with exuberant rage, the young incendiaries broke down the doors of the warehouse, doused the already highly flammable jumble with gasoline and torched it. Almost instantaneously a roaring inferno engulfed the warehouse, driving the rioters back from the onslaught of intolerable heat they themselves had created.

"Several of us American officers had been sent from the ship to signify US approval of the operation, observers really.

Even at our distance we turned our faces away from the heat. Within minutes the warehouse collapsed on itself, its contents unidentifiable in the intense glare. But one piece stood briefly above the fire, a single cross-membered strut that once supported the ridge of the roof that had fallen away into the fire below. The survival of this one piece of the structure would've been enough to cause amazement, but what caused a horrified gasp was the fact that a body was suspended from the strut, blackened, arms and legs hideously distended, the whole corpus charred, welted and warped. It didn't hang there for long. The base of the strut cracked and gave way. But the body didn't plunge into the fire because the strut fell back over the edge of the quay into the bay. Maybe it sizzled, but the drumming of the fire, though now somewhat lessened, made it impossible to hear.

"In my mind, perhaps in others', was the fate of the body in waters infested with sea serpents. Later the question was whose body was it, burned beyond identification. Was it a self-immolated Arab? Was it a retainer or member of the Sheik's household captured and fastened to the strut? A thorough roll call of Marines and police revealed no missing personnel. A half-hearted attempt was made to fish the body out of the bay, but the corpse fell apart, already half eaten by crabs and serpents that clung to it tenaciously. So the mystery remained.

"A week later we set sail for Abadan. Before our departure an elaborate myth had taken hold. Witnesses insisted that before the body fell they saw that the face was a luminous blue, unmarred by the fire, the aquiline nose bronze, the eyes obsidian, the cilia gold and, above ruby lips a silver mustache. Was it the mask of an angel or a devil? Maybe it was made of precious metals and gems. The waters were searched again but yielded nothing. The witnesses were nuts. That was the consensus aboard ship. But the face appeared to me in a dream. It said, 'In many a smiling mask death shall approach beguiling thee.' A line from my old friend Walt Whitman. But I was young then and not ready to yield to the mask of death."

Naughton slumps visibly.

Mother Martha says, "Charlene, you have your fire. Now we have to take Mr. Naughton to his room for a rest."

Charlene slowly leans back against the cushion in her wheelchair. "Fire," she says, this time quite clearly.

"Yes," says Mother Martha, "you have spoken fire and the fire has been in your eyes. Cherish it."

In his room Naughton lies down on his bed. "My apologies."

Mother Martha says to Sister Claire, "You see that Mr. Naughton attends to himself and eats right."

"Yes, Mother. Mr. Naughton has a compact with life."

"Yes. Under current circumstances, Mr. Naughton, you are not free to die. Do you understand?"

Naughton smiles and nods feebly.

"If we live we don't live for ourselves. If we die we don't die for ourselves. You have a responsibility."

"It's not just death, Mother."

"I know that. I've seen it in your eyes. I've seen it in others' eyes. It's the fear of and longing for utter annihilation, nothingness. Understand, Mr. Naughton, there's no such thing as nothingness. Dead or alive you and I will never know nothingness. That's only for fallen creatures of the highest order. So you'll stay with us and tell stories."

"It gets harder and harder, Mother."

"No matter. It's what you're here for. Charlene has to give birth, also hard."

"I'll fail her."

"No you won't."

"I've failed everybody. My sister, my parents, my children, my aunt, my wife, my wife's circle. You could even say I failed Vogt and his mad revolution. I failed Walt Whitman. When we lay side by side it was like an inexorable yeasting. I thought I would be swallowed up and baked into a huge loaf of love. I fled." The enumeration of his failures has briefly animated Naughton, but now he lies back in a state of complete enervation.

"Go to sleep now, Mr. Naughton. Vera will wake you up after a while and give you some supper and you will eat it."

Naughton says nothing.

"You won't fail this time. And don't fear your dreams. You're not a prophet."

But Naughton is blessed with neither sleep nor dreams. They beckon by the wall but give way to a dense parade of black letters, thousands of them, enough for a sizeable novel.

A Wall in Rizzo's Print Shop

The phone rings. "Get your ass here, Pepe. One last job."

Cam says, "Go. Then this is done."

Entering the shop, Peter says, "I thought on this last day of our long professional association you could call me by my right name."

"Peter is a dick name, Pepe, and I ain't calling you Pietro due to my asshole cousin Pietro."

"OK, Mr. Reetzo."

"And you, you egghead prick, could call me by my real name, Reezo."

"If I called you Reezo, then I would have to go down to Mario's and order a peeza. If you pronounced your name right you might rise up in the world. You could even jazz it up with a little rubato—Rreetzo."

"Sounds like a fucking mobster."

"What I said. You might rise up in the world."

"You fucking college dick. I'm Italian and you tell me how to pronounce my name."

Peter looks around the shop. "In some ways I'm going to miss this dump, smell of ink, paper and trays of type all over hell and gone, crumbling old posters tacked to the wall, and Martyne of course, the best mulatto typesetter in the country, an artist."

Martyne is sitting at the linotype setting type with a cigarette hanging out of his mouth long ago extinguished by spittle that has stained the paper dark brown.

"OK, what's the emergency?"

"The emergency is you ain't found me a writer and I got orders."

"I sent you an English grad student with straight As."

"Yeah and he was writing English English or some other highfalutin shit."

"OK, I'll make another call or two, but it's not easy to find somebody willing to write down to your clients."

"Down! I got the best Catholic schools in town."

"You don't have Sacred Heart."

"Stuck up bitches. Fuck em."

"What about the Jesuits?"

"Don't want the fucking Jesuits. Uptown French pricks. Anti-war. They got conscious objectors. The Pope don't want em either, but he ain't ready to make a move on em. Dead grunts don't matter to fucking Jesuits. Going to heaven. What about the Cong? They got their own heaven? But you don't have to worry about this shitass war, Pepe, because you got two kids and a high number. And Martyne is too old. He ain't got a birth certificate, but they can tell from the rings around his dick he's too old."

Martyne smiles. "Rizzo's got three exempts—age, illiteracy, and colorblind."

"Martyne knows I already fought under the stars and stripes in World War Two. Navy. Where I learned to curse so good. Besides, I ain't too colorblind to see you ain't white, Martyne, and took you on anyway and pay you good. I was paying Pepe good too, but his wife got a wild hair up her ass to go west. Get nearer to Asia, right, Pepe?"

"Right. You can pick up the smell of it on the coast. Like soy sauce."

"Actually, Pepe, I ain't got nothing against color. Take my man Martyne. Biggest cocksman in Darktown. They all want a piece of that little yellow dickie-bird. I ain't saying nothing against any of them. People got to live. And I don't say this with no malice. Orientals are also good. Different yellow from Martyne's though. Color is beauty. Whites ain't white either down in the lower precincts where it counts." Rizzo wags his head, revving up his monologue. "I don't mind doing business with nobody. And everybody wants to do business with me because I'm the best layout man in town. Like Schuman, fucking Nazi, but the best photographer in town. Got X-ray eyes. Girls at Ursuline and the nuns feel it. Like ginger in a horse's ass which is illegal, but perks em up. The Kraut puts just a hint of them things on top of their heads. What do you call it?"

"A nimbus."

Rizzo laughs. "Martyne has a nimbus over his dick, which also ain't legal, but the cops can't see it."

"Right," says Peter. "And Schuman can make the crosses and the priests' collars shine with a supernatural blue light."

"Pepe, it's a dumb fucking idea to haul everything out west. I told you I don't have nothing against orientals, but you don't know what's behind them eyes. Opposite of Schuman's, which are bulging with X-rays. The fact you got a high number don't mean you have to go to whatever asshole place she wants."

"My wife says numbers aren't a good way to solve anything."

"Don't knock numbers, Pepe. Numbers got us bingo posters. Numbers is how I pay you and Martyne and still have some left over for Melie's clothes so she ain't nothing but a printer's wife that smells like a goat with black fingernails."

"Goats don't have fingernails. They have cloven ungulate hooves."

Martyne laughs. Rizzo can't help himself and bursts out laughing. "I should've hit you on the head with a hammer, Pepe, the minute you walked in here and knocked out all them words that ain't to the point. It ain't clove or unglued that's under my fingernails. It's black. Ink. Which is OK for me and Martyne, right Martyne? But it ain't OK with women. Black is for the hidden parts, them little puffs."

"OK, what's my final job, Reetzo?"

"You're writing something, Pepe, because words is the only thing you know how to do. I ain't got time for it or I'd do it myself." He hands Peter a paper that outlines the assignment. He is to doctor an account and scraps of an interview with an Ursuline nun who went on a pilgrimage to the shrine of the Virgen de Guadalupe in Mexico City. Not the kind of thing that Ursuline nuns typically did, but Sor Luciana, a name she was permitted by the Mother Superior to use after the pilgrimage, had a vision of the Virgen. In the vision the Virgen was calling to her in three languages, Spanish, English and pidgin Latin. So Peter sits at his scarred and ink-stained desk and writes the story of Sor Luciana on her knees, one hundred yards to the shrine. He uses a poetic refrain, bone on stone, Sor Luciana climbing the steep stairway of atonement, the stark striking of her knees, bone on stone, sending up her delicate frame flames of pain and expiation. And so forth. It takes him hardly twenty minutes. He hands it to Rizzo, who reads it slowly and nods. "The nuns'll love it. Suffering and forgiveness. You got a knack, Pepe. It ain't great but it ain't average. So get your ass out there and find me a writer the same as you. You owe me. Think of all them freelancer jobs I got you, pamphlets and ad copy. House of Repose, Saint Anthony's Grot, Dolorosa Shop of Religion, Saint Francis Pet Shop. All that. You owe me."

"At the pet shop you could buy a snake, under the counter, that would curl lovingly at your feet, like St. Francis. I should've put that in the ads."

"You didn't need to put it in the ads. You fucking eggheads don't even know what you're writing. What the fuck do you think it meant when you wrote every creature was placed on the earth for our use and instruction. And was you looking for an unusual pet? What the fuck did you think it was, a crawdad or an alligator?"

Peter feigns a look of deep suffering, but when he speaks, a genuine tone of regret creeps into his voice. "What do you suppose my Jesuit teachers would think of this sanctimonious crap I've been writing for you all these years?"

"I already told you what I think of the fucking Jesuits. You should've gone to Holy Cross for high school."

"I was meant for higher things. At one time I could recite twenty lines of Homer. Rhododactylos Eos, rosy-fingered dawn. Oinops pontos, the wine-dark sea, and the plashing oars of Odysseus' sailors. And Virgil. Arma virumque cano."

Rizzo gives Peter a serious look. "It ain't good to think back over shit like that. It ain't good for you. Martyne had a wife and a kid once, but he's smart enough not to think about it. Right, Martyne?"

Martyne spits the sodden butt out of his mouth onto the floor. "Right."

"You ain't looking all that good these days anyway, Pepe. Moving could kill you. You're going to end up on some seashore and look around and not know where you are or who you are. Me and Martyne ain't much but we know."

"I'm not sleeping too well."

"You could sleep like a baby if you got faith and stayed put. We all stinking sinners, Pepe. I go home. My wife tells me you smell like a goat, Marco. I tell her, you can't say that, Melie. It's in the Bible, the sheep and the goats. The goats ain't no good.

But I shower. You can't take your wife in your arms if you're a goat."

"Catholics aren't supposed to read the Bible."

"Who said I read it? Any asshole would know you can't have your wife if you smell like a goat."

"Agreed."

"Can you do one more for old times' sake?"

"What is it?"

"Bingo night at St. Teresa of the Little Flower parish hall."

"Which flower?"

"You don't need to know the fucking flower, Pepe. Just write the ad."

Martyne says, "I gotta have the flower in mind to set the type."

"You're lucky you got any mind left, Martyne, blowing your brains out with them Black jazz bands in the Quarter and smoking whatever shit keeps you blowing."

Peter says, "It's a good thing, Reetzo, it's not St. Teresa of Ávila. She would've driven the numbers racket out of the parish hall like Jesus drove the money-changers from the temple."

"Well, it ain't that other St. Teresa. There's probably a hundred of em."

Peter doodles. "Come ye one and all, worshippers of Goddess Fortuna, study numerology, pick your cards carefully in accordance with the demonic divinations of combination and permutation. And upon the announcement of the fifth in line on your card shout lustily, Bingo, Hallelujah!"

"I'm going to kick your ass, Pepe."

"Everybody believes in luck, destiny, fate, kismet, whatever. A divinity shapes our ends, rough hew them though we may."

"I'd rough hew your end, Pepe, but you've already done it to yourself, leaving your mother city and the best print shop in it."

"Consider, Reetzo. Of the billion spermatozoa provided by the inseminator only one gets into the egg. One person's number has come up. The other nine hundred and ninety million, nine hundred and ninety thousand nine hundred and ninety-nine spermatozoa get flushed down the toilet. And compound the odds of Lucky Luigi's mother's and his father's numbers coming up, and their forebears' numbers. What chance is there of any of us existing? We don't. We're imagining each other."

"Bullshit, Pepe. Would I imagine an egghead prick like you and a yellow hophead like Martyne? You got decided up there. The divinity. You said so yourself. And you also said your wife said numbers don't mean shit. But you gotta keep her happy by going to the Pacific Ocean. I been to the Pacific Ocean. It ain't nothing special. We sat off the coast of North Korea lobbing sixteen-inch shells into the fucking hills and what was left of the trees. The only good thing was liberty in Yokohama where you could fuck any sixteen-year-old slant you wanted to. No offense."

"OK, I'll write that at St. Teresa of some little flower or other each card has only an apostolic twelve possible winning combinations out of thousands, but some lucky old lady gets it. Bingo, Hallelujah! Twenty-five bucks to the lucky little lady in blue, who knows in her heart that she's favored by God because she was never screwed by anybody but her husband and never took any pleasure from it."

"Don't be a sacrilegious asshole, Pepe. You no good at it. Jesuits got you. Touch them fuckers and you're a lifer. Now write the fucking ad and go to the Pacific, but find me a writer that knows what real Catholics want to read."

Peter writes, but just as he's finishing, a veil lifts.

Father Donnelly writes on the blackboard "Casus Contra Petri." He turns to the class. "I have told you the story of Peter Naughton, how after graduation from our campus in New Orleans he severed himself from all his classmates and left the

137

Church. He spent four years at Tulane University as a frat boy drinker and paradoxically successful scholar. He served three years in the Navy as a Supply Officer and then came back to New Orleans and matriculated in the PhD program at Tulane specializing in Walt Whitman. He dropped out and went to work in a print shop writing ads and pamphlets. During that time he married a Eurasian woman and they had two children. He now lives in Bellingham, Washington. At our campus in New Orleans he was in writing skills the most brilliant student I've ever had."

A hand goes up. "What about Moreau?"

Moreau sits stolidly near the back of the classroom.

Father Donnelly says, "Moreau is our best. Terse, cutting, accurate. Naughton had a totally different style—lyrical, metaphorical, always reaching. Maybe a regional difference in part, Louisiana and Wisconsin."

Kraus says, "Was he as moody as our Morose Moor?" K is referring to the rumor that Moreau's family came from Oran.

"He was withdrawn and uncertain of himself."

Carroll says, "I wish I knew what he looked like."

"He didn't look unusual really," says Father Donnelly, "but his face was oddly inexpressive. His classmates called him Doctor Logos and The Great Stone Face. His voice was generally subdued, but on rare occasions he could be acid. I think he never felt he fully belonged. But we're straying from the point. The indictment is as follows. It is sinful to seek mortification by debasing one's principal gift. Why?"

"The gift was God's."

"The corruption of the best is the worst."

"In Latin, please, Minser."

"I don't know it."

"Corruptio optimi quae est pessima."

"Very good, Moreau."

"Mortification should not be in extremity," says another student.

"In fact, all of your answers are good, but let's go deeper. How do we do that?"

"Apply the doctrine of the seven deadly sins to the casus," says Ratner.

"All right. That's a start. Let's make the list."

Various voices contribute as Father Donnelly writes on the board:

Luxuria—Lust
Gula—Gluttony
Avaritia—Greed
Acedia—Sloth
Ira—Wrath
Superbia—Pride
Invidia—Envy

"Who votes for Luxuria? None? Good. For Gula? None? Good. Avaritia? None? Good. Acedia? One. Why do you say so, Litthauer?"

"Because said Petri was too lazy to work out his salvation slowly and painfully."

"Excellent. What about the sin of Ira? Two. Speak, Foley."

"Petri is angry with those who work out their salvation within the normal penitential bounds of the Church."

"Worse," says Kunow. "Petri is angry with God for giving us the free will to sin and wants to show Him the consequences."

"Terrifying. What about Superbia?"

Many hands go up.

"Adamson, speak for all."

"Easy. Petri is practicing an act of supererogation, which is always an act of pride."

"Excellent. Invidia?"

Two hands.

"Inform us, McCrae."

139

"Petri cannot stand the sight of those who seem to him to have a surplus of grace. He is like the older brother of the prodigal son."

"Splendid. But now we have a problem. If Petri's act covers so many mortal sins, doesn't that suggest an even deeper corruption below, Moreau's corruptio optimi?"

In the silence that follows it's clear that everyone believes the answer to Father Donnelly's question has to be yes. But what is the deeper corruption? Father Donnelly waits. At last Moreau speaks. "I know what it is, but I can't put it into words."

"Well spoken, Moreau. Our human languages, which fall far short of the Word, cannot express everything. What are we to do in the casus contra Petri?"

From somewhere near the back of the classroom comes a harrowing sound that combines fear and lamentation. It's Donohoe.

"Where did you hear such a sound, Donohoe?"

"At a wake."

"Why is it called a wake, Donohoe?"

"I don't know, but I'm sure it's not to hope we can wake the person from the dead."

"But the person will wake someday. What day?"

"Dies Irae," says Moreau.

"Exactly. Donohoe has led us downward where words are insufficient, but we have to say something. What can we say?"

"Petri est mortuus," says Moreau.

"Dead to the world? Dead to God's grace?"

"Deeper."

"Deeper. How, Moreau?"

"Petri amat nullitas."

Father Donnelly's eyes darken. "I cannot say it better. Petri is in love with nothingness. He has gone among swine to lose his very being. Or at least to lose his humanity. To put himself out of sight of God. This cannot be done. Darkness is not infinite. Let us all bow our heads and pray that he comes back. Let him be smeared with the offal of hogs. Let him be pox-ridden. But let him come back and write again the words he once wrote with almost godlike brilliance. And let us pray for deliverance for ourselves, for we also walk in darkness." All lower their heads. Mr. Donnelly recites.

"If I ascend up into heaven, thou art there: if I make my bed in hell, behold,
thou art there.

If I take the wings of the morning, and dwell in the uttermost parts of the sea;

Even there shall thy hand lead me, and thy right hand shall hold me.

If I say, surely the darkness shall cover me; even the night shall be light about me.

Yea, the darkness hideth not from thee; but the night shineth as the day: the darkness and
the light are both alike to thee."

Naughton is en route to Charlene's station by the hall window when Ms. Trask comes out of the door of her room, Sister Kathleen by her side. Ms. Trask has a four-legged walker, each foot encased in a tennis ball. Naughton stops. As Ms. Trask proceeds out into the hall she bounces the walker violently against the floor. "You can't make a noise," she says. "How do you know where you're going?"

"The balls are to protect the floor," says Sister Kathleen mildly.

"Floor! At the end we never knew if we had a floor." She looks up at Naughton. "Here's Mr. Nobody. You ever been in a house without a floor, Mr. Nobody?"

"I don't think so, Ms. Trask. When one enters a house, a floor is something you tend to take for granted."

"Maybe we were granted a floor, but it was gone. Gone under objects and trash so thick you couldn't plumb it with a poker."

"Well that explains it, Ms. Trask. The objects had replaced the floor, joined by hooks and eyes just as explained by the ancient Greek atomist Democritus."

Sister Kathleen says, "I think maybe the floor was hiding under the objects."

"No reason to hide," exclaims Ms. Trask. "Nobody came. Lloyd was the last to get out of the door before it jammed." Ms. Trask resumes her assault on the floor. "Blue rubber baby buggy bumpers. Can you say that, Mr. Nobody?"

"Blue rubber baby buggy bumpers."

"Caw haw haw!" Ms. Trask crows in mockery and triumph. "I knew it. Anybody that gets it the first time is an idiot savant."

Sister Kathleen says, "Mr. Naughton has unusual mental powers."

"Piff! Jeanette would've shared Lloyd with me, but Lloyd wasn't a railroad man. You could tell by his stride. A railroad man's stride is exactly the distance between two ties."

"Very perceptive, Ms. Trask. I've observed in the course of time that your bathroom tile-layer has a very mincing stride."

"That may be, Mr. Nobody, but time has no course."

"True."

"Even if it did, you wouldn't know it with this contraption." Ms. Trask thumps the walker against the floor. "Here's an old one for you: Boing boing bounce bounce! Jump jump pounce pounce!" Ms. Trask bobs up and down, starts to fall backwards out of the walker.

Sister Kathleen catches her. "That was amazing, Ms. Trask. Let's see if now we can bounce our way down to the end of the hall."

"Mr. Nobody's not coming, is he?"

"No, he's going the other way."

"Lloyd was always going the other way. Even front on he was going the other way like a speck on the horizon."

Naughton finds Charlene slowly wheeling her chair, but the left arm is stronger than the right so the chair traces a hesitant clockwise arc. Vera stands aside, letting Charlene struggle with the chair. Naughton, out of sight at first, waits for the progression of the chair to bring him into Charlene's sight line. When she sees him, she works her mouth into a smile, the lips searching laboriously for proper alignment as if she has to taste the smile before she can form it.

"Well, Charlene, soon you'll go wherever you want to. There're some interesting people here you'll want to meet. And I see you're dressed for it." Naughton refers to a flowered gown with pockets and a blue sash around the waist.

Vera says, "You did not say anything about her hair."

"The raven tresses took my breath away."

"Stowy," says Charlene forcefully.

"She has been waiting, Mr. Naughton."

"It seems like only yesterday we were engulfed in flames."

"No, it was day before yesterday you told it."

"Then what happened to yesterday? Have you hidden it in your pocket Charlene?"

The laborious smile comes again and fades. "Stowy."

Naughton closes his eyes. "I have to let my mind's eye wander where it will. It can't be forced." He pauses for some moments in an inward-looking state. "I see an ocean I wish I had never seen. The color harrowing and exhausting. On the surface it seemed an ordinary blue, but some force of nature or a pernicious god had tinctured the water with an insidious palette of green tones. Maybe djinn subtly inscribing Arabic characters with poisonous ink. The Arabian Sea. Too warm for our evaporators to make fresh water for personal use once the boilers and galley were supplied. We sweated profusely, sucked salt tablets. Forced to take showers straight from the

143

waters of that inimical sea, we emerged briefly dry, glittering and faceted like diamonds, subhuman creatures slowly acquiring carapaces of crystalline rigidity. We couldn't look at each other's naked bodies. I was reminded of the glowing green June bugs of my childhood. We would steal from my grandmother's sewing box a spool of her thinnest thread, a number approaching one hundred, filament so fine that when dropped in the air of a still summer afternoon it would swoop and slide along currents so delicate we couldn't feel them on our skin. With the thread we would tie a fisherman's knot and cinch it to the creature's back leg and then send it aloft. Briefly assured of its freedom, it would fly up and away until at last the weight of even that fine thread wearied it and brought it back to earth." Naughton stops. "Sorry, the flight of the June bug is from another story."

"Gruen sea stowy," says Charlene.

"Right. So. We were lost sailors yearning for home but plunging ever eastward into that necrotic sea."

Charlene releases the rim of her chair's wheel, lifts her arms, allows her hands to fall down quivering into her lap.

"That's exactly it, Charlene. When one is the victim of an inexorable pull toward a place he doesn't want to go, mind and body lose their strength and begin to decline toward a state of listlessness, fatality. Read the stars, we said to the navigator, and tell us where we're going. The sky is murky, he said. Then what can you tell from dead reckoning? The seas are fickle, the wind hidden, he said. And so, eastward we sailed—perhaps this time really to the end of the world."

Charlene executes an arduous lifting of her right hand as if she might point toward the end of the world. Naughton holds a hand under the index finger. She lets the tip touch Naughton's hand, which he quickly withdraws as might a too forward admirer. "Do you remember, Charlene, when the ancient mariners thought they might sail west to the edge of the known world?"

Charlene nods with hardly a hint of bobble.

"What do you suppose they thought they would encounter there? The God of Job maybe, holding back with a hand wider than the horizon the unruly waters yearning to spill into the void. Or maybe just his mighty breath, a wall more adamantine than steel. But we weren't sailing west. We were sailing east, far east of the land of Job and his God. Not so, Sister Claire would say. God is omnipresent. But she has not sailed the Sea of Arabia."

Naughton stops, his breathing a little labored.

"Go on, Mr. Naughton. And let this be a lesson to you to eat right, just as Mother Martha says."

Charlene nods, her eyes bright with a fierce luster, eager anticipation of what's coming, fear that Naughton will flag.

"Do you understand what I have to do to tell this tale?"

Vera says, "I can see it in your face, but you have to go on. No story ends in the middle of an ocean."

"No story ever ends."

"All the stories end, Mr. Naughton, at the second coming."

"Right, Vera. I'd forgotten. Then they all get wrapped up as one big multi-foliate rose."

"I never heard of that, Mr. Naughton, but it is all right if that is the way it is."

"Co . . . coll . . ." says Charlene.

"White," says Naughton. "The rose is white." Now he pauses for some moments. "Charlene and I are intimates in a ward where women and men alike labor to give birth. Kind women in white and sky blue shine their eyes down on us, but we aren't allowed to climb the lattice of holy light until our labor is done. So we must go on, Charlene, to landfall or to the bottom of the sea. We don't have to worry that our bones will turn into coral or our eyes into pearls. The sea serpents will make quick work of us. Impressive dualistic creatures. White with numerous black stripes, one for each of our two hundred bones. As for our soft tissue, think of pretty streams of iridescence gracing the anemones and sea grass while manta rays and turtles swim overhead creating shimmering effects."

Naughton allows himself a moment of silence, perhaps to reflect on this image. "Landfall was not pretty, Charlene. The Port of Karachi. We had sailed up a winding way from the sea, a long inlet said to have been formed by a river, but we saw no flow. The water seemed to us stagnant and glutinous. What if the mouth of the thing closed behind us as the Suez had only a few months before? What would it be like to be swallowed like Jonah into the maw of a Muslim nation not even a decade old? What hideous contractions and corrosive digestive juices would squeeze us and break us down, white offal left over from a corrupt and decayed empire?

"Our bosun threw a monkey fist to the dock. Pakistani workers in skirts and head rags pulled over our mooring lines and secured them to ill-formed bollards that looked like worn camel backs. We winched the ship alongside and installed a gangway. A dignitary came aboard with two attendants. They wore turbans. The chief emissary's was startling—all white with a sash hanging over his right shoulder and a cleverly folded lank of fabric that sat atop his head like a blanched cockatoo. We were to attend a performance of the Royal Lancers the next afternoon. We would be gathered at noon. A provisioner would arrive later to help with our commissary needs. With that, emissary and attendants turned smartly about face and departed."

Naughton rubs his face. "What I tell you next was seen through a veil of heat and humidity so thick that even now memory wavers and dithers like faces across a campfire—the umbered earth of the flat field, the roan horses, the lancers caparisoned in gold-striped maroon jackets, the dark gray turbans of dizzying loops and folds, the burnished khaki of the jodhpurs terminating in the black shine of boots, the polished stirrups glancing in the sun, the red-and-white striped banners at the tips of the lances lifted on high and made to ripple by the cantering of the horses in air otherwise as still as death. Then the show, each rider spurring his horse down a marked track toward a hapless cabbage-size ball of yarn swinging from a rope like the decayed fruit of a guillotining. Lance lowered and aimed, no horseman ever failed to impale the offending orb and toss it away disdainfully to be gathered by half-naked fetchers. This went on interminably while we officers and a group of highborn Pakistanis applauded and broiled in our bleacher seats. At last a finale. A sudden tantara from a trumpeter we hadn't seen until that moment. He stood across the field from us sheathed in a black shalwar, the skirted blouse long, the pantaloons tightly tied at the ankles. A pennant hung from his horn. We learned later that it was embroidered with a black ram and a white ram, symbols of death and the death of death."

Vera says, "The death of death is the resurrection."

"Yes, Vera, but we had sailed deep into the maw of Islam. God help us. Anyway, the symbols were appropriate because the last target hanging from the standard at the end of the track was a replica of a Janus-faced head. When the rider, obviously one specially honored, struck home with his lance, a great spume of crimson jetted from the object, and when it had been flung aside and was rolling across the barren earth it left a sporadic trail of clotted red. It seemed to me that suddenly the ground tilted, because the head rolled on and on releasing with each revolution another gout of thick red. Great cheers from the spectators and the horseman's fellow lancers.

"From the sunbaked stadium we went to what was no doubt meant to be a greensward but was mostly browned, the sparse dry grass crackling underfoot. A large tent without sides had been set up. There was no breeze but at least there was shade. A long table was laden with a feast for us guests. I remember little of the various colorful dishes—lentils, large flats of nan, dips of yogurt and of harissa, the red of which gave me qualms. The pièce de résistance was a neatly stacked pyramid of small birds, quail perhaps or partridge. The mass was quickly disassembled piece by piece and served to us with a dollop of something pink and fiery. These birds, we were informed, were not raised domestically, netted or shot, but were snared midair by royal falcons. By now the swarming heat was as much mental as physical. The burning air outside the tent was laced with gliding and plunging accipiters, wings golden in the sun, silver talons as precisely honed as Toledo stilettos."

Naughton stops. Charlene has thrust herself well forward in her chair, hands gripping its arms of black leatherette. Vera watches closely. After a long pause she speaks. "And then what happened, Mr. Naughton?"

"Nothing ever happened, Vera. There was a field of horses, a bloody head rolling eternally across the dun earth, small birds and the beautiful instruments of their destruction." He looks at Charlene. "Charlene understands, herself an eaglet quivering on the edge. Stet."

Unseen by Naughton and no doubt by Vera and Charlene as well, positioned so as to create no reflection in the window, stands Sister Claire. She has been there for the whole telling. Now she steps into their loose circle and looks at Charlene. "I don't know about you, Charlene, but I find it hard to make the long leap from here to the terrors of Mr. Naughton's tale and back again."

Charlene makes no acknowledgement of Sister Claire's words. She has repositioned her hands to the center of the chair's arms and now begins to push her body upward, slowly forming the shape of a sigma. Her head remains down looking, for balance perhaps, or to focus her eyes on something below. Her whole body quivers. Vera moves closer to her. Quickly Charlene's strength is spent. Vera helps her fall gently back down into the chair. But Charlene continues to bend forward, looking down.

Naughton says, "One of the difficulties, Charlene, with a spent story is that you can't use it to hold yourself up. But you will stand soon. Now I have to go, spent."

An hour later Sister Claire knocks on Naughton's door. Naughton is lying in bed looking up at the ceiling. He raises himself.

"Don't get up, Mr. Naughton. Rest." Sister Claire sits down in a chair not far from Naughton's bed. "I don't mind a little rest myself."

Naughton sinks back in his pillow smiling.

"What amuses you, Mr. Naughton?"

"I'll tell you, Sister, because you're a person of great understanding. My always errant mind went sailing back to medieval Italy and a quaint picture, maybe an illustration from an old edition of Dante or more likely Boccaccio. A young man lies abed. He's not really ill but lovesick. His feigning of illness is very adroit. A slender arm hangs over the edge of the bed, deprived of animation. Pent up desire has enervated him. He makes himself pale and focuses his eyes on the empty air of the middle distance. The object of desire, lovely in a trailing white gown, has come to his bedside, moved perhaps by something more than solicitude. And so on."

Sister Claire smiles. "Yes, it's an old story. I wish you were a would-be seducer, Mr. Naughton, but I'm afraid you may be really ill."

"How can that be? Mother Martha has ordered me not to be."

"Yes, and she's not to be underestimated, but illness can overcome us even when we're most vigilant. A doctor will come, one who serves us here and at our other house. But I think your illness comes from fatigue. Telling Charlene stories has exhausted you. They're trying stories. And then come the walls, also trying, the last one echoing with foul language and reeking of ink and sweat, and then damnation."

"Never underestimate the smell of ink, Sister. It's addictive. I think Cam figured that out and knew we had to move, though she had other more powerful reasons."

"What other reasons?"

"I don't know really. But I believe she knew something was waiting for her in Bellingham. An intuition of the sensations coming up from the salt chuck, as they call it there. Much more deeply addictive than ink. The brine in the wind, the redolence of spent sea animals when the tide is slack and the water laps lazily on the shore. The addiction of the promised peace of the oceanic." Naughton pauses. "I'm trying to remember some lines of Walt's.

Return in peace to the ocean my love,

I too am part of that ocean my love, we are not so much separated

But we were separated. Or not really separated, because we were never together."

"How is that connected to the ones waiting for her, the ones you've spoken of?"

"I don't know. I don't even know if it was exactly ones. I think maybe it was something much larger, a wide circle of fulfillment. I know that things started coming together for her as soon as we got there. The stand of bronze-trunked madrones on the ridge near our house whispered to her in the wind. Their shining leaves smiled at her and their red berries kissed her."

"I believe Whitman sometimes connects the ocean with death, seductive death. Do you think she wanted death?"

Naughton's eyes widen. "Ah, you've been reading him, Sister. So you'd understand me better. How generous of you, because he's hardly of your persuasion."

"The way I read him, he's a fellow seeker looking for the divine in everything. But what about my question? Was Cam seeking death?"

"No. She was seeking a whole new way of living I had no way of understanding."

"But you do understand now?"

"A little. Peace beyond understanding."

"And would this be through a new lover?"

Naughton shakes his head apologetically. "I can't unravel that. The new lover, if there was one, led her to a circle. Circles are always places of completeness, but you have to be inside. I never have been." He frowns.

"Now for some reason I'm thinking of Alexie. Did she know what was happening?"

"She would come closer than me. But the only one who really knew was Cam herself, and she never has depended on words for anything important." Naughton pauses. "Stella might tell you something, but that's another story."

"I won't press you. I don't want to cause you pain."

Naughton lifts his hands, a motion of inevitability. "Knowing is pain."

There's a long silence. Then Sister Claire says, "Where do your stories for Charlene come from?"

"What I'm thinking, Sister, is what if I hadn't lost Alexie?"

"The stories would be different?"

"Who knows. Maybe they're the only stories I know. But I want you to know that Alexie and I aren't really estranged. She just needed to move on." Naughton smiles. "Even from cats. I'm sure there was never a Man Three."

Sister Claire gazes silently at Naughton, who says, "I don't know where she is. Maybe Josh told you. But I'm not asking."

"Josh didn't tell me. I don't know if he knows. You didn't answer me about your stories."

Naughton breathes deeply, his eyes aimed upward. "They start from memory, Sister, but memory isn't satisfying. So they veer off wherever they have to go. I think of Charlene and her hungry black eyes and I think I have to pick the exact story and tell it perfectly for her. But it doesn't do any good. The story comes as it will, the bit in its teeth."

Sister Claire nods. "The stories are extraordinary. I like to believe the Spirit has taken hold of you and infused your stories. That way I can accept the darkness in them."

"I'm glad," says Naughton, and then after a long silence he chuckles. "Your doctor won't find anything wrong with me but age and the general disintegration of the whole apparatus. He'll prescribe pep pills and protein bars and drinks that taste like the memory of mother's milk."

Sister Claire smiles. "I know. But you'll take them and whatever else Vera brings you."

"Yes. Because I want to see it to the end with Charlene."

"So do I."

In a dream the doctor comes to Naughton's bedside. He's wearing an alb-like garment of white so blinding that it hides the cincture that must be keeping it tight about the waist. The oil from the cruet is sweet. Angels. Not yet, doctor! The healer recedes, leaving behind only the blanched air of his garment.

An Apartment in San Francisco

"Look what we have here!" says Aunt Ettie, her voice croaky, eyes emerald bright in a skeletal face. She stands in the middle of a threadbare oriental rug. She wears a calf-length kimono, green with indeterminate black-winged creatures swooping along the folds and flats. Her legs are blanched sticks.

"Hello, Aunt Ettie. Here they are, just as I promised, Cam, Josh and Alexie."

"Well, they make a beautiful picture." Aunt Ettie motions them in, her arm lost in the sleeve of her kimono. "Come right in. Sit down." She smiles at Alexie, who is hanging back. "I'm not a witch, even if I look like one." The smile, ramshackle tobacco-stained teeth, blotchy receding gums, is not reassuring.

There's a musical chairs muddle. Aunt Ettie says, "I'm afraid I have to claim the recliner. Bad back."

Josh sinks into a formless sofa, Peter and Cam sit on knobby cushioned chairs, the under strapping sagging, shreds hanging down. Alexie sits on the floor and places Man Two between her knees on the rug amid broken and discolored

153

octagons. Aunt Ettie sits in her recliner, back forward. "What a beautiful cat. And blue eyes."

Alexie smiles. "My daddy told us you have green eyes."

Aunt Ettie leans toward Alexie. "Well, did he get it right?"

"Yes."

"Your great-grandmama Helen didn't approve. You must've done something to them, she said, because nobody's born with green eyes."

"Did you do something to them?"

"Maybe. Met up with the green-eyed monster. What is it, Peter?"

"Jealousy. Shakespeare."

"I knew he would know. Isn't your daddy smart?"

Alexie nods.

Josh, slouching in a deep recess of pillows, says, "Very smart with words," his voice muffled, flat.

"And what are you smart at, Joshua? It is Joshua, isn't it?"

"Yes."

"Good. I'm not a big fan of nicknames. Even the French have gotten into the habit. Sobriquets they call them. Isn't that right, Peter?"

"Yes."

Alexie says, "Then you can call me Alexandra."

"I'll call you Alexandra and think of Egypt. Why would I think of Egypt, Peter?"

"Because of Alexandria, a great city there."

"Didn't something tragic happen there?"

"A famous ancient library burned down."

Josh says, "Libraries are filled mostly with myths and misinformation."

"No doubt, Joshua, but I've never heard that being a library arsonist is a lucrative field." Aunt Ettie turns to Peter. "Weren't you there once with the Navy?"

"No. We sailed into the harbor of Port Said and south through the Suez Canal into the Red Sea."

"The Marines could've told you it was a foolish deployment." Aunt Ettie looks at Cam. "Does he bore you to death with sea stories, Cam?"

"No. We're not so much interested in the past." Cam's reply is forthcoming and pleasant, nothing more.

"That's wise. In the South everything is in the past. Meet yourself coming the other way. But tell me about this great move you're making."

"We're going to Bellingham in the State of Washington." Cam provides the information with a hint of pleasure.

"Well I'm sure it's an exciting place, but I don't know much about it."

"It's on Puget Sound, which is part of the Pacific Ocean," says Alexie.

"Now that does sound exciting. You think your cat will like it there, Alexandra? The name sounds more like Egypt."

"That's what a lady in the desert said, but it's not a she. It's a he."

"What's his name?"

"Man Two."

"Mantoo. It's pretty. I'll bet it's a name from the mysterious Orient. Did your mother suggest it?"

"No, it's spelled M-A-N-T-W-O. He's named after your cat, Man."

"Oh my word! Man would be surprised to hear it. He was a plain orange cat, disreputable, I'm afraid, and never answered to his name." She turns to Peter. "Mama wrote me when he died. But I've forgotten the circumstances."

"He lost a fight. Thelma found him near her back porch."

"He was too old to keep on caterwauling. Mama should've kept him in nights."

"He would've howled the house down."

Aunt Ettie nods. "But Thelma's yard. My Lord. It was just like Man to die in the yard of a person suffering nerviosa or

155

whatever they call it. Anyway, whatever happened to that poor woman?"

"I don't know. I lost track."

"I'll tell you. She twitched to death. The only known case in medical history of death by nervous vibration." Aunt Ettie gets up and goes to a small mahogany secretary, opens a drawer and takes out an opened pack of cigarettes and hands it to Peter. "Remember these?"

"Picayunes."

"Papa's brand. You have to get them from a catalog now. Pass them around. Everybody take a sniff. Have you ever experienced such fragrance? It comes from exotic tobaccos, latakia and perique. Latakia is from Cyprus, an island somewhere near Turkey. Is that right, Peter?"

"Right."

"What's perique?" says Josh, smelling the cigarettes with interest.

"Yes. What is it, Peter?"

"The story is that it's grown only in Louisiana and fermented in logs by French monks."

Aunt Ettie laughs. "What I liked to do was invite one of my Marine friends up and give him a shot of one hundred and eighty proof rum from some Caribbean island and light up a Picayune for him. And see if they passed the test. One, a small beautiful little Filipino, passed out on the spot. Right there where your cat is, Alexandra. I hated to move him, the design was so pretty, yellow against maroon."

Josh says, "He should've known by smell not to fall for it, but the olfactory part of the sensorium has been suppressed."

"Why has it been suppressed, Joshua?"

"Cultural evolution probably. Sensitivity to odors became less important to survival than sight."

Aunt Ettie's eyes brighten. "You have a budding scientist, Peter. But I can tell you this, Joshua. If a man could be accurately tested by rum and tobacco, the world would be a nicer place."

Josh laughs. "If they didn't pass, what would you do with them?"

"Send them to Goat Island, or is it Devil's Island, Peter?"

"Probably Devil's Island."

Joshua looks skeptical.

"How would you test them, Joshua?"

"Cognitive science is working on it."

"They're not working fast enough. All you have to do is look around. It's not just orientals passed out on rugs."

Peter says, "I don't think race has anything to do with it."

"That's right. One of my guests brought a Black friend with him. I don't remember his name though he became big in the jazz world. It was a totem name. Jimambo or something like that, Black and Indian. He took a Picayune and struck a kitchen match by raking his thumbnail along the fire line. He said he could teach me how to do it. I told him I didn't smoke anymore. That's all right, he said, but if you go to a roadhouse and strike a match that way it will shoo off the cruisers. I told him I left roadhouses back in Alabama."

"What do you do in roadhouses in Alabama?" Alexie asks.

"You dance. The jukebox throws a lot of rippling light around and makes your dress look pretty even if it's not. But roadhouses are passé now, even in Alabama." Aunt Ettie waves roadhouses away. "We were talking about eyes. I want to give you something, Alexandra." Aunt Ettie goes again to the drawer in the secretary and after a while fishes out an object on a thick black string. "You know what this is?" she says handing it to Alexandra.

"No, but it's pretty."

"It's a cat's eye stone. A friend brought it back to me from Saigon because my eyes are green."

"Did Man have green eyes?"

"Yes. But if you'd asked your great-grandmama Helen, she'd say she didn't know, and that would be the truth because she never looked Man in the eye. It would've been too dangerous. Then she would write me and say when are we going to see you again? And Man misses you too. And Lizzie, my sister and your daddy's mama, and your grandmama, would write her from New Orleans and say let's go see her in San Francisco. We could sell the family silver and take a limousine across Highway 66 and stay at famous seedy motels where they've made shoot-em-up movies. But Mama Helen didn't want to see me that bad. Lizzy thought she could tempt her by telling her she could get in the movies playing a rich widow with an ivory cigarette holder and ropes of pearls."

Peter says, "I don't think Mama Helen really wanted to see either one of you. Big-city gals."

Aunt Ettie looks at Cam in a kindly way. "You've been good for him, Cam. And these children are charming. They've got your dark eyes and your beauty." There's a brief pause. "They won't get your quietness, though, because they're too American. They don't understand that still waters run deep."

Cam smiles. "We divide it up. Peter knows how to write and talk and I've learned how to do things with my hands."

"Lots of things," says Alexie.

"I'll bet. It's easy to spot talent across a room."

Cam says nothing to that.

Aunt Ettie redirects her attention to Josh. "What are you smiling at, young man, buried in my couch?"

Josh says, "Your desk man, Mr. Lacroix, is an interesting type."

"Maurice! What did that old rascal tell you?"

"Dad asked him if he was happy here in San Francisco. He said he was because where he was before he was locked in a nasty story and couldn't get out."

Aunt Ettie nods reflectively. "If you were to talk to him some more, though I wouldn't advise it, he would tell you a lot about his self, capital S, and how they tried to take it away from him. Here he has what they call a supportive community, which is nice for him."

"Do they have parties?" Alexie asks.

"Oh yes, in different apartments mostly right around here. Birds of a feather."

Josh says, "There's no scientific evidence that there's a self."

Aunt Ettie makes a face of mock surprise. "I remember spying on my daddy hiding a pint of bourbon in a pine tree in our backyard. I remember having fights with my sister, your grandmama about my lifestyle and everything else I could think of to gall her, but she was a world-class talker and beat me every time. That's where your daddy gets it from. To go on from there. I remember marrying Tom, my Marine husband. I remember finding out he was killed at Tarawa. I remember all the friends I've made here while I was looking for somebody like him. And all that time it was always me, the same me, Joshua. If you don't call that a self, what is it?"

Josh nods noncommittally. "It could just be a string."

"It would have to be a strong string to hang all the things I've seen and done on. We might as well call it a self. Maurice would tell you they did everything they could to break the string of his real life and tie him up with another one."

Alexie has begun to stroke her cat nervously. Her face is full of puzzlement and sadness. "Who did?"

"I suppose his mama and his daddy to start with and then all the children on the playground. Once people start ganging up on you everybody piles on." Aunt Ettie leans forward solicitously. "Don't worry, Alexie. Your mama is a good protector if there ever was one. Anyway, Maurice changed the story of his life and forgot the old one. Otherwise memories would overwhelm him. Nobody tells the exact truth about themselves. They couldn't stand it."

Josh says, "The best thing is not to get locked up in any story, whether you make it up or somebody else does. Stick to the facts of your life."

Peter speaks. "The trouble, Josh, is that stories are everywhere. If you want the kind of freedom you're talking about you'll have to find a mythical place where there're no stories. Or you'll get caught, a character in somebody's story and have to get out of it. Over and over. And you'll leave a trace behind every time so they can track you down."

"Not George Washington, but Joshua Naughton slept here," says Aunt Ettie. "Listen to your daddy, Joshua."

Aunt Ettie smiles at Cam. "I'm honored by having you, Cam, sitting here and casting a rare calm on this room." She pauses. "You know something, Joshua, just having a name is already a story stuck on you like a mole. Joshua fit the battle of Jericho, Jericho, and the walls came atumbling down. You would have to go all the way back and be named Nobody."

"You haven't said anything about my name," says Cam. The statement injects into the room an element of surprise and suspense.

"No, I haven't. I wouldn't have said anything about Joshua either, but we were having a little fun kidding. But since you ask, I'll tell you. I like that it's short and to the point. But it also seems a little clipped, if you don't mind my saying so, like your mama and daddy didn't quite finish it. But it goes just right with your eyes. If you have a name like Marietta and green eyes, everything is right out front for anybody to comment on. Calm goes out the window. It gets to the point where you can tell by looking in a mirror how you're going to affect people you haven't even met."

The room is quiet. Alexie asks, "Do your friends like your eyes?"

"They don't say. But one friend I had said he liked my eyes. We were both reformed smokers. That's what drew us together while everybody else kept blowing smoke in our eyes.

160

It's a song, I think. He was from Vietnam and knew French. He said he thanked God that he gave up smoking Gauloises or Gitanes. Leave it to the French to name a cigarette after gypsies. And then the government wanted to ban them because they were turning smokers into communists or existentialists. What's an existentialist, Peter?"

"The idea that we live in an uncaring universe so we have to exercise our free will without any guidance from anywhere except ourselves."

"No wonder the French government wanted people to stop smoking those cigarettes. How would we've known to fight the Nazis and the Japs in an uncaring universe with nothing but ourselves to depend on?"

"A big subject, Aunt Ettie, that goes way beyond cigarettes."

"Don't insult me, Peter. The cigarettes were a joke."

"I know what communism is," said Josh. "A theory of common ownership distributed by the State."

"You're a smart boy, Joshua. But the difference between being a communist and an existentialist is that if you show communist tendencies, they can haul you into court and make you swear under oath, hand on the Bible, one way or the other. Isn't that right, Cam? Especially if you come from another country."

"The law doesn't make anybody swear on a holy book," said Cam.

"Is that right? What can you swear on?"

"You can just swear to tell the truth."

"I'm glad to hear it because I couldn't remember ten words from the Bible."

A veil falls in Peter's mind. It's made of scrolling smoke darkly streaked as by bristles of black hairs. "Peter, recognize these swirls of smoke? They're for when I want to fling certain words emphatically out into the air, like now. I've always saved my best words for you because you're smart. I whispered words in your father's ear, which thrilled him, but he didn't know what I was saying. All Greek. Mama Helen was fun to tease but it's not much of a challenge if somebody falls for everything. Now Titta was worth the effort because she could spit back. Funny I find you sitting now in her decommissioned bordello. And she's talking as if butter wouldn't melt in her mouth, except for a little item like the Filipino passed out on the rug. Your Josh is a wiseass, just like you were. Serves you right. Alexie could become another Stella, patron saint of cats. But it's your wife that interests me." A cigarette in ambered fingers circles around as if searching for the right orbit, leaving behind a slowly dissipating coil of smoke. "What is she, Peter, some kind of female Buddha? Titta can't get a rise out of her. Her eyes are like black stones. Does she ever say anything or just blink and lower her eyes because you already know what the command is? A minute ago she smiled, a pasted smile like you could buy at a novelty store and stick on your mouth like a fake mustache. I don't see any breasts. Bound oriental style maybe. What does that color of skin look like in moonlight? You don't want to say? I'll tell you. Mushrooms. We're opposites, Peter. I married an ape. You married a porcelain mystery. Eyebrows sketched with a calligrapher's brush with five hairs or whatever the Chinese mystic number is. I wouldn't dare touch her. Titta warned you. Everything'll be a mystery. Like taking you and the kids off to some corner of cold ocean she's always known about. Rocks and cliffs and bent trees." A huge burst of coughing and smoke bellies the veil. "I thought you were smart. Flunking out and hiring on at a sleazy print shop was bad enough. OK. Some kind of rebellious romantic Whitman thing. Man of the people and the cosmos. But being a manservant to an oriental goddess or whatever she imagines she is. That's the limit. I'll come back when everything goes to hell in a handbasket out there by the ocean. Which it will. I'm your mother."

"Peter, where've you been? Cam was telling me that in the Orient a cat's eye stone brings good fortune."

"Sorry."

Alexie says, "Did it bring good fortune to your friend?"

Aunt Ettie shakes her head. "I'm afraid he gave the good fortune to me. They tracked him down and sent him back to Vietnam and I never heard from him again."

"Then I have to give it back to you or you could be sent somewhere."

Aunt Ettie smiles thinly. "You're a kind child, Alexandra, but don't worry. Nobody's going to bother to send me anywhere. Where would it be? Tarawa? To see if I can find the ring I put on Tom's finger? Nothing was ever found. Eels and such. I can't think about it."

"Oh," exclaims Alexie.

"Never mind the war. I don't have anything against Asians." Aunt Ettie looks at Cam.

Cam says, "I don't know what part of Asia I come from."

"Of course not. None of us know where we come from. Peter and I are part English, part Irish, part Cajun, part Black and part Indian, Cherokee probably. Our ancestors are buried in sacred mounds outside of Tuscaloosa. University students stole out there one night and dug up bones, but a curse fell on them."

"What happened to them?" asks Josh.

"Various things, flu, malaria and yellow fever. One got an earwig that bored straight through his brain." Aunt Ettie leans back in the recliner, brooding. "Maybe that's what fascinated your mother, Peter. Your daddy wasn't from anywhere. A wild man, hair head to foot." She waves her hand. "I shouldn't have said that in front of the children." A ruction rattles her throat. Something comes up into her mouth but she swallows it down. She looks at Alexie. "Speaking of stories, Alexandra, your story is a beautiful tale about a girl a cat was looking for over centuries and finally found her."

"It just showed up at the door right before we left for Bellingham. Did Man look for you a long time?"

Aunt Ettie laughs. "Whatever Man wanted he found it in a minute. But you never told me, Peter, if you gave Man a proper burial."

Peter smiles. "We did, under the pines in the backyard with all attendant obsequies."

"Tell me."

"Papa and I dug the grave and laid the noble animal to rest on soft pine needles amid great lamentation."

Aunt Ettie produces a raspy laugh. "Lamentation, obsequies. Children, watch out. Listening to your daddy, you won't be able to talk like a normal person."

Peter continues. "Papa said he would read a passage in the Bible about cats and bats and birds sitting on the heads of pretenders to godliness, but Granny vetoed it. So I made up a tombstone epitaph. Here lies Man, terror of toms, who now roams free the great ancestral savannahs of his primordial home."

"Beautiful. You got the knack from your mama." Ettie turns from Peter to the others. "I used to call him at the fraternity house just so I could listen to the flights of words. But when he moved in with that horrible man Volt I gave up because Volt would answer with a voice like a cement mixer. Whatever happened to him, Peter?"

"I don't know. We lost track of each other."

"I don't think he had a track. I believe he just went around being mean like an alley cat until a meaner cat killed him. Probably a little crime notice came out in some local paper."

"Could be."

Alexie looks deeply pained.

Peter slaps his thighs. "We'd better be going, Aunt Ettie. We promised the kids we'd take them to Golden Gate Park to see the bridge and some fog."

"You can't miss it. Fog is the best thing about this city."

Naughton encounters Ms. Trask outside her door. She's motoring toward the end of the hall that looks out toward the gate that marks the end of the entrance path. "Out of my way, Mr. Nobody. Get off on a siding or I'll run you down."

"Just think of me as an old caboose they've made into a diner, Ms. Trask. There's one in every town."

"I don't think of you as anything. You or Jeanette or even Lloyd. You're all back at the last stop. But if I meet Cornelius on my track I'll trask him. Hooo!" Ms. Trask is either overcome by her own cleverness or is merely exuberantly in motion. The walker veers to the right. Naughton continues to walk warily beside Ms. Trask.

"The old Commodore can be a formidable foe, Ms. Trask. Semper Paratus."

"Him, yes. The rest of them came to nothing—wild women, horses, museums, fashion, that kind of piffery."

Vera comes the other way carrying a tray, waits until there is safe passage.

Naughton says, "An angel of vengeance has been loosed upon the world, Vera. Let the wicked beware."

"You stay with her, Mr. Naughton. Sister Kathleen is with Mr. Gerrity."

"Ms. Trask's company is a treasure."

"Treasure! All the treasure came from what it cost to ride the rails. Whatever the traffic will bear. We're going to meet him in a tunnel under the Erie Canal." Ms. Trask begins to sing, "Got an old mule named Sal, fifteen years on the Erie Canal. Low bridge, everybody down, must be getting near to town."

"Beautifully sung, Ms. Trask. I'm with you all the way."

"You couldn't get into a tunnel even if you existed. Here we go! Watch out Cornelius!" Ms. Trask slams the walker into the wall. It takes her a moment to regroup after the shock. "There." She rubs her hands together briskly. "Down like a house of cards. I knew it. You know how I knew, Mr. Nobody?"

"Tactical superiority catching him in a tunnel, meeting of steel and water."

"Don't talk to me about steel and that craven Carnegie, sold out to J. Pisspot Morton."

"Is Morgan next on your Doomsday role, Ms. Trask?"

"I have to do my calculations."

"Of course. One can do marvels with pencil and paper. It's all it took for Einstein to invent the universe."

Ms. Trask takes no interest in that. Her breathing is mildly labored as she makes her way back to her room along an erratic path. At the door, after seeing that she is safely seated by her table, Naughton says, "It was a privilege to witness your campaign, Ms. Trask." Naughton turns to go.

"Duck, you old fool. Tunnels ain't made out of cotton." Ms. Trasks laughs. "Here's a riddle for you. How did Uncle Remus know that a nobody has a head?"

"Give me a little time to ponder the answer, Ms. Trask."

Ms. Trask caws triumphantly. "You'll never get it!"

Naughton exits Ms. Trask's room and stops at the door of Mr. Gerrity's. "Come in," says Sister Kathleen. "You may find this interesting. But first, how did you find Ms. Trask?"

"I accompanied her on a mission to destroy Commodore Vanderbilt, and I fear there may be more carnage to come."

"Probably a good sign. From numbers and charts to history. Come in and see what we have for Mr. Gerrity."

Two steel stanchions have been secured to Mr. Gerrity's bed, one at the head and one at the foot. From the top of one stanchion to the top of the other runs a thick round bar. From the bar there hangs on a heavy chain an equilateral triangle fashioned also from thick round rods.

Sister Kathleen says, "Mr. Gerrity's going to lift himself."

Mr. Gerrity's face is flushed with excitement. Sister Kathleen lifts one hand and then the other and closes the fingers on the bottom of the steel triangle, his arms half extended upward, his fingers clamped as fiercely as the talons of a hawk on its prey. "Now lift, Mr. Gerrity."

Miraculously, arms aquiver, Mr. Gerrity manages to lift his upper body until his head is framed by the triangle.

"Now relax for a moment, Mr. Gerrity."

Mr. Gerrity lowers his body but maintains his claw-like grasp on the bar.

"Once more, Mr. Gerrity."

The same lift is accomplished but the quivering of the arms is more pronounced.

"Beautifully done, Mr. Gerrity! You can let go now. Two today, three tomorrow, until you lift yourself right out of here."

Mr. Gerrity's fingers tremble, but Sister Kathleen has to unfasten them from the bar.

"Astounding," says Naughton, touching the iron triangle. "Do you know what you have here, Sister?"

Sister Kathleen, flushed with success, laughs a laugh that is tuneful, almost girlish. "I like to think of it as Mr. Gerrity's barre."

"As in ballet?"

"Yes." Sister Kathleen strokes Mr. Gerrity's arm fondly. "Someday Mr. Gerrity will dance right out of here starting with a perfectly executed pirouette."

"Did you have some training in ballet, Sister?"

"Ah, Mr. Naughton, I thought you were wiser. Was there ever a girl child who in her dreams didn't twirl and sail across a stage in her tutu and silken pointe shoes?"

"You put me to shame, Sister. How could I forget? Once in a dream of my own I saw my sister Stella turning in a white gown on a tiny stage atop a music box. Someone, probably Stella herself, was playing Chopin on the piano, one of those sad Preludes."

"And then you lost her."

"Yes. I suppose Joshua has given some account."

"I'm sorry for your loss, Mr. Naughton. Anyway, it was a bit silly of me to think of Mr. Gerrity's exercise apparatus as a ballet barre."

"Nothing truly imaginative is silly, Sister. However, may I make an observation?"

"Of course."

Naughton looks into Mr. Gerrity's face with studied kindness. "When Mr. Gerrity lifted himself, I believe I observed the following. He was elated, and rightly so. Not, however, only by newly found strength but also by his ability to get high enough to look through the iron triangle."

Sister Kathleen says, "I missed that. But I think you may be right. While I was off in an old childish dream, you were watching more carefully. Can you say more?"

"Would it be too much to suggest that for Mr. Gerrity the triangle is a holy squint? Not that he's likely to have articulated that to himself."

"I think I know what you're referring to, Mr. Naughton, but please go on."

"I'm referring to an opening, sometimes called a hagioscope, through which can be seen the sanctum sanctorum. I believe I have it right."

"Yes that's right, Mr. Naughton. In my training we were taught that what's visible through the hagioscope is the priest's elevation of the host. But I don't remember any instance of a triangular hagioscope."

"Nor do I, Sister, but you're a Trinitarian. Couldn't it be appropriate for a holy squint to be triangular? Somewhere in Christendom there must be or must have been a triangular holy squint. If not, with your Irish inventiveness you can create one right here in Mr. Gerrity's room."

Sister Kathleen is taken with Naughton's suggestion. "A fascinating idea, Mr. Naughton. Let me think about it and broach the subject with Mother Martha."

Naughton strokes his chin. "With all due respect, Sister, the idea is now in its infancy and is fragile. The introduction at this point of the great weight of the magisterium might be more than it could bear. Why not make further observations? I believe Mr. Gerrity himself will show the way."

All during this exchange Mr. Gerrity has exhibited an unusual degree of animation.

Sister Kathleen says, "But when he raises himself and looks through the triangle he sees nothing but a blank wall."

"Yes. Imagine how terrible it would be for an anchorite to look through the holy opening and see only a blank wall. Such an image of nothingness might shake the strongest faith."

"I'll have a crucifix hung on the wall. Someday maybe Father Schneider could come and celebrate Mass."

"That would be appropriate in every way, Sister, but a crucifix is a very difficult thing. Your experience of it is much deeper than mine of course. Still, it imposes itself powerfully even on viewers distanced from the faith—the vertical of eternity, the horizontal of time, the maimed sacrificial figure forever impaled on that unresolvable paradox. No darkening of the sun to assure us of the presence of a watchful Father. No pietà. Just unthinkable suffering persisting until the end of time, and all caused by our relentless sinfulness."

Mr. Gerrity listens with eyes bright, lips peeling back, then closing, incisors nibbling, signs perhaps of an incipient mincing of meaning, but he cannot speak.

Sister Kathleen looks from Mr. Gerrity to Naughton. "What you say is not in strict accordance with the teaching of the Church, Mr. Naughton, as you know." She pauses. "But in terms of imagery it has a harsh truth to it." She nods. "So, what shall I use to relieve the blankness of the wall? I have to think about it."

"May I make a suggestion, Sister, and then I will leave you to your patient and your thoughts."

"Make it, Mr. Naughton."

"Place yourself in Mr. Gerrity's triangular field of vision."

"What? And perpetuate a sacrilege?"

"There's an old doctrine of degree, Sister—animal, human, angel, divinity. Nobody gets to leap from the bottom to the top."

As Naughton steps out of Mr. Gerrity's room he looks down the hall. At the end is Charlene in her wheelchair. Outside the sun-drenched window the lawn, the border shrubbery, the underbrush, everything is overwhelmed by the fiery green of late June. Even the leaves and the frayed bark of the yellow birches are aglow with glistening green. Naughton hesitates, then slowly walks down to Charlene. "This is too much of a good thing for an old man like me. I mean all this verdant opulence. Does it suit you?"

Charlene turns her wheelchair and lifts her eyes to meet Naughton's gaze. She shakes her head definitively.

"I thought not," says Naughton. "Sudden awakenings, especially those that pierce us with lances of angelic light, are painful. To the point, I have just come from Mr. Gerrity's room, where by an agonizing call upon every atrophied muscle and sinew Mr. Gerrity has raised himself up to look beyond the horizon of his dementia. What will he see there? Some brave new world, or just a different kind of confusion? What do you think?"

Charlene disengages her fingers from the rims of the wheels of her chair and lifts her hands palms up. This gesture, along with a clear facial expression of uncertainty, shows her grasp of the ambiguities.

"I think I should not have said dementia. Is the mind really gone? Let's ask Vera about it."

"I heard you," says Vera from just inside Charlene's room. She steps out into the hall. "Whatever Mr. Gerrity sees, knowing is better than not knowing unless you try to know what humans are not permitted to know."

"That's what happened in the garden, isn't it, Vera? And Eve fell for the serpent's line, thinking to become wise. And none of us has become wise ever since."

"That is mostly right, Mr. Naughton, but it does not mean we should not use what wisdom we have."

Charlene leans forward and shifts her weight, interested but impatient.

Vera goes on. "Whatever happened in the garden, Mr. Naughton, happened according to God's plan for us."

"Then you're a believer in the doctrine of felix culpa, Vera, the fortunate fall, which necessitated the redemption of us sinners by the death and resurrection of Jesus the Christ."

"You are showing off, Mr. Naughton, whether what you say is true or not."

"I confess. I'm showing off. But that will be my last attempt at theodicy, I promise. And a lame one at that."

"You are supposed to tell Charlene stories. That is what she wants to hear, not theodicy, whatever it is. That is Sister Claire's job."

Charlene nods.

"Right," says Naughton. "At eighty-six the wisdom promised by the serpent is as distant as it was when I was younger, if not more distant."

"Take care of yourself, Mr. Naughton. That is what God wants. The rest will come."

"Right, Vera. So my job is to tell stories. A beginning has come to me. I think it will be a little parable, Charlene, followed by a sort of riddle or dilemma. When I come again you can give me your answer. You know the story of the Good Samaritan, how a man was beaten and robbed and left in a ditch to die, how the Samaritan came to his rescue after others had passed by heartlessly."

Charlene nods, fully engaged.

"The Samaritan took the victim to an inn and made sure that he had medical care, food, and clothing and then went on

171

his way about his business. After a time the injured man recovered sufficiently to return home to the loving arms of his family. Now it chanced that a few months later the innkeeper overheard in his dining room a conversation that revealed that the masked assailants of the victim had been a jealous brother and some companions in evil. What was the innkeeper to do with this terrible knowledge? Tell the authorities? Tell the victim himself? What, he thought, would be the effect on the victim's renewed happiness? Should he depend on a divine instrument of justice to wreak vengeance on the criminals and keep his knowledge a secret to be buried with him in his grave?"

Vera says, "Sister Claire will know."

"I don't mean it as a general question, Vera. I'm asking Charlene what she says, from her own life experience."

"We will have to wait a while for that," says Vera.

Charlene manifests an extreme agitation for some moments, her body twisting, her arms moving erratically, her fingers quivering claw-like. And then suddenly she relaxes, only her eyes fiercely bright and focused on something near the window.

"Maybe not as long as you think, Vera." Naughton turns to Charlene. "You can be thinking about it, Charlene. So will I, and no doubt Vera. I'll return soon."

Charlene seems at once fiercely focused and reconciled to the delay.

Naughton walks slowly back to his room and lies down on his bed. Outside his window the greenwood edges close to Maison Cristina, but Naughton looks only up to the ceiling, which has no cracks, welts or discolorations for the imagination to play with and is consequently vulnerable to invasion.

The Family in San Francisco

Peter, Cam, Josh and Alexie are sitting at a table in a dubious storefront café with a huge sheet of glass on which is painted in chipped gilt the name of the establishment: La Pente.

"Let's guess what it means," says Alexie.

"All right," says Peter. "You go first."

"It's a place where they keep big animals, not cats." Alexie tickles Man Two's ear and makes it twitch. She smiles.

"What do you think, Cam?"

"Some words make the mind move. This one does nothing for me."

"Josh?"

"I don't know what it means, but whoever put up the glass had no idea how to figure wind load. In the first big storm it's coming down. So, what's the answer, Dad?"

"I was guessing it had something to do with thought, but I believe that's wrong. Now I'm thinking it has something to do with the number five."

"That would explain why it does nothing for Mom. Not even human digits." Josh chuckles to take the edge off of his remark, but Cam looks at him coldly.

"Let's ask the waitress," says Alexie.

Summoned, the waitress appears tableside wiping the palms of her hands on her apron. "What can I do for you folks?"

"What does pintay mean?" asks Alexie.

"You mean the name of the place?"

"Yes."

"I think it's something like pont, French-like. What it means? I don't know." The waitress goes off to the kitchen door, opens it and shouts, "Hey Jose, what does the name of this place mean?"

Jose shouts back. "Pontay! Es stan fo pussy la comida en su boca. Poot de foods in you mout."

"I should've guessed," says Josh.

The waitress comes back. "Sorry. Jose likes to act ignorant."

Peter is laughing. Cam shakes her head mildly.

"It's not what it means," says Alexie.

"That's right, honey."

On a street of low marginal buildings they walk in a loose group, Josh in the rear. "Are we near Haight Ashbury?"

"About a mile away," says Peter, "according to the map."

"What's Haight Ashbury?" asks Alexie.

Josh says, "The capital of hippiedom, USA. If we went there we could see flower children."

"What are they?"

"Kids that've learned to grow roses and marijuana out of the tops of their heads."

"We're going to see Aunt Stella."

"Right."

They pass under a large marquee lit with bulbs that go on and off in rotation even now in mid-afternoon. Some of the bulbs are burnt out. Live Nude Girls!

"Better than dead nude girls," says Josh.

Cam stops. After a moment of shuffling confusion the others stop. "Joshua!" Cam says. That's all, but her naming of her son has begun harshly and proceeded syllable by careful syllable as if this strictly parsed pronunciation might call him to a better self.

"Sorry, Mom."

Alexie strokes her cat. Peter appears perplexed.

They walk on in silence. Presently Peter checks a paper with a number on it. "We're close."

They stand in front of a rough wooden door graced by an ornate knocker, a brass ring hanging from the mouth of an angelic face around which is a circle of weathered stars. Peter lifts the ring and taps it against the metal plate beneath. A Black man with a mottled gray beard stops and looks at them. "You have to hit it hard if you spect anybody to answer. They stay in the back."

"Thanks," Peter says. "Are you familiar with the people who live here?"

"I wouldn't say nobody was familiar with them. Some kind of women group. Keep to themselves."

Peter gives the knocker three good hammering blows.

"That might do it." The Black man lingers behind them, curious.

The door opens. A woman in a white dress stands inside looking at them sternly. Though half in shadow, the woman's face is visibly hardened, pocked and marred, one eyebrow cropped by a scar, the right corner of her mouth elongated. Her black hair is closely shorn. Beneath the stubble a knobby cranium. "Sister Lelan's family?" The woman's teeth, those that are visible, are almost methodically serrated—tooth, blank, tooth, blank. Her gums are faintly spotted.

Peter says, "We've come to see my sister Stella. I sent a letter."

"There's no Stella here anymore. Wait."

After a while the woman comes back and lets them in, locking the door behind. She leads them through a narrow entryway and into a small room that contains several old wooden chairs. She goes away into the interior of the building. Immediately Sister Lelan appears, Stella, also in simple white, blond hair also cropped. Her face is pale and benign, her eyes faintly blue, lips virtually colorless. "Tell me who you are."

"I'm your brother Peter. This is my wife Cam. This is your nephew Josh and your niece Alexie."

"Sit down. I'll let in some light so I can see you." She adjusts a wide-slatted old wooden blind in the single window of the room. Two of the slats are stuck and don't move.

Each finds a chair. Sister Lelan remains standing, surveying them with a pleasant if cool look. Then she steps forward and stands before Alexie. "May I pet her?"

"It's a boy," says Alexie, "but everybody thinks he's a girl."

"Of course. Your father can tell you why that is." Sister Lelan reaches out and touches the cat's forehead gently. Man Two moves his head back against Alexie's shoulder but otherwise suffers Sister Lelan's stroking calmly.

Alexie says, "His name is Man Two, M-A-N-T-W-O."

"After your great-aunt Ettie's cat?"

"Yes, because I wanted a family name. But Aunt Ettie said he doesn't look anything like Man."

"You've seen Aunt Ettie then?"

"Yesterday."

Sister Lelan steps back and sits in a chair facing them. "I would like to hear each tell their own name. Voices reveal much. I remember your voice, Peter. It was plangent like the sudden striking of a harp, unusual for a child. I thought you might become a great poet known for elegies. Every death is

176

worthy of music." She is silent for some moments and then nods to Alexie, who says, "Alexandra Naughton."

"A very noble name."

"Aunt Ettie said it's Egyptian."

Sister Lelan nods, turns to Josh.

"Joshua Naughton."

"Biblical. You know the story?"

"And the walls came atumbling down."

"What walls?"

"Jericho. Nationalist Judaic propaganda. Not a shred of archaeological evidence."

"Are you interested in archaeology?"

"Not really, but if you get stuck with a name like Joshua it makes you temporarily curious."

Sister Lelan turns to Cam.

"Cam Naughton."

"And before Naughton?"

"Nobody knows my real name."

Sister Lelan nods. There's a pause while the two women study each other. "Are you surprised I didn't ask you what Cam is short for?"

"It's not short for anything."

"That doesn't stop people from speculating, does it?"

"No. Why doesn't it?"

Sister Lelan pauses, then speaks knowingly. "Because your name will always be a mystery to them, something trailing off toward a place they can't see."

"I wouldn't think they'd bother."

"But they do. And they want to look into your eyes without being obvious, because they're deep, black and beautiful."

Cam raises her voice very slightly. "What could I do to keep them from wanting to know and to look?"

"Nothing." Sister Lelan pauses. "Now I'll name the four of us. Sister Kandin, who met you at the door, Sister Plantina, and Sister Tentiva. Our names, which we invented, don't mean anything. They're only pleasant sounds. So we don't have to worry about walls and horns."

Joshua nods approval. "Does your community have a name?"

"No. We're just each ourself."

Cam says, "What do you do?"

"The answer will probably disappoint you. We try to immerse ourselves in our beings and understand how each of us is part of a larger Being."

"The answer doesn't disappoint me."

There's a silence during which Sister Lelan and Cam gaze at each other.

"How do you do that kind of immersion?" asks Joshua.

Sister Lelan says, "We do it through simple small things, cooking, eating, washing, cleaning, sleeping. They connect us to each other and to a larger Being."

"Are you looking for more members?"

"No. When someday there're only two left they'll take care of each other and then there'll be none."

"Do you meditate?" asks Joshua. "I have a friend who meditates. It seems to make him happy."

"Happiness is a distraction. But if you mean do we sit in some special posture. No. Our daily activities are our meditation." Sister Lelan turns abruptly to Peter. "Why did you come here, Peter?"

"I wanted my family to meet my only sister."

"If I wanted to be unkind I would say you came to confirm Mama and Daddy's suspicion that I would end up strange."

"They probably suspected something like that."

"It may surprise you to hear me say I honor them for being true to their selves."

Peter smiles. "Nothing you say surprises me. It never did."

"They were destroyed by things around them and within them, but they were always who they were."

"It was hard for me to see through the haze of booze and smoke and the antics. But I should tell you that Cam and I have a pact not to talk about our pasts."

"Then I'll say no more. But how did you find Aunt Ettie?"

"The same, older, thinner, maybe a little less cynical, probably for the kids' sake. True to her being you'd say."

Alexie looks up from Man Two, who seems to be tranced by his mistress's fond stroking, eyes narrowed to blue slits, a hint of purr. "Did you live with Aunt Ettie once? That's not Mommy and Daddy's past."

"Yes, for a short time when I first came to San Francisco. She was very kind to me and fixed up a room for me."

"Did she have lots of friends then?"

"Yes, but they never bothered me."

"I don't think I could live with her."

"Why not?"

"She's so thin. I don't think she has many friends now except the man at the desk named Maurice, who she said had to fight for his being."

"We met him," says Josh. "He's odd."

"He came after my time there," says Sister Lelan. "Odd? Fighting for one's being is our common fate."

Alexie says, "Aunt Ettie said they tried to take it away from him."

"That too is common."

The room seems inert now. Alexie says, "Do you miss playing the piano?"

Sister Lelan smiles. "No, because I still play."

"Where is it?"

"In another room."

"Can you play something?"

Peter looks troubled.

Sister Lelan gets up and goes through the door into the interior of the house.

A filmy surface descends over Peter's eyes. He sees his sister Stella standing just inside the doorway of her room. He is on his way down the hall to his room but stops. Stella is holding her white skirt up and out from her legs. A small trickle of blood is slowly making its way down her thigh. She holds her underwear in one hand, a shoe and a sock in the other. "I don't want it to ruin anything," she says.

Peter turns away.

"You're not supposed to understand," Stella says. "Nobody's supposed to understand."

"Ask Mama."

"Mama doesn't understand. She calls it the curse."

"That doesn't mean anything. It's just a saying."

"What does the blood mean then?"

"You said I wasn't supposed to understand."

"Yes, but do you understand?"

"It's something that happens to girls."

"Did something happen to you?"

"Not yet."

"Did Daddy tell you about it?"

"Yes."

"What does it mean?"

"It's something that has to happen to boys."

"Does it have blood?"

"No."

"Nobody wants this to happen."

"Boys want it to happen."

"Why?"

"I don't know. I have to go. You'll be OK."

"No I won't."

Peter turns to go.

"Stop."

"I can't do anything. Nobody's here."

"Yes they are. They're in the kitchen drinking and smoking."

"You want me to tell them?"

"I want you to listen to me play the piano."

"No."

"Why?"

"You have to clean up." Peter pivots away from Stella, goes to his room and shuts the door. He opens his pants and looks at himself. Nothing happens. From the living room downstairs comes the sound of Stella playing the piano.

Peter snaps his head as one whose eyes have gone out of focus. He says, "In one tribe they decorate her hair with beautiful marabou feathers."

Josh says, "You were spacing out, Dad."

Sister Lelan reappears. "Please come into the next room."

The interior room is much like the front room. The shutters of the single window are half closed so that narrow beams of light, passing unaltered through motes of dust, fall on the floor in bright stripes. An antique upright stands to the left of the doorway, ornate, the legs Greek columns, the upper front board a carved arc of vines under which three Muses in long robes are grouped, gesturing upward with their hands. Botticelli. A thin crack runs across the lower right corner of the board, the result of long cycles of humidity and heat.

Against the far wall to the left of a door that leads farther into the interior three women stand side by side. Sister Lelan says, "Here are my three sisters I told you about. Besides Sister Kandin, whom you met at the door, there are Plantina and Tentiva." Both are also in white, also shorn. Tentiva is remarkably beautiful, light-brown skin, sharp features, dark secretive eyes like a face in a harem in a nineteenth-century British academic painting. Plantina has a round unmarred face, with wide nostrils and generous lips, eyes mildly red-rimmed, white teeth revealed by a smile that seems probably habitual.

Sister Lelan says, "We have a song we sing every day. Today we can sing it for you."

181

Cam says, "We'd like that."

Sister Lelan sits down on the piano bench. From the floor beside her she picks up a small dulcimer and plucks a short melody that slowly rises and falls. Then, as the last note of the dulcimer dies, she quickly sets it aside and plays on the piano a rich chord in lower register with sustained pedal. The sisters begin to sing, not a song but a chant. "O . . ." it begins and then slides into a gentle series of glissandos, diminuendos and crescendos, each ebbing softly before reaching its extremity. The words, if they are words, are composed entirely of liquids spooled from one to the other until they approach an undivided humming. Sister Lelan continues to play chords and a repeated but elusive melodic line with subtle variations. The voices of the four women are distinct. Sister Kandin's voice is a surprisingly pleasing mezzo, as is the voice of the beautiful Tentiva. Sister Lelan's voice is a sweet soprano. Sister Plantina chants in the high register of a lyric soprano. All is sung in close harmony entirely without polyphony. It's clear that the four have chanted together very often. The chant goes on for some minutes and then ceases at the end of a long diminuendo, the piano going silent simultaneously.

After a long spell of stillness and silence the distant noise from the street reasserts itself. Sister Lelan gets up from the piano. "That's our offering."

Cam says, "It's very beautiful."

"I liked it," says Alexie. "Man Two liked it."

Sister Lelan says, "Peter may be disappointed that it wasn't a Chopin prelude."

"No. That would've made me sad. It always did."

Josh says, "Did it say something in words?"

"Not exactly. Think of a lotus floating in a pond."

"Are there fish?" Alexie asks. "Man Two gets excited if he sees a fish in a bowl."

"There may have been little goldfish deep in the water. Did you hear them swirling?"

"Yes."

"And now you're off to a city named Bellingham, Peter said in his letter. By the water."

"Yes," says Cam.

"Go to the water often."

Outside the door of the house, the light is dimming. It's a little misty. Across the street a neon sign flashes. "Payroll Advances."

Naughton finds as he enters Sister Claire's office that the slant light from the window affects his balance adversely. Sister Claire rises from her desk, steps forward, takes Naughton's hand and leads him to a chair.

"Thank you, Sister. I seem to be a little wobbly."

"I want to talk to you. Should we go to your room, where you can lie down?"

"No. I'm fine, Sister. I like this office. The light is soft."

Sister Claire nods. "That's good because what I have to report is not so soft. There's been a change since you left Charlene and Vera yesterday. Charlene became agitated, wheeling around erratically, then trying to get out of her chair, arms outstretched, to what purpose Vera doesn't know. But Vera is strong and kept her from hurting herself."

Naughton frowns. "I don't know what to say."

"I'd like for you to say something, however speculative."

Naughton breathes deeply. "Memory," he says.

"All right, memory. What about it?"

"You and I have memories, distinct histories. In my case a failed husband and father, and later an arsonist. No doubt all in Joshua's report."

"Go on please."

"What if Charlene has been robbed of memory?"

"Is it possible to be robbed of one's memory entirely?"

"I don't know." Naughton moves his head in a circular motion, like one with a stiff neck. "I'm thinking of Joshua."

"And? Why are you making me tease everything out of you, Mr. Naughton?"

"Because the moment I say something it seems improbable, even in cases where I've always thought it to be true."

"Say it anyway."

"I could say that my moment as a firebrand was an instance of felix culpa. It led Josh to bring me here where I find myself among gracious company."

"Thank you, but is that what you started to say just a moment ago?"

"No."

"Then please say it."

"All right. Joshua introduced me to the idea of retro-causality." Naughton pauses and looks carefully at Sister Claire. "I don't know anyone other than you that I would mention this to."

"I'm privileged. Go on."

"Joshua drew me a diagram. It was quite artistic, waves and a blue squiggle off to one side. In the middle square a small e was drifting backwards in time. As I said, a random recollection."

Sister Claire smiles. "You're fortunate, Mr. Naughton, that you're not confronted by Father Schneider, the echoing Grand Inquisitor of your cubist vision. He'd say, stop dallying with us, Naughton. What's the application of this diagram? How would you answer him?"

"I'd be struck dumb."

"Then answer me so you don't have to answer him."

"All right. What if we in the here and now have to accompany the little e into Charlene's empty past and supply her with memories?"

"Interesting. Are your stories meant to supply her with missing memory?"

Naughton smiles. "We know better than that, Sister. I told you I just tell what comes to me. At the most the stories might supply her with stuff to create her own memories."

Sister Claire leans back, folds her arms across her chest, and looks out above Naughton's head. Presently she leans forward again. "Comes to you from where, Mr. Naughton?"

"The stories? I don't know."

"Suppose I said that your stories are anything but random, that you're an emissary from the Holy Spirit."

"I would rather not suppose you said that, Sister."

"Of course you would. It's a terrible burden. But we have evidence. Charlene is awakening. She eats so she can stay alive. Her body grows stronger. Speech, though halting, is returning. None of this was happening until you began telling her stories."

Naughton rubs his face vigorously as if to dismiss an annoying prickling. "I would say to Father Schneider, a logical fallacy, post hoc ergo propter hoc."

"It might work with him, Mr. Naughton, but it won't work with me." Sister Claire softens her look. "We're too much together. And it won't work with Mother Martha, who already told you that your storytelling is divinely appointed."

"This is out of my depth, Sister."

Sister Claire goes on with a harder insistence. "I begin to think that this recent instance of Charlene's frustration and vehemence is a metaphor. She's testing her wings, but she can't get off the ground yet and that's frustrating her." Sister Claire nods emphatically. "That's in keeping with what you've told her, that she can take flight, like an eagle, and stoop on her prey, and no ordinary prey you say."

Naughton shakes his head apologetically. "If you've had literary training, Sister, the world is strewn with metaphors."

"No doubt. So what's Charlene's prey?"

Naughton gives Sister Claire a straight and narrow look. "Whatever powers you think I have, Sister, are vastly exaggerated. But I'll answer. Whatever she was trying to reach when Vera had to restrain her."

Sister Claire leans back and breathes deeply. "All right, here's where we are, Mr. Naughton. You go on with the parable and other stories." She looks steadily at Naughton. "And you've got to take care of yourself. You've gotten thinner. Mother Martha would say that's irresponsible given your task."

"I eat everything that Vera brings me."

"That troubles me. Why are you losing weight?"

"Maybe my mass is the same, only more compact, like one of those fabulous metals Josh tells me about, listed on the periodic table but not yet found in nature."

Sister Claire makes a wry smile. "I'm surprised, Mr. Naughton, that you make abstruse jokes when the well-being of another and yourself is at stake."

"I apologize."

Sister Claire nods. "All right, let's go to Charlene."

Charlene and her wheelchair are not to be seen at the end of the hall. Sister Claire steps into Charlene's room calling, "Vera. Are you there?"

"Nooo!" This elongation of sound in Charlene's speech is persistent now, as if she lacks an articulatory governor.

Sister Claire enters Charlene's room, Naughton close behind. The wheelchair is empty. Charlene is standing upright, her hands locked on the steel bar at the foot of her bed. She wears a short white chemise-like sleeping garment that reaches to the middle of her thighs. She is very thin but a taut wiriness runs from her neck to her feet. Her legs, like her hands, are locked in place. Her head is steady. Only her upper torso moves, as in the first moments of a ritual dance. Actually the movement is an involuntary quaking. Still, at the moment there appears to be no danger of her falling, the rigor of hands and legs firm.

Sister Claire says, "This is wonderful, Charlene."

Charlene does not move her head. She appears to be looking straight at the wall beyond the head of the bed where a simple wooden cross hangs.

Naughton says, "I told you, Charlene, when you're up and about, there are some interesting people you'll meet here."

"Tellll!" says Charlene. The command is extended until the breath invested in it has been fully exhausted.

Sister Claire says, "Charlene wants you to tell a story, Mr. Naughton." During the last few moments Sister Claire has moved closer to Charlene, ready to catch her if her strength fails.

Charlene shakes her head emphatically.

Naughton says, "I think she may mean that she wants the injured man in the parable to know that it was his brother who robbed and beat him."

Charlene nods.

"If he finds out, Charlene, there'll be consequences."

"Tellll," says Charlene, the utterance as demanding as before.

Vera comes into the room. Sister Claire nods assurance that she can catch Charlene if she loses her balance. "Go on, Mr. Naughton."

"All right. The first thing that comes up in a crime story is witnesses. The detectives look for the diner the innkeeper overheard saying the chief assailant was the victim's brother. But the innkeeper didn't get the diner's name. The detectives search high and low, but they can't find the diner. They find the priest and the priest's assistant who passed by the man in the ditch. They grill them about what they saw. All the pair can say is that they saw a beaten man in a ditch and hurried on because they didn't want to get involved. Disgusted, the detectives release them. They focus on the Samaritan. Maybe he saw the culprits fleeing the scene of the crime, or maybe he heard mutterings from the injured man before he lost consciousness. After much fruitless inquiry the detectives find out that the Samaritan is a traveling salesman of a unique sort, a restorer and interpreter of dreams." Naughton looks up at the ceiling. "I'm reminded that in an old Italian epic forgotten dreams are kept on the dark side of the moon along with lovers' sighs and letters never posted."

Sister Claire says, "You're wandering from your story, Mr. Naughton."

"True, Sister, but sometimes it's on the sidings in an old abandoned caboose, to use a metaphor from Ms. Trask's world, that one finds a nugget."

"Go on with the story, Mr. Naughton."

Charlene nods emphatically, bouncing her chin off of her chest.

"You might think that the detectives would have little trouble locating the Samaritan because no one else in the land offers his particular services. They find a few former clients, but they're not forthcoming because it's hard to get people to talk about fashioning their lives after the utterances of soothsayers, crystal ball gazers, mediums, tea leaf readers, Ouija board operators, not to mention haruspicators where animal entrails are readily available."

Sister Claire says, "You've named a number of foolish ways of directing one's life. They all depend on some misguided notion of destiny outside of God's providence. Please go on."

"Yes, that's true, Sister. It puts me in mind of the centurions dicing for the robe of Jesus. What do you think happened to the winner?"

"The Bible doesn't even tell us his name, Mr. Naughton, much less his fate."

Charlene produces a huffy sigh.

Sister Claire says, "We're off the path, Mr. Naughton."

"Where were we? Oh yes. The Samaritan is elusive because of the nature of his trade, which can be very rewarding but also very dangerous. Some of his clients, their dreams restored and interpreted, experience the lifting of a great burden and a renewal. But some are plunged into painful memories and self-examination that's too much for them. My beloved old poet called unchained dreams the far-darting beams of the Spirit." Naughton sighs. "I'm an old man myself now. May I claim the privilege of age and sit in your wheelchair, Charlene?"

"Yesss." Charlene's posture at the foot of her bed seems steady, but Sister Claire remains close by. Vera stands vigilantly just within the door of the room.

Naughton seats himself in the wheelchair. He releases the wheel brakes, wiggles the chair about, and laughs. "I look forward to the day when I can wheel around the hall. I'll challenge Ms. Trask to battle, mano-a-mano, I in my careening chariot, she in an old Flying Scotsman steamer. Homeric."

Charlene smiles. Sister Claire says, "You're years away from a wheelchair, Mr. Naughton, and almost as far from your story."

"All right. Apropos of the Samaritan's trade, do you dream, Charlene?"

"Eestraum," says Charlene.

Naughton jerks forward in the wheelchair. "Ha. Dream, traum, trauma. The German has alerted us to connections, don't you think?" He scans the faces of Charlene, Sister Claire and Vera. "A dream is always a wound. If it's happy, it leaves an unrequited longing. If it's a nightmare it leaves a gash that never quite heals."

"You are straying again, Mr. Naughton," says Vera.

"Not entirely." Naughton looks fondly at Charlene. "When you dream, Charlene, do you dream as Charlene or do you dream by the name you had before you came here? Kristin? Frieda?"

Charlene moves her head ambiguously. Then says almost explosively, "Samaaaaa."

"Right. Back to the Samaritan. We ask, how could he recover his client's dreams when they themselves had

189

forgotten them? Did he lay his clients down on a couch in Vienna, the wall hung with inscrutable geometries, the inquirer's clothes reeking of cigar smoke, his desk a jungle of grotesqueries from Africa, hominids with tigerish mouths, bulging bellies, pierced noses?"

Charlene makes a fluty sound. Her body waggles. Sister Claire readies her hands to prevent a fall.

"No, we're not in the famous studio on Berggasse, Charlene. The Samaritan simply looked into their eyes. I know this sounds strange. But what escapes memory's gray coils cannot escape the eyes. In the eyes subtle tinctures remain, flecks, maps of veins, straits, tidal bores, fading reds like the rims of sleeping volcanos. All obscured by the veil of forgetfulness. But the Samaritan grasps a thread, utters a prompt, maybe just a single word. Language, that clever vaudevillian, turns the worm in the lock of memory." Naughton keeps Charlene's eyes locked in his gaze. "The door opens on the forgotten dream. Trauma." Charlene hitches back. Sister Claire touches her shoulder reassuringly.

"There lies the client's old dream like one of those corny pictures of a skeleton in a dungeon with the shackles still around the wrists and ankles. The skull has fallen off and rolled out onto the stone. It appears to have oriented itself expectantly toward the door." Naughton looks at Sister Claire. "Is anything ever totally forgotten, Sister? I mean consigned to oblivion? What about that dusty white powder on the top of the cranium, finer than a lady's talc?"

Sister Claire says, "Nothing is lost forever. The Samaritan's dreamers will all find what they need, and the detectives will find the Samaritan. Right?"

"Yes, they find him."

For some moments now Charlene has begun to inch along the foot of her bed toward the side where Naughton is sitting in the wheelchair. She achieves this by sliding her hands slowly along the bar at the foot of the bed and moving her feet beneath her to match the motion of her hands. Neither Naughton nor Sister Claire comments on this, but Sister Claire keeps repositioning herself to stay squarely behind Charlene. The long fingers of Charlene's hands, curling around the bar, seem like the six-jointed legs of a spider.

Naughton says, "The Samaritan it turns out does vaguely remember a group of three men on the road not far from the injured man, one of them a huge man with a scar on his face. Inevitably, though the detectives mean to be prudent, word gets out to the injured man that it probably was his own brother and two fellow miscreants who beat him, robbed him and left him in the ditch to die."

"Naammm!"

"I would like to oblige, Charlene, but in parables there usually aren't names because parables are universal stories."

"Naamm."

"All right then we'll call him Nam."

Charlene shakes her head. "Name." The word is clear.

Naughton pauses. "Name? His name is Name?"

Charlene nods and immediately resumes her inching.

"All right then, Name demands to know the truth. Was it his brother? The testimony of the innkeeper is hearsay. The Samaritan's memory is inclusive. The brother has been questioned and claims to have been in a far country the day of the attack. Can the case ever be successfully prosecuted? Name begins to have nightmares in which he wears the armor of his Roman oppressors, breastplate, skirt of mail, greaves. His helmet is crowned by a coxcomb made of the barbules of eagle's feathers dyed red. A hinged lappet of steel protects his ears. He carries an impenetrable shield and a finely honed sword. But his most prominent weapon is a long steel projection that thrusts out from his helmet like a predator's beak. In his dreams he tracks down his brother and buries his beak in the hated fratricide's heart. The dreams drive him to the edge of insanity. He must kill his brother or go mad."

191

Charlene has come to the corner where the bar at the foot of the bed meets the side bar that protects her from falling out of bed at night. Here she must stop or negotiate a ninety-degree turn. Her fingers explore the small space between the two sets of bars.

Naughton continues. "Name has a daughter of great wisdom, wisdom of such depth that it has made her face long. No man will have her. She tells Name that he must not act until she has communicated with the spirits of night. Name says he's afraid she'll be lost in the netherward black of night."

Charlene has managed now to grasp with her right hand the end of the bed's side bar, her arm effectively extended, but her quaking torso and her feet not yet in place. She seems frozen in this posture, an eternal reach across an unbridgeable chasm. Sister Claire keeps close.

Naughton says, "When I was a young man, Charlene, stricken with what I thought was love, I wrote a poem to my loved one. The two lovers were separated by a deep ravine. How were they ever to meet? A bowman of immense strength would have to come and shoot an arrow across that vertiginous space, an arrow with a thin cord attached behind the feathers. To this cord his loved one would attach a thicker rope and to it a yet thicker and so on until she wove an unbreakable bridge that joined the two lovers. But I couldn't finish the poem. The bridge was never woven. Do you know why, Charlene?"

Charlene remains quaking at the juncture of the bars of foot and side. Her thin fingers, white against the silvery gray of the steel, seem hopelessly inadequate to the rigor of the passage. She looks down at Naughton. "Rannn," she says and then, "vannn." She's breathless.

"Exactly," says Naughton. "I thought only of the bridge hanging there in midair. I gave no thought to the ravine itself, the thick mist that rose from its depths down where the boulders sweated day and night with dew. There's no bridge that can span ignorance and disregard."

Sister Claire says, "We've come to the point in the story where Name's long-faced daughter must commune with the spirits of the night."

"Thank you, Sister. The question for the daughter is which of creation's many nights would she encounter. Would it be the familiar desert night where under the moon the winds drop to a whisper and the echo of the shofar continues to spend itself among the dunes? Would it be a night along the Euphrates in which divine peace and Eros lie side by side? Or the night of Hecate riven with howling revenge? Or the midnight that lies below the midnight? O Mensch gib acht, was spricht die tiefe Mitternacht? Would it be the night of the exact instant when God with his thumbnail drew a line across the hours, dark on the one side, day on the other? O let it be what it will be, said the long-faced daughter to herself and went out into the night. But what if she never returned, and her father, bereft, wreaked revenge upon his brother and then turned his beak against his own breast." Naughton stops and rubs his face fiercely.

Charlene tightens her grip on the side bar, tendons and sinews quivering. Drops of sweat roll down her arm. It seems that the outworks of her willpower are destined to be washed away in a drenching exhaustion. But slowly the sinews tighten. Blue veins pulse along the musculature of the arm.

Naughton goes on. "The long-faced daughter passes through an even greater variety of nights than she had imagined. Nights of lovers' sighs, nights of peace, of dreams, nights where the red eyes of wolves shine like dying embers in a Sultan's brazier, nights where witches pluck the cords of their throats, paying homage to Hecate. But none of these is the night of nights, the pot of black from which God painted all the nights, the darkness before time, the only darkness, she knows, that can speak the word that will save her father. She descends deeper. She thinks there'll be a gate, a huge mastiff,

193

a black river, a portcullis of invisible fire. But no, the guardian of the inner dark is Fear, which has no form. Her legs and feet become leaden, her breath broken. Her heart thumps and skips. But she goes on. Until at last her will fails her. Even the blind, we know, can sense a solidity they can't see. But she senses nothing."

Naughton stops and looks up at Charlene, who has now made the turn from the railing at the foot of her bed to the side railing and is sidling toward him. But now the quaking of Charlene's body is more intense. Sister Claire says, "Charlene, I'm going to hold you now and lower the railing so you can get into bed for a rest. Let go of the bar."

Charlene doesn't resist, but it takes some moments for her to signal to her fingers that they must relax their grip. "Vera, pull the lever." Vera moves quickly. The side bars come down. Sister Claire lowers Charlene onto the bed and gently moves her to the center. "You're all right now, Charlene. You showed wonderful strength today. God be praised. Mr. Naughton will come back tomorrow and finish the story."

Charlene lies still, breathing heavily. Sister Claire feels her pulse. "Don't be afraid of the dark. Mr. Naughton is there with you."

"And the long-faced daughter of great courage," says Naughton.

"Eyes," says Charlene with remarkable clarity. She tries to shut her eyes, but the lids have been so long locked open that they come down only partway, flutter, and go back up again. This goes on for some minutes. The struggle has the same character as the movement along the bars of the bedstead, a strenuous battle of small fractions against an old resistance. Vera looks carefully at her charge.

"Charlene has performed a heroic feat today," says Sister Claire.

Vera nods. "Mother Martha would like to see you in Mr. Gerrity's room. I should have told you when I first came, but

Mr. Naughton was in the middle of his story." She smiles thinly. "Mr. Naughton says there are only middles to stories."

"We'll require him to get past the middle this time." Sister Claire takes Charlene's hand in hers and looks into her eyes, the lids still fluttering like the wings of a fledgling. "The Spirit is moving within you, Charlene. That fills us all with great joy." She leaves the room.

Vera pulls a chair up to the bed. For a long time she and Naughton watch Charlene's eyelids. Naughton says, "What courage Charlene has, Vera. You and I open our eyes wide though we fear what we may see in the dark of our rooms. She wills to close hers though she fears what she may see in the dark of her mind."

Vera says, "What is on the outside or what is on the inside can make us afraid."

"Yes. And now Charlene can choose."

At last Charlene succeeds in closing both lids. A small tear slides down from her left eye. Nothing in her immobile face tells whether it's a tear of joy or of some other emotion or merely a reflex of the tear ducts.

"Sleep," says Vera.

Naughton lies in his bed looking up at the characterless ceiling. He rubs his head, looks at his hand and notices that a strand of three gray hairs has attached itself to his fingers. To him they seem like a strange cross between animal hairs and the lines of destiny fortune-tellers say are etched in the palm. Of course one cannot pluck out the lines of destiny as he can the hairs of his head, if he chooses.

The Burial of Man Two

The four of them sit around an old Army blanket, thick and gray, that has been spread out on the hill above the house. Several large stones have been placed along the edge of the blanket to keep it from billowing up in the stiff breeze that blows in from the bay. In the middle of the blanket lies the corpse of Man Two. Next to its head lies a gray-green cat's eye stone. It's obvious that the animal's death has been preceded by a ravaging illness because large patches of its skin are bare, and there's hardly any flesh on the bones. The lips are drawn back, the teeth exposed in the grim rictus of death. Alexie says, "I tried to close his mouth but it wouldn't stay closed."

Overhead the June sky is a deep blue. The half-closed eyes of the dead cat catch the color. Every so often a cloud tumbles by like a swatch torn from a larger mass far to the north. The bay to the west rolls southward making small cusps of white. The sparse madrones bend obediently. They look like old people trying to balance themselves with arms extended.

"You're going off to college," Alexie says to Josh. Her tone suggests a fading regret.

"Not just any college," says Peter. "MIT."

Cam says, "We're proud of you."

Josh smiles. "Come on, Mom. You don't believe in science."

"I believe it's a good thing to do well what you've decided to do. Now we have to help Alexie with whatever she decides to do with Man Two."

"You buried Man," Alexie says to Peter.

"Yes, under the pines in my grandmother's backyard."

"I don't want to bury Man Two. He didn't die in a fight in a crazy woman's yard." Alexie stops herself. "Aunt Ettie said the woman twitched to death. Man Two twitched before he died."

"That was his body letting go," says Cam.

Josh says, "If you want him to return to nature, you could lay him on the seashore."

Alexie looks at her father, who says, "Yes, the gulls and eagles would come. The sea would clean his bones and take them out on the tide, maybe to some blue grotto."

More than Josh Alexie has inherited her mother's darkness, especially the eyes. But she's not as small-boned as her mother, and her breasts are filling. She has tied her hair in a black knot on the back of her head, but she can't suppress her womanhood, or the beauty she's destined to have. "I didn't think he'd die in the summer," she says.

"He didn't think of time," says Cam. "There isn't a season to letting go."

"Letting go sounds like falling."

"It's not falling. It's floating out."

"Out where?"

Cam sighs. "Season, where, you ask, Alexie. Man Two is free of them."

"Will everybody be free?"

"Yes."

"Josh doesn't believe it. What about Aunt Ettie? Is she free now?"

Josh says, "You have to say free from what. Free from everybody saying something about her green eyes? Free from the friends who dropped in and left? Yes."

"What about Maurice?"

Cam says, "He's free from things people put in his mind."

Alexie says, "I would like to be free before I die." She touches the forehead of the dead animal. "What would Aunt Stella do?"

There's a silence. Peter says, "When I was a child and she lost something she would play a beautiful piece on the piano. When she went away she left a book of music. I tried to learn my favorite piece in it, but I couldn't." He leans back as if to look at the sky. "It began with five notes. They went up like something that was defying gravity and then they failed and came back down and then they went up again and failed, and up again and failed. But one time when they went up high you thought maybe they'd grasped something like the roof beam of a chapel or a tree limb in the Garden of Eden and would stay up there, but they came down again and stayed down, deep down."

Cam says, "The music was the way it was supposed to be. The same as when Sister Lelan played for us at her house."

Peter nods. "I used to try to change it in my memory so that the notes would go up high and stay there, but I could never keep them up there."

Alexie says, "Why would anybody write something that went down and never came back up?"

Cam says, "If Sister Lelan was here to play it, we'd understand." Cam pauses, breathes deeply of the north wind. "The cherries on the tree in the backyard come up and shine in the sun and then they fall, or we pick them. They don't go back up onto the tree, but they come again."

Alexie nods. "Yes but it's only a tree. Man Two isn't going to come back up."

Josh says, "It would be unnatural. If everything just came back again over and over evolution would stop. All those cyclic religions and theories of history didn't think about that."

"It's not thinking," says Cam. "It's feeling."

Josh is ready to make a retort, but Peter cuts him off. "There's a pretty song that has a line about a cherry without a pit."

"Can you sing it?" asks Alexie.

"A few lines." Peter gives a credible rendition. "I gave my love a cherry that had no stone. I gave my love a chicken that had no bone. I told my love a story that had no end." He stops. "That's all I remember. It was a riddle. How can these things exist?"

"How?" asks Alexie.

"I think it's that a cherry has no stone when it's a flower. A chicken has no bone when it's still an egg."

"What was the story that has no end?"

"I don't remember."

Josh says, "Maybe it was a story that has no beginning. Then it can't end."

Cam says, "There aren't any beginnings or endings." She looks at Peter. "You read me a poem about an old man looking west over the sea and believing he'd come full circle."

Peter nods. "You've said all I remember about it."

"It's because he was always somewhere on the circle."

Josh remains respectfully silent.

Alexie says, "We're looking west toward the sea."

"Yes," says Cam and touches the head of the dead cat.

Alexie says, "The circle has something to do with Man having green eyes and Man Two having blue eyes." She touches the cat's nose. "Man Two is never going to close his eyes again. When he used to sit by the window it looked like his eyes were closed, but if a bird flew by, his eyes popped open. He was always looking through his eyelids. Wasn't he, Mom?"

"He was always looking both ways, inside himself and outside the window."

"What did he see inside?"

"We don't know. Maybe a darkness, but not an empty darkness. A darkness where something was always waiting."

"Could he have told if he'd been able to talk?"

"No. Nobody can tell because it's not words."

Alexie smiles. "Nobody looks inside and sees words. What would they be doing? Dancing? Marching?"

Josh seems genuinely amused. "You forgot slithering, which is what Ss would have to do."

"Ps would always be trying not to fall over," says Peter.

Silence overtakes this whimsy.

"I still have to decide what to do with Man Two."

The wind stiffens. The blanket billows, straining under its burden of rocks to take flight and join the torn clouds that, gaining speed, seem driven by a consensual fatality in their plunging southward.

A scrim falls behind Peter's eyes. Vogt appears naked among the madrones, his yellow hair and pallorous skin a stark contrast to the blue sky and the bronze of the trunks of the madrones. He moves from one tree to another as he speaks, like a restless actor who would rather be doing battle than soliloquizing. "You called, Peter. It's been years. But it's always good to hear from an old client, particularly one with your promise. I'm sorry to see you've gotten caught in the trammels of death, the subject of your call. Even if only a cat. And estranged from your wife, also a kind of death. Even if not estranged really, because you were never joined. Just as your aunt predicted. And I predicted, if more obliquely. You tasted the sweet flesh. You sired children, but you never got past the wall of black eyes. And now she and her daughter are the officiants at these obsequies, and you are a supernumerary at best if not actually an unwanted person. Once you read me a pertinent poem from Whitman. Death came to an old man as an accoucheur. Death the midwife. A potent circle. But now we have only a dead cat that can't be wrenched into a circle. You should've triced him up with butcher's twine with his tail in his mouth before rigor mortis set in."

Vogt moves to a different madrone, closer to the family, and leans toward them. "I knew you'd call me back, Peter. Why now? To tell you death is a distraction. Where I come from death has no dominion, no ontological status. Protracted absence without prospect of renewal is often mistaken for death, particularly absence of love. You'll go back to your cold marriage bed tonight and in your poetic soul you'll say to yourself, 'Death has entered my marriage.' You once asked if I had prophetic powers. No. But some eventualities are inevitable. When your daughter goes off to college, your wife will join the circle at the old house down the road. That's why she chose this far corner of the country. Somehow she knew the circle was here. The circle people are benighted but harmless. Admittedly, circles are more comforting than lines or numbers, the things that in her heart of hearts Cam hates. But you knew that. Still, you got trapped on a line, Peter. The line leads out the door of what you thought was the House of Family. And then what?"

Vogt moves higher up on the ridge and stretches his arms up to grasp a low branch of a madrone as if he might be preparing to do a gymnastic stunt. "It's been a long time since our memorable nights in New Orleans. Your spirit broken, a condition of great promise. But you couldn't stand the brokenness. You wrote poems and letters. And now you live in the house that brokenness built."

From beyond the ridge, music, echoing from the far bank of the bay, torn by the wind and furrowed by the choppy sea, threads its way among the madrones, too distorted to produce a melodic line, yet its timbres quite distinct—a mixture of the elegiac and the clangorous, like two bands on a collision course, their standards rippling in the wind.

Vogt drops to the ground and crouches expertly, motionless like a stalker from a tribe of hunters. "You've never wanted to listen to me, Peter. I'll be brief. Everything depends on your slipping out through a fissure in the story you've gotten yourself into. You can do it. Watch what your daughter does with the dead cat. Listen to her." Vogt disappears.

"Good riddance."

"You're spacing out again, Dad," says Josh.

Alexie says, "I'm going to put him up on top of that big rock where he can see everything."

"What big rock?" says Peter.

Alexie points to a very large irregular stone that marks the end of a row of madrones. "See. It has like steps going up."

"Pick another rock," says Peter.

"No. This is the one." Alexie begins to take off her sandals.

"No it's not," says Peter. "We'll find a better one."

"Leave her alone," says Cam.

Josh says, "I can take him up."

"No," says Alexie, her voice now rising against the opposition. "I'm taking him up. He's my cat."

Josh says, "I'll climb up behind."

"No," says Alexie. "I don't want anybody behind."

"Leave her alone," says Cam.

Alexie moves the stone weights from the blanket, makes a loose sling and ties it around her waist, the dead cat hanging in a pouch behind. At the base of the rock she pauses and looks up for some moments. Then with great sureness she begins to climb, using handholds and footholds as if she had planned it all before beginning to climb. Peter and Josh move together to stand at the bottom of the rock. After two changes in handholds and one false toehold that has to be corrected, she reaches the top, where she sits resting for a moment, breathing hard. The wind unties the knot of hair and blows it around her face. She takes a moment to tie it again, tighter. She loosens the blanket, removes the body of the cat, sets it on the rock and throws the blanket down. It billows and whirls in the wind for some moments before settling on the ground behind father and brother. There, still worried by the wind, the blanket billows, collapses, wimples, until Cam picks it up and folds it without taking her eyes off of Alexie.

Alexie arranges Man Two in a hollow scooped out by rain in the variable hardness of the rock, but this can't be seen from below. She breaks off some shale-like pieces of stone with her fingers and lays them on top of the body. "He's not going to blow away," she shouts.

Now a trickle of blood seeps over the edge of the top of the rock.

"Come down now," shouts Peter.

Alexie stands up and looks out over the bay. The wind pushes her and makes her change her footing.

"Come down," Peter shouts again. "You've buried him in a good place."

Alexie turns and looks down at her family. "He's not buried. He's hiding under some rocks."

It's now possible for those below to see the ooze of blood from her right foot and from the fingers of one hand.

Peter starts to climb up, his tennis shoes sliding awkwardly on the surface of the stone. Alexie holds her hand out, smeared with blood. "No! I'm coming down. You don't know the way."

When Alexie reaches the bottom, it's her mother who takes her by the hand. "Don't worry," says Alexie, "I know what blood looks like."

"Get the sandals," Cam says to Josh. She puts one on Alexie's undamaged foot. The other has an ugly wound, a flap of flesh hanging down and the blood flowing profusely.

"Put your arm over my shoulder. Walk on one foot," Cam says. "Peter, drive the car up to the foot of the walk." Peter goes for the car.

Josh has found a rent in the blanket and torn off two strips. He wraps Alexie's injured hand in one, the foot in another. Peter drives the car up and gets out. Cam looks at him for a moment, then turns to Josh. "You drive."

Peter says, "I'd drive, but I couldn't think up a plausible story for the ER doc. Josh can give a scientific account of the action of rock on human flesh."

Naughton, walking down the hall, is surprised to hear Ms. Trask's voice coming from Mr. Gerrity's room. He stops. "May I come in?"

"Come in," says Sister Kathleen.

Ms. Trask is sitting in a chair holding Mr. Gerrity's iron triangle out from her and looking through it. The triangle has been detached from the apparatus over Mr. Gerrity's bed. "How can I see it with all these cobwebs?"

Sister Kathleen waves her hand in front of the triangle. "There. Do you see it now?"

"It's not there!" Ms. Trask looks away from the triangle toward the door. "There's Mr. Nobody. Let him take a look. If he doesn't see anything it won't matter."

Naughton takes the triangle and looks through it, cocks one eye, changes the angle of his head, turns the triangle, finally lifts the triangle above his head. "There it is up by the ceiling."

"Give it here!"

Naughton surrenders the triangle.

Mr. Gerrity wiggles his feet and hoots.

"Be careful, Ms. Trask, it's heavy," says Sister Kathleen.

"Heavy heavy hangs over your head. What is it up there, Mr. Nobody? And if you get it wrong we'll chop off what's left of you."

"There's nothing left of me, Ms. Trask, but I know what it is."

"What?"

"A golden angel that's gotten loose from Sister Kathleen's hair."

Sister Kathleen slaps the top of her head. "Begorra!"

"Wrong, Mr. Nobody!"

"Look again."

Ms. Trask lifts the triangle above her head and looks up. "Egad! It's King Tut's tomb. Lloyd had pictures in a steroptician. You could see the mummy move. And the dog lying beside him and the long-legged bird over by the wall and the evil cat. They were all skulking around real spooky. I could see. Not Jeanette. Stubborn nigh to blindness. You just had to turn the thing." Ms. Trask turns the triangle like a steering wheel. "There!"

Mr. Gerrity leans up and grabs the chain now devoid of the triangle.

Sister Kathleen strokes his back. "Just a minute, Mr. Gerrity, and Ms. Trask will give the triangle back, won't you, Ms. Trask."

Ms. Trask lowers the tringle but makes no move to give it to Sister Kathleen. "Lucky there's not enough chain to hang yourself, Mr. Garrity. There's no such name as Gerrity. There's a story for you, Mr. Nobody."

"How does it go, Ms. Trask?"

"Old geezer forgets his real name, wanders the street with fake name and ends up in an insane asylum." Ms. Trask punctuates this little tragedy with a screechy laugh.

Sister Kathleen gently removes the triangle from Ms. Trask's hands, which have begun to tremble under the weight. While she is reattaching it to the chain, Naughton says, "May I observe, Ms. Trask, that in ancient Egypt cats were not considered evil but were rather pharaohs' guardians and were champions of balance and peace."

"Balance! You see anything balanced around here, Mr. Nobody? Garrity can't even balance himself on his own bed."

"I want to share with you, Ms. Trask, an interesting thing about the pyramid where King Tut was found."

"Don't tell me about evil cats. Jeanette had a friend who named her cat Tut and it almost scratched her eyes out. Her husband had just come back from the war after being attacked by Nazi werewolves."

"Here. I'll put it in the form of a question. How could the tomb builders do their work in the black midnight inside the pyramids?"

The question interests Ms. Trask. "Not flashlights. Didn't have any. Not candles. They would burn the air up. Not cats. See in the dark but can't build tombs can't build anything."

"Your inductive powers are phenomenal, Ms. Trask. Here's a clue. There were long passages into the tomb with lots of turns and steps that blocked the sunlight."

Ms. Trask narrows her eyes. "Wait a minute."

"You'll get it," says Sister Kathleen.

Mr. Gerrity has turned the triangle on its chain and is looking through it at a triangulated Ms. Trask. "Yup," he says. "Hooo."

"Lloyd once told me how it was done. Mirrors. And what's that thing that turns light around corners?"

"Prisms. You got it, Ms. Trask."

"Hahaa!" Ms. Trask trumpets. "I could go on a TV quiz show, but it always goes to the one who pushes the button."

"Alas," says Naughton. "Knowledge has given way to manual skills."

"Technology! You can fix people's brains with it. Did you try it on Garrity, Sister?"

"No, Ms. Trask. Mr. Gerrity is not a candidate for that kind of treatment."

Mr. Gerrity lengthens the distance of the triangle from his face, narrowing the image of Ms. Trask. "Pook!"

"You can run a train without an engineer, but there could be deaths."

"Every great step forward has its price," says Naughton.

"Lloyd says thousands of slaves died building the pyramids, but it increased tourism. Lloyd was a good businessman, but Jeanette drove him away by not keeping herself up."

Sister Kathleen says, "You keep yourself up very nicely, Ms. Trask."

"You think I was after my sister's husband?" snaps Ms. Trask. She gets up, grabs her walker and heads for the door, Naughton moving aside just in time.

Sister Kathleen says, "Conversations with Ms. Trask rarely end peacefully, I'm afraid."

"You do a wonderful job with your two charges, Sister. You give them animation. Look at Mr. Gerrity. Thanks to you he's got the whole world in a triangle, and he can look at it from any angle he wants. Which of us can say more?"

"Thanks, Mr. Naughton. And I hear that Charlene is standing now and beginning to speak."

"Yes. I'm on my way to see her now."

"You're doing God's work, Mr. Naughton, without knowing it. Not the first such case."

"We'll know she's crossed the threshold when she lashes out at me."

"Then you will accept your stripes as God's grace."

"If you'd only give me a less pitiless smile, Sister, I'd proceed with greater equanimity."

Naughton finds Charlene coming out of the door of her room on Vera's arm. Her steps are not so much weak as unpracticed.

"Ah Charlene," says Naughton, "if I had a cape I would throw it down before your noble feet."

"And she would stumble on it," says Vera.

"I was referencing a famous historical anecdote, apocryphal no doubt."

Charlene gives Naughton an almost accusatory look. Her facial expressiveness grows daily. "Lonfase dark," she says.

Naughton nods. "I haven't forgotten, Charlene, but you're right to remind me because a blackness as thick as the one we've entered makes one want to forget."

Vera says, "You cannot finish the story while we are walking, Mr. Naughton."

"Stowy!" says Charlene.

"It seems, Vera, that I have to be a peripatetic storyteller. In more ways than one, because we've come to the peripeteia, the reversal."

"Just tell Charlene the story, Mr. Naughton, in the English language."

"I'll do my best, Vera, but every language has its blind spots."

"There are no blind spots in God's word, Mr. Naughton."

"Stowy!"

"We're in a pit darker than night, Charlene. We reach out to the long-faced woman of great courage and wisdom. We can hear the sound of her breathing, but it seems to keep moving away from us. We're afraid to move because we don't know where the ground may end."

Naughton pauses. "This is a fearful passage, Charlene. Do you want to go on?"

Charlene nods repeatedly. She has trouble stopping, her head tethered to a flywheel of affirmation.

"I hear the chorus now, Charlene, behind us. They always show up at critical points like this. But they never get it right, paralyzed by fear and revulsion. Still, we have to listen. Who could they be? Citizens? There's no state here, no city. Maybe they're psalmists chanting in Hebrew, but Vera says the story has to be told in English. Do you know any language other than English, Charlene? Sprichst du Deutsch?"

Charlene shakes her head, only once, in a controlled motion. "Nein."

"The psalms are full of darkness and fear."

Vera says, "The Psalms were inspired by God."

"So, it's not a chorus of psalmists.

Down through the darkness

The ravening cloud

The burial cloud

The black mass spreading fast

Athwart and down the sky.

"I didn't remember it right, Charlene, but even if I had, it would only tell us we're buried in a dark place and the darkness always hungers."

"Tell the story, Mr. Naughton, of the brave woman in the dark. Do you remember why she is there?"

"Worrrr . . ." Charlene, though less often now, cannot stop until all her breath is expended.

"She's listening for the word that only the night of nights can tell her, the word that will save her father. The chorus is turning now, strophe." Naughton makes a sharp quarter turn to the left. Charlene and Vera stop.

"It is dark under the ground here

Neither evil nor pain here

Mere blank here,

Coffin and dark grave here

Turn turn turn

Gone. They're gone, at last."

"Whoever they are they do not make sense. And you are turning every which way, Mr. Naughton. Remember the story. The woman is listening for the word to take to her father. He is dreaming of killing his brother. Remember? What is the word that she finds in the dark?"

"Worrrr . . ."

Naughton presses his hands to his temples. "I can only hear her breathing. Hörst du das Wort?"

Charlene shakes her head, as before, with surprising precision. "Nein."

"There!" Naughton almost shouts.

"Nine of what?" says Vera.

"Nine the mystic three times three."

"You are not making sense, Mr. Naughton."

"She will go back to her father and say no nine times. No, you cannot kill your brother."

"Darr . . ."

"Yes, Charlene. The dark. How will she get out? Back through all those nights. Lovers, dreamers, wolves with red eyes, wailing witches, drums of doom, black mastiff, black river, portcullis of black fire. The uncreated darkness before time. She has to turn. She has to know when to stop turning and step step step." Naughton takes a mincing sliding step and then another.

Charlene sways on Vera's arm, leaning toward Naughton until she has to take a step to stay upright. Vera holds her tightly around the waist.

"The dark presses against her thighs like a river of thickening blood. She goes on. She has in her throat the word that will save her father."

"Ja."

"Days later, when she arrives at her father's house, he takes her in his arms. Her eyes are bruised, her lips purple like one who has drunk shadows. She whispers the word in his ear nine times, each iteration beating against the drum of his ear until at last he nods."

"So he does not kill his brother."

"Not then, but what if the nightmares return, the armor, the iron beak, the frenzy of revenge? No one can go beneath the earth a second time and hear the word a second time and come back again. Can they, Vera?"

"No. There is only one word and one resurrection."

"And one death?"

"That is right, Mr. Naughton."

Naughton breathes deeply. "Listen to Vera, Charlene. She is wise. Walk with her. You are coming back up."

Charlene presses against Vera.

"Turn," says Naughton. "Turn, turn." He goes back down the hall toward his room, pausing occasionally to make a ritual quarter turn, left then right. He stops to examine the wall between the doors of Mr. Gerrity's and Ms. Trask's rooms. Nothing hangs there. But down the hall from the big window comes a flickering light, the birches and the bramble ablaze in the afternoon sun.

The Story of the Fire

Josh is sitting across the desk from his father. A dim crookneck lamp hangs over a glass of amber fluid like a bit of inept stage lighting. Peter says, "I'm going to tell you about my visit to your mother's circle."

"Why don't you wait until you're sober."

"If I was sober I wouldn't tell you."

"OK. You actually went there? This isn't one of your fabrications?"

"The world consists of two kinds of fabrications, premeditated and unintentional. Same as in your trade. All those particles and waves that act differently depending on the eye."

"That's different. But go ahead."

"Wait. We haven't toasted your elevation to Professor of Nuclear Physics." Peter opens a drawer and rummages around until he finds another glass. He holds it under the light. "This is real crystal." He taps it with a ballpoint pen. A pure sound sings in the air for a long moment. He then dips his finger into the bourbon and runs it around the edge of the glass until it makes a high yodeling sound. He sets it in front of Josh and pours it quarter full. "To the Professor. Go ahead. Take a sip with me. It'll only kill a few brain cells. How many we got?"

"Hundred billion cells, trillions of synapses."

"Then you, Josh, have two hundred billion cells and quadrillions of synapses. How many are killed by a sip of bourbon?"

"Come on, Dad, tell me what happened."

"OK. We need a title. How about Der Besuch der alt Mann, The Visit of the Old Man?"

"OK."

"We can spare the auditor a description of this wretched creature. Balding, gray, cullions hanging unevenly, spindly legs and arms, marshmallow belly et cetera."

"Right. Skip it."

"So I went to the big A-frame, its peak piercing the moonlit sky. Near a cliff. The salt and the succulent sound of subaqueous multiplication rising up from the oyster beds. We are few that can hear that coupling. You know the place?"

"I've seen it from the road. You knew she was there?"

"I'd done a little sleuthing, not hard, best-known cult in the vicinity."

"So they let you in?"

Peter makes a circle in his liquor with an index finger and touches it to his tongue. "Depends on what you mean by in. A priestess opened the door, but that's not what they call themselves."

"What do they call themselves?"

"'We' is the only title they used. And 'ones,' probably capital O. Ones is interesting because I figured out that one reason my appearance caused some consternation was I made an unbalanced number, which would be a prime number, right? Like thirteen."

Josh smiles and takes a small sip. "OK, but thirteen isn't an irrational number. Like, say, pi."

213

"So then circles are irrational. Maybe intuitively your mother knew that. Anyway, I was the oddball digit."

Josh smiles a mischievous smile. "There's no such thing as a digit in and of itself, not even you. It has to be in some kind of series or relationship. A self-contained digit would be like Aunt Stella playing Chopin with one note."

"She could do it. And that note would break your heart every time you heard it no matter where you were, in the Tenderloin or on the Scottish Highlands." Peter sips. "But back to pi. I've got to get this straight or the story will get fucked up. Pi is an unbalanced number, right?"

"Pi isn't exactly a number. It's an attempt to describe mathematically a relationship."

"And the Greeks couldn't do it, right? So Pythagoras threw himself in the mouth of the volcano on Mount Etna."

"I think that was another guy, but this is your story. You're the unbalanced one."

"I don't want to ruin the end of the story, but I'll tell you I never got to be a One. Unaccepted, uninitiated." Peter is silent for a moment. "Your mother said that nothing that had any real meaning could be expressed as a number. Remember? So there you have it, Josh. You can't make a circle with numbers because you keep running into pi, which is irrational. Ergo, a circle would have an intense appeal for your mother, like a lodestone for a ferrous personage, to keep this story scientifically grounded."

"There are no ferrous personages. And I might mention that some would prefer to say that pi is transcendental rather than irrational."

"You're messing with my head, Josh, which is already slightly bourbonized."

"I wouldn't have guessed. But you always had the knack of high-end talk even when you were drunk."

"Exactly. The fumes rise up into the brain and liberate the Logos. Anyway, to switch matrixes. Matrix, a high-end concept. The Transcendentalists were irrational, but the opposite isn't true. I mean irrationality isn't transcendental."

"A case of non-complementarity."

"Exactly. But I'm thinking of Vogt. He would claim that everything could be, or already was, transcended, time, space, identity, if only I would make a move. Maybe you scientists can make a move and rid us of all those worn-out concepts."

"Maybe. Can we get back to the visit?"

"OK. What it turned out was I was number seven. Hideously unbalanced. They had six, one plus two plus three, the whole group knit together, six Ones, three females and three males, and I screwed it up."

"Numerology. But I can imagine how they felt about you."

"Right. I was like one of those Wagnerian motifs that signals the approach of death. Ta ta dum. But fortunately they didn't know I was a fraction, half tone, quarter tone, whatever, or I never would've gotten past the front door."

"What fraction are you?"

"A third. Of our little family."

"Why not a fourth?"

"Because Alexie has escaped altogether. Unless you hear from her."

"I don't."

"Maybe your mother hears from her on some frequency you and I can't tune into."

"Maybe."

"Make me a promise. Tell me if you ever hear from her. You don't have to tell me where she is if that's a secret. Just tell me you've heard from her."

"I promise."

Peter takes a sip of bourbon. "Where were we? The fractal man. So you could say I was one third of a seven, which is also an irrational number no doubt."

"It is. So you and the One that opened the door discussed all this?"

"Don't be a smart-ass. She just looked me over and told me to take my clothes off, which was disappointing, because I had dressed for the occasion—black jeans, crimson shirt, occulting black jacket with iron studs and a bolt of gold lightning on the back."

"All right, Dad. You said this wouldn't be an intentional fabrication."

Peter takes another sip of bourbon and points to Josh's glass. "Get into the spirit of it. Try to shuck your professional skepticism. I'm telling you where your mother is, on as many planes as I can."

"I'm listening."

"The divestiture took place in the front hall. There were hooks on the wall and some other garments, pungent of course. Anyway, the priestess didn't take much interest in the process or the revelations that it led to. Just as well, because we've decided to skip descriptions of the physical decay of the protagonist."

"Right."

"OK, the priestess said, we'll make a place for you in the circle. More obligatory than warmly welcoming. You want a description of the priestess?"

"I want to hear about Mom."

"Which brings up Vogt again. He told me I'd have to let your mother go and join the circle people."

"Way back in New Orleans?"

"No, he's visited me since our hall mate days. Like the day Alexie cut her foot. That's when he told me I'd have to let her go." Peter peers at Josh. "You know anything about these kinds of visitations?"

"No. The psychology department is across campus, but even if it wasn't, they don't deal in parapsychology."

"Mostly rats and electrified trip pads?"

"A lot of that but also some human subjects. Stuff better left to the cognitive scientists."

"When I was a kid I tried to bend my mother's wedding ring with brain waves."

"Did it work?"

"I don't think so, but they had to cut it off after she died. I also dabble in telepathy. For instance, I know what you're thinking now. Is the old fart telling the truth? And whether he is or not, I don't like this story."

"That's not telepathy, it's empathy and induction. Besides, whether I like the story or not I need to hear it. I can filter out most of the alcoholic invention. So, the priestess took you in where the circle was, right?"

"Yes. The first thing that hit me when she led me into the big room was the vaulting roof. They were burning incense, lots of it, and it swirled up into the peak like a spirit. There was a musical logic to it. If I were a composer I'd transform the swirl into music. Transcendent." Peter smiles an uneven smile, right side short on lift. "I could almost hear it at the time, like a distant echo of one of Stella's pieces fading off into the air, ending so softly that you could never be sure just when it did. Very elegiac. I've always been big on elegies, dead presidents, bereft birds."

"Right. But you looked down and saw Mom in the circle."

"Don't rush the story. At first I couldn't really make out who was there. They'd widened the circle and made a place for me. There was no jostling. It was as if they'd practiced many times, for other visitors, prospects maybe. There wasn't much light. The big triangular window that would've let light in from the outside was hung with a mostly opaque drape that had lots of signs on it, planetary bodies—planets, the moon, the planets' moons. Some of them trailing silver light. Everything orbital of course. No sun or stars. No doubt an astrophysicist could've told them about some more distant orbits."

"No doubt. Quit farting around, Dad. Who was in the circle?"

"Five people, the place for the priestess being temporarily empty while she brought me in and announced the arrival of a guest."

"And you said?"

"What did I say? What the hell would you say? Hi, gang? Nice to meet you? Freut mich whatever? I didn't say anything. The amazing thing was that when they made a place for me, they kept the distances between bodies exactly equal. It's not likely they used a platinum rod, the universal standard, right?"

"Right."

"Or maybe they used the length of a hip bone, which is biblical, I think, or the jaw bone of an ass. Anyway, they did it perfect. And I had a seat in the magic circle."

"OK, who was in the circle?"

"Your mom was in the circle, but guess who I was looking for?"

"Tell me."

"Alexie. She wasn't there. Do you know where she is?"

"I told you, I don't hear from her."

"She drove away to the hospital with your mother and never really ever came back. She had to wear a boot while the gash healed. Remember?"

"Yes."

"On the top strap of the boot she painted a blue eye and on the bottom strap a green eye. The eyes were always looking at you, no matter which way you moved. Remember? But she wasn't there. She'd already sent herself ahead to the place where she was going. Where do you think she is?"

"I don't know. The circumference of the earth is twenty-five thousand miles. And there're cats everywhere. Who was in the circle?"

"Your mother was the most beautiful of course, even with her hair cut off like all the rest. I'm not going into detail about her body, which would be inappropriate."

"Thanks."

"Three women and four men including me, the only one with hair on his head, not much. We sat in the lotus position, hard as hell on my bones, never mind the finger part where you hold your thumb and index together delicately like you'd got hold of a tiny red cunt hair."

"Dad."

"The sticks of incense, leaning together in the middle like a tepee, kept giving off lots of smoke. I don't know what scent. Sandalwood maybe. Your mother didn't look at me, which was OK because nobody was looking at anybody. You were supposed to have your eyes shut and meditate. But I don't know how to meditate, don't want to know."

"OK, so what did you do?"

"I peeked out of my eyelids. Naked bodies aren't very interesting. Even the priestess would've been ordinary except she had a red bush. Don't ask me if it was natural."

"I thought you were going to skip body descriptions."

"Mine and your mother's. These others are necessary to the story. The men were so thin they made me feel bulbous. They frightened me. The women were frail too. Your mother was the same as when I last saw her."

"Which was how long before?"

"How the hell would I know? Time out of mind. I waited to go look for her, thinking maybe she'd come back. Stupid."

"Keep going."

"The priestess went over to the drape and pulled it back a little. Some light came in. I could see a stand of alders outside, evergreens behind. Remember the salmon we used to smoke with alder wood? Came out all bronze."

"Yes, I remember."

"One of the women was androgynous, if it was a woman. Or maybe not androgynous. Maybe just withered away. I was getting scared that this was some kind of death cult. I remembered having read about the Albigensians, something having to do with courtly love poetry maybe, a Manichean thing. The material world is evil, created by a daemon. Only way out is manic sex and death."

"That wouldn't be Mom's thing."

"That's right. Her thing would be fierce quiescence, acceptance. Oxymoron. But as the incense sticks burned away and fell into ash, I saw what had been holding them up. A stone. A lingam. It reminded me of that stick fire at the Pueblo museum, supposed to be holy. Remember?"

"Yes."

"It also reminded me that my mother was a devotee of Eros and Chaos. That was her religion. She wouldn't have fitted in the circle. Lots of smoke and sex all right but way too noisy." Peter shakes his head like someone trying to clear out cobwebs. "One of the women was menstruating. It was a shock because then I realized these people weren't old. So then, why weren't all the women menstruating? I thought women together got synced."

"Most scientific evidence is against menstrual synchronicity."

"I figured. Anyway, a thin trickle of blood ran down her thigh. Perversely I wanted to know what it smelled like, see if I could tell if she was moribund. She was that thin. Her pubic hair was very patchy. Approach of death."

"Did somebody finally say something?"

Peter doesn't seem to hear the question. "You sit long enough in a circle of what looks like concentration camp survivors, you start to lose control of what goes on in your head. You start to think you're in one of those reverse time clips. Instead of birthing, everything was being sucked back up into those dying vaginas. Not caves, not even just total darkness. Nothingness." Peter waves his hand. "Don't bother to tell me that in science there's no such thing as nothingness."

"Right. There are voids, with something around them, but not nothingness."

"OK, this was a void with a big house around it. The three men's parts were shrunken, obviously defunct. I thought, no, it wasn't a lingam in the ashes. It was a tombstone. The inscription said Universe: Big Bang—1990." Peter goes silent. He is swirling the liquor in the glass, clockwise then counterclockwise then clockwise etc., looking deeply into the liquid as if he might read a prophecy there.

"Wasn't there any sound? What about wind in the trees outside?"

"She would've known that I hadn't come to try to get her to come back home. But now that I was there and saw the group, I wished I'd had the power to take her out of there."

"What did you go for?"

"Sound, you asked? Yes, they began to hum. Maybe it was Om. What does that mean anyway?"

"I'm not sure. Maybe some idea of the ultimate."

"Is that what Stella and her bunch were humming? Om? Big mystery."

"The idea is to solve mysteries, not worship them."

"Forget that idea. There'll always be solvists and worshippists."

"The solvers will win. But the worshippers won't lose because they'll get the benefit of the work of the solvers. Anyway, what did you go there for?"

"I told you I went there to see if she would tell me where Alexie is. You really don't know?"

"I really don't know. And you should've known she wouldn't tell you."

Peter doesn't look chastened. "Doesn't matter. I had to ask. You lose everything, you ask. You don't have any shame. Like homeless guys claiming to be vets with cardboard signs. Homeless. Help. My sign says Lost Wife, Daughter, Son. Help." He looks at Josh. "I'm surprised you came back. Why did you?"

"Classes are over. You were alone. I came to see if there's anything I could do. Practical matters. The house, bank accounts."

"The money's still coming in from your mother's trust. I wouldn't sell the house anyway. She might want it when everybody else in the circle dies. If you want to do something, go down there and strip and get in the circle and see if your mother will speak to you."

"She's gone, Dad. Moved on. Finish telling me the rest of your visit."

"OK, everybody humming. I was silent and then I started to hum. Maybe I could get in. I mean really in. You know what I mean? But the humming wasn't getting me in. So I tried a little polyphony, started singing Alexie's name, very deep, but I figured your mother could hear the name inside the hum. Maybe she'd find a way to speak to me, inside the humming or later whatever was going to happen next."

"Then?"

"It got darker. One by one they started to get up and go to another part of the house through some doorway it was too dark to see. The humming trailed off. At last it was just your mother and me. I started to get up and go to her but she shook her head. What do you want, Peter? Her voice was the same, clear, chiming with candor but nothing else. You knew there were depths inside, but you weren't invited in. Right?"

"I wouldn't argue with that."

"You think she let Alexie inside?"

"No. She let Alexie be herself. She let her go. What did you answer when she asked you what you wanted?"

"I said I wanted to know where Alexie was. She said she's all right where she is and for me not to come back. I started to grovel. I said I didn't have anything left. She said I wouldn't find it there. She got up and left. Disappeared into the dark." Peter throws his empty hands up. "There was a little light by the front door. I dressed and left. Not much of a climax to the story, is it?"

"No. But I believe it. I wondered at first."

"Well, we lit highbrows were taught that if there wasn't any action in the climax, at least there was a gain in understanding. Epiphany. Not in this story. I already knew what emptiness felt like. I didn't need to see the death seekers." Peter shakes his head. "I'm surprised she stayed around as long as she did after Alexie left. Maybe just to have a place for Alexie for holidays." Peter lifts his glass and drinks what's left, not a great quantity. He looks at the bottle on the desk, but doesn't pour himself any more. "So they were right. Vogt. Aunt Ettie. I was never going to know her and should've known it. Right?"

"Why didn't you know it?"

"Because it wasn't in my story to know it, Josh. It was in my story to look into those black eyes and imagine I saw my image. What's your story? Why did you really come back here?"

"I told you. I wanted to see if there's anything I could do."

"Like what?"

"I told you. Affairs. Lawyers. The house. What you're going to do."

"Naw. You came back to make sure your old man was a hopeless piece of wreckage that could be thrown into the bay, quick work for eels and crabs."

"Is that what you plan to do? You could launch off the very same rock where Alexie buried Man Two. High-end literary symbolism."

"That's not what I plan to do."

"Tell me."

"I plan to become a wanderer. Like in Mahler and Schubert. You know them?"

"No. What does the wanderer do? Sing for his supper in castles?"

223

"Wrong era. In one version the wanderer has lost his loved one and has to walk through meadows and look at flowers and listen to the birds and sit in the shade under trees until he recovers joy again."

"Nice."

"In another version the wanderer comes down from the mountains into a valley. The sea roars in his ears. He keeps asking where his land is, because he's a stranger everywhere. Where is it? Where? Where? Finally a ghost answers him. Over there. There. Your happiness is where you are not."

"A tautological ghost. If you're still looking for something, by definition you haven't found it yet."

"You're smart, Josh. Even college profs can sometimes recognize the real thing. But there's a third version." Peter picks up his Whitman, thumbs awkwardly, but finds the place. "Here." He moves the book away from his eyes and back until he finds the focal plane.

"Afoot and light-hearted I take to the open road,

Healthy, free, the world before me,

The long brown path before me leading wherever I choose."

"What do you think you'll find, Dad?"

Peter pours himself a goodly portion of bourbon. "You're not drinking with me. Never mind. I'll answer. Maybe I'll run across Vogt. Slip up on him before he can dive below. Grab him by his golden hair. Prophesy, you Teutonic son of a bitch. Or maybe he'll take me below like the epic heroes of old, stick a bourbon teat in Cerebus's teeth. My mother and Ettie having an epic smoking and swearing contest. My father hanging in the air on the smoke and the bitter arc of their words, laughing gaily, his hairs glistening like sable. Only human pelt to fetch a million dollars on the open market." He sips. "I'll find Alexie. I won't bother her. I'll just look in the frosted window at dusk. That'll be enough for me."

"What about Stella?"

"I've already wandered into her nunnery and heard the blessed singing of Om. See what I mean, Josh? People everywhere humming and singing Om. It's enough to make me want to join Vogt's underground revolution."

"The revolutions that stick, Dad, are in science. They go on. The others melt down in history."

"History is one of the first things that's going to disappear in Vogt's world."

"Interesting. On my campus there're a dozen who're making a living revising history. It's a good racket because you can do it over and over again. They're actually fun to talk to. One of them has it right, I think."

"What does he say?" Peter has begun to swirl his liquor again.

"He says history's not a story."

"Right. It's a form of myth parading as fact."

"He says it's a process of agglutination. A lot of things happen, most of them bad. Humanity isn't constituted to tolerate shapeless misery, so it forms scabs over the wounds. The scabs are history."

"I tip my hat to him. Fuck history. Lilacs in doorways, trains wandering across the continent, birds hiding in bushes. That's my thing." Peter lifts his head straight up, with effort. "Time for valediction. But first, don't worry. My road will not take me to your campus. Midwest gives me the jimmies."

"Still, you know where to find me."

"Right. Go back to your lab. Forget your dreams as soon as you wake up. There're no Daniels or Josephs to help you. Make those particles go around orbits of transcendent numbers. Nothing more dangerous than irrational particles." Peter stands and holds his arms out. Josh comes around the desk and gives his father a hug. Peter goes limp. Josh leads him dragging his feet to his bed and lays him down in it. Instantly Peter begins a raucous snoring. Josh stands for a moment looking down at his father, shakes his head, snaps off the light and leaves the room.

Mother Martha and Sister Claire are sitting in Sister Claire's office. Mother Martha says, "I understand Charlene is walking."

"Yes, more steadily each day."

"And talking."

"Also rapid advances."

"At one time she spoke in German, you said."

"Only a few basic words."

"So you don't attach any importance to that?"

"Mr. Naughton says her memory of German is distant and fragmentary."

"What about Naughton? He doesn't look well."

"Vera has a hard time getting him to eat."

"Not eating is often a way of getting ready for death."

"I know that, Mother."

"But you still want him to be with Charlene and tell her stories."

"Yes."

"Suppose I said you're closer to Naughton than to Charlene."

Sister Claire responds with little pause. "True. I can only reach Charlene through Naughton."

"Is that the only reason you're closer to him?"

"No. We share a deep affinity."

Mother Martha studies Sister Claire. "I think the affinities are unbalanced. I had thought to offer you a temporary assignment at the convent until the case of Charlene has been settled. But I've decided not to. I need you where you are, and I trust you."

"Thank you, Mother."

"Then let us go on. As Naughton declines, Charlene strengthens. Is this some kind of unholy ratio?"

"I hope not, Mother. I hope balance will soon be restored."

"Hope is a great virtue." Mother Martha pauses. "Here is my hope. When all this is done, you will be whole."

Sister Claire nods reflectively. "I know better than to test my strength beyond what God demands."

Mother Martha says nothing for a while. "Take care, Sister. Pray. I'll go now and visit Charlene. I'll offer her my hand and a smile. But she'll have none of it. You and Naughton and Vera are her trinity." Mother Martha gets up and goes to the door, where she pauses and smiles thinly. "Sister Kathleen tells me that Naughton also has a good effect on Ms. Trask and Mr. Gerrity. I'll visit them too." She starts to leave but turns back again. "Someday you'll be able to tell me what he is, Sister."

Ms. Trask suddenly bursts out into the hall banging the tennis balls on the back legs of her walker violently. "You're all missing the show!" Sister Claire and Naughton appear hastily.

In Mr. Gerrity's room an unusual sight greets them. Mr. Gerrity has managed to insert both legs through the iron triangle that hangs above his bed. He has grasped in his hands the horizontal bar above and is now suspended over his bed.

"Look at that!" exclaims Ms. Trask. "A trapeze artist. What's the song, Mr. Nobody?"

Naughton tunes his throat for a moment and then sings. "The daring young man on the flying trapeze, he flies through the air with the greatest of ease."

"A golden oldie," says Ms. Trask.

"Very old," says Naughton.

"What's the rest?" says Ms. Trask.

"I don't know the words but I know the story."

"Tell it."

"The trapeze artist steals away the young man's fiancée and turns her into a masculine trapeze artist."

"Bluuu! If I'd known that I wouldn't have asked." Ms. Trask turns her attention to Mr. Gerrity. "See what he's doing? He's not Gerrity. I told you. He's Italian or gypsy. What's your real name, Mr. Gerrity? Come on. Fess up. Garafalo, or Django I bet. Lloyd went to one of those shows. Django's partner didn't catch his hands. Jealousy of course. Esmeralda was her name. But it didn't work. Django had a huge handlebar mustache, which he twitched like wings and flew down onto the sand where the spotlight was."

Mr. Gerrity moves his mouth from side to side. His cheeks bulge alternately.

"That night Django buried a stiletto in his partner's throat, Esmeralda's too." Ms. Trask cackles with wild satisfaction, then sags a bit, breathless.

Sister Claire says, "Is this a new exercise you've designed for Mr. Gerrity, Sister?"

Sister Kathleen shakes her head. "No, Sister. Mr. Gerrity achieved it entirely on his own."

"Remarkable." Sister Claire turns to Naughton smiling. "And thus a holy squint becomes a gymnastic device."

Naughton says, "With all due respect, Sister, the case may be more complicated."

"How so?"

"In the distant past, when I intended to become a literary scholar, the concept of the polysemous was thought to explain many textual complexities."

"Go on."

"Simply put, any text might mean more than one thing at once, particularly in an accomplished work."

"What's your point, Mr. Naughton?"

"Nobodies don't have points," says Ms. Trask.

"A moment, please, Ms. Trask."

Naughton says, "In this case the triangle is a holy squint, an exercise device, and a trapeze."

"Ingenious, Mr. Naughton."

"Not genious," Ms. Trask declares. "Mr. Gerrity, who isn't Mr. Gerrity, isn't polymous."

"Oh I believe he is, Ms. Trask. Observe. Sometimes he's as placid as a sloth hanging from the limb of a tree. At others he thrashes against the hated bars of imprisonment like a caged panther. At others he flies through the air with the greatest of ease. Most remarkably he gazes through the triangle at the sanctification of all ordinary things."

"I don't let him gaze at me. Italians and gypsies, black magic, lechers. Tights that don't hide anything."

Naughton winces. "It's true that Mr. Gerrity's exertions have wrenched his robe and undergarments into disarray so that they fail at the concealment for which they were intended."

Sister Kathleen cannot suppress a laugh. "Unintended consequences is the current phrase, I believe."

Sister Claire says, "You're doing wonders, Sister. None of us fully understands the consequences of our most charitable actions."

"Whoo boy! You could understand if you kicked Mr. Nobody out and defracked Mr. Gerrity, who isn't Mr. Gerrity. If Lloyd was here he could teach you how to unsteam letters open, which was how he found out Jeanette was sending money to a faith healer who wasn't even near enough to touch her."

Sister Claire says, "Dear Ms. Trask, our hope here is not to evict or defrock people but to restore them to their true selves."

Mr. Gerrity, who has been thrashing about and swinging, now assumes his sloth-like posture, looking benignly out into a space that may or may not be occupied.

"I was my true self until they dragged me out of the house and put me in this insane asylum."

Sister Kathleen says, "I'm hurt, Ms. Trask. I thought you and I were partners, rolling down the tracks of olden days, confronting greedy scoundrels, breaking down the walls of privilege."

Ms. Trask sulks.

Sister Claire says, "I'm going to visit Charlene, alone. I hope you won't be offended, Mr. Naughton. I want to try to see Charlene in and of herself. Non-polysemous so to speak." She departs.

Ms. Trask has lost interest in sulking. "Where do they keep the papers? That's what I want to know."

"What papers, Ms. Trask?" asks Sister Kathleen.

"You know what papers I mean. The ones that tell how we got trapped and how you keep us here. Django up there on his trapeze doesn't know he's here, so it doesn't matter. And Mr. Nobody is nowhere. Charlene's in the dark with the Devil. But I'm a personage to be reckoned with." Ms. Trask moves the arc of an evil eye throughout the room. "Lloyd will find me, you know, and there'll be hell to pay." Ms. Trask bounces her walker against the floor.

Mr. Gerrity makes an owl-like sound of disapproval.

"Aw shut it, Django." Ms. Trask wheels around to exit. "Never mind. I'll find them. Lloyd taught me how to tap on walls for the tell-tale hollow."

Back in his room Naughton detects a timid tattoo on the wall of his bathroom. He gets out of bed to investigate. He encounters his face in the mirror above the sink. A double image. Peter Naughton as a young father. Peter Naughton old, grizzled, wearied by the search for understanding.

The Family in San Francisco, Reprise

The Naughton family of four is walking a familiar street in San Francisco in June. The sun comes down between tall buildings, through tainted air and lands on their shoulders. Their shadows move along the concrete in broken patches. Josh says to Alexie, "How does it feel to be a certified artist?"

Alexie pinches her upper arm. "It doesn't feel like anything." She's wearing scintillant jeans, running shoes on which she has painted spiraling eyes that match the ones on the breast of her shirt. Her hair is unartfully cropped. It approximates that of a patient not destined to recover from chemo. Her face is quite beautiful, eyes slightly extended toward her temples, her skin a porcelain off-white.

Peter says, "You crossed the stage like the queen of harlequins."

"I would've worn a cap and gown in honor of tradition, but the cloth was some kind of cheesy crepe."

"We wouldn't have known who you were," says Josh.

"A queen in any habiliment," says Peter.

Alexie cocks her head. "What shall I reign over?"

"Your self," Cam says.

231

"Not much of a kingdom," says Alexie.

"The largest," says Cam.

"And now we get to go slumming with royalty," says Josh.

"We're not slumming, bro. We're looking for our aunt Stella."

"Why're we looking for our aunt Stella?"

"Because she didn't make it to the graduation. I sent her an invitation, and it didn't come back. So she must be here."

Cam says, "I think she's here, in the same place."

"That was a long time ago," says Peter. He looks around. "Restaurant La Pente isn't here anymore. It appears to be a vintage clothing shop now."

"Great," says Josh. "We can all buy some hip threads and join the counterculture with Alexie."

"Unlike you, I'm not a member of any group."

"What group am I a member of?"

"Nerddom. Nerddom is the most uniform group in the world, held tightly together by orbits and numbers."

Cam smiles.

"Mom doesn't believe in numbers."

Cam says, "Numbers exist. But they don't mean anything."

They arrive now at a wooden door. Peter says, "It looks just the same, but the knocker is gone."

"Try knuckles," says Josh.

Peter raps on the door. No answer.

"Who you looking for?" says a Black man coming up behind them.

Alexie turns. "You're not the same man."

"What same man?"

"That told us how to knock before."

"There ain't no secret knock."

Peter says, "Is there anybody living here?"

"There's probably somebody in there. Living is another thing."

Peter knocks harder.

The Black man shakes his head. "They ain't coming out. Try just letting yourself in and hold your nose. Cops don't care."

Alexie steps forward and pushes on the door. It bends in but does not swing inward.

"Lift up some."

Josh says to Alexie, "You sure you want to go in there?"

"I didn't come all this way to get scared off."

Josh gets his toe under the door and pushes. The door swings in a couple of feet. "After you," he says to Alexie with mock gallantry.

Peter says, "Call, Alexie, before you go in."

"Sister Lelan. Sister Lelan!" Alexie turns to the others. "I heard something."

"You heard your own echo," says Peter. "Let's say we tried and let it go at that."

"Tried what?" says the Black man.

"Tried to find my aunt Stella."

"There never was no Aunt Stella here."

"She called herself Sister Lelan."

The Black man says nothing to that.

Alexie steps into the house. Cam goes in behind her.

The Black man laughs. "Ain't you boys going in?"

"How about you?" says Josh.

The Black man shakes his head. "Nose too delicate."

From within Alexie calls, "It doesn't smell like death."

The Black man frowns. "How she know what death smells like?"

Josh says, "Everybody knows what death smells like. It's an evolutionary defense." He steps inside the door. Peter comes in behind. The first layer of odor is acrid but not as of urine. The second layer is of mild mold. Another layer suggests decaying fabric or wood.

"Is anybody home?" calls Alexie.

There's a stirring from the other side of a large room that's faintly lit by the collapse of two slats of a wooden shutter. A figure in white appears in a wide space created by the partial opening of a pocket door. Behind her it's dark. The woman is Black. Her garment, though tattered, has retained its whiteness. The pale shreds lie against her brown flesh like slashes of muted light.

"I'll paint that," Alexie whispers.

"You never painted anything that looks like anything," says Josh sotto voce.

"Is Sister Lelan here?" says Peter.

The white-striped woman stands still in the doorway as motionless as a statuary mime, even the eyes, large and white-rimmed.

"You're Sister Plantina," says Cam.

The woman nods, her first movement.

"Is Sister Lelan here with you?" asks Cam.

The striped woman makes a ruction in her throat, a test before she speaks. "Mmmm . . . don't like be called from this side."

"Nobody does," says Cam. "But her niece has come a long way for her blessing."

The woman turns and disappears into the dark.

Alexie says, "I didn't say anything about a blessing."

"You didn't need to."

"Right," Josh says. "There's no sense coming to a nunnery if you don't want a blessing."

"I don't mind a blessing," says Alexie, "but I just came to see her."

"You never told us why," says Peter.

Cam says, "You might get her to say something, but she couldn't tell you."

The four are silent. After a long while Sister Lelan appears in the doorway exactly where Sister Plantina had stood, as if the substitution has been carefully choreographed. When she speaks, her voice is also rusty, but clear. There is little noise from the street. "A second time then."

"I wanted to see you," says Alexie.

"You don't have a cat."

"No, not anymore."

"If you had a cat you wouldn't have to paint yourself with cat's eyes."

"I'm not a cat," says Alexie, matter-of-factly.

"What are you?"

"My daddy says I'm a queen."

"Were you just crowned?"

"No. I just graduated from art school. I sent you an invitation."

"I thought of coming as the ghost of your father's youth."

"I wish you had. None of the other families had a ghost."

Sister Lelan laughs. The sound seems to come with even more difficulty than her words. "What did you do with your cat?"

"It died and I buried it on top of a big rock in the sun and wind."

"Who was that in myth, Peter?"

"You may be thinking of Beowulf, who was burned and his remains raised up in a barrow on a high mountain."

Sister Lelan nods. "And no doubt many other famous mountain burials."

"Like Moses and Robert E. Lee," says Josh.

Sister Lelan smiles. "I'm glad to see you haven't changed, Joshua. Constancy is admirable." There's a silence. Sister Lelan speaks. "There're only two of us now. And I can't offer you a song." Silence again. "Did you want to say something to me, Alexie?"

"I didn't think of something. But I'm going to paint you and Sister Plantina."

"Don't worry," says Josh. "Nothing will be recognizable."

Sister Lelan nods. "I like that kind of painting. Better than the three Muses that were carved on the piano. Remember?"

"What happened to the piano?" asks Cam.

"It fell into disuse so we sold it."

"And the dulcimer?"

"The same."

"I'm sorry. Your song was very comforting."

"Sister Plantina and I sing it in our heads. You don't need instruments."

Alexie says, "I'll think of the sound of the dulcimer and the piano."

"Don't think of anything. Just listen to the O as it goes its way up and down, out and back again."

Peter says, "It's hard for me not to think of you at the piano."

"It's hard, Peter, not to think of a lot of old things. But it must be done if we're to remain present."

"How do you forget them?" asks Cam.

"You can't forget them because they're always there. You just lay them on an altar in the back of your mind."

Cam nods.

Sister Lelan says, "White dust will settle on them like the fog that hides the ocean north of here."

"That's how I'll paint it," says Alexie. "Like Kandinsky when he's not geometrical. You can imagine you glimpse things you might recognize, but the paint has overlaid them forever. There could be a sly green pretending to take the shape of a cat's eye. That's why I never got another cat."

"Beautiful," says Sister Lelan. "Le Monde sans Chat." She lifts her hands, a clear signal that the visit is coming to an end.

Alexie says, "I would ask to see Sister Plantina again, but I'll look for her on the altar."

"That would be better. Sister Plantina wouldn't like to be thought of as a model."

Cam says, "What should we say to tell you good-bye?"

236

"Adieu is pretty and was once holy. But saying nothing is better. A slow parting, the sound of breath lingering a little while."

Charlene and Vera are traversing the hall, from the door of Charlene's room toward a door labeled "Maintenance." There they turn about. Naughton makes his way slowly toward them, smiling sunnily. Charlene is supporting herself with a metal walking cane that has four feet. "Well," says Naughton, looking down, "I see that you and Vera have acquired a gecko foot."

"What is that, Mr. Naughton?"

"Litzart," says Charlene.

"That's right," says Naughton. "We all came up through the saurian world."

Vera shakes her head but says nothing.

"Telll story," says Charlene. "Truue story."

"You know, Charlene, I would do anything to please you, but I don't know any true stories."

Charlene smiles but nods insistently. "You remember," she says.

"Yes, but memories don't make true stories."

"Truue memory."

Naughton considers. "If I tell you a true memory, will you tell me one?"

"Something."

"All right. But I'll have to use fictitious names to protect the innocent." He smiles. "Vera doesn't believe in innocence."

"We are born into sin."

"I thought there were Holy Innocents."

"King Herod killed them all. Go on with the story, Mr. Naughton."

"All right. Shall we continue your stroll as I talk? The story itself is a bit peripatetic. About a wanderer. We'll just call him

Wanderer." Naughton nods. "We begin, in media res, like all stories, even Genesis."

"Do not commit blasphemy, Mr. Naughton."

"I'm warned, Vera. Wanderer was for some time dazed and distraught by a conflagration of his own making."

"Why?" Charlene demands.

"If we go back to the motives for the arson, Charlene, we'll have to go back to the wounds Wanderer suffered and who gave the wounds and why until—you see?—we arrive at the snake in the garden and why he was there, if you will pardon the reference, Vera."

Vera speaks, unruffled as always. "All sin began in the Garden of Eden. That is the beginning of the human story."

"Hasen hool," says Charlene.

Naughton nods. "Right. Let's go on from the point where we've begun. Wanderer was dazed by the violence of his act. He couldn't believe he'd done it. He kept glancing to his right and to his left, thinking to see the Doppelgänger that had done the evil, but afraid of what the creature would look like. In the old movies, remember, the actor begins to change as the moon rises. His face grows hair. His eyes burn. His teeth lengthen and sharpen. The wolfman, what the French call the loup garou."

"Der werwolf."

"Exactly, Charlene. But if Wanderer couldn't see the creature walking beside him, then maybe it was inside him. This horrible thought made him believe he should've immolated himself in his own fire."

"Was bren . . . no what buurr?"

"A house. Wanderer believed that the house was the home of an ungodly cult that had stolen his wife from him. So, he burned it. Now he wanted to undo the burning the way you can run a film backwards until the flames fold back into themselves and the house rises up out of the ashes."

"Can."

Naughton is silent, his brow bent.

"What she means, Mr. Naughton, is that forgiveness is always given to us. It wipes away the sins of the past, and it changes everything."

"Ah. Of course. But Wanderer didn't know that. He went to the top of a high jagged wall of granite with the idea of throwing himself onto the rocks of the bay below. But as he stood teetering atop his perch, a strange thing happened. A sea hawk came winging its way up from the bay with a young salmon in its beak, the scales bright even in the mist. The span of the hawk's wings was wider than Wanderer was tall. He fell to his knees. The belly of the fish grazed his head, leaving a slick of oil. He was anointed. In a state of wonderment he began to climb down from the wall but he slipped and fell. The ground was soft with damp leaves. He lay there for a long time. He had known this soil in a different time, but the memory of it eluded him. He got up. He now knew he was destined to do something other than kill himself. He packed a knapsack with deer jerky, hard cheese, and dry bread and hung it on a stick from an ash tree and carried it over his shoulder, as he had seen in a child's picture book."

Charlene lifts her walking cane up from the floor and holds it out for Naughton to see. "How many claw?"

"Four."

"The sea hawk."

"Yes. That's right. Four claws with the strength of a vise."

"And eagle?"

"Four. You're an eagle, Charlene. I'm the story man."

Charlene points the stick at Naughton. "Story."

"All right, I'll go on with the story, but remember your promise, story for story."

Charlene nods.

"The memory buried under the leaf-covered ground kept silence, but Wanderer knew what he sought, a beloved face with one silver stud in the left nostril and three silver studs in each ear. She had sworn never to relinquish them to the vagrancy of time. Samantha. But he knew the name was of no use because, unlike the silver, she would've cast it off long ago. How will he find her? He remembered her description of a painting that would guide her all her life. Kandinsky was the artist's name. The painting was a grand chaos of brilliant colors, proto-creatures, including a half-bird, half-serpent caught, whirling, squirming, and clawing at an old net, drawing its own blood, the brightest of reds. The primordial violence of creation." Naughton stops and rubs his jaw vigorously.

"That is not the creation in the Bible, Mr. Naughton."

"No, it's not, Vera, but artists are always picturing the power of creation over and over again since they're not allowed to see God."

Vera says nothing to that.

Charlene lifts her walking stick and inscribes on the air a calculated image. Claws crushing prey, or a painter's brutal impasto of thick crimson, or the thrust of a magic wand, or the recumbent eight signifying eternity?

Naughton doesn't gloss the gesture. "It didn't take long for Wanderer to find the Kandinsky. It was in a glossy coffee table book he bought at a high-end librairie in a city to the south. He took the book to the local library and photocopied the painting in color. Then he made a gift of the book to the library because it was too heavy to carry in the backpack he'd replaced the knapsack with. The librarian thanked him and showed him a book with pictures of the work of Jasper Johns. He found a painting of the number eight. It was refigured to look like a teapot without a spout. It was surrounded by ghastly white that had leeched up all color and hidden it in its aura. He thought his wife Jing would approve of the painting—the only worthwhile thing to do with numbers, empty them into white fog. He would've photocopied it too, but he never expected to see Jing again."

"Numbers are necessary," says Vera.

"Why?" Charlene points her quadrupedal device at Vera.

"Clocks. What would be the use of a clock without numbers?"

"That's a different artist," says Naughton. "Clocks flopping over the edge of tables like flapjacks running loose in the kitchen."

Charlene emits something between a laugh and gargle, which creates a brief moment of choking.

"Be careful, Charlene," says Vera. "You are learning everything all over again, and laughing is a hard one."

"Vera is right on both counts, numbers and laughter. For instance, Wanderer, though very careful with money, still needed to use numbers. There was a long string of numbers on the card he inserted into ATMs, and he had to key in four digits before the machine would give him cash from the trust Jing had set up for him. The ATMs put on little shows. Bulbs circled the screen like the marquee of a clip joint. A disembodied hand entered stage left and pointed to the slot for the card. An extraterrestrial top spun at warp speed center screen to assure the customer of assiduous attention to his request. Fingers riffled digital bills like a card sharp. Sounds varied—pings, bells, jingles like an old cash register. The best show was a stork swooping down with a sling. Instead of a baby the sling was filled with bills of various denominations."

Charlene laughs an unthrottled laugh. Vera laughs with her. "Mr. Naughton, your head is like one of those horns that spills out everything."

"You've made my day, Vera. No one has ever compared me to a cornucopia."

"Youu will run out," says Charlene. "Story."

"OK. Wanderer took his turn at library computers and searched the web for any gallery handling an artist whose work resembled Kandinsky. He was amazed to see how many still sold paintings of cows, mountains, trees and people. He found nothing on the web, so he made a pilgrimage south to many galleries along the West Coast, sure that it was Samantha's natural habitat. He showed owners the famous Kandinsky and asked if they had ever handled the painting of an artist resembling this. The gallery owners were eager to help, and to sell, but none produced a likely lead.

"At last he found in the catalog of a small gallery situated at the estuary of a stream in southern California what he was looking for. The paintings featured primary colors and proto-organisms, with tell-tale touches, bursts of silver and verdigris that evoked Samantha. He took a bus south. When he got off at a tiny roadside station, the salt air striking his skin transported him back to his house by the bay. He remembered a towering rock that Samantha climbed. There was a dead cat and some other animal, maybe overhead."

Charlene thrusts her stick out again. "Eagle. Fish. Claws. Catch everything. Story."

Naughton rolls his head. "Once upon a time a girl had a cat with blue eyes . . ."

"You are well past that, Mr. Naughton."

"You're nowhere, Mr. Nobody."

So engaged in storytelling have the three been that they've failed to see Ms. Trask bearing down on their right flank, scooting rapidly, tennis balls sliding silently along the tile.

"It's always a pleasure to see you, Ms. Trask. But you're mistaken about lack of location. We're somewhere near forty-five degrees north and seventy-three degrees west."

"Hooo! That may be where the rest of us are. But you're nowhere, and I hope the staff will handle it speedo."

Vera says, "Nobody is nowhere, Ms. Trask."

"That's what I said, wasn't it? Mr. Nobody is nowhere. Jeanette used to twist my words. She got lock-jawed and Lloyd had to take her to a vet because he was the only one who had a big enough needle."

"I mean nothing God has created is ever lost."

Ms. Trask twirls a hand in the air above her head. "Never mind that. I know where the papers are." She produces a shrewd look.

Naughton says, "I've often wondered where they are."

"Yours is a blank sheet of paper, Mr. Nobody. They tried holding it over a candle in case it was written in lemon juice, but nobody could see anything." Ms. Trask turns sharply to Charlene. "What've they got on you, sister? You'd have been better off just lying there playing dead."

Charlene smiles a warped smile. "War crimes."

"You're not old enough to commit war crimes. Besides, there's no war now."

"That's not a fair assertion, Ms. Trask. There's a war somewhere in the world every day, like rain."

"I wrote Lloyd a letter and slipped it out past the guard. He's coming with a drill. I know the exact spot in the wall. Whatever they cooked up on me will be exposed for the slander it is. Speaking of exposed, Mr. Gerrity has escaped from a zoo and is hanging upside down with his privates in full view. Don't ask me about his other ape doings."

Vera says, "Swinging is better than lying and looking at his feet all day."

"Sister Kathleen gave him a triangle to look through, which should've been enough, but no, he has to swing on it hooting and grabbling. Sister Kathleen says he's making progress, learning to talk, and she a nun having to look at you know what. Talk! If you start with hooting, it'll take you centuries to talk. Evolution. Even the Church doesn't deny it."

"The Church never denies what is true," Vera says.

"You better read your history, kiddo." Ms. Trask squints slyly. "Don't bother to try to intercept Lloyd's reply. It's registered mail, like a diamond ring, and if you mess with it the federal government will come down on this place like an eagle on the fold. Shwush!"

Naughton says, "Sometimes, Ms. Trask, I think you don't hold us in Christian charity."

"You're the charity case, Mr. Nobody. The nuns all pretend you're here, even Mother Martha. Why, I don't know. Jeanette would go out of existence sometimes and Lloyd and I would have to go looking for her. Jeanette! Jeanette! We would call and she'd come back out of nowhere until one day she didn't. But I tell you this, Vera. You and the nuns had better stop pretending Mr. Nobody is here. You could be charged with harboring a criminal null set. Lloyd was good with numbers. He could spot a null set in a minute, today, tomorrow, ad ignitum."

"Not coming back will happen to all of us someday, Ms. Trask," says Vera.

"Let it happen to whoever you want it to, but Lloyd is coming with the drill and I'm out of here. The rest of you can stay and not come back." With that Ms. Trask lifts her walker from the floor, does an about face of military precision, and heads back up the hall carrying the walker in front of her like a battering ram.

The three left behind in the tailwind of Ms. Trask's departure stand silent for a moment.

"Story," says Charlene, gazing fixedly at Naughton.

"No, Charlene," says Vera. "You are not a hypnotist. And Mr. Naughton has told enough for one day. He is worn out."

"Perhaps Vera is right, Charlene. I believe that the shape of the story is clear in my mind, but at the moment it's a bare bone that must be fleshed out."

Charlene lifts her walking instrument again. Using one hand as a cradle for the shaft and turning the handle with the other, she succeeds in spinning the device rapidly, creating the illusion that the four-clawed terminus is drilling into Naughton's psyche. "No story mine until you end."

"Agreed, Charlene."

A Report from the Underworld

Naughton prepares to lie down for a nap but looks up to find Vogt in his doorway. "You called, Peter."

"Did I?" asks Naughton uncertainly.

"Most certainly."

Naughton squints and shakes his head. "You're not old."

Vogt makes his sizzling laugh. "At our last meeting, Peter, by the rocks and the sea, you were obsessed with death. I assured you that death has no status in reality. Now I tell you that neither does age or time."

Naughton thinks for a moment. "OK, I get the logic. If there's no death, there's no time. But if there's either, then there's both."

"If logic had any salience in reality, that would be well argued, Peter. But these matters, though seminal, are not what you called me for."

"What did I call you for?"

"You wanted a report from the Unterwelt."

"So?"

"Your Aunt Ettie has gathered a group of like-minded green-eyes. Very cohesive. I had a hard time detaching her until I told her I had news of her beloved nephew. She approves of your search for Alexie."

"That was a long time ago."

Vogt wags a finger.

"Sorry. Timeless. I forgot."

"Anyway, your Aunt Ettie wishes you good luck with your search but feels you've skipped a step."

"What?"

"Look in San Francisco, she said. Stella is probably dead, but Alexie would want to visit the old nunnery, a believer in auras and afterglow."

"OK, I'll consider doubling back."

"About Stella being dead, she was wrong. I would've seen her."

"You can see all the dead at once?"

"Yes, but that would be ineffective. I set coordinates. In this case they were wide enough I would've caught her."

"Maybe Stella has declined to join the inhabitants in your precincts."

"I never rule out anything, Peter, but our catalog is complete." Vogt shrugs. "Anyway, as we chatted, Ettie was curious to know if Josh is still a know-it-all smart-ass. I told her he betrayed you."

"He saved me from jail." Naughton smiles. "I thought you'd end up in jail or a nuthouse, a messenger from the Underworld. Maybe in a special ward housing prophets and Jesuses."

Vogt returns the smile. "Such a thing could happen theoretically, but my traffic between the Unterwelt and this world is carried out with great discretion."

"Of course. But tell me. Does everybody have a rep from your shop?"

"Everybody that wants one, but most of you terrestrials decline, afraid. You're a rarity, Peter." Vogt pauses. "I'm not surprised to find you here. You have stubbornly refused my invitations. Maison Cristina. A haven of repose after a bit of arson. Bourbonless, no doubt."

"Yes."

"But I see they've let you keep a copy of *Leaves of Grass*."

"Yes."

"Do you read some of the more succulent passages to Sister Claire? She's hooked on you, you know."

"No she's not."

Vogt shrugs, steps forward and picks up the Whitman. "Let me see if I can find it." He checks the table of contents, finds a page. "Here. A seer came to him and told of eidolons.

Ever the mutable,

Ever materials, changing, crumbling, re-cohering,

Ever the ateliers, the factories divine,

Issuing eidolons."

"The old boy got pretty close, Peter. In our precincts even the most dogged in their ways are experiencing relentless change in their being."

Naughton nods, but absently. "What about Cam?"

Vogt shakes his head. "Not with us yet. I would've seen her if she'd been there, given the coordinates I'd set."

"Coordinates. What do you mean?"

"A metaphor, Peter. We use the terminology of geography to designate degrees of presence and absence. I didn't see Cam, but I saw her adoptive parents."

"Really. What did they look like?"

"The mother flat-faced, a Korean I'd say. The father an unhandsome instance of black Irish with a wispy coal-black mustache, inexpertly tinted. I could've spoken with them if I'd adjusted my coordinates, but I wasn't motivated."

Naughton's face darkens.

"You wouldn't have wanted to either, Peter. What you really want to know is the story of Cam, where she came from originally, what she was, what she is, right? To complicate matters, the two of you had a pact. No talk of family. It made you want to know her story all the more. You know what the moral of that is, Peter?"

"What?"

"Stay out of stories." Vogt pauses. "And yet I have to admit these yarns you're spinning Charlene are right for her."

Naughton waits for Vogt to go on.

"They're right because they keep sailing off out of space-time. But watch out, Peter. Stories have a childish way of clinging to old forms—beginning, middle, end—their mother's milk." Vogt looks at Naughton and nods. "Well, Cam avoided that trap. Give her credit, but she got caught in another one."

"What?"

"Circles. Everything everywhere a circle."

Naughton nods.

"I came here, Peter, to answer your call for information from below. I'm glad you called, but for a different reason."

"What?"

"You're a study, perfect example of liminal man."

"What does that mean?"

"I mean you're caught on the threshold between the old Adam the Jesuits taught you about and a new kind of creature."

"I feel anything but new."

"Observe yourself more carefully. Especially when taking flight on the wings of one of your stories for Charlene."

"It sets my teeth on edge, Vogt, when you speak of Charlene. Is she a client?"

"No."

"Of some other operative from your place?"

Vogt shakes his head. "I'd know." He pauses. "She's the child now, Peter, of your stories. She was locked in what's called in common parlance the past. The past is an illusion, an ugly one. You knew that."

"Go on."

"I've seen her father."

"Did you speak to him?"

"No. Our shared field was thin, and I chose not to adjust my coordinates. I knew any exchange would be negative."

"What do you mean?"

"I mean he was a disfigured specimen."

"How?"

Vogt awards Naughton a thin suture-like smile. "For one thing, he sported a mensur scar on his left cheek, not likely administered by a fellow student at Wittenberg, more likely self-inflicted." Vogt pauses. "That ends my report from the Unterwelt. Now to your stories."

"I don't want to hear any predictions."

"We don't engage in prophecy, a self-contradictory term predicated on the notion that there's something not yet in existence."

"All right. Go on."

"I say simply, using ordinary language with you as I must, that she's being detached from him. A few scraps of German. They will fade. Credit your stories."

"If the father is only a cheap counterfeit, why was she near death when she came here?"

"Counterfeit doesn't mean inconsequential." Vogt pauses, musing. "When you called me in New Orleans, I thought you were merely a broken failure, but with promise. But actually you were always getting ready for Charlene."

Naughton frowns reflectively but says nothing.

"I'm on my way, Peter." Vogt smiles. "We're getting caught in verbs, tenses, unavoidable for talk, but not to be encouraged. Keep storytelling, my liminal friend. Call me any time."

Vogt pushes himself slowly away from the door jamb, turns and walks away.

A scrim rolls down across the door. A vocalise arises, far away, barely audible, a cross between a whisper and a breeze. Perhaps it's Li Po's butterfly escaping from Cam's mouth, beginning its impossible journey from the distant South. Now the vocalise comes forward with incredible speed and transforms itself into an image on the scrim, the nexus of a three-point perspective. One sight line vanishes down the long hall of Maison Cristina. Another is lost among the ranked trunks of the golden birches beyond the window. The third enters the door of Charlene's room and quickly finds its terminus in a dark cul-de-sac lined with thickly leaved linden trees. But what is the object in the foreground from which the lines of sight radiate? It slowly takes shape. Vogt. His outlines are clear, a darkly golden edging that marks him off from hall, woods, room, the gold borrowed from his thick locks, which fall in tufts like the unshorn hair of a Grunewald peasant aghast at the foot of the Crucifixion. Within the edging of the body everything has been cleaned out, heart, lungs, viscera.

Quickly silence and black shadow paint the scrim.

Naughton leaves his room and begins his slow walk down the hall to Charlene's room. The big picture window, sheeted with rain, gives the appearance of being bowed inward by the weight of water and wind. The greensward is inundated. One imagines black cypress knees thrusting up amid the muted gold of the birches. Sister Kathleen intercepts Naughton. "Mr. Gerrity wants to talk to you."

"How wonderful. Of course."

Mr. Gerrity is sitting straight up, gripping the sides of his iron triangle with Euclidean precision. Near the foot of his bed Ms. Trask, sans walker, sits in the guest chair of worn fabric, leaning forward with an air of defiance and expectancy.

"Top of the morning to you, Ms. Trask."

"If an ape can talk, I can walk without bouncing Betsy."

"I don't doubt it for a moment, Ms. Trask."

"The talking part isn't true."

At this point a series of sounds comes from Mr. Gerrity's mouth, carefully aimed through the triangle at Ms. Trask. The series is broken into parts, very much like words in a sentence being taught to one unfamiliar with the language under study.

They're unintelligible, but if one were to make a charitable guess it might be something like lulu lemon ululate.

"Remarkably cogent, Mr. Gerrity, given the complexity of the subject."

Ms. Trask says, "Lululu. Don't tell me you're one of those interpreters of tongues, Mr. Nobody."

"No, Ms. Trask, I'm not gifted."

"Lloyd would've known what the ape wanted to say. He was onto animal speech, like Dr. Doolittle. Subliquids he called it. If you ask me what the ape man is saying is he wants to use the loo instead of doing his diapers."

Sister Kathleen shakes her head dolefully. "That's very unkind, Ms. Trask. I'm surprised at you. Surely you wish Mr. Gerrity well on his way forward."

Ms. Trask cocks her head. "Maybe he's one of those time-lapse cases. You take snaps twenty years apart. You know what I mean, Nobody?"

"Yes, a long process is compressed into a series of rapidly changing images."

"Up in his bed, then on a trapeze. First thing you know he'll be on all fours barking for supper, then luluing words a mile a minute."

Mr. Gerrity wiggles his feet at Ms. Trask provocatively.

Ms. Trask laughs wickedly. "You aren't nowhere near that yet, buster."

Naughton says, "I must be on my way, but this has been a wonderful treat. Please keep me informed, Sister. And, Ms. Trask, I congratulate you on your new sure-footedness."

"On your way is right, Nobody. You're on the way down faster than Mr. Gerrity is on the way up. Evolution isn't for everybody, especially if they're consorting with a witch."

Naughton finds Charlene in a darkened room. She's standing by the window running with rain, but she's not

251

looking out. Her face, in silhouette, is a black featureless cut-out. So is the rest of her body, encased in a long gown. "Setzen Sie, Herr Naughton." Charlene's diction is without defect, the Ss crisp Zs. But it has a slightly distant, ventriloquistic quality.

"I'm afraid I'm not permitted, Charlene. We'll have to wait for Vera."

"Vera's got a dayy."

"That's true, Mr. Naughton." Sister Claire has come behind and stands now just inside the door. "Wouldn't you like some light, Charlene?"

"You cannn truss Mr. Naughton."

"Of course we can trust Mr. Naughton, Charlene, but Vera would be very disappointed if she didn't get to hear the end of Wanderer's story."

"Vera alllready knows the end."

"Yes, Vera is very perceptive," says Naughton.

"Everybody knooows, but him." Charlene has lifted a hand and points toward Naughton.

Naughton says, "In most stories, Charlene, at least our human ones, the end is not known until it comes, if at all. The world is full of contingencies."

"Bible," says Charlene with a sharp laugh, an almost doglike yelp. "I'm Vera."

A silence ensues. Sister Claire says, "I think often of your own story, Charlene. Are you looking forward to leaving us?"

Charlene turns now and looks at the two standing in the doorway, but there's little light on any of the three faces. A painting of thick sfumato. "When?"

"Some physicians must come and make a judgement."

"Judgement?" Charlene pronounces the word accurately but lengthened by an exploratory tonality.

"Yes, and there must be a place and someone for you to stay with."

"Someone." Charlene imbues the word with an almost mocking improbability.

"Yes. Do you have someone in mind?"

Charlene says nothing.

"See if you can remember someone, Charlene, a relative or a friend. None was on record when you came to us."

"Came?" This very pointed.

"Two women, lay members of our order, brought you with some men willing to help."

"Where wasssss I?" The question is almost fearful.

Sister Claire smiles, the smile marginally visible by a slant light of unknown source that has come into the window behind Charlene, perhaps a security light lit by a sensor. "Your coming had an oddly picturesque quality to it. Our companions found you sitting under the arched lintel of an old brick building. They thought you weren't safe. The bricks were old and crumbling. They spoke to you, but you didn't reply. They motioned you away from the doorway, but you didn't look at them. They asked passers-by about you, but no one said they knew you. They took your hand, but it didn't open to them. It remained clutched though there was nothing in it."

Backlighted, Charlene's face is impossible to read. She says nothing.

Sister Claire goes on. Her account has something of the quality of a practiced recitation. "After more efforts at making contact with you and failing, our companions enlisted the help of some men, assuring them you'd be welcome here at Maison Cristina. The men became hesitant when they discovered that your body wouldn't bend. But in the end they brought you here in a sitting position like a grand lady borne by liveried bearers who'd lost their litter."

"Hahahahhh." Charlene's laughter, at first genuinely jolly, declines into a barking cough.

Sister Claire steps forward to steady her, but Charlene pushes her away.

Naughton says, "Vera has said that laughing is one of the hardest things to relearn."

253

"No doubt," says Sister Claire, "but Charlene has great courage and strength and will not give up, will you, Charlene?"

"Haha ha." This time Charlene's laughter is contained.

"So, Charlene, for a while you were our lovely lady of difficult angles, but now you're supple."

Charlene wags her head. "Sehr komisch."

A long silence follows. Sister Claire says, "We'll leave you now, Charlene. If someone comes to you, even in a dream, let me know."

"Story."

"Yes, Mr. Naughton will resume his story, but now I have to take him away and talk with him about his own prospects."

"Time," says Charlene. "Dümmlich."

"I can't contradict you, Charlene. Time plays tricks on us, and our plans often seem foolish in retrospect, God knows. But that doesn't excuse us from trying to look ahead and prepare for the future as best we can. Wouldn't you agree?"

"Der Abschied ist süss."

Naughton chuckles. "Are you playing Juliet to my Romeo, Charlene?"

Charlene mimics Naughton's chuckle. "Ja." Now she addresses Sister Claire. "His prospects. Not much."

Sister Claire touches Naughton lightly on the shoulder. "Mr. Naughton isn't as diminished, Charlene, as outward appearances might suggest." With that she turns and pushes Naughton gently along. "Tomorrow then."

In Sister Claire's office Mother Martha is waiting. As soon as greetings have been exchanged and Sister Claire and Naughton are seated, Mother Martha says, "You're thin, Mr. Naughton, and your voice is reedy. I believe your health would improve, mind and body, if you sent your friend Vogt away for good."

"He's not a friend, Mother."

"What is he?"

"I don't know."

"Let's say he's a demon. We could summon an exorcist. But you could be your own exorcist."

"I wouldn't know the ritual, Mother."

"Never mind the bells and incantations. Just tell a story in which Vogt is banished. Then concentrate entirely on the stories that bring Charlene to the light, though I don't understand how they do." Mother Martha turns to Sister Claire. "Do you understand how dark tales bring a person to light, Sister?"

"No, Mother, not really. Some principle of salubrious reversal maybe."

"Salubrious reversal. There, Mr. Naughton, you have a wordsmith equal to your own verbal powers."

Naughton smiles. "Greater powers, Mother, more incisive."

"You've cast Charlene as an eagle. What a beautiful and fearful creature." Mother Martha leans back and creates a silence that clearly belongs to her and is not to be broken by another. At last she says, "This is a good moment to tell you, Mr. Norton, that we have a communication regarding Charlene. You have earned the right to know what we know, however murky."

"Thank you, Mother."

"The communication is a paste-up. The sender has glued cutout letters to a white sheet of construction paper. The words say, 'I have known her. I am coming.' It's unsigned."

Naughton says, "A very old device in mystery stories. The sender ensures that his hand script or his typewriter keys can't be traced. And even computer printers leave their fingerprint. May I see it?"

"The original paper has been given to the authorities, but here's a photocopy." Mother Martha hands Naughton a paper. "You will notice the possibility of sexual references."

"Yes. Both old, one no longer in use."

Mother Martha says, "Apart from salacious wordplay, what do you make of the message, Mr. Naughton?"

Naughton receives the paper and examines it. "I'm reminded of an ingenious method of coding. You write a letter in, say, German. The recipient has a template that fits over the text revealing a message in English. Very difficult to construct, but . . ."

"Mr. Naughton, we're asking you what you make of the actual message we have."

"On the surface it seems pretty clear, Mother, one breach effected and another threatened. But have you thought of an anagram?"

"Neither Sister Claire nor I see any such thing."

"What about German?"

"What about it?"

"I have little German." Naughton studies the paper and slowly pronounces a list of words made from the letters of the epistle. "Klein . . . Höhle . . .will . . .willkomen . . . ich hack . . .ah! heimlich . . . in. So, what do we have? 'Welcome to the little hole I hack.' I think we're missing an article."

"What might that mean, Mr. Naughton? More sexual imagery?" Mother Martha is clearly put off but interested.

"Maybe not. Hack is not right. Maybe the writer is claiming to have hacked through the defenses of Maison Cristina."

"Our security here is very tight," says Mother Martha. "We've met all code requirements and more."

"No doubt," says Naughton respectfully. "But maybe the hole is not physical. If an attack fails at the outworks, the assault may turn to an agent within."

Mother Martha hitches back in her chair. "Go on, Mr. Naughton."

Naughton thinks. "We're obviously not thinking of a mole. What about a metaphorical breach? A hole in the psyche, like amnesia."

Mother Martha directs a penetrating gaze at Sister Claire. "What are you thinking, child?"

"A very strange thought, Mother."

"What is it?"

"That the writer will materialize."

"Materialize? What do you mean exactly?"

"That he will come within our walls. Maybe by way of Mr. Naughton."

Naughton is taken aback. "If you mean . . ."

"I don't know exactly what I mean," Sister Claire says. "In one of your stories or visions."

Mother Martha says, "Go on, Sister."

Sister Claire continues to look steadily at Naughton. "We believe Charlene will follow your Wanderer, but we don't know where that leads."

"I don't know either, Sister, but I believe she'll follow Wanderer only as far as it suits her purpose."

After a while Mother Martha says, "We're done for now. We all need to think, think and pray. The Devil may be among us. Finish the story, Mr. Naughton. Sister Claire will report to me."

Naughton goes back to his room. A large white butterfly beats against the outside of his window. A world of air is everywhere around it, but the butterfly beats against the glass. What treasure can it sense within the shadowy enclosure of Naughton's room? Naughton walks to the window and moves his eye close to the glass. The wings of the butterfly expand until the window is filled with an expanse of delicately veined white.

A Presence in the Trees

Dusk has dimmed the golden ranks of the birches. A breeze makes them restless. They move to and fro as if seeking a winning alignment in a board game. "These trees would burn just as hot as the ones you set on fire. Remember the wind? Red embers blew over the top of the hill. Some were still alive when they hit the bay and hissed like snakes. There were no bones to be found among the ashes. We knew that. We watched the officers rake through remnants of our robes and shoes. You were not there to witness your handiwork. You were wrapped in an alcoholic haze not far up the road. One officer said, a bunch of ignorant hippies burning green wood in an open fireplace. What would you expect? An explosion of blistered wood and boiling sap. And the chimney looked like it had never been cleaned. The flue was caked with tar."

The speaker now appears between two ranks of trees, bringing with her a conical ray of mild light whose apex is out of sight above the birches. She wears a long white gown and leather sandals. Black hair falls below her shoulders. A thick rope terminates under her breasts in an intricate series of overlapping knots. "Yes, Peter. I'm a kind of nun." The face, porcelain in its purity, allows a thin smile. "You can't get away from us. Sugary nuns in Rizzo's pamphlets, in love with Julian the anchorite and her famous brown nut, then with Stella your sister nun. But the strangest of all your nuns is the man-woman Vogt. But I was the one you wanted most, my body a scroll of secret characters that would unlock all the mysteries if only you could read them. A gift from the Orient."

The speaker moves to another opening, the light following her faithfully. "I joined a circle. You burned it up. But I have my own circle now."

The speaker moves again, the light with her, the birches still but tense. "In a circle time goes to sleep with her lips apart. You can hear her gentle breathing and catch its fragrance. You can share her dreaming though in the circle each person's dream is different."

The speaker is silent for a while, stoops and laves her face with imaginary water. Then, like a mother herding her flock, she gathers up the remaining burden of her talk. The porcelain of her face is undisturbed. "You believe I know where Alexie is. I don't."

"I don't even know where you are."

"I'm out here in the woods."

"When?"

"That doesn't matter. I'm not where or when I can know where Alexie is. That's the story you have to tell." The speaker sighs. "I don't know where she is. In all of our years together did I ever lie to you? Did I ever tell you I loved you?"

"No."

"Then don't lie to yourself, that you love Alexie. You need to find her. That's as it should be, but it's not because you love her. It's because you need for your stories to come full circle. The story of the wanderer is necessary but it won't bring them full circle."

"I don't want my stories to come full circle."

"What about the one about a woman coming up from the pit? It's your real love story, after many false starts."

A silence follows. The white figure seems still but is moving within herself.

Naughton says, "Vogt saw your step-parents in the Underworld. He knew they never could've produced anything as beautiful as you."

The porcelain face is marked briefly with the etching of a smile. "You never stopped believing I was beautiful, Peter. I had to be, in your story." The speaker pauses. "Did I ever tell you a story?"

"Never. You didn't even follow the story of our lives. You left it."

"Because it wasn't my story. Do you want me to tell you a story?"

"Yes."

"There was a girl child born with a caul over all of her head so that a hole for the nostrils had to be snipped open quick. The caul was made of silvery lace. Cauls, it was known, were woven by witches and given only to royal infants. A caul would be stored in a jar of pure spring water kept fresh with a pinch of salt. The parents showed the child the jar with the net shining in the moonlight. She wanted to wear it like a crown, but they didn't let her. She grew up like any other child in the village until they sent her away. At first she thought maybe they were sending her to a throne in a castle because she was way up in the air. But she came down into a very hot and damp city by a river. She thought maybe they'd taken the caul out of the jar of water and spread it over the whole city. But it was just the air. At first she didn't want to breathe it, but she learned how. She grew up."

"That's it?"

"It's like your stories. They go up and down and end in the dark, still searching."

"Searching for what?"

The speaker lifts the knot of white rope under her breast and drops it, a gesture merely of punctuation perhaps. "Your stories are looking for a name, because the one she has is borrowed."

"What's in a name? The question is what is she?"

"She's one of us nameless who got stitched together. Men think we're secret scrolls. They want to read us."

"I never read you."

"You were busy making up a story about a man and his mysterious beautiful wife Cam and their two brilliant children."

"What were you doing all those twenty years before you opted out of the story?"

"I didn't opt out of the story. The story was like the smoke over the house you burned. It just disappeared."

It's now revealed that the shifting of the birches under the conical light doesn't create a new pattern each time but repeats certain alignments. The speaker again lifts and drops the knots of her cincture. "I'm going now, Peter, but I'll answer your answer. I was watching over Alexie. Josh was safe in his world of facts and numbers. You were living a story. I hated to destroy it, but once Alexie was off to college, my story as mother and wife was finished."

The cone of light now follows the speaker back among the trees. "Good-bye, Peter. I'm happy for you. You have ex-changed marriage vows, story for story, with the one you love, the only one you have ever really loved."

The conical beam dims. The speaker disappears in a fading glimmer of white light.

The scrim descends, this time like a shattered window made of reinforced glass, a thousand pieces, but none of them fall. The figure on the other side seems to be made of many green shards. If it moves its head, lime flecks shift like the sharp-edged platelets of a monochromatic kaleidoscope. "What did I tell you, Sonny? You will never know her. Love, you said. Like it was something everybody knows the meaning of. Love. She never said it. Also your mother, a master word cynic, never said it. The main thing she had in her life was black hair. I admit I can imagine a certain thrill in having that bristly mat come down on you. Very different from my little yellow smoothies. And now you've got yourself another mystery. Is Charlene real, or did all of you nuts and nuns trapped in that weird house dream her up? Did she come up from the grave? Is she a Kraut? OK, she's a more interesting case than Cam, whose name and normal feelings were whacked off at birth. A caul like a crown. Whoever heard of such a thing? And now you've got another one without a real name. But you figure you can get inside and untwist her bony self and see what's down there by telling weird stories." The platelets shift. Head and hands bend across the edges of green. "You might ask why didn't I just stay down in the fog with my green friends. Keep everything simple. But no, I said, I've followed him this far, from womb to tomb as they say. I want to see how this all ends. I know how to dodge Vogt now. He's prowling around my place. Once he caught me unawares and tricked me into talking to him, which I would never do when the two of you were housemates. I couldn't tell for sure from listening to him on the phone whether it was a man or a woman. He won't catch me again. You can smell him a mile off. What about your new girlfriend? You've gotten your nose close. Question is, is she already dead? If she's dead, there's a law against meddling with corpses, you know. I shouldn't have said that. But talking to you, Peter, can sometimes bring out the worst in a person. You also tried to penetrate Cam, but she was technically alive and your wife, so you were at least within the law." The face comes closer. A green eye, sliced in half and misaligned, seems to struggle to reintegrate itself. "Also, there's no law against penetration with weird stories, unless you kill her. Right now the nurse is keeping her alive on soup and crackers. But watch out, Sonny. You already have a criminal record as an arsonist, which would've landed you in jail if it hadn't been for your smart-ass boy Joshua bringing you here. Nuns love crazies. Birds of a feather. An interesting mix. I'm sticking around for the ending, Sonny. This is a house call. Vogt can't answer. And you can't hang up on me."

From the window to the entrance of Maison Cristina the hall seems to narrow rapidly, perspective foreshortened. Charlene is standing in front of the window pointing her walking stick straight down the hall. Vera stands aside. No danger now of Charlene falling. She is wearing her dark gown, which in the light of the window is revealed to be not simply black but a complex color that contains a tincture of mauve. But in the folds of the garment black reigns. Charlene walks up the hall, her gait still showing the lingering stiffness of protracted immobility but now marked by a slow almost regal pace.

As Charlene approaches the three doors leading into the quarters of her fellow residents, Naughton emerges from his room and looks at her, his face revealing an intense expectancy. Charlene walks on without looking at him. Now Ms. Trask appears at her door and quickly takes in the scene. "Whoo! Up from the dead. Where does she think she's going?"

Mr. Gerrity appears strapped into a wheelchair pushed by Sister Kathleen. He hangs over one arm of the chair, his mouth and tongue working vigorously like a dog lapping the wind in the window of a moving car.

Ms. Trask crosses the hall and falls in behind Charlene and Vera. Sister Kathleen pushes the wheelchair across the hall and rolls it along behind Ms. Trask. Naughton walks toward Vera.

"Get in line, Nobody! No breaking in."

Naughton drops back and walks abreast of Sister Kathleen, who says, "This is a queer parade if there ever was one."

"Lularoo!" calls Mr. Gerrity.

Naughton says, "If he can add one more phoneme we'll have a werewolf."

"Werewolves were invented for the Nazi Wehrmacht," says Ms. Trask. "Everybody but Nobody knows that."

Charlene walks on, unperturbed by the talk behind her.

"What do you mean, Mr. Naughton, one more phoneme?"

"You're not familiar with the terrifying loup garou, Sister?"

"No."

"The French, I believe, for werewolf. Mr. Gerrity came very close to hitting upon this term for lycanthropy."

"Ah! In Irish it's the foulad or something like that."

"Very interesting. But the French will be easier for Mr. Gerrity. The p is probably suppressed."

"Nothing is easy for Mr. Gerrity! He's not evolved."

Charlene, approaching the entrance, lifts her four-clawed walking stick and aims it at the brass security bar that goes from wall to wall across doors.

"It's not going to open for her," says Sister Kathleen sotto voce.

The door shudders. The exterior sleeve of the security bar begins to slide away from the interior and then stalls.

"My Lord!" exclaims Sister Kathleen.

"Oolulumu!"

Charlene holds her walking stick in place, but the door remains shut admitting only a thin ray of light, knife-bright even in the well-lit hallway.

Sister Claire emerges from the door that leads to the nuns' quarters. "Did you want to see through the door, Charlene?"

Charlene thrusts her cane forward.

"All right." Sister Claire keys in a code on a pad to the left of the door. Sleeve and interior of the security bar slide apart. The double doors swing slowly open. A shallow portico guides the eye straight down three steps to a path of gunmetal-blue shale pavers, which in turn lead the eye to a plain iron entranceway, ungated, a dozen feet wide and about the same in height, topped by a grilled arch. On either side of the entrance an undulant green lawn runs left and right to a border of widely spaced arbor vitae interspersed among unruly masses of underbrush. Beyond the pavers, through the entire lawn, a path, barely visible, rarely trodden, runs away from the eye, turns and disappears behind a more orderly rank of arbor vitae.

Charlene walks toward the door. The two panels of the door close swiftly together. Charlene turns angrily toward Sister Claire, who says, "It was not me that closed the doors, Charlene. See the two little pillars you have just walked through? They let no one out. Only Mother Martha can deactivate them."

"Lloyd could fix that."

"Then we must take extra care when Lloyd comes, Ms. Trask."

"Loiooo!"

"Lloyd's not going to stick around this looney bin. We'll go straight home."

"That's prudent, Ms. Trask."

Vera moves over and takes Charlene's elbow in her hand. Charlene tries to jerk away, but Vera holds fast. "You and Mr. Naughton made a vow. He is going to finish the story of the wanderer and you are going to tell him your story." Vera's words put an end to Charlene's pulling away. She turns slowly and begins to walk back down the hallway toward the large window at the opposite end, retracing her steps with the same stately gait. Those who have lined up behind her go back to their rooms, except Naughton, who follows Charlene and Vera down the hall. The large window, yellowed with light from without, grows larger and brighter until even the folds of Charlene's gown give up their shadows to a darkling mauve.

Once more in her room Charlene lifts herself onto her bed, but with such a deliberate and supple motion that the bed is made to seem a royal couch. Naughton sits in his accustomed chair. Vera has brought a chair into the room and is sitting near the door. Naughton breathes deeply for a while. "Well, Charlene, what did you think of Sister Claire's pillars?"

"Noo," says Charlene. It's hard to tell whether this is a comment on the pillars or a refusal to speak on the subject.

Vera says, "They are for the safety of the residents."

Naughton nods. "But if you like allusions, you might think of the Pillars of Hercules or the sealed gates east of the Garden of Eden or the Gates of Paradise."

Vera shakes her head but says nothing.

"You might think of them as a weir. You can swim in but not out. Do you remember how you entered, Charlene? No, of course not, and neither do I. One minute I was in my son Josh's car. A long sleepy trip. And then I was looking up at Mother Martha and Sister Claire. A pleasant enough wakening but hard to prepare for." It appears that Naughton might go on with his memories of his arrival at Maison Cristina but he turns aside. "This proves again, Charlene, the advantage of being an eagle. Nobody nets an eagle."

Vera says, "The eagle is St. John, nobody else."

"Wanderer," says Charlene.

Naughton nods. "Where were we? Ah, I remember now. Down in southern California. Salt air tinged with the fragrance of mussels and clams and barnacles. And, of course, this brings back old memories like the object of Wanderer's quest and the high rock with her dead cat. A train of associations well known."

"Not well known," says Charlene.

Vera chuckles.

"Wanderer was searching for his daughter. In the little town, really just a settlement, near the bus stop he found the gallery. Seaby Art was burned deeply into a weathered plank that hung over the open entrance. The gallery was half on solid ground, half perched on stilts buried in a mixture of mud and sand at the far end of a lagoon. Sandpipers darted over water and sand, lit, pecked, flew up suddenly as if caught in disgraceful acts. He showed the gallery owner the Kandinsky. I thought you might come, she said. Angie called from Mendocino.

I was never in Mendocino.

Word gets around. A nut schlepping a Kandinsky from gallery to gallery. The woman's hair was dyed red and teased up to look like flames. You want to see some paintings? They walked around the gallery, which was a kind of warren of nooks and extensions, lathing with plaster bulging out, arty rustic, the floor creaking under their feet. She took him to the sea room. The paintings were all over the map—benign seascapes, turbulent seascapes à la Turner with waterspouts and smoke rising up out of the ocean and ascending to the heavens."

"That would be the Second Coming," says Vera.

"Not yet," says Naughton. "There was a room of flowers, some tastelessly suggestive. A room of human figures, stalwart seamen to lapsing nudes. A room of wood sculptures made from driftwood, the idea being to work the gnarls and the cracks into the human figures, not easy to execute if the artists were to avoid anatomical grotesqueries, which they didn't always succeed in doing. Then finally, the gallery owner having cleverly contrived this delay and climax, the room of abstracts. Wanderer saw a large canvas he knew was painted by the beloved Samantha. There was no background, middle ground or foreground. Everything had already arrived at once, colors melding, muscling each other around, envenoming each other, auto-injecting. Maybe it suggested the oceanic, the march of gray across the bottom of the canvas a rank of castellated sea rock, but the shapes were almost irrelevant. Everything was color and light. A true daughter of Kandinsky, just as she vowed years ago."

"Aus der rabbit hool."

Naughton has to pull himself slowly out of the story. He speaks with a hint of consternation. "Is everything into or out of the rabbit hole, Charlene?"

"On earth," says Charlene. She lifts a hand, which not long ago was crimped like the talons of a dead bird. Now she cups it with the index finger extended in a gesture mixing elegance and command. "Story."

Naughton sinks back into his chair, gathers up his powers, comes forward and resumes.

"Five thousand dollars, said the owner.

Underpriced, said Wanderer.

Then you can pay more.

I will if you can arrange for me to meet the artist.

Can't.

Why?

Artist's instructions.

Wanderer and the owner looked at each other for some moments, a kind of joust of eyes. Don't offer me money, said the owner.

I wouldn't think of anything so offensive. But I've come a long way with many fruitless stops. In my search this gallery will be the center of a circle. I'll work my way out until I find her."

Naughton is in full sail, the story billowing.

"If you make a circle from here you will drown in the Pacific Ocean before you find her.

Then I'll adjust the circle.

A shape with a half-moon cut out of it isn't a circle.

I don't mind what it's called. I have a son who, though not a topographer, could give us a formula if not a name.

The owner nodded disinterestedly. I can point out for you a couple of spots to skip. Merriman has a mastiff. Portman has a rack of rifles and shotguns six feet high. I'll tell you where they are.

I appreciate it. First, can you tell me where I can put up, motel, whatever.

There isn't any motel. The whatever is Mom's Eatery and Hostelry. That's right, Mom's.

Then I guess that's it.

Did you ever eat a leather pancake?

No.

The owner looked Wanderer over. You can stay here unless you're worried about your reputation. But nothing else is included.

I'm not worried. But if I wanted to be insulting I'd ask how business is for you.

You may find it hard to believe, but clients come from some distance. Just yesterday a guy from San Diego came to buy some flowers and beaches. Hotel lobby probably. I don't ask. You'll have to fix your own grub. I'm on a strict diet. Sludge Number 5. Last resort from a diet witch. I don't have a stomach. I can see you're thinking cancer. It could've been cancer or I could've been born without a stomach. I don't remember which. Nobody's memory is perfect."

"Hahaha." Charlene has begun to master a throaty laugh that reserves to herself a superior grasp of the humor of the subject.

"What does it taste like?

It tastes like the color gray, but if you use your imagination you can conjure up clam, or lavender in the spring. I understand you're a literary man.

Ex.

Didn't they used to go around and sing for their supper?

Yes. I couldn't carry a tune in a bucket, but I could recite you a line or two of poetry.

That would be real nice. I'll sit down here, you stand over there and recite.

I'll try not to get stage fright. Wanderer stood and tugged off his backpack, which he had kept on until this moment. He

269

rummaged around and found a book, *Leaves of Grass*. He quickly found the page he was looking for. Ready?

The owner smiled, swallowed up in haphazard cushions that failed to hide the twisted wood of the chair. From flaming hair to veined feet, neckless tie-dye blouse to unhemmed sweats to flipflops, she was spare and angular. Ready.

Wanderer read in a kind of plainsong, undulant, rhythmically irregular.

This is the female form,

A divine nimbus exhales from it from head to foot,

It attracts with fierce undeniable attraction,

I am drawn by its breath as if I were no more than a helpless vapor, all falls aside but myself and it,

Books, art, religion, time, the visible and solid earth, and what was expected of heaven or feared of hell, are now consumed,

Mad filaments, ungovernable shoots play out of it, the response likewise ungovernable,

Hair, bosom, hips, bend of legs, negligent falling hands all diffused, mine too diffused,

Ebb stung by the flow and flow stung by the ebb, love-flesh swelling and deliciously aching,

Limitless limpid jets of love hot and enormous, quivering jelly of love, white-blow and delirious nice . . .

As he finished the recitation Wanderer looked out as if into the distance beyond the head of the owner."

Charlene lifts a cupped hand, the index finger extended as before, wiggling a little.

Vera says, "This is not fit."

Naughton says, "It was written by America's greatest poet."

"That does not mean it is fit." Vera gets up and leaves the room.

Charlene signals peremptorily with her finger.

Naughton goes on. "The owner said, If I thought you were reciting that stuff to me I'd remind you that I said nothing else is included.

Wanderer was away off somewhere, his eyes still fixed on something above the owner's head.

Where are you? asked the owner, bemused, curious.

I was thinking of an old friend, not friend exactly.

What exactly? An old love?

No. A revolutionary. He dreamed that all gender would come to an end.

And then what?

I'm not sure. We would all intermingle in ecstasy, something like that.

Nice but crazy."

Sister Claire comes into the room, Vera close behind. The two have been waiting outside the door. Sister Claire surveys Naughton and Charlene, who scowls crookedly. Sister Claire says, "Vera says that you've come to a good stopping place in your story, so I can have Mr. Naughton for a while. He has his own needs."

Charlene rewards this with studied silence. Naughton rises obediently and departs with Sister Claire.

In her office Sister Claire says, "That was quite a passage the wanderer recited for Celina. A little ripe, maybe overripe, even for Whitman."

"Yes, Emerson advised him to trim his sails." Naughton holds a hand up. "If you're worried about Charlene being exposed to some salacious episode in the wanderer's story, please don't be. I'm sure nothing will transpire between the wanderer and Celina."

"But you say you never know where your stories are going."

"Yes, but I have a sense of their general tenor, and there's nothing like that coming."

"Good." Sister Claire pauses. "I've wondered from the first if Charlene has been the victim of sexual predation."

"So have I, Sister."

"I remember Vogt's claim that he saw Charlene's father in the Underworld, a hideous man with a mensur scar."

"Yes, but I don't know where to go with that."

"Neither do I." A pause. "The cutout message. Vogt's work?"

Naughton shakes his head. "The cutout is light-years from his style."

"That's what I thought." Sister Claire lifts a brow quizzically. "I expect to meet him some time."

"You have already met him through me."

"I mean on my own. By the door to my office or my room. He likes doors."

"Yes. A very liminal devil."

Sister Claire nods peremptorily. "In the meantime we have the wanderer's story, our coin of exchange for Charlene's true story. I assume the wandering will come to an end."

At this moment Ms. Trask appears. She cocks her head plaintively. "Give us a little sunshine, will you Sister?"

Sister Claire says with unusual crispness, "There's sunlight in every window of Maison Cristina, Ms. Trask. It was built that way by design."

Mr. Gerrity rolls up in his wheelchair. He's working his fingers furiously on the shiny rim provided for the occupants' self-locomotion, but in fact he's being pushed by Sister Kathleen, who, the moment she's in sight of Sister Claire and Naughton, shrugs and makes a face of self-acquittal.

"Ssssooon aloo!"

"Another phoneme," says Naughton, "a sibilant and a fierce one at that."

Ms. Trask says, "Mr. Gerrity and I crave sun not through glass. Lloyd could tell you glass robs the rays of half their powers."

Naughton says, "I'm afraid she has a point, Sister. Josh used to lecture me regularly about vitamin D deficiency, insufficient exposure to sunlight."

"Rickets!" cries Ms. Trask.

"Only in children, Ms. Trask," says Naughton, "but in us adults weak hearts."

"Hearts in nobodies!" Ms. Trask hoots. "Or tin men! There's a good one." She pauses to catch her breath. "How about some rays straight from the sun, Sister?"

Sister Claire shakes her head. "I'm surrounded." She and Naughton and the two petitioners, followed closely by Sister Kathleen walk down the hall to the entryway. Sister Claire enters the code on the keypad to the left of the door. The double door parts. A long widening shaft of light lances the hall from the door to the far end, where it gilds the window and paints the greensward and the birches with an aureate glaze, the sun above the peaks of the arbor vitae at the end of the lawn mixing blood red and gold in a slow swirl.

A figure appears on the walk. Backlighted, sharply silhouetted, it appears to be a Chirico-like cutout of a man, its ink-black shadow thrown askance onto the lawn five times as tall as the figure itself. Nowhere is there texture, the sun having flattened all into twin monochromes of black and green-gold. Presently an arm and hand move stiffly until at last the hand touches and lifts a black hat from the cutout's head, which is also black above a face that is featureless.

"Lloyd!"

The silhouette returns hat to head and turns slowly until it's barely a slice of black, which widens as it continues to turn until it appears much as before, only backside now. Then it begins to move away from Maison Cristina down the path toward the arbor vitae. A waggle in the legs and bobble of the head signal that the figure is walking as it diminishes in size, its shadow following but sliding slowly to the other side of the path, responding, it would seem, not to the sun but to another powerful mobile light not visible to the watchers, who remain motionless inside the house.

"Lloyd!" There is nothing mournful or desperate in the cry. If anything, it's an almost ecstatic cry of recognition.

"Loo Loo!"

In a matter of moments the sun, pierced by the spires of arbor vitae, begins to relinquish its dominance of earth. The alternate light, from whatever source, also dims. The cutout, diminished in size, deprived of light, loses its sharpness. Soon all that is left is the shadow, which performs an antic zigzag contraction and fades out.

Charlene has come to the door, Vera by her side. She points her walking cane toward the door. "No!"

Sister Claire activates the keypad and closes the doors.

"Too late, Sister! Lloyd's onto this place now."

Sister Claire, her voice steady, says, "Ms. Trask, please return to your room. I'll come to you later. Sister Kathleen, take Mr. Gerrity to his room."

"Rhum!" The r with an impressive ruction in the throat.

Ms. Trask turns to go down the hall. "Got a motor in his throat now. Gerrity's idea of evolution."

"Come along, Ms. Trask," says Sister Kathleen.

Vera steers Charlene away from the door, against a resistance that is surprisingly unenergetic.

Moments later Sister Claire asks Naughton, "Do you believe in the Devil, Mr. Naughton?"

Naughton speaks as one under painful compulsion. "I don't really believe in much of anything, Sister."

"What can that mean?" asks Sister Claire in a tone of exasperation.

Naughton lowers his head apologetically. "I mean when I leave this office in a moment I believe I will probably step onto the hard tiles of the hall, but I'm never sure. It could be the edge of a cliff."

"The world is not as insubstantial as you'd like to imagine, Mr. Naughton, but in your mind the cliff is never far away, is it?" Sister Claire shakes her head. "We'll come back to that. But now, what do you think that was?" In voice and face Sister Claire begins to reveal a deep consternation.

"A hologram maybe."

"How would that work?"

"Josh could tell you in detail. Something to do with diffracting light from an object and projecting it elsewhere."

"Who does it?"

"The holographer, whoever."

"Where does he do it from?"

"Out of sight, so he doesn't ruin the illusion of the reality of the object."

"The figure never looked real."

Naughton nods dolefully. "No, it didn't."

"What could be the point of projecting an unreal object?"

"For this, Sister, your stories are better than mine. The Tempter in the desert, master of the unreal. The point? Damnation, isn't it?"

"Are we sure this isn't Vogt's doing?"

Naughton nods. "Yes. The sowing of mere confusion wouldn't be like him. If he were going to put on a show, it would more likely be a panorama of a world outside the normal imperatives of space and time."

Sister Claire, who has throughout this exchange been leaning toward Naughton, now pitches back in her chair in profound vexation. "I have to report this to Mother Martha. What am I to say?"

The question is so charged that Naughton cannot escape its force. He encloses the fist of one hand in the clutch of the other and breathes deeply. "You can tell her that five of us saw some kind of apparition, created by the lights and shadows of sunset."

"If I stopped there, I would be withholding the full impact. I can't do that." Sister Claire doesn't wait for a response, but suddenly gets up from her chair. "Five of us. Yes." She leaves the room and in a short time returns with Sister Kathleen. "Sister Kathleen is here to tell us what she saw. Sit down Sister."

"I'd rather stand for now. I don't know why."

"As you wish."

"What did I see? I saw a queer little manikin all in black with a long shadow on the pathway to our house. He walked away into the sunset."

"What was queer about him?"

"He was all one piece like a cardboard doll. He didn't move naturally. And his shadow wagged like the tail of a dog."

"Who do you think he was?"

"I don't know that there was any who to him, Sister."

"Whatever it was, what do you feel about it?"

"It made me feel that something unholy had come onto our grounds. But the minute I saw it I knew Ms. Trask would insist it was Lloyd."

"Do you think it could be a version of somebody we know?"

"I told you, Sister, I don't think it was human." Sister Kathleen sighs impatiently.

"I'm sorry to have pressed you so hard."

"I understand, Sister. It's a hard matter. Not to know what a thing like that is. What does Mr. Naughton have to say?"

"He thinks it may have been a projection, an optical illusion."

"Where does he think it came from? Because it wasn't a natural trick of the eye."

"Maybe somebody contrived it. Is that right, Mr. Naughton?"

"Yes."

"Then I'd like to have a word with that somebody. I'll never quiet Ms. Trask down. And Mr. Gerrity's already infected."

"What do you mean by that, Sister?"

"He used to hoot at her. Now he listens to everything she says and tries to imitate her words. And she eggs him on, talking about his evolution."

The three of them remain silent for some moments. Finally Sister Claire says, "I'll need both of you to be with me when I report this to Mother Martha tomorrow."

Neither demurs.

"And we." Charlene stands in the doorway, Vera beside her.

Sister Claire, startled into silence for a moment, at last says, "Come in."

Sister Kathleen moves aside. Naughton gets up to relinquish his chair, but it's not necessary. There are enough chairs for five. Still, Vera, like Sister Kathleen, stands.

Sister Claire says, "Vera, were you and Charlene close enough to see the figure?"

Charlene nods peremptorily, a snap of her head. Vera says, "We came up before you closed the doors and the thing disappeared in the sun."

"What did you make of it?"

"Nichts," says Charlene, holding up a finger. The finger has assumed a remarkable range: Listen! Do as I say! Mark this well.

"Not Old Nick!" hollers Ms. Trask, pushing Mr. Gerrity into Sister Claire's office. "Lloyd."

"Nooolorrr!"

"Lloyd's collapstable hat." Ms. Trask holds her hands apart and brings them together with a loud clap. "Sharp as a butcher's knife." She curls her hand back and flings it forward as if launching a frisbee. "Whish! One time an undesirable came to the door, wouldn't leave. Lloyd backed him down to the sidewalk. Then!" Ms. Trask gives another flick of her wrist. "Off with his head clean as a slice of baloney. Slisht!"

Charlene, now in possession of an ever enlarging repertory of expressiveness, laughs a gusty laugh. "Schnitte! you mean."

Naughton, preempting a response from Ms. Trask, says, "You father taught you a number of German words."

"Father? I have no father." Charlene speaks matter-of-factly.

"Well, biologically speaking, Charlene, everybody has a father. But I suppose you're speaking of a different kind of father."

"Once you, but not." The eloquent finger flicks Naughton away.

Sister Claire says, "You have a father in heaven."

"Heaven?" Charlene does not speak mockingly.

"Not a place exactly but a condition that is promised to all of us."

Charlene turns from Sister Claire to Naughton.

"Remember story," says Charlene, pointing an uncrooked finger directly at Naughton. "Wanderer. Auf Deutsch."

"Der Vanderer," says Naughton.

"Gut, Vater." Charlene laughs a laugh that hovers at the edge of derision, turns away, and begins to walk back down the hall. Vera follows.

Sister Claire breathes deeply. "I think we may part now. Remember everything you can about the figure. Mother Martha will want to hear full details."

A Scientist at Maison Cristina

Naughton tries shutting his eyes, lowering a curtain of black membrane over the entrance to the optic nerve, but the manikin keeps walking toward him. He can't make it go back down the path. He opens his eyes and looks at the wall. Josh appears. He's wearing a long white lab jacket, black hair slicked back, a monocle on his left eye. "Greetings, Dad."

"Oh for Christ's sake, Josh, what kind of get-up is this?"

"Science. Pure and applied. At your service."

"I don't need your services."

"You need them more than ever."

Josh is standing in a small yard delineated by waist-high shrubs, boxwood maybe. A small wooden object stands behind him, half obscured by his body.

"Where are you?"

"Just outside the window of Sister Claire's quarters."

"And what scientific enterprise are you pursuing there?"

"Measurements. My monocle is calibrated. I can tell you that Sister Claire is almost perfectly proportioned for a woman of fifty-three years. I'll use inches since you're unconverted. Sixty-five inches tall, waist twenty-nine, shoulder forty-five.

Breasts firm for her age. A little dry below, as expected after menopause."

"What makes you think I want to hear this?"

"I thought, given your closeness to the good Sister, you'd want to be informed of facts not easily ascertainable by you personally. Anyway, regarding that last observation, I've left a small tube of lubricant on her desk, Angel's Touch is the brand, zinc based." Josh steps aside so that the wooden object behind him is now fully visible to Naughton.

"It's not a desk, it's a prie-dieu."

"Ah. I should've known. Note the scrolls on the side pieces. Do they remind you of anything?"

"Nothing in particular. Scrolls are very common."

"They remind me of the scrolls on the front board of Aunt Stella's piano before it was sold into less holy hands. But you're right. Scrolls are everywhere. Why do you think that is?"

"You know what, Josh. As you used to say, there's a lot of heavy stuff coming down here. I appreciate your visit and the measurements, but I need to concentrate my mind elsewhere. Would a postponement be possible?"

"No. The timing of these various visits you're having has to be propitious. Let's pursue the matter of scrolls. Quite a history—Egyptian accounts of sun gods, the Torah, Dead Sea Scrolls. You know this stuff better than I do. You could be making a scroll of *Leaves of Grass* in your spare time here. There're a number of outfits that make paper from grass. Yours would be unique. Black ink, of course, with just a hint of red. The fragrance might take you back to the good old days at Rizzo's shop. But the question we're addressing is why the fascination with scrolls?"

"Am I supposed to answer that, or do you want to go on with your dissertation?"

"I'd be interested in your answer."

"OK. Because in the early days of writing there weren't books. There were long sheets of papyrus which Chinese scholars didn't want to drag behind them like dragon tails so they rolled them up in scrolls."

"Of course, but why the persistence of scrolls today, on temples, piano legs, silverware, sorority pins, wedding invitations and the like?"

"A species of gauche antiquarianism."

"Go deeper."

"I might say an image of the metaphysical complexity of the universe."

"Get rid of metaphysical and universe and you might be close. Science is discovering that we image not just the objects around us but also our interior attributes like, say, the involuted coils of the brain."

"Watch out, Josh. You're drifting toward art."

"Art is not a scientific term, but the things produced in its name are amenable to scientific investigation. But more to the point, I have observations about what you call the heavy stuff coming down here."

"Like what?"

"Like the fact that your theory of a holograph for the little black man on the path won't hold water."

"Why?"

"Too many technical improbabilities—distance, electricity, installation of equipment, just for starters."

"You have another theory?"

"Hysteria."

"Five people all becoming hysterical at once and all sharing the same image? Now who's being improbable."

"There's nothing improbable about a group of people becoming hysterical at once. Hysteria is contagious. And anyway, they didn't all share the same hallucination. You and Sister Claire perceived that the figure was, however queer, animate. Sister Kathleen saw a paper doll. Ms. Trask saw her beloved Lloyd with his guillotine-sharp hat. Mr. Gerrity is likely to have been guided by Ms. Trask. Charlene saw her father or quite possibly saw that the rest of you were deluded."

"Why just at that moment and all of us together?"

"Simultaneity in science is explained by quantum entanglement, particles separated in space acting alike. We could analogize that principle to the common experience among you of the little cardboard man."

"You're saying that though we were separated we all perceived something in common."

"Yes."

"Why?"

"Some force has to be adduced. Then the seemingly unconnected consciousnesses enact a simultaneous illusion."

"What is the force in this case?"

"You really don't know? Guess."

"Give me a hint."

"What is the one thing here that most occupies everybody's attention?"

"Charlene?"

"Charlene and the weird stories you're telling her. Approved by Vogt, but let's come back to him later."

Naughton cups a hand over a fist and places them under his chin. "Weird, you say."

"Weird and dark. Fatal falls, ingestion by sea serpents, murder, arson, werewolves and now the manic wanderer. Dark stuff."

"What's the scientific definition of darkness?"

"There is no such thing as darkness per se. It's the vulgar term for the absence of light. There is only light and no light, though I might add it's virtually impossible to create a space in which there is absolutely no light." The monocle drops from Josh's eye. Unattached to a string, it falls from sight below the window of Naughton's room.

"There you have it, Josh. The absolute divide between science and reality. Here's the Bhagavad Gita: 'In the night of all beings, the wise man sees only the radiance of the Self; but the sense world where all beings awake, for him is as dark as night.' What's the scientific definition of Self?"

"There isn't one in the absolute sense you mean. But back to Charlene. Do you think you're restoring her Self?"

"What you said. I tell her dark stories."

"Still, she needs a story that restores her. Do you think Wanderer's story is going to end in a restorative darkness?"

"I never know the end of the story. That would be a falsification of the role of the storyteller."

"Good science. A proven datum is no longer a hypothesis to be tested. Here's a hypothesis. The meeting of the wanderer with Samantha, alias Alexie, will not be sufficient for her restored health."

Naughton responds with alacrity. "Do you know something about Alexie that you aren't telling me?"

"I know that your Wanderer is geographically close to her."

"How do you know?"

"An art prof at my U mentioned something about a southern California artist that rang a bell, but when I tried to follow up with him he didn't know any more."

"The wanderer has to keep looking."

"He's in a dangerous part of the world, Dad. Armed nationalists, snakes, soupy wetlands. And you're not in great shape. You've lost a lot of weight. Your color's not good. Do you even have a compass to find your way out and back on your forays?"

"No. Wanderers don't use compasses."

"What I figured." Josh goes on, unsmiling. "Why don't you call up your friend Vogt. He's got coordinates on everybody living and dead. Well, not dead since there's nobody dead in his universe."

"Do you think there're alternate universes?"

"No. They aren't necessary to explain anything we don't know."

"Not necessary but how about useful?"

"At the moment all plausible hypotheses can be constructed without positing alternate universes. But I admit the question is not closed."

"Do you believe in Vogt?"

"You mean that he exists? Of course. Mom mentioned him once. And he came to our house in Bellingham."

"I don't remember any such thing."

"He didn't come to the house. He stayed up on the ridge by the madrones, swinging on them like some kind of weird clown. It scared Alexie and me. Anyway, why not call on him."

"I don't call on him. He says I do, but he comes when he wants. And besides, what good would coordinates do if I'm out in the middle of nowhere?"

"That's what they're for, but you have to plot them on a GPS."

"Wanderers don't have GPSs. Anyway I think you're farting around with me, saying stuff you don't believe, which is a form of filial betrayal."

"It's not. I know you have to go your own way."

Naughton nods and then after a pause says, "Suppose Wanderer finds Samantha. You have a message for her?"

Josh thinks about that. "Tell her to just keep doing her thing."

The scrim comes down, opaque. A young man stands in the foreground facing Naughton. Black hair piled up on top of his head, cascading down onto his shoulders. Black beard, crudely cut. Eyes dark. Around his neck a string of seashells. He wears a tank top tie-dyed so that a sunstar from some other galaxy radiates from his solar plexus. Jeans cut off raggedly at the knees. Sun-darkened skin. He begins to sing, accompanied by an electric guitar and a drum. Dylan-like, "You ain't got to be nothing, babe, but what you are, cause all them others are what they ain't . . ."

The young man snaps his fingers and moves his torso with a practiced insouciance. The song goes on for another verse, fades. The scrim gives up its opacity and with it the image of the young man. Only the wall remains.

Naughton sits uneasily in a chair facing Sister Claire, who says, "He's been back."

After a pause Naughton says almost absently, "I'm not terribly surprised."

"You're not with me. He's been back. Where are you?" Sister Claire's agitation cannot be disguised.

"I'm in southern California. I have an intuition of a painting of the beginning."

"Beginning of what?"

"The beginning when everything crawled out of the dark."

"From Wanderer's story."

"Yes."

"How does it apply to the figure on the path? Do you know how disturbing this is? I've summoned everybody to report to Mother Martha in a few minutes, about the first appearance, and now there's another."

"She knows nothing about all this?"

"Just the first appearance. I've given her the gist of it."

"But no explanation?"

"No."

"That's good because any explanation is a thicket."

"Mother Martha will dive into the thicket whether I offer an explanation or not. She has conferred with Father Schneider. She wants to question each witness separately."

Naughton shakes his head sadly. "Then so be it. But this second occurrence. Who saw it other than you?"

"Nobody."

"What did he do?"

"He smashed his hat flat, just as Ms. Trask described, and threw toward me. I tried to close the doors, but they're slow, as you know. It slipped through with a silvery whirling and flew down the hall. I don't know where it landed."

Mother Martha arrives and seats herself firmly across from Sister Claire's desk. "We're to have a hearing," says Mother Martha in a juridical tone of voice. "The sighting of an uncanny figure has been reported. The question before us—is the figure physically real, or the product of a shared psychological aberration? I will question each of the witnesses separately except for the two of you. Also, you will be present during the testimony of the others." Mother Martha pauses only briefly. "Sister Claire, on the occasion of the sighting you and Mr. Naughton were together."

"Yes."

"You report you saw a diminished black figure in the shape of a man on the path to the entrance. After a while he doffed his hat and then walked down the path toward the arbor vitae, where he was lost to view in the sunset. His shadow was long and did not follow the laws of optics. Is that how you have described the incident?"

"Yes, Mother."

"Mr. Naughton, did you observe that the figure was flat and cardboard-like?"

"Yes. That was revealed when he turned."

"Did you comment on this to Sister Claire at the time?"

Naughton thinks for a moment. "I don't think so. I think I assumed we saw the same thing."

"Is it true that you and Sister Claire have shared other visions that come to you?"

"Yes."

"You may be surprised to hear that I do not ask how you share. Father Schneider suspects demonic traffic. He would be with us today, but he's conducting a retreat at Saint Gervais. I am postponing this aspect of the inquiry for now." It's clear that Mother Martha has prepared her questioning well. She keeps it precise, but a hint of aversion creeps into her voice.

"Would you, Sister, put the appearance of the little black visitor in the same class as other of Mr. Naughton's visitors? Or is it possible that this could be a collaborative invention?"

"The visitor was different. We simply saw it simultaneously. That's all."

Mother Martha addresses Naughton, her tone insistent. "Surely mere simultaneity cannot explain anything to a master storyteller. Tell us the story of this apparition."

"No offense, Mother, but my stories are compelled by Charlene and by no one else." Naughton tilts his head. "Of course, I could spin a yarn about the manikin coming stealthily to the other end of the building, slipping past Vera, appearing in the window of Charlene's room or in her dreams. And so on. But it would be ill told and have none of the spontaneity of my stories for Charlene."

"Never mind spontaneity. Is the story you are now telling Charlene about a wanderer in search of a lost daughter authentic?"

"I believe it is, but I couldn't tell you why, Mother."

"Vera believes it will be your last story. Do you agree?"

"Yes, probably."

"Back to the manikin. Do you think we can expect more visits from this creature?"

"No."

"Why is that?"

"Because I believe Charlene has dismissed the manikin."

"Has she also dismissed the composer of the cutout? You say the figure was himself a sort of cutout. Are they the same?" The staccato of Mother Martha's questions is relentless.

Naughton takes a while to answer. "I think not the same, Mother, but of the same matrix if that makes any sense."

Mother Martha gives Naughton a long look, then turns to Sister Claire. "Sister, please ask Sister Kathleen to come to us."

Sister Kathleen seats herself with admirable composure.

Mother Martha says, "We won't ask you to recount again what you saw the afternoon of the manikin's visit unless you've thought of some detail you haven't yet shared with Sister Claire."

"I don't think of any, Mother."

"Then tell us what you think you saw."

"I've thought of that, but I hardly know where to go with it. The idea of a demon came to mind."

"Do you believe in demons, Sister?"

Sister Kathleen smiles. "Are you putting me to the test, Mother? There're demons in the Bible."

"Of course, but skeptics have argued they're really metaphors for mental illness."

"Have the skeptics ever seen a great herd of swine dashing out of a psychiatrist's office and plunging into the sea?"

Mother Martha smiles. "The demons you cite invaded the body of a self-lacerating wretch, but the manikin had no such occupants as far as we know."

"That's true, Mother, but I suppose demons come in many forms, as they did in the Bible. In Ireland my favorite is the Banshee because my grandmother used to say when I got very angry I screamed like a Banshee."

"You think the manikin might be an Irish demon?"

"Oh not at all, Mother. He was something of a dandy doffing his hat and pivoting on his feet like a Beefeater. I'd say he was British. But I don't know if there ever were any Anglo-Saxon demons. Were there, Mr. Naughton?"

"There was Grendel, a monster really, rather than a demon."

Sister Kathleen says, "Maybe he's just a little cardboard imperialist then."

"And what about the hat compacted into a lethal discus?"

"A gift from Ms. Trask."

"Well then," says Mother Martha, "why don't you bring Ms. Trask here."

Sister Kathleen shepherds Ms. Trask into the room rather forcefully, there having been apparently some resistance. Ms. Trask stands leaning defiantly on a cane, two hands on the handle. The cane is of carved wood, the handle a natural twist in a stout branch. She's obdurately quiet and stiff.

Mother Martha says, "Have we seen your cane before, Ms. Trask? It's handsome indeed."

"Lloyd carved it out of pignut hickory, same wood as Chinagook made his bows and arrows out of, nothing like the yellow scrap wood you got out back."

"A noble shaft indeed, Ms. Trask, and one about which I'm sure you might tell us many tales, but . . ."

"Tales is Mr. Nobody's thing. This cane is because Miss Black down the hall has got her claw-footed walking stick and is pointing it at everybody. She won't get past this." Ms. Trask waves her cane threateningly.

"I'm sure you're safe, Ms. Trask. But just now we've been talking about the appearance of the black-suited man on the front path."

"Lloyd, you mean?"

"From what you've said recently of Lloyd we had in mind a more stately gentleman."

"The more to bumfuzzle the jailors."

"You can't mean the good sisters, Vera and me."

"What they say, if the shoe fits wear it." Ms. Trask cackles. "Lloyd wears black shoes high polished. Didn't you notice? In the Navy the officers had stewards to spit polish their shoes. But Lloyd wouldn't put them to it. Lloyd never put on airs."

"But it seems he could put on a disguise."

"For a house of crazies deviosity is necessary."

"Which made us wonder if you yourself have learned from him the art of deviosity and disguise."

"How could you disguise yourself with a nun poking in your room every minute?"

"I'm surprised to hear you refer to your good friend Sister Kathleen that way."

"I got nothing against the Irish. Lloyd never spoke unfavorable about the Irish—Micks, Paddies, Bog-trotters and the like. If Sister Kathleen were just a gal in the neighborhood, I'd call her Red. But here I respect the propers even detained against my will." Ms. Trask snaps her head. "Wait a minute. Disguise you said. What's that all about?"

Mother Martha nods weightily. "I must tell you, we have no record of admitting a Ms. Trask."

Ms. Trask crows and points her cane at the nun. "Then hand me the keys, Mother, and I'll be moving on."

"To whom should we say we're handing the keys?"

"Pick a name, Mother. Smith, Jones or if you like colors, Brown, Green."

"The name has to match the one on the admission papers."

"Fine. Give me the name and I'll wear it out the door."

Mother Martha gives Ms. Trask a shrewd look. "It would be irresponsible, and we might fall under the law, if we discharged a person who doesn't know her name."

"Well then, Mother, either you can give me the name or Lloyd will have to break in. And then there won't be any stopping him. He'll let everybody out of here like Bastille no matter what name they have. Mr. Nobody'll disappear whether he's somebody else or not. And Miss Black by whatever name you gave her will go off into the night, inky dinky parlay voos. And Gerrity can be sold to a zoologist."

"A primatologist," says Naughton.

"You don't need a home, Nobody. They can just cut a hole in a dictionary and let you worm your way in."

At this moment Mr. Gerrity wheels himself into the room, chair bumping against the wall and Ms. Trask at the same time.

"Oh dear," exclaims Sister Kathleen. "I thought I'd locked the wheels."

Ms. Trask laughs raucously. "The old geezer has invented the wheel all over again. Evolution!"

Sister Kathleen pushes the wheelchair against the wall and steps hard on the brakes of both wheels.

Mother Martha smiles at Mr. Gerrity. "What have you come to tell us, Mr. Gerrity?"

Mr. Gerrity holds up the iron triangle he's taken from his exercise bar. It has until that moment been hidden under the folds of his robe. He looks through it at Mother Martha. "Loolooshsh." The sibilants are harsh.

"You're frightening me, Mr. Gerrity."

Mr. Gerrity now looks through his iron squint at Ms. Trask and then back at Mother Martha and then back. It seems that the alternation may never end.

Mother Martha says, "I take your meaning, Mr. Gerrity. I must help Ms. Trask, by whatever name."

"I'm Ms. Trask and nobody else. I don't care what the papers say. Lloyd is onto this place and knows where they are. He's not coming to tip his hat next time." Ms. Trask takes a deep breath of exasperation. "Names! It doesn't matter who Gerrity really is because he's too far down the chain to be named. And Mr. Nobody is not nobody else. Who cares? As for the lady in black, you're going to have to rename her because Charlene sounds like a dessert, which she's not."

Mother Martha says, "What would you name her, Ms. Trask?"

"You could try Beth, rhymes with death, but it wouldn't stick because she's coming on."

"What do you mean coming on, Ms. Trask?"

"If you don't know when somebody's coming on, I can't help you." Ms. Trask cocks her head shrewdly. "The story oft is told of old, the kidnapped learn to love their hole."

Mother Martha nods stoically. "Let's come to an end, even if only temporary. Let's agree that what we have seen is a shared hallucination and let it have no effect on our conduct here."

"Nooo!" Mr. Gerrity pivots his triangle around an imaginary axle.

Ms. Trask chuckles. "He isn't as dumb as you think. Also when you find Lloyd's hat, notice the band of little beads. They help with the rotation. Advertisement! Handle with care, as the French say."

In Charlene's room Naughton finds that she has mastered a new posture. She lies on her side, head held up in her hand, elbow crooked below. The bed's coverlets have been rolled down so that her bare legs are visible below the hem of her nightgown. Before Naughton has a chance to comment, she says, "Story. Woman with head on fire."

Naughton says, "Actually for a while we're going to part company with the owner."

"Name."

"Celina, self-named. Only eight in ten thousand women in America are named Celina, she said. I didn't want any lookalikes. She pointed Wanderer toward the one store in the settlement. Used to be called the country store in the old days, she said, firearms forbidden."

"Name."

"Lager House. Celina said the current owner inherited the place from his father, a German who got run out of town during World War Two, swastika on the lawn, that kind of thing. Peaceful out here now. So Wanderer went to the store because Celina had nothing in the house but Sludge."

Charlene, propped up on her elbow, smiles ingenue-like. "Gray or lavender."

Vera says, "You ought to cover yourself, Charlene. You will catch cold." She moves to pull the covers up, but Charlene shoos her away.

"Right. Gray or lavender or clam. Wanderer went to the Lager House, climbing up the stairs staying close to the handrail because the treads were suspiciously bowed. The sound of a raspy electric glockenspiel announced his crossing of the threshold. Inside he was greeted by the owner, a squat little man with a pointy hat and a leather skirt. A figurine from the Munich Town Hall clock. What can I do for you today, sir? No accent. Wanderer loaded up his backpack with bread, cheese, Thuringer and bottled water. He bought beer. The owner said, it's illegal to drink the beer on the premises.

Where do the premises end?

At the tip of your nose.

Wanderer drank thirstily, paid and left. Back at the Seaby he unloaded his backpack except for a few items for the day's search. Nothing but imperishables, he told Celina.

You're what's perishable, she said. A few inches south of here are Baja bandits, a few inches east a desert microecology, finger of the Sonora. Everything is protected—jackrabbits, kangaroo rats, roadrunners, rattlers, prickly pears, scorpions. Between here and anywhere you're likely to get to are about four palo verde trees, all the shade there is, a skeleton under each one. Before you die out there you might have a chance to see a flock of Harris Hawks hunting down a rabbit like a pack of wolves. Just hope the rabbit doesn't run your way.

I'll find my way back.

Right. Just follow the sun late in the day. You'll come to the ocean. But remember not to drink from it.

Wanderer decided to go north, not because of Celina's description of desert hazards but because he figured Samantha would want to stay near the water and the few rocky outcroppings just east of the beach. But as he passed near the Lager House he spotted the young man of the scrim coming out. He decided to follow him."

"Scrim?" says Charlene.

"It's a word I use for dreams I have, see-through dreams."

"I have them too."

"Will they be in your story?"

"Yes."

"The young man was unmistakably the one in the dream, tie-dye tank top, shell necklace, ragged jeans, floppy hat wide as a sombrero. Wanderer kept a good distance behind the young man and readied himself to flop down on the sand if the young man turned. The young man, determined to reach his destination with his backpack of goods, kept straight ahead. The sand made for silent footing. A warm downdraft of desert air muted what little noise Wanderer made.

The sharp crack of a rifle came from Wanderer's right. The sonic trace of the bullet sliced the hot air.

Fuck you, Portman! shouted the young man. But Wanderer wondered if the shot was a warning for him."

Vera says, "Mr. Naughton, there are ways to indicate bad language."

"Right, Vera."

Charlene in her new role of youthful nonchalance betrays neither pleasure nor disturbance, supremely relaxed in a posture that might last forever, congealed into a Goyaesque maja vestida. But the eyes are not Goya's languid eroticism. Instead, a half-hidden avidity shines bright in the obsidian of her eyes.

"Suddenly a small animal ran across Wanderer's path. A wild scene ensued. A kangaroo rat leapt high in the air. A snake had struck. The rat kicked. The snake fell back, repelled. The two animals went their separate ways. Wanderer walked on, but shaken. He looked up. The young man was barely in sight. The light was fading." Naughton's voice cracks.

Vera says, "Would you like some water, Mr. Naughton?"

"That would be nice, thanks."

Vera goes into Charlene's bathroom and brings out a plastic glass with water. Charlene says, "Why didn't Wanderer bring water?"

"He did, in a canteen in his backpack, but the young man was walking so fast he didn't have time to drink any." Naughton downs a plenteous gulp of water and makes a theatrical hawing of satisfaction.

Charlene smiles. "Was it a rattlesnake?"

"I think it must've been. Wanderer broke into a trot to keep up. Fortunately, the young man's tank top remained visible in the gloaming. But then a strange thing happened. The young man seemed to be ascending into the sky. Wanderer shook his head violently, rubbed his eyes, slapped his face, wake-up things he'd read in books or seen in movies. The young man kept ascending in a snake-like pattern, curving left, right, but always up. Wanderer pushed forward over a growing fear that threatened to paralyze him. The young man, keeping to his sinuous path, climbed higher and higher. Wanderer perceived that the sky into which the young man was ascending was darker than the surrounding dusk. That told him the young man wasn't ascending into the air but climbing something solid. But what steep solid thing could be out in the middle of the desert? Now the young man stopped climbing and disappeared. Had he gone down the other side of whatever the thing was?

Wanderer, gathering up his slack courage, hastened on. At last he saw what the young man had climbed. A berm five or six times his height. Some structure was on top of it. Nightjars began to fly around, luring Wanderer's eyes into their swift orbits. He stood and waited for a sound, which soon came, but first came a wavering yellow light in an opening in the structure on top of the berm. The light came forward. He saw that the structure on top of the berm had the rough outlines of a geodome. The light-bearer was a woman. She doused the light. A guitar sounded. A male voice began a song. The woman joined in. Wanderer could catch only fragments. Here comes the sandman . . . don't give him yo hand . . . When the wind blows the sand in yo eye . . . don't give him . . . There was laughter. The two went inside.

Wanderer moved up to the base of the berm, touched it gingerly, pressed his finger against it." Naughton prods the air carefully with a finger. "You could do this better, Charlene."

Charlene obliges, thrusting the imperious finger against an unknown mass.

"Exactly," says Naughton. "What did Wanderer discover? A mixture of sand, silt and decayed vegetation pressed into a dense thatching baked by desert sun. Wanderer smelled his finger. Redolence of the sea. His mind went whirling. Did the builder of the berm dig deep under the desert sand and find a postdiluvian deposit of rich mud? Did he train shore birds by the thousands to fly from the lagoon to the growing berm, dropping from beaks and claws fragments of their habitat? The mysterious matter of the berm created in him a mixture of reverence and dread. He heard from above an ecstatic cry. Not of a maiden breached, he thought, but of a warrior woman crushing the flanks of her man between her thighs."

"Mr. Naughton."

Naughton holds up a hand, suing for forbearance. "What should Wanderer do? Even if he could follow the young man's circuitous path up the side of the berm, what would he do at the top? Announce himself as the long-absent father come to reclaim his paternity? What reception could he expect? He found a slight depression at the base of the berm and like an old dog scratched and burrowed until he had a place to sleep. He took from his backpack the canteen of water and drank. He didn't open his cheese or cured meat for fear the smell of them would lure predators. He tucked his pants into his boots, slid his hands up into his sleeves. But he imagined rattlers and scorpions readying themselves for a nocturnal feast. How would he protect himself? Eventually exhaustion from the day's rigors brought him sleep."

"That's a good place to rest before finishing the story, Mr. Naughton." It's Sister Claire.

Naughton smiles. "I thought I heard you listening, Sister. Well, there's not a great deal left, I don't think."

"Nevertheless, let's pause here. I would like to have a word with you in my office."

Charlene says, "Vera and I can play a guessing game of the end."

Vera shakes her head. "Not me, Charlene. I never know which way Mr. Naughton's stories will go."

Charlene says, "God is not at the top."

"God is everywhere," says Sister Claire.

"This top is not in everywhere." Charlene maintains her languid posture, but her eyes brighten.

Sister Claire says, "If you mean the top of the berm is only in a story being told by Mr. Naughton, God is still there, in the words."

In her office Sister Claire says to Naughton, "I took a stroll down the front walk, the first time in years. It was instructive. You remember that at the far end the path turns and disappears behind the arbor vitae into a dark wooded area. You remember in your youth not taking a path into the woods."

"Not taking a path into the woods?" Naughton thinks. "Yes. And I, Doc Logos, quoted Dante to my classmates. But I don't remember now exactly how it goes."

"I'll read it to you." Sister Claire opens a copy of *The Divine Comedy*.

"Halfway through the journey of life
I found myself in a dark wood.
The path that led straight was lost.
Oh how hard it is to say how
wild and forbidding this woodland was.
The very thought of it makes me fearful.

"But he makes himself enter. Why?"

"Because he has to," says Naughton without hesitation.

"Why?"

"So he can get to the other side of darkening life."

"But you didn't at the lake. And neither of us did here. We just stood and watched the little man, whatever he was, disappear into the trees."

Naughton pauses. "I was hoping you would tell me that this time you walked all the way to the end and took the turn into the woods."

"I would've had to go back to the middle of my life, which is past."

"Where is the past?"

"Where is the past?" Sister Claire thinks. "It's somewhere. You couldn't tell Charlene stories without it."

"I make them up."

"Yes, from your imagination and scraps of memory. Only God can make something ex nihilo."

"Are we sure there was ever a nihilo? But finish telling me about your walk."

"I want you to listen carefully and say something when I'm finished." Sister Claire speaks with intensity. "The first thing I noticed was the tilting slates and the pleated gravel under my feet as if some burrowing creature was coming up from below. I'd assumed the walk would be firm. But it wasn't. I was unsteady. Some of that comes from your descriptions of people losing their footing and falling from high places."

"Those are from other stories, not yours."

"Nevertheless, it seemed to me that the edge of the walk marked a precipitous plunge." Sister Claire pauses. "I want you to listen to this carefully."

"I am."

"When I'm finished I want you to say something."

"I'll try to say something meaningful."

"I expected to encounter the little man in black. It was late afternoon. If I looked back I could see my shadow. It was angled as it should be. That was comforting. But what is more insubstantial than one's shadow? A cloud might pass over the sun, or the sun might impale itself on the peaks of arbor vitae and drop, airless, to the ground."

"Sister . . ."

"Don't interrupt me, Mr. Naughton. I'm practicing your art. So I walked down the walk. And like a high lady under a parasol I imagined I'd encounter a proper little gentleman in a dark suit who'd doff his hat and award me a pleasantry. But I was quickly enmeshed in a confusion of lines and edges in which the gentleman appeared fleetingly in fragments on shifting planes. I couldn't focus clearly. And worse, among the acute edges of the little man ran, half hidden, the abrupt border of the walk where the earth seemed sheared away. It was paralyzing."

Sister Claire struggles to keep her voice even. "Remember the way the manikin on his first appearance turned in the sunlight as if he were on a spindle? Remember? And displayed himself as something wickedly angular and acute." Sister Claire leans back, comes forward again. "It brought back to me a vivid memory. Three of us naughty students at St. Cecelia got hold of a forbidden book of modern art. There we found in the table of contents a painting called nude descending stairs or something like that. We hoped to see in the painting a prophecy, our pubescent breasts swelling against an elegantly flocked wall and our dainty little puffs grown to fulsome black bushes, everything artfully half hidden by a carved balustrade. Imagine our horror to discover that the artist had broken the nude into innumerable sharp metallic plates and assembled them precariously. The edges scored our eyes and the tenderest places of our body." Sister Claire pauses. "Are you listening carefully, Mr. Naughton?"

"Yes."

"I believe you are. Growing up as a male is utterly different from growing up as a female. In this culture it has to do with looking at or being looked at. A female cannot look at herself the way a male can look at himself. She needs a mirror or a painting. Paintings are best, but not the one we naughty students found. You look at me strangely. No, I haven't wandered from the front walk of Maison Cristina. I'm still there entangled in those planes, lady on a stroll, wandering nun, hysteric. I was supposed to be the stable one here, keeping in balance an Irish demonologist, a mad self-named widow, a creature who hoots like an owl, a catatonic awakening into God knows what identity, an inspired but dark storyteller, what else? Oh yes, a doctrinaire Germanic priest." She pauses, changes register. "A wonderful old matriarch who would be deeply saddened to hear me now." Sister Claire looks sharply at Naughton. "So now we have the key to the mystery."

"I don't know what you mean."

"I mean I'm the hole."

"What hole?"

"The German hole you found in the cutup message."

"Oh that. I was just playing with words, showing off my tidbit of German."

"That doesn't matter. The Spirit guided you. And now we have the revelation. The breach the little black man made here is me."

Naughton rubs his face. "You can't know that, Sister."

"I need to know it. You, Mr. Naughton, can live in a world where men are butterflies and vice versa, where walls are theaters of rearranged memories. But I have to know something. I have to know that I'm the broken flesh that let the black manikin in."

"Why? So you can confess and get absolution?"

"That too."

Naughton inhales deeply, speaks with studied care. "Do you remember what Charlene said when she saw the manikin?"

"Something in German, wasn't it?"

"Nichts."

"All right, Nichts. A gloss please, Mr. Naughton."

"I think she was telling us and the manikin himself that he is nothing."

"Maybe she's a sybil. So we have a hole and a nothing."

"Yes, but they're different things. A hole has stuff around it. Nothing is absolute. In any case, you're not the hole that let the manikin in."

Sister Claire looks uncertain.

Naughton says, "I agree with Charlene, he never was. That's what Mother Martha perceived."

Sister Claire thinks about that. "I was taught that absolute nothing is the Devil."

"Of course. Because absolute nothing is unimaginable. We need the Devil."

Sister Claire is silent for a while. "So I lost my footing on the walk and some odd things happened. Sometimes I think, Mr. Naughton, that I'm a character in one of your stories."

Naughton shakes his head definitively, then smiles. "No, but you may be a character in Charlene's story."

Sister Claire returns Naughton's smile. "You believe she has a story and will tell it."

"Yes."

"All right, but I don't want to be a character in anybody's story."

"That's not possible. But in your own story you're the principal character, if that's any consolation." Naughton pauses. "That day the manikin came back, did you walk on?"

"I tried. I took little baby steps as in a game of Mother May I. I didn't know where the edge of the walk was because the shimmering black planes followed me, pranced around me doffing, bowing, spindling, little black shapes from a geometry primer skewed and animated by a malevolent magician. So I had to turn back and seek safety here in the house." Sister Claire wears for a moment a grimace of shame and then dismisses it. "I refuse to believe that the adolescent peccadillo with the art book followed me all my life to the perilous walk. You promised to say something."

Naughton nods assent. "Did you ever actually feel anything physical?"

"If an imaginary incision is so vivid you actually flinch, it's physical."

"Nearly. But if it's not going to be merely a sensation there has to be blood."

"Blood. I told you I am past the middle of my life."

Naughton is silent for a while, then nods reflectively. "I wonder if for all of us there's just that one tiny slice of time when we can enter the dark wood and go through."

"And if we fail the challenge, what happens to the rest of our lives?"

"We keep to the middle of the walk, stay inside the house, imagine things, dream."

"And tell stories that make up for our failures."

"Stories don't make up. Vera chides me because my stories don't end right. I tell her that stories never end." Naughton smiles, not a condescending smile. "Vera's faith is perfect. She knows that in the End Time all the stories will end, even mine. But I think she might agree that meanwhile imperfect stories have their uses."

"We're back to the case of Charlene."

"Yes, but also Ms. Trask, who lives a storied life as a member of a famous railroad dynasty and has a brother-in-law who is a famous polymath."

"I admit all that, but I have to say I don't like this story you're in the middle of."

"I wouldn't have thought you liked any of them."

"I like your retelling of the story of the Good Samaritan and the brave long-faced woman who went into the dark. But this story you're telling now seems dangerous."

"More dangerous than the others?"

"Yes, because we know that for some time Charlene thought of you as father."

"But she's disavowed me."

"True, but in the wanderer's story the father's passionate quest for his daughter could create in Charlene a dangerous sense of absence and longing."

"Charlene is not one who will step back after taking a step forward."

A Mirror in Maison Cristina

Naughton goes into his bathroom and looks at himself in the mirror. There's a defect in the silvering. He moves his head. The defect relocates itself on his face. By his ear it appears to be a common rash, on his chin a shaver's rough, on his nose the venous mapping of a drunkard's progress. Above his eye it's the supercilia of a British Lord, on his forehead the faint suggestion of the stigmata of a crown of thorns, on his cheek a mensur scar.

"Well, which will it be, Peter?" Vogt has come to the door of the bathroom. Unclothed, he is clad in a semi-transparent sheathing of musculature. Veins and bones appear beneath as if behind a scrim that is inconstantly lit so that the eye moves uneasily from the thewy integument into the blood-suffused interior and out again.

"None of the above, Vogt. But what are you now, somatically speaking."

"Let's just say I'm transitory."

"You look like an anatomical drawing done by a trippy medical illustrator. Don't tell me I called you."

"You did, or I would have gone about my business on the other side of the mirror."

"You've been reading children's books."

"Not necessary. People are looking into warped and de-silvered mirrors all over the world."

"OK, what did I call you for?"

Vogt wags his head. The cervical vertebrae realign themselves. "You wanted to talk about the world of Charlene before she arrived here at Maison Cristina."

"Does it have to do with the little black man on the walk?"

"Not my style, Peter, just as you told Sister Claire." Vogt laughs a barking laugh, different from his previous hissing. Supple muscles pull up the sides of his mouth. The larynx closes. A rosy banner unfurls rapidly over his brain and just as quickly flies away. "Apropos of Charlene, I'm sorry you took me out of Wanderer's story."

"What in hell do you mean by that?"

"I mean in one version, which you ditched, I was Celina's twin brother." Vogt grasps a hank of his red hair, the follicles visible above his skull.

"Celina doesn't have a brother."

"She did once. Remember? She sent him out into the desert as part of a search and rescue team to save Wanderer. We were headed toward a colorful finale. I was sorry to be excised."

"There's no such thing as a finale."

"Agreed."

"But I did have in mind a different eventuality. Wanderer digs in the berm and finds the seeds of time."

"You just now thought of that, but go ahead. What's he going to do with them?"

"He's going to wait until the sun is at the meridian, at which moment he will expose the seeds to solar gravitational warp. A geomagnetic storm will occur. The desert as a microcosm of the heliosphere will flare and tilt momentarily.

That will be the signal that the seeds have begun to bind all humanity into eidolons of connectivity."

Vogt laughs. The crescent of his diaphragm arcs acutely. "Very imaginative, Peter, but Wanderer isn't the right agent. It would be out of character."

"Don't tell me you're the right agent."

"No, I'm not."

"Let's get back to what you say I called you for. What do you know about Charlene before she arrived at Maison Cristina?"

"For that we need to take a little trip."

"To the Underworld, I hope, because that's where you're at your best."

"OK, call it the Underworld. Not far from here. A decayed old brick building."

"Sister Claire already told this story."

"She just told the part about a passer-by discovering Charlene and the litter-bearers carrying her off."

"And you're going to relate the prequel? To tell the truth, Vogt, I don't have much faith in you as a storyteller. It's not your medium, but go on."

"Before Kristin, aka Charlene, was brought to Maison Cristina, she was a prisoner in the old brick house. Take it from there, Peter. You're the storyteller. Describe the interior."

Naughton laughs. "Can I change the finale?"

"Of course, but like a true storyteller you'll stay true to the course of events."

"OK. I see the interior as a large rotunda with two dozen open cells around the base floor and a second-story gallery from which twelve sleepless watchers constantly observe the activities in the cells. Each of them wears a small pair of binoculars strapped to his head with black elastic bands. How am I doing?"

"Very good, Peter. Your words are all that's holding up the gallery. The brick pillars crumbled a long time ago. Keep going."

"The onlooker who has just entered this unpromising space has a keen sense of expectation. He understands there's a living creature of some kind in each of the cells though none is visible. He sees shadows moving fitfully inside. Misted suspirations disturb the air near the entrances, punctuated by the wavering blue of suppressed wails. In the gallery above, the tense forward-leaning posture of the watchers lends urgency to the air of expectation. Lean forward, Vogt, so I can get it right."

Vogt leans forward intently, taking his assignment seriously. His eyes bulge in their sockets. Tensors contract.

"There. Though strictly speaking the bodies of the watchers are not visible, the onlooker detects the subtle compression of the sternum, the partial closure of the suprasternal notch, the forward crook of the cervical vertebrae. At this point everything is enchained in a painful waiting. The inevitable questions insert themselves into the onlooker's mind. What are these in the cells? Who's coming through the ogival door at the far side of the rotunda? Whoever it is, he'll have to trip some mechanism that opens the iron portcullis that bars the doorway. The terminals of the verticals of the portcullis are spiked and penetrate the rubbled stone of the floor. OK so far?"

"Actually it was just a heavy wooden door bolted from the other side."

"OK. I get it. This isn't medieval. It's an eighteenth-century panopticon."

"Right."

"The sound of metallic wrenching penetrates the room. The door opens. Out steps a grandee, hair gathered in a blue ribbon tied in a bow at the neck. Dark jacket and velveteen knickers, white stockings, buckled shoes. What is this he has in his hand? A whip? A riding crop? A baton? A miniature épée? He gives it a shake. The shank of it trembles and disturbs the air with an incisive whine. From the cells comes a medley of woe—whimpering, sniveling, moaning. The grandee whips the air with his instrument. Louder! Now arise cries, howls, screeches and keening that split the air. OK?"

"OK, but focus. We're only interested in one of the inmates."

"Understood. The grandee stands now in the middle of the circle of cells and turns slowly, pointing his instrument at the cells one by one, eliciting from each an outcry peculiar to the occupant, yelp, breathless gasp, scream, gargle of strangulation et cetera. Polyphonic atonal opera."

"We're only interested in one of the inmates."

"Right. Though he's the focal point of a continuous chorus of lamentation, the grandee succeeds in isolating the single silent cell. Ha! He signals a subordinate to go to the source of silence, an oxymoron."

"There's no element of wit here."

"The onlooker has not been aware of the subordinate until now because he is attired very much like his commander and thus easily perceived as the object of a doubling trick. Apropos, as the subordinate approaches the silent cell, his superior seems to diminish. It's as if to substantiate the one the other must contract. The subordinate drags from her cell a warped wretch from whose mouth a viscid saliva streams and with it a slobbering protest. The subordinate rips open the back of the woman's tattered robe. The grandee, now brightening into focus again, steps forward with his instrument."

"This is good, Peter."

Naughton throws his arms up. "It's hideous, Vogt. It's an idiotic cliché. You're putting it into my mind."

"No, Peter. Neither of us believes in telepathy." Vogt's cerebellum darkens.

"Or believes in this stale scene. I'm letting this faux Marquis de Sade stand there with his lash for all eternity. I'm not moving him an inch."

"An unacceptable stance for an ace storyteller, Peter. Let's say that after a good whipping the Marquis directs his subordinate to drag her out of the hall and deposit her on the steps, which is where Sister Claire's story begins."

Naughton glares at Vogt and speaks angrily. "Go ahead, Vogt. You're the storyteller now."

"OK. Jump to a post-Naughton Charlene. She returns to the rotunda, a black predator with wings wider than the grandee's lash is long." Vogt lifts his arms. Bone and blood brighten. "She wreaks vengeance on her tormentors and on the watchers in the gallery. Isn't this what you've been telling her?"

"I've been telling her stories. She can do with them what she wants. Please depart, Vogt."

"I will, Peter, soon. But a call has its own integrity. I have to hold you a bit longer."

"You can't hold me, Vogt. You've decorporealized yourself and can't hold anything."

"Don't confuse power with materiality. The question still hangs in the air, what have we learned from our visit to the Marquis' torture chamber?"

"We've learned that you don't know how to tell a story."

Vogt begins to turn away from the door. Axes are formed, left and right, front and back. Muscles flex, extend, contract. Balls turn in sockets. Planes form and shift. "That's not what we learned. Think about it, because in the case of Charlene, if you don't get it right, there are consequences. It's in your hands. You're the storyteller."

Naughton says, "It's hard to think seriously about anything, Vogt, with this anatomical showbiz going on."

"Make a move, Peter. Step over the threshold." Vogt exits.

Naughton is on the way to meet Charlene and tell her the end of Wanderer's story. Sister Kathleen intercepts him just outside the door of Mr. Gerrity's room. "Do you have a minute?"

"Of course."

"Mr. Gerrity would like to have a word with you."

In the room Ms. Trask is sitting in a chair leaning forward with great expectancy. "I bet he can't do it."

Mr. Gerrity rises from his wheelchair, Sister Kathleen holding it steady for him. Now he commences a series of exercises, each one done with great concentration, Sister Kathleen standing by to make sure he doesn't fall. He reaches toward the ceiling, first with one arm and then the other. He makes his hands and arms rigid and thrusts them forward as if to fend off an attack. He lifts one leg and then the other in a slow march. Moves his mouth in a rolling motion and hums several tones, major and minor. He then relaxes, head and arms hanging down, and breathes deeply. Naughton nods appreciatively. Ms. Trask says, "He hasn't tried the hard part yet." Sister Kathleen stands by.

"See," says Mr. Gerrity, widening his eyes. "See."

"Very good, Mr. Gerrity," says Sister Kathleen.

"See what?" says Ms. Trask. "Or is it just alphabet? ABC."

Mr. Gerrity points at her. "See him."

"I'm not a him."

Mr. Gerrity points at Naughton. "See her."

"He's never going to get the hims and hers straight."

Naughton says, "The distinction between genders may not be as important, Ms. Trask, as the concept of personhood."

"Concept of personhood! That's what you are, Mr. Nobody, a concept. You were never conceived, you were concepted. Your mother, Miss Nobody, used a device."

"What a terrible thing to say, Ms. Trask!" Sister Kathleen's shock is overdone.

"Not at all," says Naughton. "Ms. Trask understands that the difference between the word and the flesh is crucial."

"Him!" intones Mr. Gerrity ending the pronoun with a rich elongated hum. "Her!" with an impressive growl.

"Congratulation, Sister," says Naughton. "Pronunciation, grammar, expressiveness. He's on his way."

"I'm on my way out of here. They've hidden the papers. The courts are backed up. My case is down in the docker. But Lloyd is on it."

"We'll miss you terribly, Ms. Trask. Won't we, Mr. Naughton?"

"It will be as if a star has fallen from the sky."

"Haw haw," says Ms. Trask disdainfully. "You got your playmate in black down the hall. You don't need me."

"Every soul is precious," says Sister Kathleen.

"Indeed." Naughton exits.

Charlene is waiting in a mid-length dark blue velveteen gown. Across the front in the shape of a broad baldric is a splash of avian images, bright silver shapes giving way to thinning glyphs that form brief arabesques and then disappear. The entire design, the creatures and their traces, appear painted rather than embroidered. Naughton nods. "Fetching."

Charlene smiles. Vera says, "It came in the mail. Sister Claire said she could wear it."

"From whom?"

"It did not say."

Charlene says, "Guess."

Naughton lifts his brows. "I would say from an admiring ornithologist who has spotted you from afar with his field binoculars."

Charlene laughs an arch naughty laugh. "Celina. Somebody painted it for her."

"Where was it postmarked?"

"Sister Claire did not say."

Charlene says, "P.O. Box 123, Sonora desert."

Vera shakes her head. "All this storytelling. Things were going to get mixed up."

Naughton smiles. "Stories are always a conspiracy among the teller, the hearer and the characters in the story."

Vera says, "I will thank God if your characters stay in their stories."

Charlene says, "Tell the story of Wanderer." She speaks with a charming simplicity, mixed. Queen, ingenue, adept in skyey mysteries. Charlene settles in the chair that Naughton has been accustomed to sit in. Vera takes her usual seat. Charlene smiles, nodding toward the bed. "You can have the bed. The head is up."

"I've never told a story from a bed."

"We're all doing things for the first time," says Charlene.

Vera says, "It is not the time that matters. Is it the right thing?"

Naughton says, "If I'd known I would've worn my robe."

Vera says, "A gentleman does not wear a robe in a lady's room."

"Nor does he occupy her bed."

That statement would seem to create a stalemate, but Charlene says, "The first time. And once."

Naughton sighs and stoops to unlace his shoes. Charlene nods with satisfaction. Naughton climbs up into the bed and rests his head on the raised pillows. "I'm afraid I may doze off."

Charlene says, "Wanderer is waking up from sleep against the hill that the birds made."

"Yes. He began to wake up. It wasn't just the sun lighting up the sand that awoke him. It was also the intuition of an intruder. He slid the lid of his left eye up very slowly, leaving the right closed. In front of him on the sand not far from his feet a snake began to coil. Wanderer knew it would be futile to try to jump away. He had none of the spring of a kangaroo rabbit. Now the snake began to flick its tongue, a long blue two-tined fork. Its strike could be only a moment away. Then came a zing in the air. The snake turned to strike, too late. The heavy head of an ax cut deep into the creature's body just below the head. There followed a hideous coiling and spurting of blood. The ax head fell once more and severed the head from the body. The coiling stopped but the head continued gnashing wildly for some moments, its fangs glistening, before its jaws finally closed and it lay quiet on the desert floor.

Wanderer looked up. Standing before him was the young man he'd followed into the desert from the Lager House. He was cleaning the head of his ax with sand. Under his wide hat his face was darkly shadowed. I was hoping he might've gotten a baby rabbit, a two-fer, but I can tell you before I clean him there ain't nothing in his belly. The young man laughed. He almost got you, but you don't look too edible.

I think I better thank you for saving my life.

My name is Jep. I think it's short for Jeptha. I don't know what that snake was thinking about. He got your dander on his tongue, but he had to know you're too big for him to kill and eat. You must've been flailing around in your sleep and threatening him. He was genuine pissed. You saw the head didn't want to give up, and if it had gotten to you it wouldn't have mattered the body was gone.

Maybe I was having a bad dream. I thank you, Jep, for saving my life.

Not necessarily. If he'd struck, you would've had a hell of a time, hollering, puking, gasping for breath, blind staggers, but you would likely have survived. Zora would've nursed you, but she wouldn't have been too happy about it. Now the best thing you could do would be go back the way you came.

Go back without seeing her and her painting after I came all this way?

I don't know how far all this way is. What's your name?

Just tell her a wanderer came to see her and talk to her.

I'll see what she says. Jep picked up the snake, which was limp now, and tucked it into a leather pouch tied around his waist.

Wanderer watched him climb up the side of the berm. There were footholds and knobby protrusions that served the climber like pitons. He made swift progress. Wanderer tried to imprint in his mind the path, but it was too complex. Jep reached the top and disappeared into the house. There came a curious kind of braided silence, the wind intermittently worrying the sides of the berm, a whispering of airs among the miniature dunes and hillocks of sand. Wanderer was left with his thoughts, which he didn't welcome. He'd have to think about what he was going to say to Zora. So he came up with something else to think about."

Naughton lifts his head slightly and resettles it on the pillow. He looks straight before him, a sight line leading to the intersection of the wall and the ceiling, pale green against shadowed white. He remains silent.

"What did he think about?" asks Vera after a while.

"What she was then or now," says Charlene.

Naughton nods. "He thought about her walking down the street of a hilly city wearing beads and a shirt with a sunburst on it. She was like a bird let out of a cage. Her mother let her out. The street was steep. If she'd wanted to she could've leapt up and flown away. She was free. Her mother had been only a temporary protector. Her brother believed that art is an irrational excrescence. Her father said things, but she couldn't remember them, didn't try. There was no cat. A nun spoke of a world without cats." Naughton stops there.

Charlene says, "There will always be cats, the more people kill them. What happens?"

"Just when Wanderer thought that those above wouldn't speak to him again, Jep's voice came down to him. You can come up. I'm coming down so you can follow me back up.

At the foot of the berm Jep said, give me your pack.

They begin to climb the berm. Jep took it slow so that Wanderer could locate footholds and handholds, but Wanderer was breathing hard. A little farther and there's a ledge I made. Wanderer rested for a minute on the ledge and caught his breath. By the time he pulled himself over the edge at the top he was spent. Jep went into the house leaving him to lie on his back and pant. It seemed to Wanderer that the fire he set a thousand miles up the coast was now burning in his chest and would never go out.

Come in and get out of the sun.

Wanderer rolled over on his side and looked up. There stood Zora naked from the waist up, cutoff jeans below. He thought maybe he wasn't seeing right. Her right breast was missing. The scar tissue was painted, a green cat's eye. Zora smiled. No, I didn't have the ambition to be an Amazon. Cancer. A close call. She bent closer to him. The cat's eye narrowed. He said, you thought you were never going to have another cat.

I don't know how you know what I thought. But I didn't think I was going to have cancer of the breast either.

Wanderer sat up and tried to take in the image of Zora. She was brawny and evenly bronzed. The color reminded him of the madrone trees in a place where he'd lived far to the north. The aureole and teat of the good breast were darker, a color she might've created by mixing magenta and black. Or the darkness was created by a shadow cast down from her hair, a wild black bush.

It's not all from sun, she said.

What is it then? Did you paint yourself?

Not exactly, but constant proximity to pigments rubs off on you. Zora shook her head. Poor wanderer, you thought you'd find a wild artist girl that was beautiful.

Jep said, she is beautiful.

Yes, said Wanderer.

What did you think you came for, Wanderer?

Wanderer struggles to his feet. I came to see you and the painting.

Come into the shade and drink some water. Your lips are too cracked to talk right.

Jep laughed. He wasn't having much luck talking that rattler out of striking.

Wanderer moved into shade thrown by a thatch overhang and sat in a chair made of large sticks planed smooth and tied together with leather straps. He drank water from a jar Jep brought him. He said to Zora, where have you been?

Lots of places. I painted my way from Vancouver down here. Sometimes a meal was all I got for a canvas. I specialized in bodies on their way to being ghosts. A nut in Portland Oregon hired me to teach a class in life drawing, in the back of his gallery, as if the authorities cared. He was the model. Michelangelo rummaging around with his gravediggers couldn't have done worse.

And Jep?

Jep laughed. She dug me up just south of Costa Linda.

Zora nodded. It was Jep's idea to build the hill and the house with walls for me to paint. Celina sells enough of my stuff for us to live on. It took a long time to build the hill.

I want to hear that story some time, but right now I want to hear more about your paintings. I saw one in Celina's gallery. It's what you always said you'd paint.

No, what I always wanted to paint is inside. But you need to rest and eat something.

Jep said, in his pack he's got some cheese and meat stuck together like Siamese twins.

We can do better than that.

At least until I fry that snake. Then we got some real eats.

Wanderer ate some bread and pickled cactus strips.

You like the bread? Jep asked.

It's very tasty.

It's from a goopy starter the old Kraut gave us. Then it picks up desert spores, virgin grass, paloverde, mesquite, cactus, who knows what else.

After a pause Wanderer said, when you painted your way down through San Francisco, did you see any family?

No. Everybody in my family is dead. Besides, I was moving south fast. I knew there was something here.

I was thinking about your mother.

Nobody knows anything about my mother. That's the way she wanted it.

Wanderer breathed deeply. Sorry, but I need to lie down.

Zora and Jep helped Wanderer to a bed made of ropes tied across two thick pieces of timber and overlaid with a mattress that mixed the odor of human bodies and desert grass. Wanderer fell into a deep sleep."

Naughton looks at Charlene and then at Vera, who says, "I was that hot one time."

Charlene says, "Wake him up."

At the doorway Sister Claire shakes her head. "He's tired. Let him rest a while."

A Makeshift Room in San Francisco

Stella is sitting on the foot of a bed in the room her Aunt Ettie has made for her. A doorless alcove actually. A two-piece makeshift white curtain on a rod has been installed for privacy. It's pulled back halfway on both sides. Stella looks like a character on a stage just as the curtain opens in the proscenium arch. A man is walking back and forth on the other side of the alcove. If one reverses prospective, Stella becomes the audience watching a character pacing restlessly along the front edge of the stage's apron.

The pacing man says, "This ain't no place for you, kid." He's wearing a gray T-shirt with USA stenciled on it. What little hair he has on his head grows in cropped patches the color of a bruised orange. The skin around the patches is rashy and broken. It's as if his pate has been worked over by a lawn thatcher. On his upper right arm is a faded tattoo of a shield with US Army printed on it. Perched atop the shield is a bird, no doubt an eagle but the tattoo has been so badly damaged by the sun that the details are bleached. The man says, "I see you looking at me like I'm a weirdo, kid. It's because I was burned half dead by the Sahara sun, which ain't no place for man or beast except Berbers and camels."

Stella sits quietly, her hands in her lap. She wears a calf-length white dress with lace at the neck and wrists. She says, "I like San Francisco."

The man paces to the left, momentarily out of sight, and then comes back center. "Ettie says you wanted to be a nun, but they wouldn't let you in."

"The Mother Superior said I didn't have a calling."

"Calling! Jesus Christ, kid, there's a million things you can do in life without a calling." The man laughs without opening his mouth, snorting. "Me, I got a calling. I got called up. So I got to chase the Desert Fox across the Sahara."

Stella nods. "The country owes you a lot."

"Maybe, but you ain't of this country, are you, kid? You aim to be a level up, or is it maybe more than one level up?"

"I have to start my own order."

"If you still mean nuns, you don't have to start nothing. There's convents from one end of this town to the other, Caramelites, Josephines, whatever. Go knock on doors."

"I already did that. The door was not opened."

"OK then, you can call your order the Sisters of the Little Star. There's even a song, Stella by Starlight. You know it? Just out." The man sings, "'A song the robin sings through years of endless springs.' You like it?"

"I'm not going to call my order anything."

The man nods emphatically. "The song is crap. But not calling your order anything is going to be hard for people to get. Sisters of No Name."

"Not even that. Nothing."

The man paces across the curtain's divide and returns center. "Wait a minute. You really mean nothing, don't you? Pure nothing. You think I don't know about nothing? I've seen it plenty. You wake up in the middle of the night. You don't remember where you are, probably because you don't want to.

319

You look out from your pad. Nothing. There can't be nothing, you say to yourself. You shake your head, blink your eyes. But there it is. Nothing. That's what you mean, isn't it?"

"What I mean has to be in a song."

"What song?"

"I have to compose it. It's just coming into my head."

The man leans toward Stella. "Are you a musician?"

"I play the piano."

"So this song. It comes after nothing?"

"There's a nothing beyond the nothing you're talking about. And then there's something beyond that."

"What is it?"

"That's what my order will be about."

The man rakes his fingers through his clumps of hair. "I don't know, kid. People might think you're deep. But they also might think you're just looney."

Stella nods. "I like you."

The man makes his nasal laugh. "You got any idea how dangerous it is to say something like that in a place like this to somebody like me?"

Stella smiles but makes no reply.

The man makes a precise pivot and crosses the open space between the curtains with military steps, but it doesn't seem like an act. It seems more like the unconscious enactment of an old discipline. Back center, he says, "I'm not one of your aunt's boys."

"I didn't think you were."

"You have to be a Marine." He snorts. "My qualification is that I'm homeless. Mustering out pay all gone. Whiskey, women, dope." He reflects. "Your order could do a real service. Introduce homeless and whacked-out vets to the nothing beyond nothing and then the something, if you find it. But just nothing would be better than what they got." He pauses. "Your aunt is good hearted, takes in stray cats. Temporary."

"When she left home to come out here she left her cat behind in Bedford Mississippi. It died and my grandmother and grandfather had to bury it. My grandfather wanted to give a funeral oration, but my grandmother wouldn't let him. My brother Peter, who is a great reader, thought that was a great shame. Once he read me a poem about a pussy cat and an owl who got married. I think he was half in love with me."

The man shakes his head emphatically. "You watch out, kid. Every man that sees you is going to think he's in love with you. Get your nun's clothes as fast as you can."

"My aunt wants me to get a job. It's not the money."

The man doesn't seem to have paid attention to that. "Love. What is it?"

"My aunt loved her husband before he got killed, but I don't think she's been able to love any man since."

"What she had ain't love. It was just a good match, and she can't find another good match." He pauses. "She says you had to grow up with alcoholics."

"Yes, but they were a good match."

"It's easy to be a good match inside alcohol. It's called codependency. I got that from a counselor, free through the VA. I could tell you everything I am in exact terms. Addictive, antisocial, aggressive, anxiety-ridden, and that's just the a's. They did say, though, that some conditions could be ruled out, like bipolar, schizophrenia, phobias. That was good to know."

"Did they ever tell you to get back to that time in the desert when there was nothing in the way?"

"In the way of what?"

"In the way of leaving the war for a while and being yourself."

"No, they never said that, but there was one shrink that did an interesting thing with me. We sat across the room from each other. You had to lay your hands face up on your thighs like you expected something good to come down from heaven. Then I was supposed to identify my spirit animal. I said I

321

wanted to be a fixed cat. She asked me why I wanted to be a cat. I said so I could sit and look out the window and never do anything. If somebody picked me up I'd just hang there like a rag and not purr or cuddle and not be any fun and they would put me back on the windowsill."

"What did she say about that?"

"She said I was confusing the spirit animal with the physical animal."

"What did you say?"

"I went off the rails, halfway on purpose. I said my body was so wracked with pain and hunger and thirst that it didn't have any idea what a spirit was, animal or otherwise." The man takes a deep breath. "Let me ask you, kid, but you don't have to answer. Didn't you ever see your mom or dad start to get the shakes before they got another drink?"

"No, because they always had plenty in the house."

"Smart. That's the first thing an addict has to learn. Every morning know where your supply is coming from that day. If you're on the street, which your mom and dad weren't, that's your assignment. You're on the substance detachment today, sergeant. Yes sir." The man starts to salute and then pulls his arm back down. "Your aunt has supplies, but I have to leave here."

"Why?"

"Too much military traffic, jarheads. I leave as soon as they come, but sooner or later there'd be conflict. When you see her again, which may not be until tomorrow morning, tell her you and Sarge had a nice talk. And thank her."

"Where're you going?"

"Out onto the streets of this great city to join up with my comrades in arms for the next attack. Tank guns. Your ears ring. You might forget the guns for a while if you can get hold of the right substance, but the ears remember."

"I would tell her we talked about cats, but I think she misses having a cat."

"She's too busy to have a cat."

"It's not that. Man was the only cat in her life, like Tom was the only man in her life."

"It doesn't stop her from looking. If she found a man she could get a cat. Order of things."

"I would tell her we talked about holy orders, but she doesn't approve."

"And it's no use telling her we talked about nothing, because she hasn't gotten there yet. So, good-bye, kid. I'll look you up at your new convent. It might be hard finding the convent of nothing because there's nothings all over this town."

Naughton looks around the room. "I appreciate your waiting while I got a little snooze."

"You were dreaming of your sister Stella."

"Did I say her name in my sleep?"

"Stern."

"What is that?" asks Vera.

"Star," says Charlene.

"Etwal, my mother said," says Vera.

Charlene says to Naughton, "Your eyes were open."

"Vera says you slept with your eyes open."

"That was before. And I wasn't asleep. I was resting and watching."

"Good idea. But let's press on to the end of this story. It's already too long."

"It's wandering," says Charlene.

"Oh no. If you've gotten wordplay from me, Charlene, I beg your forgiveness. Words are full of pitfalls."

"You're good at falls. Story."

"Briefly then, they ate the rattlesnake, boiled and then fried, and bread and something green, not cactus. The house was open at both ends, but not much air passed through. They sweated. It was afternoon. Wanderer said, can we see the paintings now?

Zora looked out the door. The sunlight is good.

They walked across the main room of the house and into a long room on the other side. There was painting para- phernalia—brushes, palettes, trowels, rags. The floor was multi-colored, splotched. A very large work-in-progress extended over half of the length of the house, three panels, each about six feet by six feet. They were lit by an oblique but powerful light coming down through a series of skylights. In the first panel against a black background a large white circular shape was spinning so fast that its borders were warped and distended. Colored bubble-like shapes were either born from the mother circle or were gathering for an invasion. This would become clear momentarily, Wanderer thought, and then he realized this was a painting. Paintings, he knew, could suggest motion, like the speeding glyphs of speed and flaming wakes in the works of the Futurists, but they couldn't actually move. Nevertheless, Wanderer said, is it solar powered?

Zora smiled. Jep said, you talking about your head?

Wanderer shook his head, slapped his face. Maybe it's the rattlesnake.

Jep said, it ain't you, man. It's the painting.

Wanderer popped his eyes wide open and froze his lids, but he couldn't stop the wheeling of the white circle or the massing of tense energy among the small objects. He said, are the small ones going in or out?

Zora said, out, but they're waiting for time to start.

Who's going to start it?

I am. Follow me.

They moved toward the next panel, which was separated from the first by a line so thin that the eye could barely make out that it was a vertical spectrum, red at the bottom, violet at the top and at each end a vibratile tail like a miniature rattlesnake's. Wait, said Wanderer. I missed something. He went back to the first panel and now saw something barely visible around the spinning white circle and behind the smaller bubbles, a moiling churn of no color or shape, pure agitation. It was as if a desert wind had invaded the house and layered the panel with a dusting of pure energy. He thought he should wait for a fiery combustion.

Jep said, you have to move on. Everything has to move on.

Wanderer said, what is that stuff you can't see?

Zora said, dark energy, but that's just words, not the stuff itself. You have to move on. I almost got stuck back there. If you get stuck everything goes around and around. The brush in your hand starts spinning. You have to move on.

Back at the juncture between the first and the second panel Jep said, pointing to the razor-fine line, that's one billionth of one trillionth of a second.

Wanderer peered at the line and nodded.

The second panel bore some resemblance to the painting Wanderer had been carrying for some weeks in search of the artist. Shapes had begun to emerge.

Later, said Zora. Many laters.

Of course, said Wanderer. It was always in the paint. The paint remembers.

Unlike the first panel, the second had no background color. Everything in it was middle or foreground. The dominant and central figure was a huge white creature rearing up from a bed of vibrant primary colors. It seemed to be straining skyward barely conscious, an amorphous being moments after birth. Off to the left side of the panel a large stony white outcropping fronted the creature. Silhouetted against the outcropping was a set of four small figures, almost identical in size and shape but variously colored, each topped by a head-like shape—steles or proto-humans. Oddly shaped saurians of various colors crawled around the lower foreground. Elsewhere homunculi appeared, some lying on streams of yellow liquid light, others struggling upright and waving to show they'd arisen. Sprinkles of primary colors represented seedlings of vegetation yet to appear. But one tree-like growth perched precariously atop a buttery gobbet. One head and many yellow trunks. Above all the images a narrow band of truncated sky strained to assert its continuance against the burgeoning life below. Jagged rays of sun, bolts of lightning and gray clouds limned by the secant border of the panel jostled each other in a cramped space.

Wanderer stood still, gazing at the painting. Zora stood beside him. Jep kept well apart. After a long time of intense looking, Wanderer said, this is how I found you.

Zora said nothing to that.

As early as a tie-dye T-shirt winding through the streets of San Francisco. Your mother saw it before I did.

No she didn't. She just knew that first there had to be space and air.

Wanderer said, we could stand for hours and never exhaust what's here.

Move on, said Jep softly.

Wanderer looked for a transitional stripe between the second and the third panels, but there was nothing but the sawn edges of the two pieces of contiguous wood. The background of the third panel had been painted a sickly gold marred by careless-seeming brush strokes laid on in various directions. Wanderer thought of a hazy desert, a foul breath coming from the distant lagoon. Near the upper right corner shone a necrotic moon, clouded with nauseous green. Near the center a commanding acute triangle descended inexorably on the unseen world below. Everything seemed at once uncertain and indelible. Wanderer didn't want to look at it. He turned to Zora. This one you'll have to invent. The paint can't remember what has not yet been.

There's nothing that hasn't yet been. Where would it be?

I don't know. But I'm glad I'm not the one who has to paint it.

This is the third start.

I'd like to claim I saw pentimenti but I can't.

When it's done, if it's ever done, it won't be possible to see the old layers, but it'll be apparent to the viewer that they're there.

I won't ask you what you'll do with the triptych when it's done. Or what you'll paint next or do with yourself.

Zora smiled. We don't get to know that.

Wanderer turned to Jep. What will you do?

Jep shakes his head.

He's writing a song. I'm not sure he knows it, but I can hear it."

Suddenly Charlene says, "Who's in the paintings?"

Naughton, jarred from his story, is silent for some moments. "Suppose I said it's just all color and shapes."

Charlene shakes her head. "Who's in the paintings?"

Naughton yields. "If anybody's in the paintings it would have to be the mother. But be patient. They went back into the part of the house for cooking, eating, and sleeping. The odor of the fried rattlesnake was still in the air. It took Wanderer back to his boyhood in New Orleans and the smell of fried frog legs. He said, I have to go back now.

Why? said Zora. We can make you a place to sleep here. It's nearly dusk.

I have to go. It's time.

All right, said Zora.

Jep picked up Wanderer's backpack. I'll take you down and back over to Celina's place.

It'll be dark, said Wanderer.

I could walk it blindfolded.

Zora folded her arms over the maimed and the good breast. I would say come back. But I think you're done here.

Yes, said Wanderer.

They went to the edge of the level surface on top of the berm. Jep said, it's trickier going down. You have to feel everything more. I'll be above you.

They descended slowly. From time to time Jep, looking down, prompted Wanderer to move his foot to the left or to the right. They reached the ledge and stood there together to rest for a couple of minutes. Wanderer got his wind back. Has anybody else seen the paintings? Celina?

Not even the Man in the Moon.

They resumed their descent. Wanderer made a false step, struggled to hang on with his hands but fell and landed in the sand on his back. Jep hurried down. You all right, man? Can you hear me?

Wanderer looked up. He saw the moon winking behind a coy lace of nighttime clouds.

He came to in Celina's house. He blinked. He remembered falling. How did I get here?

Jep put a hand on Wanderer's shoulder to keep him from trying to get up. We got some guys from the marina and made a canvas litter once we knew you weren't busted up. A doc from Costa Linda has been by.

Bones?

None broken. Don't know how bad your guts got shook up. Time will tell.

In time Wanderer healed. Celina said, I think you better head back north. Lagoon and desert aren't good for you. You had to come, but now you need to go back.

Wanderer nodded. That's good advice.

You got what you came for. Most aren't that lucky.

I came to see the paintings.

Or you came to find out if it was the paintings you came to see.

It's hard to know what to do next.

What I said. You didn't really know what you came for, so whatever you found was going to be what you came for. When you go north you won't know what you're going for, but whatever you find, that'll be what you were going for.

Wanderer let that go.

Who knows. You might find a place like I did and just stay there and let things come to you. Or maybe that's not your nature.

Wanderer doesn't know what to say. He's never thought of himself as having a nature though he thinks he knows the meaning of the phrase. After a while he says, Wanderers don't have natures.

I don't think being a wanderer can be a permanent job, though I admit there's more places in the world than you could wander through in a lifetime.

The law of wandererhood is that you can't know where you're going more than one step ahead."

Charlene laughs a genuine laugh.

Naughton says, "Some would find that more pathetic than comic, Charlene."

Vera says, "Something has to make sense to be pathetic or comic."

"Never mind sense. I've told my story and now Charlene owes me hers."

Charlene doesn't say anything. Vera says, "Like all your stories, it does not have an end."

"I said stories never end. They begin in the middle and end at the beginning."

Charlene laughs.

Naughton says, "I'll be coming to hear your story. Vera wants to hear it too. Everybody wants to hear it."

Charlene says, "We will tell it."

Naughton doesn't ask who the we is. He rouses himself from his nest of pillows and swings his legs out over the edge of the bed. "If you'd told me I could get through a story in bed I would've said that Morpheus, god of dreams, would've put

---

me to sleep. Then you'd have to get inside my dreams to find out what happened to Wanderer."

Vera says, "There is only one God, but you did sleep and dream."

"Right. Poor Morpheus, bottled up like all the pagan gods."

"Morphine," says Charlene.

"And on that note of cognate perception, ladies, I must take my leave, repair to my own bed and rest from my wanderings. I'll live now in delicious anticipation of your story, Charlene."

A Rundown House in New Orleans

Naughton lies down in his bed and looks at the broad band of sky outside his window, gray clouds and patches of blue. Gone now the dry heat and brazen sun of the desert. The wild painter with the cat's eye scar way off in the alternate geography of dreams. How sweet to sleep safely in Maison Cristina, where no vipers flick their tongues, no scorpions hold their poisoned tails up proudly over the burning sand.

Suddenly Naughton is up in the air, seized by a transportive force that conveys him south. Lakes and streams glint in the landscape below. Clouds roll by outside his window or are torn apart to make way for his passage. The sun slides slowly toward the front of the conveyance, which presently wheels about and dips, offering a glimpse of a fan-shaped estuary. A crescent appears upstream. The descent of the conveyance sharpens and soon there is a bump and a brief roar of engines.

A second more leisurely transport takes Naughton through streets that seem to disappear at a vanishing point ahead but then abruptly veer off into another equally narrowing way. The transport stops at a corner. The door opens for some moments, then closes. In the seat next to Naughton the air is warped. "You called. You wanted me along for your revisit," the new occupant says. Vogt.

Naughton says, "I never know whether I've really called you or you just come when you want to. But anyway, what are you now, Vogt?"

"You don't have a word for it. Joshua would probably say I'm a highly flexible polymer. But whatever I am, I'm gradually taking leave of you."

"Why?"

"Because you don't need me anymore. There aren't any more options."

"What does that mean?"

"You know what it means, Peter. During the early parts of a story there're lots of forking paths and then there's only one path left. The story line has gotten control of everything."

Naughton is silent for a while. "OK, a little detail to make this story a little more believable. How did the driver see you?"

"He didn't. The pick-up was prearranged."

"By whom?"

"Thousands at his bidding post over land and sea."

"Oh for Christ's sake, Vogt. It's a little late in the game for you to become a literary adept. And you didn't get it right."

"Then your tutelage has been imperfect. But all is forgiven."

"Did you arrange for my transport here?"

"You willed it. We obliged. At your request, we even arranged for several deceased to join the gathering. A rare accommodation. Actually I wouldn't have advised it. The city is different from the charmed days of our midnight conversations in the old house on Lisle Street. I'm going to get out now for a brief conference with another client. I'll join you at the house." A rear window rolls down a few inches. Vogt slides out, a faintly hinted reconfiguration of thickened air conforming its shape to the glassy aperture and then disappearing.

His old home is barely familiar to Naughton. The house that used to be next door, also a shotgun, has been sheared off. All that's left of it are a few stones and a depression where the crawlspace was. Missing from the still-standing house are three of the four pillars that held up the extension of the roof over the little porch. The intricately wrought bric-a-brac that ran from capital to capital of the pillars hangs loose and misshapen like a winter spiderweb. The front doorway and the door are rhomboidal, reshaped by the sinking of the house. Naughton would've preferred not to enter, but conscience requires him to step across the threshold.

Inside, the house is deeply shadowed. Cigarette smoke and spiritous fumes thicken the air. As Naughton's eyes grow more accustomed to the dark he's able to make out five figures. They're arrayed in an arc defining about a quarter of a circle, but he can't see any chairs or sofas. So the figures are elongated busts hanging in the air unsupported by pedestals. One of them speaks. Behind them a planar patch of wall shimmers waywardly. Vogt.

"Gray smoke is one of the hardest things to paint, especially if you want to put something inside it." Naughton recognizes Alexie.

"You don't have to worry about that here. There's nothing inside it." Ettie.

"Don't be snide, Titta." A fingerling of ash falls down, disintegrating as it descends.

Naughton says, "What about painting alcoholic fumes, Alexie?"

"Easy. You just have to make the stuff on the other side wobble like a funhouse mirror."

"Please keep that in mind. I may have a promising subject for you." Ettie.

A sound comes from an invisible piano, a brief series of diminished chords.

"That, Stella, was somewhere between sweet and funereal." The words swirl in the smoke.

Stella says nothing.

A voice diminished by time and distance says, "I warned you about green eyes, Marietta."

The great tiger cat Man swims briefly into view. Perhaps it's in Ettie's lap, but that part of her body isn't visible. "I thought you'd decided to stay dead, Mama Helen, but now that you're here, you'll remember the way the fur of the forehead spells M, for Man and Master."

Mama Helen pishes. "You were always a wayward child, Marietta. I warned you not to marry a Marine in the middle of a war even if you got a widow's pension. And you were no better, Elizabeth, marrying a Cajun lowlife. Bedford wasn't good enough for either of you. So you ran off to big cities and made bad marriages."

"Don't worry about Titta, Mama. She's looking for another husband every night. As for me, didn't I give you two grandchildren and two great-grandchildren?"

"Where's the mother of the great-grandchildren?"

"You might as well ask where the wind is," says Alexie.

"Blood is thicker than water," says the mother. "We're all blood kin here." A fire flaring in front of her face produces a round red glow. "Say something, Peter, if that's you standing in the door. My God, you've aged."

Naughton says, "Blood lines. Understood. So Cam's not invited. What about Josh?"

"Men don't have blood, Peter. They have words. Words are the only reason you're here, to tell us a story."

Naughton, compelled, steps forward.

The mother turns to Stella. "Some intro music for our guest speaker, honey."

From Stella's vicinity comes a comic thirty seconds of piano that mixes a march and a gigue.

The mother applauds, dropping ash. Behind Stella Vogt has draped his warbled transparency across the end of an imaginary piano like a jellied cocktail-lounge vamp. The mother says again, "Tell us a story, Peter."

Naughton steps forward and closes his hands under his chin.

"That's an old Chinese mark of respect for the gods," says Ettie.

Naughton says, "Right. I'm calling on the gods to help me sing a family saga. We begin with our elders, Mama Helen and Papa Beau. Beau in his case wasn't a synonym for suitor but a sobriquet for Beauregard. Both Mama and Papa are now happily buried in the Bedford Cemetery."

"Yes," says Mama Helen, "with Confederate veterans on either side of us. And just down by the creek is the nigra graveyard. Rosa is down there. All of us very sociable. We never understood what all the talk about race was."

"What about the flood, Mama?" Ettie.

"Oh the flood was terrible. The creek rose up and coffins floated out of their graves because the nigras didn't dig deep enough. It was said some floated all the way to Pearl River. It was sad because they were our nigras, not those troublemakers from up north."

"Pearl River in China?" says Alexie in a voice of feigned wonderment.

Naughton says, "No, in Mississippi. The one in China was named after ours."

"I told Papa Beau not to go down to the creek, but he did anyway, but when he came back I told him not to tell me anything about it."

Naughton says, "To veer away from alluvial matters, I'm trying to remember something I may have heard about an oddity in Papa Beau's burial wishes."

"There was an oddity. He wanted to be buried in a winding sheet in the bare earth. Have you ever heard of such a thing? He got it from looking at some strange pictures an English poet painted with tree roots all around the dead. Maybe you know of him, Peter. Anyway, it was after Papa's second stroke. Reverend Ross and I did the right thing by him. A nice coffin with brass rails and satin lining."

The mother says, "You were lucky, Mama. Marty and I didn't like where we were buried, above ground out by Lake Pontchartrain. It was always damp. Then one day a stranger came by and offered us an alternate resting place. We took him up on it."

"What did he look like?" asks Naughton.

"I remember him well, a redhead, blue eyes, bony, lots of angles like he had extra joints. I can see by the look on your face, you know him, Peter."

"We were housemates."

A tittering laugh, like a dime rolling across glass, comes from the far end of the room, but nobody seems to notice it.

"He was horrid when he answered the phone," says Ettie. "I almost gave up calling Peter. Where on earth did you let him take you, Lizzy?"

"That's my business. But here's a clue. Not exactly on earth."

Naughton says, "We'd better round out the burials. Marietta nobly gave her body to science. Researchers will examine the connection between brain and Eros, looking beyond the already well-established role of the hypothalamus. Alexie is still alive. She has given up cats for pictures of the cosmos in various states of development."

"Don't knock stuff that's over your head, Daddy."

"Did I knock the cosmos? Shame on me. But to go on. Stella is also still alive, in a state of advanced sanctification not known to the rest of us. She may be the only hope we have for getting into the realms of the blessed."

Stella says, "Everybody is already in, Peter. You will understand that later."

The mother says, "Hypothalamus, cosmos, blessedness. Does this story have a plot, Peter?"

Naughton says, "For family stories you don't want a plot. Think of the great family stories of the ancients and the Bible— fratricide, patricide, matricide, incest, filicide. Interestingly nowadays more children are killed by their mothers than by their fathers. Working-class Medeas springing up all over the place."

"Peter, if you don't have a story, you might as well go back where you came from."

Ettie says, "He doesn't know where he came from."

"Proximately I know very well, but nobody knows where they came from ultimately. A small door in eternity opened and somebody shoved us through, usually with a lot of hollering and slime."

"I can tell a story," says Ettie. "Once upon a time a man child came into the world. He was neither luckily or unluckily born, which is the case with most of us except ones at the very high or low end. Anyway, he made his way through a lot of smoke and fumes into childhood and later adolescence. His older sister taught him, probably without giving it much thought, about beauty and love, or as much as he could absorb. And then she went away to a higher calling. I happened to be a brief waystation, not up to the task. But I don't blame myself too much because few are allowed to touch an angel."

"I hate to interrupt, Titta, but if you're just going to stick to the facts you're not going to tell a very interesting story. You've got to pep it up with some invention."

"Not in Peter's case, Elizabeth, because there's a quirk that runs through the factual story toward a thrilling end."

"I'll believe it when I hear it."

"Then shut up and listen."

Naughton says, "Ettie is equipped better than any of us to wear the buskin. Remember, her warrior husband was not borne home on his shield but was lost in the sands and coral reefs of Tarawa. Full fathom five thy husband lies. Those are pearls that were his eyes."

"Beautiful," says Stella.

Naughton says, "What Ettie got was a beautiful purple heart with a profile of George Washington, though he wasn't at Tarawa unless you believe in reincarnation."

"Let's hear Ettie's story," says Alexie.

Mama Helen says, "The story of Peter really begins when two sisters decided there wasn't enough to do in Bedford and ran off to big cities and got lost."

"If we keep going back, Mama," says the mother, "we'll get to Adam and Eve, which, come to think of it, at least had a plot."

Ettie says, "I'm going on. So Peter, already lathered up with love and idealism from Stella, went to school with the Jesuits and learned to say love in many ways—amo, amas, amat. The Jesuits took him with Aeneid to the Underworld, where they were still waiting for Peter's father to show up, which wouldn't be long because tobacco and booze were doing their work. Peter was also exposed to the worship of Mary with beads and the like. From there he did an about face and joined a fraternity at Tulane University, an outfit specializing in parties and heavy petting. He got there on a Navy scholarship, taking a test that featured words and a few numbers. In college he learned more words and stored them up, probably top one percent of Americans."

"This is a wordy story, Titta. Hahaha."

"From Tulane he went into the Navy to spend his obligation as a Supply Officer on a ship in the Mediterranean that ferried sailors from one port to another to sample what European whorehouses had to offer. In the Navy the new words you learn don't have much use in public life—portholes, hatches, scuppers and the like. He did learn a few numbers so he could count the government's money. From the Navy he went back to Tulane for graduate school in English, our native tongue, but you can never have too many words, Peter figured. He got hung up on a queer dead poet who threw a net of words over the whole world and from there went on to the cosmos."

"Are we coming to some kind of climax, Titta?"

"Definitely. But I need to say that Peter's aptitude for words, as shown by a number of tests from grammar school on up, came from his mother. There are lots of old-timey maternal curses leading to crime and insanity, but his mother's curse was unusual. Logomania is what he himself called it. The victim might break into a cold sweat if he couldn't talk or write for a long time. Are you OK now, Peter? No. You look a little pekid. Go ahead. Say something."

"Just one thing, a quibble maybe. The tongue the protagonist of your story learned from his mother wasn't ordinary English but a distinctly Bible State dialect laced with dashes of Louisiana. This particular dialect was not highly favored in general society. It could even lead to misunderstanding. For instance, you all as pronounced by his mother might not easily be understood by an unaccustomed ear as merely allophonic but might be mistaken for the designation of a sailing boat. And other instances could be adduced, but go ahead with the story, Aunt Ettie."

"And see if you can come up with an exciting plot, Titta."

"We were talking about a queer dead poet. Isn't that a good plot hook?"

"Not in New Orleans, where queers are a dime a dozen."

Alexie says, "It could be a plot hook if, say, the protagonist kept the queer dead poet's body in the attic and slept with it."

Mama Helen makes a choking sound. "And you were such a pretty baby, Alexandra."

"Sorry, Mama Helen. It's a story we read in high school. Forget I ever mentioned it."

Ettie says, "We're not going to use the gay phrase anymore because it upsets Mama Helen. We'll give Peter's poetic hero a specific name. How about Quim. Peter's mentors in graduate school didn't approve of Peter's choice of a romantic literary figure in general and of Quim in particular, especially when Peter said he planned to go to places associated with Quim's great odes—Illinois and Montauk, which is somewhere by the New York ocean."

"What was the matter with that?" asks Alexie.

"You don't do literary research in actual places. You do it in books. Actual places can't be depended on to stay quiet, especially in Quim's work, which features a lot of wind and birdcalls in specific locales."

Stella says, "That's not something to make fun of, Aunt Ettie. Some shamans have conversed with birds. Ravens are gifted with speech."

Naughton says, "But you have to get a wolf to translate for you. They hunt together."

The mother says, "Good Lord, Peter. It's no wonder they kicked you out of grad school."

Ettie says, "I'm going on. Peter gave up on grad school and instead went in pursuit of a beautiful Asian girl who didn't share his enthusiasm for Quim but preferred a Chinese poet who proved that it was impossible for any person to know whether he was a human or a butterfly, and that actually it didn't matter much. Does this seem to you a good basis for a marriage? Peter did. And the girl went along with it. They had two kids but the mother wouldn't have said two because she didn't believe in numbers, even small ones. Anyway, the marriage went on for x number of years and then when the children were independent, the mother disappeared. Peter found out that she went among some hippies, countless in number at the time, so he set fire to their coven or whatever you call it. His son Joshua saved him from the law and put him

340

in a Catholic asylum where the nuns weren't familiar with Quim."

"You left out the part where he came looking for me in the desert."

"I'm coming to that. In the asylum Peter befriended two nuns, a Mother Super, a Creole keeper and three fellow nuts. This is where you come in, Alexie. It's where we all come in, plus an unimprisoned nut named Vogt, the one who reburied you and Marty, Lizzie. At Peter's call we all started appearing on the walls of the asylum, which doesn't actually hurt you, but it's like being in a movie that somebody is filming without asking you. But never mind the walls. The plot involves Peter and one of the other nuts, a dark young woman the nuns dug up out of a French dungeon run by a lunatic obsessed with whips. The plot turns on the question of whether Peter will bring the woman up from the dark or whether she will drag him down with her. There's a little black guy, not a Black but more like the Shadow. Remember that old radio program? It's thought the little black guy may be in cahoots with the dark young woman. Anyway, Peter has been helping her up from the dark by telling her shady stories, with lots of extra words of course. The last story he tells is the story of a wanderer looking for his artist daughter. Alexie thinks it's her. And it may be, but the stories tend to yaw this way and that. Anyway, it's now the turn of the young woman to tell a story. That's the plot so far."

"Wait a minute, Titta. Even though it's not much of a story, you can't just leave us hanging like that."

"I've told his whole life story, Lizzie. I can't tell his death while he's standing right here in front of us."

Mama Helen says, "He looks like he's fading to me."

"Peter, you come right back here."

"Can't, Mama. My car's waiting for me."

Ettie says, "Probably with his buddy Vogt already in it."

Alexie says, "You already spilled the beans. You might as well finish."

"I didn't spill the beans. That was a joke about his death like everything you could tell about him is a joke."

"Thanks, Aunt Ettie. On that wisp of macabre humor I'll take my leave."

"Give our regards to Vogt. Tell him that your mother and daddy are happy where they are. She just came up here for this little meeting of us family women. Maybe the last one."

"Be all right with me," says Alexie.

"Glad to have been of service," says a voice in the back of the room, warbling like a bird that's having trouble perfecting its mating call.

"Now he's throwing his voice," says the mother. "Think of it. If he gets real good at it, he could fill the whole world up with his words and get everybody and even the animals to say what he wants them to."

"Good-bye all."

Naughton and Sister Claire are sitting opposite each other in the center of her office. The top of her desk is very tidy. It's quiet, but something seems to be stirring the air. After a lengthy silence Naughton says, "I went back."

"Yes, I know. What did you learn?"

"That nothing has changed."

"Do you think we're allowed to change the past?"

"Allowed, I don't know. But it's a major occupation of historians."

"So. The story we're about to hear from Charlene, will it be the real or the changed past?"

"The real past is every moment of every leaf of grass, insect, human that ever was. Nobody could tell that story but your God. And even if you zoom in on a single person, the welter of the moments of a life is virtually infinite. I once read a story about a boy who could remember his life in every detail. He sickened and died of the surfeit of memory."

Sister Claire frowns. "An odd story, but I don't think Charlene will sicken and die amid her memories, horrible as they may be."

"I agree."

"But her story. Will we know if it's factual memory?"

"Setting aside the difficulty if not the impossibility of factual memory, there's a test we might use. If it's ragged it's probably factual. If it's well made it's probably fabricated."

"Raggedness. That's how we know your stories are true?"

Naughton laughs. "True? Yes. You can hear in the telling I'm trying to fix them up."

"What do you call a story that may not be actual but makes something actual happen?"

"Intentionally?"

"Whether or not."

"It's a mistake to tell a story to make the listener do something. If you just tell the story as it comes to you, whatever she does is not at your feet."

"The storyteller gets off." Sister Claire softens the challenge with a smile.

Naughton nods. "Usually, unless he's a bad storyteller, in which case he might have his head chopped off."

There comes an authoritative rap on the door. Sister Claire invites Mother Martha in. She circles behind Sister Claire's desk and seats herself. "As I'm sure both of you know, I don't like surprises." She looks sharply at Naughton. "What are we going to hear?"

"Charlene's story. That's all I really know, Mother."

"It's not all you really know, Mr. Naughton. You cannot attend a person for months, telling stories, watching the person struggle up from darkness and dumbness to speech and consciousness and claim you don't know anything."

Naughton tilts his head. "I'm sure Charlene's story will reveal things about what caused her condition when she was brought here."

"Her condition was appalling. Is she really capable of telling her story?"

Sister Claire says, "Mr. Naughton and I were just talking about that."

"What did you conclude?"

"That she will tell a story."

"A true story or one employing the arts she has learned from Mr. Naughton?"

"In that regard we'd have to judge the story on its own merits."

Mother Martha is silent for some moments. Then she repeats meditatively, "On its own merits." She nods. "Because we have no way of corroborating any of it."

Naughton nods, speaks. "Yes, Mother. We'll have to judge the authenticity by the rough intensity of the telling."

Mother Martha shakes her head bemused. "How often I have heard theologians argue this very point. The miracles of the Gospels are proven not by their historicity but by their inner qualities of conviction." She pauses. "So we have the story of a creature virtually risen from the dead, a female Lazarus." Mother Martha waves her hand dismissively. "I'm not comparing you to Jesus, Mr. Naughton. Maybe you think Lazarus was just a case of cardiac arrest." She leans toward Naughton. "Well?"

"That's what my son Josh would say, if he took the trouble to say anything about Lazarus, but it's not what the story says."

"Good. So we'll go together and hear the story. We're in God's hands, but He has given us great latitude." Mother Martha rises and come around from behind the desk. Sister Claire and Naughton stand. "How often, Sister, have you wished to have the burden of freedom lifted from you?"

"Too often, Mother. Sinfully often."

"No doubt. Yours is a restless spirit, Sister, destined to walk along the edge, Mr. Naughton's cliffs, you might say. His coming here has not been fortuitous for you."

"Perhaps a necessary test, Mother."

"Never ask to be tested."

"I didn't, Mother, but he came nevertheless."

Mother Martha turns to Naughton. "And you, Mr. Naughton. I don't ask if you've been tested and found true, because you will launch into one of your bouts of self-abasement, foolish if sometimes moving." She steps swiftly around them, as one might navigate silent pillars, giving them no chance to show the courtesy of deference. "I must go to prayer now." She looks at her watch. "We'll meet here at half past three, the hour of gifts."

Naughton lies abed. A wall blank and silent would be a blessing. But what is more elusive than absence?

Distant bells ring.

Vogt says, "I'm glad you called. They're coming to get me, Peter." He has cranked his voice up into a falsetto caricature of feminine fear.

"I didn't call you. But never mind. But who's coming to get you?"

"Father Schneider and the local exorcism team, two doughty acolytes, all having foresworn sex for the requisite two weeks, even with each other, and therefore doubly dangerous."

"How can they get you? You're immaterial."

"It's when we're most vulnerable. Here they are now."

A cloud of incense smoke wafts through the wall beyond the foot of Naughton's bed. Vogt says, "You're honored, Peter. This is very high-end myrrh, copal and frankincense resin exhibiting distinct notes of citrus and juniper."

Now the team of three advance, led by the chief Exorcist in a black chasuble and scarlet stole, Father Schneider. He has in his hands a large book bound in brass. The acolytes are in black cassocks. The thurifer swings the thurible in an ample arc whose periods, however, are foreshortened by a rhythmic snap of his wrist. The thurible has the appearance of a hookah with the stem sawed off and the base punctured. The other acolyte keeps his fingers interlocked under his chin in an intricate ogival pattern suggestive of a Gothic cathedral tower.

"Lord have mercy," the Exorcist begins.

Vogt says sotto voce, "Now comes the Litany, Peter. It's really long. I'm going to duck out and look in on Charlene, see if she has any new costumes or poses."

"Vogt!"

The recitation of saints, prophets, evangelists, angels, virgins, innocents, martyrs and various other spirits proceeds in a slow chant. At the calling of St. Martin of Tours, Naughton's mother Lizzie exclaims, "Did you hear that, Marty, your saint, patron of the Third Republic or is it the Fourth? I didn't know he was actually in the Bible."

The Litany concluded, the Exorcist proceeds. "Lord, who consigned that fallen and apostate tyrant Lucifer to the Inferno, snatch from the clutches of the noonday devil this human being made in your image and likeness."

"I'm back," says Vogt. "Can't have an exorcism without a demon. Meanwhile, let me assure you that Charlene is in fine fiddle, actually a little too saucy for my taste."

"Vogt, goddamn you, I hope the good father erases you."

"Can't, Peter. You've already inscribed me in your story. 'The moving finger having writ . . .' Isn't that the way it goes? Anyway, this is my third exorcism and the best so far."

The Exorcist says, "I command you, unclean spirit, whoever you are, to tell me your name."

"Vogt, Father, but temporary like all the names in our realm."

The Exorcist produces a small basin of holy water and an aspergillum and sprinkles Naughton's head and the heads of the acolytes. "You are cast out, unclean spirit. Away with you. Stay far from this creature of God."

Vogt is silent.

After a considerable silence the Exorcist says, "You are rescued from the clutches of your Foe and free now to worship the one true God the rest of your days."

Naughton, Sister Claire and Mother Martha meet in the hall not far from the door of Naughton's room. Mother Martha leads the way. Before they reach Charlene's room, Vera and Charlene come out into the hall. Charlene is wearing again the dark blue gown, but in the late afternoon the blue is lightened by the sun coming in from the wide picture window. The baldric of birds flashes a sharper silver of curling flights.

Mother Martha, approaching as head of the delegation, nods. "This is quite striking, Charlene. I can almost hear the clinking of cocktail glasses and youthful laughter. I congratulate your couturier on understanding what would be just right for you."

Charlene smiles. "Not a couturier." She imitates Mother Martha's pronunciation perfectly. "A friend of his." She nods toward Naughton.

"Then I must extract from Mr. Naughton an account of his associations in the haut monde of fashion. But today we've come to hear your story. We need chairs. My old bones can't stand for long."

There's a great bustling as everybody but Mother Martha and Charlene fetches chairs from down the hall. Once the chairs are arranged in a gentle arc around the teller, Mother Martha says, "How would you like us seated, Charlene?"

"Mr. Naughton in the middle." It's the first time Charlene has used the name. "Then Vera." The rest are allowed to choose their own places. Mother Martha sits beside Naughton so that he is flanked by Vera and her. Sister Claire occupies a wing.

Charlene begins, "A little boy with black hair." She says to Naughton, "You will tell."

"This is your story, Charlene."

"Yes, but you will tell. I will give you words." It's obvious that this procedure is set in Charlene's mind.

Accordingly, Naughton says, "What color eyes does he have?"

"Black."

"Then he's like a little doughboy."

Charlene smiles. "You don't bake him."

"He ran away."

"No. He had a grandmother. Silver. You will see in your mind."

"The little boy with black hair and eyes had a kind grandmother whose hair was silvered by years. Or frost?"

"It was cold enough."

"The little boy and his grandmother lived in a cold country. I see tall trees that are green all year. There were just the two of them living there."

"They had a cat."

"The cat purred for whichever one held it. At night it went out hunting."

"No."

"They couldn't let the cat out at night because there was an eagle that claimed the woods as his own."

"The grandmother died."

"The grandmother went away into the dark. The little boy would've followed lovingly, but villagers came and took him away."

"No. He burned her and ran."

"The little boy used all his strength to try to dig a grave, but the ground was hard. If he only heaped up sticks and leaves over the grandmother, the wolves would come, or the eagle, so he made a bier of stones and pushed kindling and fallen wood under it and lit it. He couldn't stay to see the fire do its work because the villagers were coming. He ran."

"By the town a little black man."

"For a while he kept to himself, stealing bits of food from houses on the edge of the town, but he grew cold and thin. He looked in windows and saw walls pink from the glow of fires. He thought of knocking on a door, but the villagers wouldn't want an orphan who had lived with an old witch. A little black man appeared and motioned that the boy must come with him. The little boy didn't ask where."

Charlene says, "I had a dream. It was about a gold coin. It could do anything. Then you wake up. What is a dream?"

There follows a long silence. At last Mother Martha speaks. "Some dreams are prophetic, but they're very rare. I doubt you will find a magic gold coin, Charlene."

Vera says to Charlene, "Sometimes in your sleep you say some thing is coming, but you never say what."

A flash of anger crosses Charlene's face and quickly passes. "What I say in my sleep is secret."

Naughton says, "The little black man takes the little boy to a castle."

"No. Stones."

"The little black man takes the boy to a stony place like a cave made by giants. A fire burns in a pit for cooking and to keep the wolves away."

"A snake. Mice."

"A snake with red eyes guards the fire. The little black man feeds the snake mice. Over the fire he cooks meat and potatoes. While they eat he shows the boy a bag of coins. Where did he get them, the boy wants to know."

"A show," says Charlene.

"Every summer a carnival comes to the town with a tent and a beautiful trapezista."

"A doll. Bear."

"Also a life-size doll that dances with a singing bear on a big plate that goes around and around to the tune of the Blue Danube."

Charlene appears delighted with these details. Mother Martha and Sister Claire show an intense interest. Vera seems moved but it's uncertain just how.

Naughton proceeds with confidence but always at a pace that makes room for Charlene's prompts. "The little man is featured in a sideshow. The Incredible Razor Man. In the light of flambeaux he turns this way and that, from normal girth to black shadow to razor thin. Stand back! Touch and you'll be cut in two. Throw coins at his feet or he may jump down from the stage and harvest you like wheat with the scythes of his arms."

"No joints."

"The little black man doesn't have joints in his arms and legs. They extend like spokes from the axles of small wheels. The spectators are fearful that a limb will fly off and spear them."

"The meat. The knife."

"The meat on the fire doesn't have joints. The boy doesn't know what animal he's eating. After a time it doesn't seem odd to him that when the little man turns a certain way all that's left is a blade with images of the fire dancing along the edge."

"Years. Coins. Love."

"Some years pass. One night, disobeying the little man, the boy secretly goes to the carnival and falls in love with the beautiful trapezista child whose name is Vadoma."

"They must part."

"The little man motions the boy, now a youth, to go away. He gives him gold coins in a leather pouch and pushes him onto the path that leads through the dark woods to the world."

Charlene, looking at Mother Martha, asks, "Can you buy a person?"

Mother Martha says, "No one should ever sell or buy a person, Charlene, though unfortunately history tells us it has often been done. And still today."

Charlene shifts her gaze to Sister Claire. "Did someone sell you to God?"

Vera says with some sharpness, "You should have asked me that before you asked Sister Claire."

Charlene continues to gaze at Sister Claire, who at length says, "No. I came to God another way."

"What way?"

"I reeked of sin and knew that only God could save me."

"Did the other one reek too?"

"Yes."

Charlene seems satisfied with this exchange and redirects her gaze to Naughton. "The youth buys. Names."

"The youth offers to buy Vadoma from her mother, whose name is Farren. He has many gold coins in his pouch, but he has no name. Farren will not sell her daughter to a man with no name. The youth tries to remember, but if he ever had a name he's forgotten it. He goes back down the path through the woods to the home of the little man. Maybe he'll remember his name, but the little black man is not there. There's no fire. The stones are silent. He sits on a stone and thinks. What name would his silver-haired grandmother have given him?"

"Walter." Charlene pronounces the W as a V.

"He decides he remembers Walter. He goes back to Farren with a name and buys Vadoma."

"Wander."

"They wander from town to town. Neither of them knows what they're looking for. There're no more gold coins in the pouch. People turn them away."

"Carnival."

"In a field outside a big town they find laborers driving stakes, raising tents. The great lumbering wagons of the carnival come down the road. A cacophony of animal noises offends the skies. Then come the tumbrils of straw and fodder. After that the principals on horses and behind them the common workers in jostling carts. The strong man comes in his own cart loaded with black hexagonal barbells."

"The head man with the tattoo." Charlene's prompts come now with mounting urgency.

"The impresario has a handlebar mustache and a black toupee. He rides with his queen in a wagon emblazoned with the name of the carnival, *Mysteries of the Night*. All around the lettering stars glitter, comets trail off into the dark, the moon's menacing grin flashes serrated teeth."

"The bargain."

"Walter tells the impresario that Vadoma is the greatest child trapezista in the land. The carnival does not do high-wire acts. And besides, trapezistas have to be beautiful and Vadoma is a ragamuffin with rat tails in her hair. Walter tells the impresario that he and Vadoma can do many acts for him. A drama of love and death to the sound of drums, a waltz in a palace, the beast with four legs, and many more. The impresario says that all he lacks is an animal act and only for one person. How much will he pay for Vadoma? Ten D-Mark. More. Ten D-Mark and fifty pfennig. More. Ten D-Mark and eighty pfennig." Naughton has caught the ugly rhythm of the bargaining and seems ready to go on with it.

"The animal act."

"At last Walter completes the sale. He whispers to Vadoma that he will come back for her in the night and steal her away. He never does. So Vadoma becomes the carnival's animal act. She trains a white horse named Noble to count up to twelve. When she says the number, Noble paws the earth the correct number of times while his mane, gilded by the flambeaux of the big tent, shimmers in aureate splendor."

"No."

"Vadoma trains a little dog named Flip to jump through a hoop of fire. The little dog leaps four time his height. As he

352

passes through the hoop of fire, Vadoma holds on the other side a big round mirror and tilts it this way and that so that in the eyes of the audience the fire lights on their heads and dances from one to another."

"No."

"Vadoma trains an African elephant named Jumbo to stand on a stool and rear up on his hind legs. The stool is very small with a stripe of stars around the top. When the elephant comes down, Vadoma congratulates him by nuzzling his trunk and giving his front hoof a hearty handshake. Jumbo lifts Vadoma up on his trunk and carries her around the arena to the applause of the audience."

"No."

Naughton takes a breath and plunges on. "Vadoma becomes a tiger tamer. The tiger is actually Fritz in a tiger's pelt. Fritz has mastered the raspy rattle of a tiger's anger, also the movement of the head to the side and the agile leap up onto the platform. The tiger pelt has become loose and shaggy, but the audience, lost in wonder at the taming of such a dangerous beast, does not notice. Vadoma cracks a long black whip. Fritz is in love with her. He lets her put her head in his mouth."

"No."

Vera gets up and comes back with water for Naughton. He drinks it in small sips, thinking. "Vadoma learns to charm a cobra. The cobra has no name, but its hood is wide and its scales glisten. When Vadoma plays her flute the snake comes up out of a big urn. Around the sides of the urn are panels with pictures of Krishna. In one he sits by a maiden under a full moon. In another he enchants a white bull and a peacock with his flute. The eyes of the peacock's feathers wink. The bull is lovingly somnolent. In another Krishna is armored for war with embossed brass shin and breast plates. From a belt made of golden links hangs his sabre in a sheath of steel. Around his headpiece a nimbus rotates galvanized by a brilliant sun behind. If Vadoma plays Mozart, the cobra sways presto. If she plays Debussy's *Prélude à l'après-midi d'un faune*, the cobra rises languidly, the pulses of elevation so slow as to be almost invisible. This at last pleases the impresario."

"No."

"Vadoma learns falconry. The falcon's name is Prince. It is a peregrine falcon because it came wandering from a far country. Vadoma's glove is made of tightly woven mail instead of leather because Prince's talons are so powerful and sharp they would pierce any animal skin. Prince's hood does not shutter his eyes or clamp his bill to prevent him from burying his beak in his prey because he is well trained to bring the prey back to his master whole. He dives at speeds exceeding two hundred miles per hour. Vadoma releases Prince with a hiss and the command, fly! To call him back she whirls a long leather strap with a teardrop pearl in a small basket at the end. The sound of the whirling strap is high, almost inaudible to the human ear. In demonstrations at the carnival a pigeon is set free. Prince flies above the hapless bird and stoops. The impact showers feathers down. Prince returns the bloody bird to Vadoma. The crowd cheers and calls for more. There is a good supply of pigeons."

"Four claws."

"Yes, four sharp talons. The impresario is at last well pleased."

"No."

Naughton and Charlene challenge each other with hard looks. After a while Charlene says with simple deliberateness, "You know. The animal act. The cage."

Naughton takes a deep breath. "The impresario builds a cage of rude timbers with scaling bark. He covers the floor with straw. He imprisons Vadoma in the cage. She's billed as a wild woman from Borneo. He tries to get her to eat live animals, but she won't. He doesn't want her to starve and die so he hires a clever baker to make pastries that look like dead uncooked animals—chickens, rabbits, pigeons. The carnival audience watches, horrified and delighted. She dives into the straw gnashing her teeth and making grunting sounds. Make her show us eating! the crowd hollers. Her keeper prods her with a long stick, but she burrows in the straw. She is given a bluish fermented drink that effervesces evilly in a glass jar. She takes a gulp and spits it out into the crowd. They shrink back, frantically wiping the toxin from their faces and clothes. Vadoma cackles like a witch. Only ignorant villagers could fall for such a transparent act. Vadoma is dressed in rags. The keeper proclaims she doesn't have beneath the rags what they expect. Show it! The keeper flips up the ragged edge of her skirt, but she howls and dives back into the straw. Some of the crowd stand for a long time, fascinated. One day a young man waits until everybody else is gone and the sun is low. His eyes are full of pity and love. He has seen the buried beauty in the carnival wretch. The keeper tells him to move on. It's time for her pot. The young man never comes back. The novelty of the wild woman wears off. Something new must be done. Vadoma is lashed. The blood is real. The crowd is again pleased but only for a while. Something new must be done. Vadoma is fitted with a chastity belt. What a joke, a crowd pleaser, a grated view of the impermissible. The time comes when the impresario is out of ideas. He sets Vadoma free. Three of his men take her blindfolded to a crumbling old brick kiln. They put her in the furnace for shelter, but they think she will die. She does not. She . . ."

Charlene says emphatically, "That is the end of the story."

There is a long silence. At last Vera speaks. "That is how all of Mr. Naughton's stories end. They do not end."

There is a long silence.

"But this is Charlene's story," says Mother Martha. "Perhaps it ends differently from Mr. Naughton's."

Charlene looks at her but says nothing.

Sister Claire says, "We'll go now and think of how Vadoma's story will end. Maybe someday you'll tell us."

Charlene says nothing to that.

Another silence, then Naughton. "We haven't finished. There is Walter's story."

"No."

"Yes, Charlene. Walter must have his story."

Charlene gazes fixedly at Naughton but says nothing.

"Walter reeks with sin, but he doesn't know what sin is. Neither his grandmother nor the little black man never taught him, so he only knows the effects of sin, the principal one being restlessness. He's not haunted by something following him, but he is driven. To be driven is terrible, but to be driven without knowing toward what or away from what is more terrible."

"No. Not to move is more terrible," says Charlene.

Naughton nods. "No doubt, but Walter can move. He finds a river. If the water moves, it must be going somewhere. Sometimes there are wonderful curls of green meadow. Sometimes high hills make long shadows over the water. It's easy for him to steal food from farmhouses. He's skilled at stealth. The air grows cooler. The river grows wider. Small bridges are less frequent. Once the river divides. This makes him fearful, because which way will he choose, but then the forks rejoin. Whenever the river passes through a town, he finds a market at closing time. The sellers readily give him the day's leftovers—bruised apples, rusted cabbages, twisted carrots, potatoes with big black eyes. He steals eggs, which he eats raw. He never builds a fire at night. It would give him away. To whom? He would laugh at his nameless fear, but he's never learned to laugh."

"Hahaha. It's not easy," Charlene says.

Vera says, "Yes, she would begin to choke. I told her laughing was one of the last things to learn again."

"You could choke in the night," says Charlene. "Who would come?"

"I would come," says Vera.

Naughton listens patiently, then resumes. He tells Walter's story in short sentences that make breathing easy. "Walter is still young and sound of body. It's his mind that's not right. He comes to a great city with spires and a bridge. It's wide. Carriages pass each other going in opposite directions. But it's the ships that astound him. The masts make a leafless forest. All tied together with ropes. The bowsprits point out and up. They seem to him to know where they're going. He signs on as a seaman. His ship sails down the Elbe into the North Sea. He had never dreamed of so much water. Soon no land is visible. This will be his place. He says little to his shipmates. He learns how to tie knots, to haul, to set running rigging. Mainly he looks at the sea. It never in its wildest moods makes him fearful or sick. But time and change catch up to him. First the oddly rigged clipper ships, then the steamers. He cannot bear to shovel coal. He gets off a steamer in the New World and buys a train ticket. Maybe he'll find a place to be still."

"What is the New World?" Charlene asks.

Mother Martha says, "We are in the New World, child. It's everything west of Europe and east of Asia."

"Why is it new? Did God make it last?"

"No, but it was not known to us until six hundred years ago."

"How did it stay hidden?"

"The people here were quiet."

"Hahaha." Charlene looks at Vera. "Were your people quiet?"

"They were moved and then they were quiet."

"You are not quiet." Spoken with absolutely no animus.

"God and his nuns have not told me to be quiet."

"Nor will we ever," says Mother Martha.

Naughton resumes. "The train lurches from Grand Central Station. Walter wonders if he has made a mistake. Already the station had terrified him with its reverberations. They sound like rolling stones. He thinks of his home among the stones of the little black man. And the fire. The train rolls west. Green fields appear out the window whizzing by. Little towns pop up. Miniature people scurry about, in and out of little buildings. Like one carnival after another. He remembers a pretty little girl. His mind clinches. He pulls the window shade down. And never looks out again. His seaman's sense of height tells him the train is traveling high over gorges. Sometimes he hears running water and is tempted to look out, but he doesn't." Naughton pauses.

Sister Claire says, "Rest a little while."

Naughton says, "We're almost there."

"Where?" asks Charlene.

"Somewhere far north of San Francisco, California where he gets off the train. How he gets there isn't important. When he gets there he knows that he has come to the right place. The sea again, richer than the sea he had sailed. Salt in the air. The wind fresh. The rocks above the water old and clean. He walks along a ridge. Short trees hold out their arms to him like friendly brown people who love the sun. Now he only needs to find the exact stone, high above the water. He will dive down. He knows that the water will be cold. But it will change everything. He won't have to move again. Here he can be still. He finds the stone. There are grooves that fit his feet, scooped out by the wind and the rain. A large bird flies from behind him. Once out over the water it dives and comes back up with a fish in its talons. Walter doesn't know about signs and cruxes, but he feels the moment. He dives."

Naughton is sitting in a chair in his room. A mobile serving table has been rolled up in front of him. Vera stands on the other side. "I am not moving, Mr. Naughton, until you eat it all and drink the broth." Naughton lifts the mug to his lips and takes a dainty sip.

"All, Mr. Naughton."

"I would say it's the elixir of the gods, but that would offend you."

"I do not care what you call it, just that you drink it."

Naughton drinks some broth and eats a cracker topped with a soft cheese. "Already I can feel renewed energy coursing through my body."

"You have let your body get thin."

"Which is a sin, it being a temporary vessel of the spirit."

"Not temporary, Mr. Naughton. When the dead are resurrected, so will you be."

"In better shape, I hope."

"You will be perfect."

Naughton drinks and eats with a bit more appetite. "Good."

"You do not have to tell any more stories."

"Who granted this dispensation?"

"Sister Claire, with Mother Martha saying yes. They want to talk to you."

"And Father Schneider too no doubt."

"Father Schneider talks to Mother Martha and then to Sister Claire, not to you."

"Chain of command. Good."

"You need to rest for a while."

"Yes. How is Charlene?"

"Charlene is thinking."

Naughton nods. "She's had to learn to think all over again."

"She had to learn everything all over again."

"I wonder about her memories?"

Vera frowns. "I think they are not good. Even yours are better for her."

The three of them are seated in a loose triangle in Sister Claire's office. The sun is low, a big shiny orange in the window. A crookneck lamp on Sister Claire's desk shines down on some papers. Naughton breaks the silence. "There's always a little sadness in the moments when we shift from the light of the sun to light of our own making."

"Nicely put," says Mother Martha. Then pausing for only a moment, "I'm going to be very direct, Mr. Naughton. Was that Charlene's story or yours?"

"I was always totally in the moment, Mother, transported. But I know this. The story wasn't like other stories I've told."

"What was the difference?"

"Charlene took the lead."

Sister Claire says, "Is it possible that the story was a mix of hers and yours, at least until you got to the story of Walter?"

Naughton thinks for a moment and then shakes his head. "The story of Walter wasn't different. Charlene still had the reins."

Mother Martha says, "I want to go back before Walter's story. Is Vadoma Charlene?"

Naughton hesitates. "The time and the place don't fit exactly."

Sister Claire says, "In stories shifts of place, times and characters are common."

Mother Martha says, "Shifts are dodgy, Sister. We're accountable for what we are."

Naughton nods. "Of course, Mother, but sometimes we see ourselves but in a glass darkly."

"No doubt, Mr. Naughton, but let's leave St. Paul out of this and look at things as directly as we can. So, we were in Germany, were we not? But there were no German words in the story. Yet you report that Charlene has spoken German words."

"Yes," says Naughton, "but I don't think you'll hear Charlene speak any more German."

"Why is that?"

"Because she's left them behind, remnants of an old life she's free from now."

Mother Martha turns to Sister Claire. "What do you say, Sister? Is she free?"

"I think freedom is a process, Mother, not an absolute."

Mother Martha smiles. "I was half expecting you to say that freedom is an illusion. You read too much, Sister. But never mind." She turns sharply to Naughton. "In your world of dark mirrors, Mr. Naughton, I ask again, is Charlene Vadoma?"

"It seemed so in the telling."

"Indeed. An animal in a cage." Mother Martha presses on, speech scarcely waiting on thought. "Back to the original question. Was the story yours or Charlene's?"

"Charlene's."

"But you were the conduit. A perfect conduit passes its content on untainted by its own substance. Correct?"

Naughton smiles. "You've caught me, Mother. Either I claim perfection or I confess to corrupting the narrative."

"Or," says Sister Claire, "we have to deal with imperfection like everything else in life."

"But there are degrees, Sister. How much of the story is pure Charlene, how much Mr. Naughton's imperfection? How much of Vadoma is Charlene? How much is Mr. Naughton's defective piping?"

Sister Claire says, "I can't answer that, Mother. Mr. Naughton and Charlene are deeply entwined. The stories of Vadoma and Walter belong to both."

Mother Martha's patience is obviously strained. "All right then, another matter, how did the little black man get from our doorsteps to the wilds of the Black Forest? Or is it vice versa?"

Naughton and Sister Claire look at each other. Sister Claire says, "I'm afraid, Mother, that he seems to have passage anywhere he pleases."

"If Father Schneider were here he might say the little black man is an agent of Mr. Naughton, propelling the story along all sorts of outlandish paths." Mother Martha puffs as if she might go on speaking but remains silent.

Naughton sighs. "I try to stay out of the stories, Mother, or I might become a merciless onlooker outside Vadoma's cage or the besotted young man who never came back for her or . . ."

"Walter."

Naughton says nothing.

After a silence Mother Martha says, "Do you know what I found most unbearable in your story?"

Naughton and Sister Claire wait for Mother Martha to go on. "Well?"

Sister Claire ventures an answer. "The betrayals."

"No doubt it should've been. But it was the straw. Do you understand that, Sister?"

"I'm not sure I do, Mother."

"Straw on your skin, in your mouth, scarifying you everywhere, bleeding you."

Sister Claire nods empathetically but says nothing.

"Treachery that pierces you at every portal or makes its own. Did you understand that in the telling, Mr. Naughton? Did you understand how nearly you touched Charlene's wound?"

Naughton pitches back in his chair. "I understood little, Mother. A corrupted conduit, just as you said."

"You never thought, yes, I have to take her into the dark, I have to cut her to the quick to bring her back? This day and all those other days of black stories?"

Naughton is struck dumb.

Sister Claire says, "I believe, Mother, when you're in the throes of a story, you don't think." Sister Claire waits for

Mother Martha to speak. In the permissive silence that ensues she goes on. "I told Mr. Naughton a story once. It came of itself. I didn't think it."

Mother Martha speaks with surprising mildness. "Someday you may tell me that story, Sister, but I doubt it." She sighs. "We've come to the end of this. You could say more, couldn't you, Mr. Naughton? And you, Sister. I could say more. But it would all be like the birds that loop around Mr. Naughton's stories and invade Charlene's clothes. Oh yes, made by a friend of Mr. Naughton's. I never expect to hear about that either. Never mind. The point is. What has the story done for Charlene?"

Naughton says, "Charlene will be all right now. She's free of me. Vera is her rock."

At the Foot of a Bed
in Maison Cristina

Naughton concentrates on the wood of the footboard of his bed. It's common maple with a reddish stain. He says, aloud or subvocal, hard to tell, hard in fact to tell exactly what he says. Maybe something like, "I'm calling you one last time, Vogt."

Silence.

"This is my story. You can't disappear unless I consent."

Silence. And then Sister Claire appears and speaks, her voice a little distant. "He'll never come back, Mr. Naughton. You may have found some elements of Father Schneider's exorcism comical, but it was totally effective."

"A good thing," says Naughton, after a brief hesitation.

"Yes, it is a good thing. I had a brief talk with him. He told me he was going to be an angel in this God-haunted house, his words. He was going to snatch you and Walter out of midair."

"Sacrilegious, Vera would say."

Sister Claire chuckles. "You have to be religious to start with if you want to be sacrilegious."

"He had his own religion."

"Yes." After a pause. "He said you were a liminal man."

"And lots of other interesting identifiers."

"But this time he's right. Joshua has filed papers and is coming to get you."

"Really. What if I decided to stay?"

"You can't. Legalities. And we need your bed."

"You have an occupant waiting?"

"A long list."

"You won't need a storyteller. Charlene is about to take flight. I see Vera holding her up like a hawk on a simple gauntlet and letting her go and never calling her back."

"Exactly."

"Do you worry about what she'll do?"

"I might, but it would show a lack of faith to question what God has in mind for her. I think I worry more about what you'll do."

"Do you?"

"Yes. Not the early stages of your freedom. Joshua will lead you over the threshold. No problem there even for a liminal man. Down the walk you two will go. The little black man won't show up."

"Are you sure? Why won't he?"

"He'll smell science, which he hates. Religion he could stand, but not science."

"OK. And then?"

"You'll go with Joshua to the far gate and step over another threshold into the evil old world again. No more hiding behind the skirts of godly women." Sister Claire smiles.

"And then?"

"You'll thank Joshua for your deliverance. Never a parting of father and son more amiable."

"I'll ask him if he knows where his mother is. I'll say her butterfly man wants to fly back to her."

"He won't know. And besides, you're being a bit disingenuous for once, Mr. Naughton. A wanderer might find her. But you won't search. You've already found the one you really wanted to find."

"Where will I go?"

"You'll head straight across the continent. You won't stop in San Francisco to look for Stella because you and Stella parted a long time ago. You'll find your stone. It'll be the same as it was when you lived beside it. Wind and rain work slowly on stone. Call it a lodestone. The same groove, like a foothold. The same bay will be shining in the distance as you look out from your pinnacle. The same sea hawk with the same fish in its mouth. The same bronze trees bowing to the wind god. The same broken sky, blue and white."

"I don't believe in prescience."

"That doesn't matter."

Naughton is packed. He's taken leave of Mother Martha. "You'll always be in our prayers, Mr. Naughton," she says. "Father Schneider bids me tell you that he believes you are disburdened of evil spirits and will find your way. I agree."

Naughton smiles. "Is there any record of posthumous conversions, Mother?"

"Not in our annals, but there may be many."

Naughton goes to tell Sister Kathleen and her charges good-bye. Ms. Trask says, "You must be dying or they wouldn't let you out."

"We're all dying, Ms. Trask, just at different rates."

"I've slowed mine down to a crawl until Lloyd can get here and search out the papers."

Sister Kathleen says, "Life wouldn't be the same without you, Ms. Trask."

Ms. Trask says, "You'd always have Mr. Gerrity climbing the ladder toward humanity. Maybe Mr. Nobody can send us some new words to teach him. He's got plenty to spare."

Mr. Gerrity begins wheeling his chair around in a tight circle. Sister Kathleen goes to him. "If you want to go somewhere, Mr. Gerrity, you have to turn both wheels at the same time."

"Same with trains," says Ms. Trask. Then in a whisper she says to Naughton, "Call him when you get out." She slips him a piece of paper with a number on it.

"It will be a pleasure," whispers Naughton, pocketing the paper.

"What are you two whispering about?"

"None of your business," says Ms. Trask.

Naughton says, "We were just sharing our admiration for the quiet of Maison Cristina and the sweet spiritual susurrus that slides along its halls like a holy stream. To speak of it at all we had to whisper."

"Eessiss," says Mr. Gerrity.

"You ain't a snake anymore, Mr. Gerrity, crawling around the jungle. You're a quad ped now and soon you'll get up on two legs like regular homo sepals."

"Indeed," says Sister Kathleen.

Naughton says, "I'm having a hard time saying good-bye. You three have been such wonderful company."

"Zeeoot toot." Mr. Gerrity aims his wheelchair toward Naughton. Fortunately Sister Kathleen has hold of the back of the conveyance because Mr. Gerrity hasn't learned to brake yet. Now the four of them are at close quarters. Naughton says, "Even now our breath mingles like lovers. Is that too forward, Sister?"

"It isn't forward enough," says Ms. Trask lifting herself up on tiptoe and giving Naughton a peck on the cheek. "There," she says. "He is real. I thought it might be like trying to kiss the smoke the magicians pour out of milk bottles."

Sister Kathleen says, "We used to do that when we were kids. All you need is soda and vinegar."

"Did you just kiss the smoke or did you kiss each other?"

"I'll never tell."

"Kiss and tell," says Ms. Trask, "can get you in big trouble. My sister Jeanette got put in a dark closet for so long she couldn't see for an hour when she got out. His name was

Johnny Rogers. Lloyd took her away from all that and not a minute too soon given her inclinations."

Mr. Gerrity wheels about. Sister Kathleen follows him across the room to the window. He looks out longingly. Sister Kathleen says, "I think he wishes he too had a son to come for him."

"Or anybody else," says Ms. Trask.

"Be careful what you wish," says Naughton. "The world is wide. It's easy to get lost. Here in Maison Cristina you're safe. But I have no choice. When a son comes, one must answer the call."

"What's he calling? I told you Jeanette would wander off and Lloyd and I would have to go out calling her name. Unlucky it was a common name and more than one woman of the street would show up with wares if you take my meaning."

"Well, there's only one Peter here," says Sister Kathleen, "so Mr. Naughton will be the only one that answers."

"He won't be calling Peter. He'll be calling Daddy. Or what if he calls Father and that stickman priest shows up and scares him off?"

Naughton says, "I hear him coming now."

"What's he coming on that would make that kind of noise?"

"I meant in my inner ear, Ms. Trask, like an offstage post horn. And now. . ." Naughton slides out the door throwing back a kiss.

In Charlene's room Naughton finds Charlene and Vera sitting silently together. The moment he steps through the door Charlene says, "You're leaving."

"Yes, my son's coming for me."

"What's his name?"

"Joshua."

"I don't know any story of Joshua."

Vera says, "He was a Bible hero. They made a song. Joshua blew his horn and the walls came tumbling down."

"What walls?"

"The walls of Jericho."

Charlene smiles. "You will tell me the story."

"There are many great stories in the Bible," says Vera.

Charlene turns to Naughton. "Do you love Joshua?"

"Yes, as a father loves a son."

"Not more?"

Naughton smiles. "Maybe a little more."

"Who do you love?"

"I would like to think I love everybody I know."

"Do you love me?"

"Yes."

"Do you love me more?"

"Yes."

"Do you love me the most?"

"Yes."

"Do you love Vadoma?"

"I have a special love for people in stories."

"Why is it special?"

"They're like one's children."

"Joshua is your child. Do you love him more than Vadoma?"

"I love him differently."

"Who do you love more than Vadoma?"

"I love you more than Vadoma."

"Do you love Sister Claire more than Vadoma?"

"The difference is too great for more or less." Then Naughton adds, "I love Vera."

Vera says, "Love is of God. It can go everywhere."

"But not the same," says Charlene.

"No, not the same. That would not be right," says Vera.

"What about Zora?"

"I love her the most, in her story."

Charlene smiles. Then she asks, "What is making you go away from the ones you love?"

Naughton is silent. Vera says, "Sometimes you have to go on. But love is everywhere."

"Did you not have any more stories?"

Naughton nods. "No more stories."

"What happened to them?"

"I've given them to you. You're the storyteller of Maison Cristina now."

The three of them are silent for a long time. Charlene says, "Vera will be the storyteller of Maison Cristina. She has the whole Bible. I have to go away."

"Where will you go?" Naughton asks.

Charlene laughs. "Ha. I will be a wanderer."

Naughton says, "I think you'll come to a place."

"Why? Wanderers don't have to come to a place."

"But I believe you will."

"Why?"

"Because you came here from a place."

Charlene thinks about that. "Am I going back to the same place?"

Vera says, "This is one story Mr. Naughton does not know, Charlene."

Charlene listens to Vera, turns back to Naughton. "How will I know what to do when I get there?"

Naughton says, "I don't know, but you will know. I wish I was in your story."

Vera shakes her head in mild wonderment. "I will not be surprised if you put yourself in it."

"Yes," says Charlene, "for love of me."

"For love of you, Charlene, I would do anything I could, but I am being pulled away as if I were in a cart drawn by the great white stallion that Vadoma never got to ride."

"That was a different story."

"Yes. Each story has its own truth. Now I have to find the truth of my own story."

"Maybe our stories will cross," says Charlene.

Vera says, "In the end all the stories will come together like train tracks away down the line."

Charlene gives Naughton a fierce look. "Go then."

"Will you give me your blessing?"

Charlene says nothing.

Vera says, "Give him your blessing, child. We all have blessings to give. It is not just the priests."

For a long time Charlene is silent. Then she smiles and waves her hand like a fairy queen. "Did you feel it?"

"Yes. It will go with me wherever I go."

"Go."

Naughton is standing with Sister Claire in the shade of the portico of Maison Cristina. Beside Naughton is a medium-size leather suitcase. He looks at it. "This must be what I had when Joshua brought me here."

"Yes, we kept it in the storeroom because the bedroom closets are small, as you know."

"Joshua will pick it up to carry it out to the car. He won't feel any spiritual emanations."

Sister Claire smiles. "Do you?"

"Maison Cristina will always be with me."

Sister Claire moves her hands outward and apart. "I'm trying to measure the distance between Naughton pre-Cristina and Naughton post-Cristina."

"It's not distance, Sister. It's a quality."

"You were already a man of quality when you arrived."

Naughton chuckles. "I thank you for that. Nevertheless, something inside of me has shifted."

"And in me."

"Not much, or I would've lost my footing."

"We must speak of Charlene," says Sister Claire simply.

371

"Yes."

"She's come a long way, thanks in great part to you. I could not have guessed when you came that you were part of God's providence."

"Don't forget Vera, her rock."

"Yes."

"But she also needs a wall."

"We've had too many walls. Speak more plainly, Mr. Naughton."

"I mean that Charlene grows strong, almost too strong, if that's possible. She needs a falconer to limit her flight. Or she might fly away and we'll never really know her."

"You know the Bible, Mr. Naughton. We may never know her, but she'll be known and will know herself."

"What a wonderful thing. I wish it for myself."

Sister Claire makes a mildly disdainful laugh. "You're not only known, Mr. Naughton, but I believe you also know yourself."

"Really?"

"Yes. You're a storyteller whose stories animate people."

"You say so now, but you and Mother Martha worried because my stories were so dark."

"Not only dark but twisted, a challenge poor Vera has had a hard time meeting. And I also."

"You?"

"Yes. Don't act surprised. Remember the day I was compelled to tell you about my encounter with the little black man? Where did he come from but from your stories."

"Was there a little black man in one of my stories?"

"He was in the story of Walter. Probably he was in all of your stories, hiding out." Sister Claire chuckles.

Naughton seems on the verge of drawing breath to deny it but remains silent.

Sister Claire speaks now in a tone of hovering wonderment. "I've thought, what if the little black man comes up the walk with that oddly scissoring gait of his, accompanied by his antic shadow while we're waiting for Joshua? Would he drive me again to that old dizzy perch on the rim of womanhood?"

"I don't think he'll appear, and if he did, I don't think he'd have the power to cast you back."

"He's already imprinted that time indelibly in my memory. But tell me. Why didn't he affect you deeply?"

"How do you know he didn't? I was mightily buffeted. Charlene claiming ownership of him. Ms. Trask identifying him as Lloyd. Sister Kathleen wondering if he were a demon, not Irish. Mr. Gerrity looping his vowels out into the air to lasso him. I didn't have room to feel threatened. Meanwhile, you were a model of stability, managing everybody. It wasn't until later, the second meeting that you temporarily lost your balance." Naughton gives Sister Claire an admiring look that quickly darkens. "If he had come at me with his glittering knives, I would've fallen over the edge of the walk."

"No, you wouldn't because you're not a woman."

Naughton says nothing to that. Then after a silence, "According to you the little black man was in all of my stories but hidden. Then he came forward in the last story of Vadoma and Walter." Naughton pauses. "Wonderful and terrible. A story can help you hide something from yourself. It might even steal from you the real narrative of your life. Or it might be the challenge required for you to save yourself."

At that moment a car pulls up at the end of the walk.

Sister Claire says, "I've been preparing for this moment, promising myself I wouldn't say something stupidly sentimental."

"So have I. We've only got a few more moments to hold to our promises because Joshua's astringent company will relieve us of all possibility of emotional excess."

"Then I'll simply say, que Dieu te garde. Vogt be gone."

"And for you the little black man." Naughton pauses and considers. "We may be asking too much, Sister. I mean such surgically precise excisions from the soul may not be possible. We may have to carry our Doppelgänger with us until the day of our final freedom."

"Maybe, but we're absolutely required to struggle against him."

Joshua mounts the stairs, manages a smile and greets the two. "Hello, Dad. Sister, good to see you again."

Sister Claire smiles. "I should say the same, but you've come to take our prize resident away from us."

"Well, Sister, the world's full of people who've wandered from the path. One of them will find his way here."

Naughton laughs. "He means the path of reason."

"Right, Dad." Joshua turns to Sister Claire. "Don't worry, Sister, I'm incapable of corrupting him. Once a mythographer always a mythographer."

"I'm sure you're right, Joshua. Here we've done nothing to cause him to swerve from the strict imperatives of the imagination."

"Right. I'll take him to the train station and say good-bye. Finis. Neither of us will attempt a reorientation. But I'll certainly not leave without saying thanks to you and your staff."

"I'm glad you brought him here. He's been with us only a year, but his stay will stretch long into the future."

Joshua nods and picks up his father's suitcase.

"It's good-bye then, Mr. Naughton."

"Good-bye, Sister."

"Let us hear from you."

"Of course, if there's anything to tell."

"Ha. What a thing for a storyteller to say."

Dear Reader,

Please stay with me one minute longer. But first, thank you very much for reading *Maison Cristina*. I know you have a world of choices and limited time and I'm very grateful you've chosen to take this journey with me.

Ralph Ellison's magnificent novel *The Invisible Man* ends with a question: "Who knows but that, on the lower frequencies, I speak for you?" I believe every writer's fervent prayer is that he or she has spoken to the reader on the lower frequencies, the shared motifs that echo below the words. So, perhaps you, too, have been a caregiver, have wanted passionately to be a healer, have believed in the healing power of stories. Perhaps you or a loved one has wanted to reach back and redeem an imperfect past or to perform an act of profound goodness. Maybe you have wanted a counselor for a loved one or for yourself, a spiritual guide capable of leading those in her care out of self-doubt and the fear of an empty death. If the story has spoken to you about some of these or other refrains echoing on the lower frequencies, you'll understand why I spent four years writing *Maison Cristina*.

If you've found this story meaningful, I'd like to ask you for a few seconds of your time. I want to share this story with as many readers as possible and I can only do this with your help. So I will be forever grateful if you would consider sharing your reading experience with other readers. You can do this by writing just a few words about *Maison Cristina* and posting them on Amazon.

If you are on Goodreads, a few words about your reading experience would be deeply appreciated there as well.

With many thanks,

Gene Garber

To learn more about the author and his work, visit:

http://www.eugenekgarber.com

To learn more about Transformations Press, visit:

https://transformationspress.org

About the Author

Eugene K. Garber has published seven books of fiction and is the creator, with eight other artists, of EROICA, a hypermedia fiction for the web. Garber's fiction has won the Associated Writing Programs Short Fiction Award and the William Goyen Prize for Fiction sponsored by *TriQuarterly*. His fiction has been anthologized in *The Norton Anthology of Contemporary Fiction*, *Revelation and Other Fiction from the Sewanee Review*, *The Paris Review Anthology*, and *Best American Short Stories*.

Made in the USA
Middletown, DE
06 August 2022

70706711R00229